STATE OF CONTROL

A VIRGIL JONES NOVEL

THOMAS SCOTT

GODBOLD & WHITEMAN - PUBLISHER OF MYSTERY,
THRILLER & SUSPENSE NOVELS

GODBOLD & WHITEMAN
Publishers of Mystery, Thriller & Suspense Novels
Godbold & Whiteman

ThomasScottBooks.com

Giving up control is one of the hardest things I've ever done. In truth, I'm sure I still have a lot of work to do. But I have wonderful teachers who continue to guide me and show me the way forward.

Joe, Tori, Zachary, Lauren & Joshua...You guys are the absolute best. You've taught me more than you'll ever know. I'm so proud of you all. This one is for you. From the bottom of my heart, thank you.

Control |kən'trōl| noun

THE POWER TO INFLUENCE OR
DIRECT PEOPLE'S BEHAVIOR OR THE
COURSE OF EVENTS; A GROUP OR
INDIVIDUAL USED AS A STANDARD OF
COMPARISON FOR CHECKING THE
RESULTS OF AN EXPERIMENT; A
MEMBER OF AN INTELLIGENCE
ORGANIZATION WHO DIRECTS THE
ACTIVITIES OF A SPY

CHAPTER ONE

In the end things turned out the way they did because of their shared history, a time from decades ago when choices were simple and clear, balanced by a fundamental certainty that truth, integrity, and innocence weren't just words, they were a way of life. But it was a history filled with markers that remained fluid and resonated with energy, with them at every turn like a Klein bottle or Möbius strip, Euclidian in nature, its affine properties rewriting their future at every turn. Ultimately it left them with the kind of choice no one should ever have to make, much less carry to their grave.

Had things gone differently, taken a turn somewhere along the way, it might not have happened at all. But where did you draw that line? Especially with Virgil Jones.

Virgil...always pushing. Always in control.

THE WATCHER FELT out of place. It was an odd sensation because in a way he felt like he belonged up front, maybe even sitting right there in the front row next to the family. But he wasn't. He was lost in the middle of the crowd under a sea of umbrellas, though he was still close enough to see and hear. The hearing wasn't so important because like almost everyone there he'd heard some version of it all before. The same predictable speech, varied with the utterance of a proper name and a specific prayer: *ashes to ashes*, or...whatever.

But the seeing mattered, in a guttural way. It was a need, a fixation he could not escape. He caught himself standing up on his toes to get a better view past all the umbrellas, then forced himself to relax and keep his heels on the ground. Reminded himself that he was surrounded by an army of cops.

The whole affair took longer than he thought it would, most of it spent waiting for everyone to shuffle into place before they could begin. It looked like every cop in the state was present. The city and state cops wore dress blues, the county cops in brown and tan, their Smokey Bear hats covered with clear bonnets. The bonnets reminded him of his grandmother's old shower cap... and the crusty expression that went with it. Even the DNR guys were there. Their uniforms were dark green with some sort of ceremonial sash that angled over their shoulder and then down around their waist. It looked impressive enough from a distance but up close it was all pressed polyester and faded sweat stains that smelled of fear and dry-cleaning chemicals. They were all probably thinking the same thing: *That could be me.*

He fell into a rhythm of bowing his head every few minutes like he might be praying or reflecting on some long forgotten memory of the deceased. Then he'd raise his head slowly, always in a slightly different direction. Doing so gave him almost a full one-hundred-eighty-degree view of everyone around him. Not that he needed it, really. There were only a handful of people he was actually watching and all of them were knitted together in a tight little group under the tent, right in front of the casket.

And out of the whole of that group he was really only interested in one person.

The little boy.

THE NEWS of the cop's death had stunned him, mostly because he'd been planning to do it himself. He'd spent years trying to figure the whole thing out, but he wasn't quite smart enough to pull it off...to get all the pieces in the proper order. He'd gotten away with killing before, plenty of times—so he wasn't dumb, he was simply...uncreative. And a little lazy. The lack of creativity paralyzed him and the laziness justified it all, day after day, until he woke up one morning and was hit with two stark realizations: The paralysis had cost him six years of his life, and the chief cause of that paralysis was dead. Now here *he* was, standing in the middle of a crowd at the gravesite of Major Crimes Unit Detective Ed Donatti, with storm clouds on the horizon, surrounded by what looked like every cop in the state of Indiana.

He was lost in thought when the preacher said something with finality and people started forming a line to walk by the casket. Some of the mourners touched the flag that covered the coffin. Others saluted or crossed themselves. Some looked like they didn't know what to do or say so they just walked on by, eyes straight ahead, their hair and jackets and skirts and ties blown sideways as the storm moved closer. Many of the women paused to hug Donatti's wife or place their hand on top of the boy's head before they walked away.

As the line moved forward he let himself drift toward the back. He didn't want to be seen here even though the only person who would recognize him wasn't really in a position, much less a state of mind to point a finger and start screaming his name. Why risk it?

Besides, he'd done his research over the last few years and he knew who all the players were. He saw an attractive blond woman named Sandy Small move away and wait by the line of cars. She was a tasty looking little tart...one of those broads who simply *oozed* sexuality. He wondered what *that* would be like. Maybe he'd have the chance to find out.

He watched Virgil Jones sit down next to Pam, and the boy, Jonas. Pam said something and then Jones said something to her, though he couldn't hear exactly what. Too far away. Then Pam shook her head and said something back. It looked like they might be arguing.

The rain started up again, then Virgil Jones moved to stand up, but the boy climbed on his lap and hugged him and held him down for a few more minutes. The boy might have said something, though it was hard to tell. When he glanced at Small he saw her bury her face in her hands.

Then the rain came hard and the whole thing was over and he turned away, thoughts of his past lurking at the back of his brain...his abusive father, the beatings, the emotional scars, the war. These thoughts were swallowed whole and undigested, left to rot in the septic of his soul. Everything should have turned out so different, yet it hadn't. What was the greater message here? Probably nothing at all. You left your mark or a mark was left on you.

The rain on his face tasted like saltwater and he couldn't understand why until one of the cops saw the look on his face and patted him on the shoulder as he walked past. He flinched without meaning to, an odd look on his face. He'd been crying and didn't even know it.

Hell of a storm coming.

CHAPTER TWO

Harvest time now, the dead season right on its heels, the calendar running short on breath, a couple minutes of light peeled back every day like logs pulled from the winter cord. It'd be downright cold soon—a brittle slap in the face that carried a four-month sting. The leaves had already turned and gone, ripped away by an early polar vortex that swept in from the Northwest on the ass end of a ruinous year, a dry death that every farmer in the state of Indiana would speak of for generations to come.

Every farmer except Charlie Esser, that is.

THE FIVE MEN met in secret. They sat around a plain wooden eight-by table in the central meeting room of the Shelby County Farmer's Co-Op, in Shelby County, Indiana. The co-op was a squat, single-story cinderblock structure that much like the men in the room, was showing some age. The building, painted with two coats of barn-red every year by the 4-H club whether it needed it or not was now so thick and heavy with the stuff it looked like the cinderblocks themselves were no longer necessary for structural support.

The men: Henry Stutzman, Angus Mizner, Basil Graves, Cal Lipkins, and Vernon Conrad. All were board members and stakeholders of the county co-op. The only member not present was the board's chairman, Charlie Esser. It wouldn't do to have Esser at this particular meeting, thus the secrecy.

"Just so we're clear, we all know what were talking about here," said Stutzman, the vice-chair of the six-man board. He tapped his finger on the table for emphasis. "The deadline is tomorrow. If we miss it, the deal is gone for good and we're toast. If we make it, all operations would essentially cease."

"That's not exactly accurate," Graves said. "There's no 'essentially' about it. We'd be done with our farms. Forever."

Lipkins rolled his eyes in a dramatic, almost valley-girl sort of way. "For fuck's sake, we all know that. How many times are we going to go over this? If we take the deal, we won't *need* to farm anymore. Our biggest worry will be what color umbrella we want in our rum punches while we sit on the beach and calculate the interest."

"And keep track of the royalties," Conrad said. "That'll be a full-time job, right there." A little light in his eyes.

"I'm sort of worried about finding the least crooked funds manager," Mizner added. "Fund-wise, I've got it narrowed down to Fidelity and Vanguard, but the people who run them—they're all a bunch of thieves."

"Let's try to stay focused," Stutzman said. "We've got to find a way to get Charlie on board or there won't be any colored umbrellas and crooked fund managers to deal with. Or royalty checks for that matter."

They all ran mega-farms, including Charlie Esser, the lone holdout on their multi-million dollar deal. When Charlie married Martha Shultz, he married into just over two-thousand acres in the southern part of Shelby County, most of it bordered on the Flatrock River. The Flatrock ran diagonally through the county where it eventually hooked up with the Wabash and Ohio rivers before draining into the Mississippi. Martha's great-grandfather had purchased the land a section or two at a time during the course of his life over one hundred years ago and her family had farmed it ever since. Her grandfather went on to start the co-op, Hank Stutzman's granddad right there with him. Together the two men had turned a small farming community into an agricultural powerhouse.

The Mizner, Graves, Lipkins, and Conrad families took up a year or so later, after the fact. Over the decades that followed their influence and voting power had grown strong and allied, though they were no different from any other farmer. They were all cash poor and land rich. When the last of the Shultz men were dead and buried, Charlie Esser found himself at the head of the table, in charge of an empire...one he ran with an iron fist that was as hard and solid as the forged blades of a twelve-bottom plow. But that was about to change.

Maybe.

Their season had been bad, the worst any of them had ever seen. No rain to speak of...*not a fucking drop* was the way almost everyone described it when they weren't in church. There were a few brief showers here and there, along with one ferocious storm earlier in the year that spun up a small tornado, but it wasn't nearly enough. When the Flatrock flowed to no more than a trickle, the co-op brought in drillers who worked in triple shifts boring deeper and deeper into the water table for irrigation, and then, there was that faint whiff of sulfur in the air and everything changed.

———

THE DRILLERS HAD HIT a pocket of natural gas. Charlie Esser and Cal Lipkins were standing next to one of the drilling platforms when the foreman started shouting and hit the rig's kill switch. Two seconds later they smelled the stench of sulfur and Lipkins' face lit up like a kid on Christmas morning. A geological survey crew was called in —no one really knew who made the call, though everyone suspected Lipkins had greased those particular skids—and a week later a lawyer representing a natural gas consortium made his pitch to the board. The first one had not gone well, but the lawyer hung around and chipped away at them in a divide-and-conquer sort of way. He was making progress and he knew it.

"The bottom line is this," the lawyer had said. "You're all sitting on a mountain of money, especially you, Mr. Esser."

"I own over two-thousand acres of land," Charlie said.

"Land that's been in my family for generations on end. I've been sitting on a mountain of money since the day I married my sweet Martha."

The lawyer almost laughed at the absurdity of his statement. Another country simpleton. "Yes, sir, I understand that. I really do. But if I could be brutally honest with you, Mr. Esser...with all of you, we know this hasn't exactly been your best year in terms of yield. You've all turned more than ninety percent of your crops under, the drillers have pulled out because they're not equipped to deal with the dangers of gas pockets this large, and the Flatrock doesn't show any signs of returning to normal levels until next year at the earliest. Maybe not even then. In addition —and I know all of you know this, but I'm going to just go ahead and say it anyway—even if the Flatrock were at normal levels, you couldn't pull enough water out of the current without having every town and county municipality to the Southwest breathing down your necks for overuse. Quite frankly, I'm having trouble seeing the alternatives. Why not just take the money? You'll still own the land. The people I represent are only interested in the mineral rights."

They called him City. He drove a fancy car that never seemed to get dirty, and wore expensive suits with pinstripes so subtle they acted like eye magnets. His hundred dollar haircut looked like it had been photoshopped from a magazine cover.

"You're talking about fracking, aren't you?" Charlie said.

City gave them an answer that said absolutely nothing, the kind of answer a politician might give a TV reporter when asked to state their position on congressional term limits. "We prefer to call it by its proper name, which is hydraulic fracturing, and it has been used as one of the key methods of extracting unconventional gas resources since 1947. They don't tell you that on the evening news, do they? All they talk about are the dangers. Well, let me tell you something gentlemen, natural gas extraction by way of hydraulic fracturing is the future of this country. Without it, we'll be right back where we were in the seventies...at the mercy of the middle-east, or worse, the Russians. Everyone thinks Putin is just a figurehead, but I'll tell you just as sure as I'm sitting here, they've already claimed the Arctic Circle as sovereign territory and even with the mid-terms out of the way, we're coming up on a lame duck session. The bottom line is this: Washington is afraid to even blink, let alone try to stare down the Russians. Or maybe they just don't care. I'm not entirely sure. But the industry is concerned. Very concerned. They are in fact, as concerned as I've ever seen them and I've been in this business a long time."

"Fuck a bunch of Russians," Charlie said. "I don't give two shits about the Russians...or the Arabs. We export more food to them than we keep for ourselves. Let 'em eat their oil. Here's *my* bottom line: My land is all I've ever had, all I've ever wanted, and all I'll ever need. Playing the patriot card with me won't work."

The other men nodded their agreement. "Charlie's right." Stutzman said. "Our families have farmed this land for generations. We're doing something good. We're feeding people."

This time City did laugh. "So are we. But ours have a

much bigger appetite, I guarantee it. You know what else they don't tell you on TV? The easy oil is gone and it's been gone for a long time. We're pulling natural gas out of shale and tar sand because other than going five miles deep in the Gulf for low-grade crude, that's what we've got left.

"What you've got left is exactly this: Bank notes you can't pay in full because your crop insurance only covers you up to fifty percent. Yes, that's right, I checked. It's part of my job. And while fifty percent might cover your nut through the winter, you won't have any money to buy the fuel or seed you'll need to plant next spring—rain or no rain. The hard truth of the matter is I'm all you've got left. This isn't a high pressure sales pitch...it's an accounting of the facts. You're each being offered two-million dollars up front, with a guaranteed cap on back end royalties that'll triple that number inside of two years. Let me be blunt: The people I represent? They're heavy hitters. That's a polite way of saying they don't fuck around. A week from now you'll be sitting down at the greasy spoon talking about do we or don't we and they'll already be gone and you won't even know it."

Then, trying to sound like a farmer: "I'd think it over, right quick, I were you."

THEY THOUGHT about it for three days, both individually and together, the clocks in their heads ticking down like a time-bomb. The bomb wouldn't explode with a loud bang... it'd fizzle out like a dud, but the end result would be the same. They'd all be dead, financially speaking. Eventually they all came around...except for Charlie Esser. And Charlie's hold-out was what brought them together again this morning.

"I just don't see it," Mizner said. He looked around the table. "I've talked to him, one-on-one, and I know you all have too. He's not going to budge."

"The hell he ain't," Lipkins said. "There's just too much at stake. I won't have it."

"Well, it's his land, Cal. We can't exactly force him to sell," Conrad said.

"What about Martha?" Graves said. Martha Esser was Charlie's wife, who had recently taken a nasty fall on a set of hardwood stairs with an even nastier blow to the side of her head on the way down. She was currently in the hospital, floating in and out of consciousness.

"What about her?" Lipkins said. "Martha's a mean old hag who never worked a day in her life."

"Jesus Christ, Cal, that's a little over the top," Conrad said. "How many times has she cooked for you?"

"Fuck you, Vern. She's a vile bitch and always has been. You think Charlie married her because he loved her? He married her to sit at the head of this table. And I'll tell you something else, just because you used to roll her when you thought no one was looking doesn't mean you get to—"

Conrad was across the table and had Lipkins by the throat before anyone knew what was happening. The other men jumped up and pulled them apart, but not before Stutzman caught an elbow in his left eye.

"That's enough," Stutzman shouted after they were pulled apart. He rubbed at his eye. "Goddamn it, that hurts."

"You're gonna have a mouse," Mizner said. "And a good one at that."

Stutzman pointed at Lipkins and Conrad. "Sit the fuck down. We gotta figure this out."

They all sat the fuck down and eventually Graves said, "So what are we going to do? I was asking about Martha. Wouldn't Hank need her signature or something too? She might be a mean old hag..." He glanced at Conrad when he said it. "But Cal's right, Vern. It's just as much her land as is Hank's. Maybe even more so if they had one of them there pre-nups."

Conrad didn't want to hear it. Wasn't even listening. "Fuck you, Basil," he said. "And you too, Cal. So we've had a little fun along the way. So what? Besides, it was before they was married...mostly. I'll tell you all something, I still sort of have feelings for her. She weren't never mean to me, so I'd appreciate the hell out of it if you all would show just the smallest bit of respect for the woman."

"Oh for Christ sake, Vern" Lipkins said. "Give it a rest. I think I speak for everyone here when I say nobody gives two genuine shits about your feelings. This is a county co-op board meeting, not a group therapy session. We've worked all our lives for what we've got, and I for one am not going to just sit here and let one bad season and a heavy-handed board chairman ruin us."

They all thought about that grim little nugget for a while.

Then Conrad said, "You guys know that Charlie beats on her."

Graves: "He does not."

Conrad: "He does."

Mizner: "That rumor's older'n you are, Vern."

Conrad: "Ain't no rumor, Angus. She's talked to me about it. I seen the bruises too. Hits her where it don't show."

Lipkins: "So she's not just been cooking for you, huh Vern? Sounds to me like she's been *cooking*."

Vernon Conrad pointed his finger at Lipkins. "I swear to Christ, Cal, if you don't shut your trap, and I mean right fucking now, I'm gonna shut it for you."

Lipkins sensed that he'd hit Conrad's limit and held up his hands, palms out, though a ghost of a smirk remained splayed across his mouth. Conrad turned away, his face red.

"I still don't believe it," Graves said. "Besides, knowing Martha—no offense, Vern—if there was any violence, it was probably self-defense on Charlie's part."

Conrad shook his head. His forearms rested on the table, his fists clenched.

Stutzman looked at Mizner and Graves. "I'm ashamed to admit it, but Vern's right. It's not a rumor. Charlie knocks her around, time to time. Nothing too serious, and not very often, but he does like to let some steam out once in a while, especially if he's been drinking."

Conrad shot Lipkins a look. Mizner too. "See. Like I said, ain't no rumor. He beats her." Then to Stutzman, almost as an afterthought, "And just how in the hell do you know about it?"

Stutzman ignored the question. "I'll tell you something," he said, "and this is a little weird, but right after she fell, Charlie got pretty hammered one night down at the Flat-Tap." The Flatrock Tap & Grill was one of the nicer establishments in the area, if your definition of nicer was someplace that didn't have dirt floors and indoor picnic tables. "I didn't think much about it at the time because, you know, Martha was hurt, and he *seemed* upset, but now that I think about it..." He let it drift.

Conrad leaned forward. "What? What'd he say?"

Stutzman rubbed his swollen eye. "He was good and drunk, talking out of turn. Probably didn't even realize what he was saying. But he told me that they'd always had power of attorney papers—him for her, and her for him—in case anything ever happened. Said they had plenty of life insurance too. Million dollar whole-life policies, one for each of them. Said they'd had 'em for a coon's age and if anything ever happened to her, he'd be set for life."

Conrad leaned back and crossed his arms. "So what? I got life insurance. Plenty of folks do. Though mine ain't no million dollars."

"It wasn't as much what he said, but what he left out," Stutzman said. "He said if anything ever happened to *her*. He sort of went on and on about it. Never said a word about if something happened to him...that she'd be set for life. Sounded like he was sort of hoping something *would* happen to her. In fact, the more I think about it, the more I'm beginning to think that maybe Martha didn't fall down the stairs all by herself. Maybe she was helped down the stairs. Head first."

"You know what?" Lipkins said, his rugged face turning sour. "It's no wonder he doesn't want to take the deal. He doesn't need to."

"What do you mean?" Graves said.

"I'll tell you exactly what he means," Mizner said. "He

doesn't want to take the deal because when Martha goes, he's going to have all the money he needs."

"Be leaving quite a bit on the table if what City says is true," Conrad said. "We've got the deal in black and white, on paper."

"That's true," Lipkins said. "But think about it for a minute. He wouldn't be leaving *that much* on the table. We're getting two million up front, plus a percentage on royalties that'll triple our take in two years. That's six million."

"That's what I'm saying," Conrad said. "He'd be leaving five million on the table over two years."

"But it's not five million," Stutzman said. He'd caught the logic right away. "Not from Charlie's perspective. He's got over two thousand acres of land. That's almost half as much as the rest of us combined. Anybody here besides me talked to an accountant yet? That two million you're hoping to get? Uncle's going to take almost half of it right off the top. Now you're down to a million and change."

"Still gonna get the royalties," Graves said.

Stutzman nodded. "Yup. And that's a lot of money, I'll grant you. But that's where the land comes in, especially from Esser's point of view, because it's the *amount* of land that matters. That's why the gas people only want the mineral rights. We'll still own the land, but we can't farm it. In fact, once they start the extraction process the only thing we can do, and in fact will *have to do*, is pay taxes on it. So between the tax on the two million in front money, the land taxes, plus the tax he'll have to pay on the royalties, he'll be better off if Martha is gone. Charlie's got over two-thousand acres that'll no longer qualify for the farm tax-break because you actually have to farm the land to get the credit. The life insurance settlement is tax free."

"Here's something else to think about," Mizner said. "If he holds out and doesn't take the deal, *and* Martha is out of the picture, we're fucked, each and every one of us. Charlie's gonna collect a big fat life insurance check for a million bucks—tax-free, mind you—and ride out the winter in style. When spring rolls around he'll offer to buy us out for pennies on the dollar. And you know what? We'd have to sell. City's right. We might make it through the winter, but come spring, we'll be busted."

"Esser, that Jew bastard," Lipkins said. "I saw him talking to City day before yesterday and they were laughing and back slapping like long lost buddies. I'll bet that son of a bitch is putting a side deal together with him. He buys us out next spring with his life insurance money, then signs with the gas people. Now instead of two million up front, he's getting twelve, plus the royalties...all from our land."

"He'll still have to pay the taxes," Conrad said.

"He'll be able to afford the taxes, you moron. The interest on the royalties alone would pay the taxes and he'll still have the after tax portion of the original twelve million. I'm guessing he could somehow squeak by on that."

"I'm not a moron."

Lipkins ignored him and spoke directly to Stutzman. "What're we gonna do, Hank? Hell, for all we know, he's over at the hospital right now with a pillow over Martha's face."

"I don't know," Hank said. "But we better think of something, and quick. What we really need is time—an extension on the offer. If we could get more time out of City we'll have some room to maneuver...to plan. We're all supposed to meet here tomorrow morning anyway—regular business—so I'll call City. Maybe I can get him and his people to extend us some time and we'll all make one more push together at Charlie in the morning. Agreed?"

They all nodded in agreement.

Vern, still thinking of Martha, had tears in his eyes.

THE NEXT MORNING Charlie Esser climbed out of his pickup and walked across the gravel parking lot of the co-op building, dawn still more than ninety minutes out. Inside, the overhead fluorescents buzzed to life, the flickering light ricocheting off the windows as he made his way to the coffee supplies. He filled the basin with fresh tap water, separated a paper filter from the stack then filled the basket with few scoops and set the machine to brew.

A few minutes later he poured himself a cup and carried it back outside. He set his coffee on the rail that fronted the co-op's porch, leaned against the side of the building and lit a cigarette. A crisp breeze swirled against the front of the building and it had some teeth. A fat squirrel ran past and stopped next to the steps, its cheeks packed with food. It sat up on its hind legs for a moment, checked its surroundings, then scampered away.

Morning in the country.

The others would be along any minute now. Charlie sipped his coffee and waited.

HE DIDN'T HAVE to wait long. Henry Stutzman arrived before Charlie was finished with his smoke. Both men were dressed alike: Oshkosh overalls, blue denim work shirts, billed John Deere hats that had once been green, and scuffed steel-toed work boots with the tread lugs mostly worn away. Stutzman was lean and solid, not an ounce of fat anywhere, though he had a bit of a drinker's nose that made his face look a little front heavy. He climbed the three steps of the porch with a measured effort. Farming did that, made you feel young and old at the same time. He tipped his head upwards then nodded through the smoke. "Chuck."

"Hank. Coffee's on. What the hell happened to your eye?"

Stutzman ignored the question. "Anyone else yet?"

"Not just yet. Any minute now, I imagine."

Stutzman walked into the building and let the door bang shut on its springs. Charlie felt the vibration race up his back like boot spurs against his spine. A few seconds later he looked out at the road and saw Angus Mizner, Basil Graves, Vernon Conrad, and Cal Lipkins coming in hard, a single line of trucks that bobbed along the gravel pack, a pale dust plume in tow disappearing into the darkness. The four men parked their trucks, climbed the steps and moved past Charlie without a word. They all smelled faintly of diesel fuel, feed corn, manure, and bacon.

Charlie pushed himself off the side of the building and ground out his cigarette under the toe of his boot. He shook his head, dumped the cold of his coffee on the gravel and followed everyone in.

Too goddamned early in the morning.

Stutzman brought them up to speed, but it was mostly for show. City had said no to an extension and hammered home the fact that it was an all or nothing deal...that they all had to agree. His reasons were complicated and his explanations convoluted, all dealing with geography and the geometry of something called angular access, which none of them really understood. Their land bordered each other's in one way or another, but the only viable access to the best pockets of gas—City had called them domes—would be primarily through Charlie's fields. If he held out, none of them would get a nickel.

So, decision time. They'd all sign or they wouldn't.

The contract was on the table in front of Stutzman. He had a pen in his hand. Graves, Lipkins, Conrad, and Mizner had already signed. Charlie had his Leatherman knife out, cleaning the dirt beneath a thumbnail. Stutzman shook his head, sighed, and said, "It's just too much money, Charlie. I'm taking the deal, and I'm begging you to take it too. We've got the auctioneer coming out next week. I'm selling it all to the highest bidder...every last piece of it, from the machinery right down to the goddamned spoons. The lowest bidder can have the rest. It's not like we'll need the money after this. Gail wants to move to Arizona and be closer to the grandkids." He signed the contract, set the pen on top of the papers and slid the pile over to Charlie.

The Leatherman was sharp as a razor and Charlie didn't look up when he spoke. "My land is the only thing I've got left and I don't intend to—"

Lipkins cut him off. "Listen to me, Esser. The deadline is today. If you don't sign, and I mean right here and now, you're going to cost us all millions of dollars and I'm not having it. None of us are. Do you hear me? Now pick up that fucking pen and sign the goddamned papers."

Conrad had heard enough. He stood up so fast he knocked his chair over. "This is crazy. We all used to be friends. Now look at us. I can't take it no more." He walked out of the room, the door banging shut behind him. The room got quiet, the only sound was Conrad's truck as it pulled out of the lot.

Charlie was still cleaning his fingernails with the Leatherman. "I talked to Carl Johnson yesterday over at Sunnydale Farms. He's bringing in two loads of feed corn this morning. He needs to store it here for a couple of days while he rotates his stock. The only silo we've got open that can handle that much is number seven." He stood from the table. "I'm going to scrape out the floor and patch the rat holes at the base if anyone wants to help."

Graves shook his head and said, "Come on, Charlie. It's over. Surely you can see that."

Charlie ignored him and spoke to Lipkins. "We've known each other a long time, Cal, and I think by now you'd know that I'm a man of my word."

"Meaning what?" Lipkins said.

Charlie looked directly at him. "Meaning exactly this: You've called me Charlie ever since we was kids. When you address me by my last name without putting a 'Mister' in front of it I take that as a sign of disrespect. Use that kind of language with me again and I'll stick that pen so far up your ass you'll be able to sign with your teeth." He drove the tip of the Leatherman through the stack of papers and into the wood of the tabletop. "There is no deal." He left the room and headed out to number seven, the handle of the knife swaying back and forth like a silent metronome.

THE SILO ACCESS doors opened inward so that when the silos were filled the weight and pressure of the silage would hold them closed. The door was six feet high and three feet wide. Two steel beams rested on four brackets that provided additional structural support when the silo was full. A heavy-duty padlock hung on a clasp just above the lever that unlatched the door. Charlie took out his keys, unlocked the lock, removed the beams, then hung a pair of work lights on a pole-stand. When he unlatched the door to number seven and pushed it open he discovered the mess was worse than he thought. The silo hadn't been used in over a year and the floor was covered with a thick layer of rotten silage and the rats had chewed through the dry mortar at the base. Charlie grabbed a shovel and got to work, scraping the floor. Once the silage was gathered together he'd cart it out with a wheelbarrow and dump it out back for hog slop.

He hadn't been working long when he heard the others leave. He stepped outside and watched them all drive away, their taillights fading into the black of the morning. He had a quick smoke then went back to work. An hour later, his task almost complete, Charlie caught the shadow of someone crossing between the work lights and the open door of the silo. The lights were bright enough that he couldn't see who stood in front of him, only their outline, like someone standing between a pair of headlights at the side of the road on a moonless night.

"You should have signed, Charlie."

"My decision's been made."

"So has mine. It's one you won't soon forget either."

"I ain't afraid of you."

"The look on your face and the sound of your voice says different."

"What's that you're holding there? I can't see you. Step out of the lights."

"I don't think you want me to do that. If I have to step outside of these lights it means you've made a choice. Why not take the easy way, Charlie? Take the money. You've earned it."

"I've made my position clear. I'm not taking the deal."

"So you're not going to change your mind then?"

"No, I ain't."

"We're talking about the deal of a lifetime here. Millions of dollars. You can't say no."

"I already have. Now if you don't mind, I've got work to do and no matter what you think, I ain't afraid. Especially of you."

The bat was a wooden Louisville Slugger and it cracked Charlie's skull with a dull wet crunch, like a watermelon dropped on concrete. The attacker pulled the blow at the last minute, the way a prize fighter might pull a punch and show mercy on his opponent in the first round.

When Charlie fell to his knees his attacker waited a moment, then pushed him forward with the end of the bat. He fell face-first on the floor of the silo. His breathing was steady...maybe a little shallow? There wasn't any blood— that was a relief, because this was only a message. The attacker squatted next to Charlie, close to his face and checked his eyes. Neither pupil was blown, which was another good sign. The attacker was no medical expert, but he'd seen a lot of crime shows on TV.

Then, the sounds of big trucks coming in, the roar of Jake-brakes as they slowed for the turn off the county road. The attacker ran outside and saw two semis, still about a half mile away and felt the anger swell up inside. What the hell were they doing here? Back in the silo, quickly now, where Charlie got kicked in the ribs for good measure, once, twice, then a third time, as hard as possible. "How's that feel? You're going to take the deal, Esser. Nobody walks away from that kind of money." The attacker kicked again...getting a little carried away with the rush of it all, the trucks getting louder by the second. Had to go. Time to get out.

He turned out the lights, pulled the silo door shut, clicked the padlock in place, put the steel beams across the brackets and hopped into Charlie's truck. The Esser farm was only about a mile away. He turned his head as the semis passed. They wouldn't have been able to see inside the cab against the glare of the headlights, but better safe than sitting in county lockup. Two minutes later with Esser's truck parked safely in the barn, the attacker switched into his own vehicle and made three or four random turns down old country roads, the highway only a few hundred yards away with no other cars in sight. He was safe.

Start to finish the whole thing was over inside of thirty minutes. It was still dark outside.

Message delivered. He'd take the deal. Might have to sign with his teeth when he woke up, but he'd sign.

THE TWO GRAIN haulers from Sunnydale turned into the co-op lot, Carl Johnson himself in the first truck and one of his hired hands, who was just a kid, in the second. The kid set the airbrakes with a hiss, climbed down from his rig, stretched, then walked over to Johnson's truck.

"Was that Charlie just went by?" Johnson asked. "Looked like his truck."

"Don't know from Charlie," the kid said, and he didn't, being new and all. "Driving like he was late for quitting time though, whoever it was. You want to back up to the chute first, or you want me to?"

The chute was a huge grate set in a concrete pad large enough to accommodate the semi trailers. It sat next to the scales under a covered opening. The way it worked, a truck would pull up, get weighed, dump their load into the grated opening, get re-weighed then pull away. The difference in weight between the full load and the empty rig equaled their total off-load. An auger carried the contents—corn, beans, grain, whatever—through a large tube and up to the top of the silo where it fell right in. But the whole weighing process wasn't necessary in this case because they weren't getting paid for their loads, just storing them. They could skip the scales and the arithmetic and just dump their loads and the auger would do the rest. "I'll go first," Johnson said. "Charlie said to put it in number seven. Go check it out, will you?"

The kid said he would, and by the time Johnson got his rig backed up to the grate he was back with two cups of coffee. "Seven's all locked up and the keys weren't on the board," he said. "Coffee's hot though."

Johnson took one of the coffees and scratched at the back of his head. "Anyone else around?"

"Nope. Must have been and gone already."

"Well, no shit. We just saw him drive by."

"How do we tell if seven's empty or not?" the kid said.

"Ideally, we'd unlock the door and push. If it won't open, it's full."

"But we can't do that."

"So, plan B," Johnson said. He pulled a pry-bar from behind the driver's seat of his rig and told the kid to follow him. They walked across the gravel lot, around the back of the admin building and up to the silo area. There were ten of them in total, all in a row, with augers running at odd angles that snaked back to the enclosed chute behind the scales. Ten silos, with ten augers. Johnson counted from his left and they ended up at number five. Then he took the bar and tapped on the side. The noised was muffled and dull.

"Hear that? This one's full. Number five." Then he walked to the next one, number six, and tapped again. Same thing. Same sound. "Full." Then they got to seven. He gave it a rap. The sound was completely different. Hollow and distant. "See? Number seven. Empty and waiting, just like Charlie said it would be. Go inside and turn on the auger for seven. I'll dump mine then you can back yours up."

"Okay," the kid said, then he stopped and listened.

"What?" Johnson said.

"I thought I heard something in there."

"In where?"

He pointed to seven. "In there. Inside."

Johnson laughed. "You probably did. Rats. They make 'em as big as dogs around here. They've got teeth the size of your thumbs." He tossed him the bar.

"What's this for?"

"The rats. If you see one, swing for the fence."

The kid shuddered and walked away in a hurry.

An hour later they were gone.

So was Charlie.

CHAPTER THREE

Sunday morning, a time to relax and reconnect. Virgil Jones was up and around by eight. Up meant out of bed wearing nothing except his boxers, with around being loosely defined as standing sleepy eyed in front of the Keurig trying to decide if he wanted the Donut Shop regular or the vanilla latte jolt.

Sandy, Virgil's wife, who was almost eight months pregnant with their first child—a boy they'd already decided would be named Wyatt—slipped in front of him and popped the latte container in the machine. The O.B. doc had said Sandy was carrying perfectly, and when Virgil looked at her from behind, he whole-heartedly agreed.

"Is that for me, or you?" Virgil asked.

Sandy hit the brew button as she simultaneously reached behind herself and cupped his boxers. "It's for you. You're going to need the extra energy. Drink up, big boy."

She walked back to the bedroom and Virgil drank up,

letting himself enjoy the sugar boost, not to mention the ego boost. *Big boy.*

The O.B. doc had warned him about this. Said it with a sly grin...the hormones and the late-stage desires. He drank the coffee so fast he burned his tongue a little. Didn't care though.

With the reconnection, and all.

———

AFTER THE LATE-STAGE desire festivities were complete, Virgil—being the gentleman he was—insisted Sandy shower first. She had a brunch scheduled with Pam Donatti and he had a schedule that included precisely nothing, which was exactly how he liked his Sundays. He dozed for a while despite the coffee, then was pulled awake by a kiss from Sandy before she left. Virgil told her good-bye, shook off the sleepiness then jumped into the shower and did the whole routine. He dressed in jeans, a crisp Red Stripe Jamaican beer sweatshirt he'd gotten from their beer distributor, and half-top brown boots. When he finished, he admired himself in the full-length bedroom admiration mirror, happily deciding he looked like he'd just gotten laid and had a nap, which was all true. He went outside, grabbed *The Indianapolis Star* from the driveway, then made himself another latte after winning a weedy internal argument on the grounds that he'd just burned enough calories to offset the extra fat.

Virgil and Sandy had settled into a comfortable rhythm over the course of the pregnancy, and while much of it felt natural, they both admitted early on, like all first-time pregnant couples do, that neither of them had a clue what they were actually doing. They'd each read the 'What To Expect' bible, and while it was packed with some valuable information, most of it was generalized and the generalization seemed to create more questions instead of answering some of the more fundamental ones they already had. Sandy's position on the matter was they were simply nervous and a little scared because it was all so new to them.

Virgil's position was a little more basic: They were lost in space. It hadn't helped that he'd actually sort of skimmed the pregnancy bible as opposed to reading it cover to cover.

After the death of his friend and long-time co-worker, Ed Donatti, Virgil suggested because neither of them had living parents they could turn to, maybe Sandy should seek out Pam Donatti's advice since Pam and Ed had the experience of their own son, Jonas. Sandy liked the idea and as it turned out, so did Pam, who, they all agreed, could use a little support anyway. The problem was, Pam had never quite forgiven herself—or Virgil, for that matter—for Ed's death. Virgil wasn't at fault, not directly, but Pam was still stuck in the grieving process and Virgil often found himself a convenient target of opportunity.

So. Over the last eight months the two women had developed a close friendship, formed over the shaky bond of Ed's death and Virgil and Sandy's unborn son. What could possibly go wrong?

He was down a half-cup with his latte and had yet to look at the newspaper when his cell buzzed at him. He tapped the screen and said, "Jonesy."

"Jones-man." It was Cora LaRue, chief of the state's

Major Crimes Unit. Cora was a former beat-cop, a no-nonsense administrator, and Virgil's previous boss until he'd been fired from the MCU for a smallish prescription drug problem he'd developed after getting a serious tune-up that almost killed him. "Are you open today?"

Virgil and his all-but-adopted brother, Murton Wheeler, co-owned a Jamaican themed bar called Jonesy's, as well as a private investigations firm they ran on the side. Murton, a retired FBI undercover special agent, and Virgil, forced out of the state's MCU, worked well together. They operated both businesses out of the same location...the bar on the main floor, the P.I. business upstairs. "The bar, or the office?"

"Both. Either. It doesn't matter." Their was an edge in Cora's voice—Virgil had known her long enough that he heard it right away.

"Bar's closed on Sunday's. The shop opens at eight tomorrow morning. What's going on, Cora?"

"The governor wants a meeting. In private."

"How about I just go to his place, or the office?"

Cora let out a breath that landed somewhere between a sigh and a snarl on the Richter scale. "You clearly haven't read *The Star* this morning, have you? I'm at the mansion now and the media is hovering at the front gate like they're expecting us to toss a carcass over the fence. They're already waiting at the office and this is Sunday, for fuck's sake."

"What do you want from me?" Virgil asked as he picked up the paper. The story was right there, front and center, above the fold. Then, without waiting for an answer he said, "Have him come out to my place. I'm alone. The bar's too visible anyway, even when we're closed. Maybe especially if we're closed."

"That could work." Virgil heard her pull the phone away for a moment, then say—presumably to the governor—"How about his place?" Back to Virgil: "How about an hour? We've got to get to the airport."

"That'll work. Has he made a statement yet?"

"We're working that out now. He wants your...input... before he says anything, hence the meeting."

"Can you get here without being tagged?"

"We're working on that too," Cora said, then clicked off.

After they'd hung up, Virgil thought, *the airport?*

VIRGIL SPENT the time getting himself up to speed, and couldn't quite believe what he saw. He read the entire *Star* piece twice, the first time quickly, then once again more carefully, looking for the not-so-subtle tinges and allusions that typically characterized modern-day reporting. Unfortunately, he didn't find any. There were no *unquoted sources close to the investigation*—which usually meant some asshole-blogger's opinion, or the ever popular *some have speculated*—a different asshole's Twitter feed—type of statements. What he found was a compact piece of investigative journalism backed up by solid research, pertinent details, specific dates, and an accurate, if not somewhat banal portrayal of the facts.

No wonder newspapers were going broke.

A quick check on-line revealed that the story had

already been picked up by the A.P. and was beginning to gain some traction on CNN and FOX, both of whom already had it on the net. That meant it either was or soon would be on TV, so if you were either an air traveler or a right-wing nut job you had just enough information to spread some social outrage.

It went like this: The governor's former chief of staff, the now deceased Bradley Pearson, had hopped into bed—figuratively speaking—with Augustus Pate, Chairman and CEO of Augustus Pate International. API was nothing more than a shell; a holding company for a variety of ventures, not the least of which included two disparate firms...one that contracted with the state to handle the sales and marketing of Indiana's lottery gaming, and another that acted as the general contractor to oversee the construction of any number of private prisons throughout the country, including the state of Indiana.

Governor Hewitt (Mac) McConnell had approved of the lottery plan on the basis of simple economics. A buck was a buck, after all. He did, however, have deep misgivings about privately held corporations running the state's penal system, and had vetoed every bill sent to him. But the legislature—McConnell being a blue governor in a deeply red state—had no trouble overriding the vetoes, and at the end of the day the resolution passed. Indiana was on its way to having one of the largest private prison systems in the country.

It all fell apart though when Pearson and Pate colluded to scam the lottery. They both wound up dead, as did the lottery director herself, in a vicious gun fight that left Virgil, Murton, and Ed Donatti caught in the cross-fire. That same battle ultimately cost Donatti his life when he was stabbed in the throat.

As tragic as it was—Virgil and Donatti had been close friends—that should have been the end of it. There was some damage control and clean up at the executive level, of course, but it was mostly for appearances because everyone who'd had their hand in the wrong end of the penal pie was dead.

But the republicans in the house and senate were more than slightly miffed. Not only was their prison deal dead, they were now on the hook for hundreds of millions of dollars in land, materials, cost overruns, and other expenditures that bloated the state's budget and placed it severely in the red. Virgil speculated it didn't help matters that over the past seven months the governor had been walking around with a smug 'I told you so' look on his face.

The republicans, in a very demonstrative right-wing sort of way went into full circus mode. They demanded a thorough investigation and voted to bring in a special prosecutor to handle the subsequent smearing of the executive branch of their own state government. Pearson worked for the governor after all, not them. What they needed was a scapegoat for their own blunder...a way to humanize the tragedy of government run amok. But it wouldn't fly. Pate and Pearson were dead. As far as Virgil was concerned it had been a witch hunt that lacked...well, a witch.

He looked at the headline of *The Star* again.

ISP UNION REP SAYS STRIKE IMMINENT
Governor Set To Call In National Guard

Clearly something else was at play because the governor wanted to meet. But why, Virgil had no idea. He was out of it and had been ever since Cora—at the direction of the governor himself—told him to pack up and ship out.

No matter what was going on or about to happen, Virgil wanted Sandy there with him when Cora and McConnell came by, brunch or no brunch. Sandy had a way with the governor. She knew how to...*handle* him. He picked up the phone to call her just as the doorbell rang.

CHAPTER FOUR

Virgil checked his watch instead of the peephole and thought, *early*. He opened the door and found Murton holding a copy of *The Star*, a grim look on his usually smiling face.

"We have what any reasonably intelligent person might describe as 'a sticky situation.'" Murton wore jeans, and despite the cooler than normal fall air, a vintage short-sleeved Hawaiian shirt adorned with scantily clad women depicted in various stages of inebriation.

"That's one way to put it," Virgil said. "Come on in. Where the hell do you find those shirts?"

"I'm not saying. People with a certain sense of style know where to look. Others, well..." He spread his hands and let the implication hang.

They settled in the kitchen, Virgil ignoring the hanging implication. "This is not something we want to get tangled up with, Murt. It's pure politics."

Murton tipped his chair back and put his boots up on

the table. Virgil saw the bottom of an ankle holster strapped to his right leg under the jeans. He knew from experience that there was a knife tucked into the other boot, and the loose fitting shirt covered a chrome-plated .45 holstered on his belt. "Of course it's politics, Jonesy. Everything is politics. And like it or not, I suspect we're going to be in the middle of it before it's over."

"Why do I get the feeling that you're already working an angle of some kind?"

"I have no idea. But since you and the governor are sort of asshole buddies, I'm thinking he might be able to offer us some sort of guidance or something. Help us get our stories straight at least."

The middle of it, as outlined in *The Star*, was this: The Indiana legislature had found a way to humanize the tragedy of government run amok, and in typical government fashion they did it by taking an aggressively passive stance. They simply waited for the other side to make a mistake. And in this case the mistake was a big one.

The day that Pearson and Pate were killed was the same day that Virgil and Sandy were having a cookout with all their friends. Given the fact that Virgil and Sandy were cops—even though Virgil had been fired—most all of their friends were cops too, with the exception of Delroy and Robert, two Jamaicans who, a few years ago, emigrated to the U.S. and were now co-owners of Jonesy's Bar. When Murton and his girlfriend, Becky, failed to show up for the party, Virgil and Ed Donatti went looking for them.

What they found was Becky beaten to a pulp, and Murton tied to a chair with the business end of a shotgun pressed against his head. A gunfight ensued and Virgil killed Pate, all while Donatti—who'd gone in through the back—struggled with one of Pate's henchmen, Hector Sigara, in the kitchen. During that struggle Donatti managed to pull his service weapon and kill Sigara, but not before he'd taken a fatal stab wound to the throat.

Pam Donatti grieved in ways that Virgil had never seen. There was a burning anger underneath it all...some of it at herself—it had been her idea that Donatti go with Virgil to Murton's house—and some of the anger was pointed squarely at Virgil. Ed might still be alive today if she'd have kept quiet, or if Virgil had been more careful. But the real mistake was yet to come.

It happened quietly, in the background over a period of months and was now bubbling up—as outlined in *The Star* —in a very public way. Because Donatti was an investigator with the state's MCU, and because his death was ruled a homicide, an autopsy was required by law. Except Pam didn't understand why her beloved husband had to be cut up and have every inch of his body, both inside and out, examined in such a harsh and clinical way when it was clear how he'd been killed and why he had died. Both cause and manner of death were clear. Any idiot could see that.

Something of a minor argument ensued between the grieving wife of a slain state police officer and the Marion County Coroner, who, by all accounts, was simply doing his job. But Pam wouldn't let it go and said something to Sandy, who then said something to Virgil, and because Virgil and the governor *were* sort of asshole buddies, the governor took care of things. Blood samples were taken and stored, the autopsy issue was quietly buried, and so too was Ed Donatti. It should have ended there.

But it didn't.

As Detective First-Grade with the state's MCU, and as a career police officer, Donatti not only made enough money that Pam didn't have to work, but he'd also dutifully contributed to the state-managed police pension fund. The fund would provide a more than adequate retirement for the Donatti's, but it also stipulated that should any participant officer be killed in the line of duty, two things would happen: the amount would be doubled, and the payout would come as one tax-free, lump sum. It further stipulated that if the officer had children, an additional fifty-percent of the doubled amount (effectively one-third of the total payout) would be set aside in a trust, managed by the surviving parent on behalf of the child.

So. As broken-hearted and angry as Pam was, she was also more than financially secure. Quite a lot more by almost any standard of measurement. Until, that is, it was time to dot all the i's and cross all the t's.

THE I-DOTTING and t-crossing came to a grinding halt when the plan administrator, a staunch, Ronald Reagan-really-was-Jesus type of conservative reviewed the paperwork. He was just about to grudgingly approve the payout to Pam Donatti, and her son, Jonas, when he noticed that an autopsy—a strict requirement before distribution of funds—had never been completed. He contacted the coroner to find out why. The coroner, who was a politic only by way of an unopposed election, had no reason to lie. He told the plan administrator that the cause and manner of death were clear and an autopsy simply hadn't been necessary, though when pressed, admitted that the governor had intervened on behalf of the surviving widow.

When the plan administrator heard that, he immediately called an influential republican state senator. The senator—who knew Reagan wasn't Jesus, but thought he was close—just happened, quite un-coincidentally, to chair the committee looking into the misappropriation of funds by the executive branch on the privatization of the prisons. The administrator was told to sit on the check, a hasty committee meeting was called and the general consensus was unanimous. They had the governor—that smug son of a bitch—by the balls.

But it wasn't the governor's first day in office. Had he gotten the coroner to sign off on Donatti without doing an autopsy? Yes, and why not? The coroner himself said it wasn't necessary and was only doing it as a matter of routine. The governor sought advice from his legal people who, after reviewing the appropriate laws and regulations, informed him that like most laws, it all came down to interpretation. "In Clinton-speak," the lawyers had said, "it depends on what your definition of 'is' is."

The governor's definition of the law sided with Pam Donatti. Her husband, Ed had been a valued member of the MCU almost since its inception, an inception by the way, that had been the governor's idea when he first took office. So the actual autopsy was waved, Donatti was buried and everyone dug in for the fight.

It was a slow fight, as fights went. Eventually, after months of back and forth between the governor's office, the plan administrator's office, the sub-committee, and Pam

Donatti's lawyer, everyone agreed that a distribution of funds would be in the best interests of all parties. But how to make that happen? There had been a significant amount of press surrounding the entire affair and with election time right around the corner there was quite a bit of face-saving to attend to.

The Governor wanted the check cut...period. The pension fund administrator wanted the letter and spirit of the law followed, which meant an exhumation and full autopsy. The sub-committee wanted a public statement from the governor's office declaring that he'd stepped over the line by intervening on Pam Donatti's behalf, along with full and complete testimony regarding the prison deal and anything else the committee deemed 'necessary and relevant' to their ongoing investigation.

Pam landed somewhere in the middle of the fray. She wanted the check, but there was no way in hell they were going to dig up Ed.

The coroner didn't quite give a shit one way or the other. He'd do the autopsy or he wouldn't once the lawyers were done arguing.

In the end, the governor agreed that he would testify before the committee, but only if they—the governor privately referred to them as right-winged pricks—would limit their questions to details specific to his own involvement of the prison plan, *and* instead of a full autopsy, limit the coroner to his relevant record of events. The administrator tried to have a say in the matter, but no one really cared what he thought. He was just an accountant, after all.

So Pam Donatti would get her check and after almost eight months it looked like everything would be fine.

Except the plan administrator was more than slightly perturbed. He wasn't just an accountant...he was in charge of a multi-million-dollar police pension fund, and he had an agenda of his own, one he took seriously.

Very seriously.

———

ACCORDING to the article in *The Star*, the plan administrator went through the entire agreement word by word in an effort to ensure that all the legal, moral, and ethical requirements had been met. What wasn't mentioned—but seemed fairly obvious—was a palpable sense that he was doing what administrators do best: He was covering his own ass.

The agreement between all parties stated that in lieu of an autopsy the distribution of funds would be approved based on the relevant record of events as listed in the police reports and from the coroner's record of findings prior to and in lieu of a full autopsy. It occurred to him that blood samples had been taken, but there were no toxicology results listed. When he asked the coroner about it, the coroner said nothing had been done with the blood because of the dust-up surrounding the exhumation and autopsy, or lack thereof.

Shouldn't the toxicology results be accounted for? The administrator certainly thought they should. Wasn't that the meaning of the word relevant?

The coroner was a medical doctor, not a politician. He worked with cops and investigators all the time. Many of them he knew on a first name basis. He was even friends with a few of them. In this case, he didn't much care if there'd been an autopsy or not, but there was a gaping hole on the form...a form that needed his signature if Pam Donatti was going to get her money. The administrator convinced the coroner that the fastest way to get the grieving widow her much needed money was to order up the toxicology and then everyone could just get on with their lives. In reality he was hoping for a miracle.

The coroner wanted the damned thing to be over, wanted the Donatti woman and her kid to get the money, and mostly wanted the plan administrator out of his life. So he ordered up the toxicology.

And that's when everything went south, because miracles do happen.

THE STATE of Indiana considers an individual intoxicated when their blood alcohol level as a percentage of the whole reaches .08 or above. Ed Donatti's level came back at .0797, and while that technically put him under the limit, it showed, according to a quote from the republican sub-committee chair, "*A significant impairment that clearly affected Detective Donatti's judgment and his decision-making ability. The negligent actions of a drunken Indiana State police officer can be tied directly to the deaths of Augustus Pate and Hector Sigara, a situation that cannot and will not be tolerated. Detective Donatti's actions have been deemed suspect after the fact, and may very well end up being defined as criminal in nature. As such, and according to the provisions outlined in the police officer's pension fund, no amount of monies will be paid or made available to the surviving family members of Officer Donatti until the situation has been resolved. The state's attorney general is meeting with the members of this committee next week to determine..."*

Like that.

Politics.

"Right in the middle of it might be something of an understatement," Murton said. "They're going to want to talk to us you know. The state's A.G., probably the sub-committee too. We're going to need a lawyer. Maybe lawyers...plural. Could get expensive."

"We didn't do anything wrong, Murt. I shot and killed Pate in self defense *after* he shot at me. You were tied to a chair with a shotgun pointed at your head. We're in the middle of it, but we're also in the clear. Hell, we were cleared eight months ago and it was all based on the facts. None of the facts have changed and they aren't going to either. They can't un-clear us."

"That's all true," Murton said. "But it doesn't explain why the governor wants a meeting with us."

Virgil had been looking through the kitchen window at his backyard, the high gray clouds reflecting off the black pond water. He snapped his head back toward Murton. "Us?"

"That's what I said. Cora called me about forty-five minutes ago and told me to get my ass over here. She can be pretty direct sometimes. You ever notice that?"

Then they heard the rotor blades as the governor's helicopter buzzed the top of Virgil's house. It made a sweeping pass out over the water before the pilot pivoted the craft into the wind and landed right in the middle of the backyard between the house and the pond.

And Virgil thought: *Ah, the airport.*

CHAPTER FIVE

Sandy thought Pam Donatti was as close to a mental break as anyone could get without sailing right over the edge. Her face was gray and waxy, there were bags under her eyes, and her hair looked like it hadn't been brushed—much less washed—in days. Brunch, Sandy discovered as she was led inside, was off. The women sat next to each other on the sofa in the living room. The vodka, orange juice, and ice sat next to each other on the coffee table. Pam, the still-grieving widow, had started her day with the breakfast of champions.

"Is this about the news this morning?" Sandy asked her. She'd caught a segment of it on the radio during her drive over.

Pam seemed to not hear the question, or if she did, she chose to ignore it. After a moment she looked at Sandy and said, "I owe your husband an apology. I've been too hard on him." Her words weren't yet slurred, but they sounded,

Sandy thought, like they had to be carefully placed in the right order before they were spoken.

"Virgil's a good man. Ed worshiped him, and I've spent the last seven months hating his guts." She held up her glass before taking a large drink. A small belch escaped her lips after she swallowed. "Hell of a way to honor your dead husband, huh? I'm sorry for that."

"Pam, no one blames you for the way you've been... handling things. Especially Virgil. He doesn't hold a grudge. You were forgiven a long time ago. Do you think I'd be here, that I'd be your friend if either of us thought this was about anything other than grief?"

"They're not going to pay...the pension or the life insurance. Our savings is gone. I'm unemployed and haven't worked for years. I'm going to lose the house. The foreclosure notice was in yesterday's mail."

"What? Why haven't you said anything? What does your lawyer say?"

"I'm filing for bankruptcy protection next week. I still won't be able to keep the house, but it'll slow them down. A little, anyway. Six months maybe. I don't know." She freshened her breakfast by adding some vodka to her glass. "Have you seen Jonas? He's been awfully quiet all morning."

"Pam, I just got here." Sandy said, then felt her chest tighten a little. She left Pam on the sofa and hurried down the hall. She found Jonas sitting on the floor next to his bed. He was dressed in a pair of dirty undershorts and one brown sock. He held a toy truck in his hands, but he wasn't playing with it. Sandy sat on the bed and patted the

mattress next to her. "Hey buddy. Come sit with me for a minute. Are you doing okay?"

Jonas let the toy truck fall from his hands, then climbed on the bed and sat down next to Sandy, his legs hanging off the mattress, his arms limp at his sides.

"Jonas?"

He gave her a shrug. Then his lower lip began to tremble. Finally he looked up at her and said, "Mommy's mad at me."

Sandy wrapped him in her arms and held him tight, stroking his dirty hair. "Oh no, sweetheart. No she isn't..."

SANDY SPENT a few minutes with Jonas, gently questioning him...when was the last time he'd eaten? *Yesterday*. When was the last time he'd had a bath? *Don't remember*. Was he still going to pre-school? *No*.

"How come? I thought you liked it there."

"I do," Jonas said. "But mommy says we can't ford it." Then, "Miss Sandy?"

"What, honey?"

"What does ford it mean? Mommy says we can't ford anything."

Sandy wasn't quite sure how to answer, but it didn't matter because Jonas didn't give her the chance.

"Mommy's always mad at me. And I miss my daddy. And mommy's mad at Daddy because he went to heaven and he isn't coming back. She's mad at everybody, even Mr. Virgil and Mr. Murt."

Sandy got off the bed and down on her knees, right in

front of Jonas. She held his face in her hands as she spoke. "Listen very carefully, sweetheart. Your mommy isn't mad. She's not mad at Mr. Virgil or Mr. Murt, or your daddy. And she's definitely not mad at you. She's just very, very sad. She misses your daddy just like we all do."

"She yells at me."

Sandy thought about it for a minute. "I've got an idea. How would you like to come with me today? We can go back to my house and you and Mr. Virgil can go fishing in the pond. How does that sound?"

Jonas shrugged again. "Okay, I guess. But mommy won't let me."

"You get your warm clothes on. Can you do that by yourself?"

He said he could. He was a big boy now.

"Okay. You get dressed and I'll talk to your mommy for a little while, then I'll come back here to get you when it's time to go, okay?"

"Okay. But mommy won't let me."

She doesn't have a choice. "Yes she will, buddy. You'll see. Wait here until I come to get you."

It took Sandy a few minutes in the bathroom to cool down and gather herself together. She'd never raised a child before, but you didn't have to be an expert on parenting to recognize a child in crisis. She rejoined Pam, who had in her short absence decided to go for the gold.

"I'm suing them," Pam said. She was shouting now. "All of them. The state, the governor, the MCU, the docs, anyone and everyone who's had a hand in this. By the time I'm finished with them they'll wish they'd have just written the check and walked away. This whole thing has gotten out of control. I've done everything they asked. Everything except allow them to dig up Ed's body and chop him to pieces."

"Pam, lower your voice."

"Don't worry. I'm leaving you and Virgil out of it, but the rest of those bastards are going to pay."

"Pam, I said lower your voice. Jonas is—"

But it was too late. Sandy caught the movement out of the corner of her eye and when she turned she saw Jonas in the hallway, dressed in the mismatched way that children do when left to choose their own outfits. He was staring at the wall, sucking his thumb, tears streaming down his face.

SHE COULDN'T DO two things at once, so Sandy chose Jonas. She walked over, took Jonas by the hand and led him into the den. She turned on the TV...if she could keep Jonas distracted with a children's program for a few minutes, she'd be able to deal with Pam, then get Jonas out of the house for a while.

When the TV came up it was on a local news channel and Sandy's brain almost didn't register what appeared on the screen because she'd never seen it from that angle. A news anchor provided the voice-over to an image that showed her own house and property. Just then the camera zoomed in and she clearly saw Virgil, Murton, Cora, and the governor. They were all standing in the backyard next to the governor's helicopter, looking up at the news station's own helicopter—and its camera.

She turned the volume up and caught the announcer: "...have been informed that the property belongs to Virgil Jones. Jones, the former lead detective of the state's major crimes unit, was summarily dismissed from the department after—" There was a brief burst of static, then the reporter was back. "Our pilot is telling us that we've been ordered out of the airspace by the FAA and instructed to return to the airport. We'll keep you updated on the situation as things unfold. I'm Jack Evans, your Eye-In-The-Sky reporter, WISH-TV, Indianapolis."

Murton waved at the camera as the pilot banked the helicopter away.

And Sandy thought, *what the hell?*

———

WHILE THAT WAS GOING ON, Pam had managed to collect herself...somewhat. When Sandy returned, Pam let out a deep breath and said, "I may as well tell you now. I'd rather you hear it from me than anyone else."

"Tell me what?" Sandy said.

"Ed and I went through a pretty tough time a few years ago. That's partly why I've been so upset with Virgil."

"I don't understand," Sandy said.

"You will. Just let me say it. When Virgil hired him, Ed was thrilled. It was exactly the kind of work he'd always wanted to do. No more third-shift patrols, no more domestic disputes, no more sitting on the side of the highway with a radar gun and a ticket book. He'd finally be doing what he'd wanted to do all along...work high profile cases as part of an elite unit. The MCU was perfect for him. And I thought it was going to be perfect for us, too."

"Pam, what happened with Ed...the attack...it could have happened to anyone. It could have happened to him if he was still on patrol. Surely you know that."

"I do. I'm not talking about how he died. I'm talking about how he *lived*. We had a good thing going. It wasn't perfect, but we made it work. When Virgil hired Ed everything changed. He was happy in a way that I can't describe. And I'm ashamed to admit it, but the happier he got, the more unhappy I became.

"We tried everything. Couples therapy, church, whatever. You name it, we tried it. But Ed wasn't the problem, we weren't the problem. I was the problem."

"Well you must have worked through it. I was watching you guys at the party—and I'm not making this up, Pam—I remember thinking how happy you guys looked, hoping that Virgil and I end up as happy as you guys are. Were. I'm sorry. You know what I mean."

Pam waved her away. "It's okay. I do. We were happy. Then. But about a year before Jonas was born, I finally ended up at the doctor's office and it turned out I was clinically depressed. I'm telling you something, I wouldn't wish that on my worst enemy. It really is that bad. And during all of it, even though he tried to hide it, I could see that Ed was happy. Do you know what that must have been like for him? He had to hide his happiness so I wouldn't be so upset. Who puts their spouse through something like that? I'm ashamed of myself. But back then I started to resent him for it. How could he be so happy when I was so miserable? The doctor put me on an anti-depressant and that just made things worse. We started arguing, then we really started fighting. Mean, hurtful, door slamming fights. Saying the kinds of things to each other that you can never take back. The kinds of things that are never forgotten and rarely forgiven. I no longer cared about being happy. I only wanted him to be less happy. But Virgil and his goddamned MCU kept him busy...and happy. I couldn't take it anymore. If I couldn't get myself up to his level, I needed to drag him down to mine. I needed him to hurt. So I...hurt him."

"Hurt him how?"

"Maybe I should say I tried to hurt him, because you know what? I never did. I made the mistake all right, I just didn't have the guts to tell him about it."

"What? What mistake?"

"When I said we tried everything to get happy, I mean we tried *everything*. We'd been trying to get pregnant for over a year anyway but it just wasn't happening. We both got checked out and all the tests came back normal, but it just wasn't happening. The doctors said it was stress. So we fought about that too. About how I was the one who was so stressed out all the time.

"One afternoon, after a really big argument, he got called out for something, some mission or operation or surveillance—I don't remember what—and I was just sick and tired of all the fighting and pretending, so I went out on a little mission of my own. I didn't know what was going to happen...I really didn't, but I took a drive out to the country and ended up at a bar. I met a guy... he seemed nice and we were just having a regular conversation like everyone does when they sit at a country bar in the middle of the afternoon. There was nothing to it. Nothing."

"But?"

"But I was mad and I was hurt and I had too much to drink and the bar was attached to a roadside motel. Do I have to finish the story for you?"

Sandy shook her head, trying to keep the judgment out of her eyes. "No. I get it. You never said anything? Didn't tell Ed?"

"No. How could I? I found out—a little too late—that I really wasn't trying to hurt him. I was trying to hurt myself. It was weird, but after that encounter, something just clicked and suddenly everything made sense to me. I threw the anti-depressants away, recommitted myself to our marriage and after two years of struggling we clawed our way back to us. So no, I never told him, and it's absolutely killing me."

Sandy wasn't quite sure how to respond, so she didn't say anything for a few minutes. Both women sat quietly and stared at the wall until Sandy said, "You know what? If I wasn't pregnant right now, I'd join you for breakfast."

That got a small chuckle from Pam. "I'm afraid there's more."

There always is, Sandy thought. "Pam, listen. Why don't we finish this tomorrow or something? Take some time to think about whether or not you want to talk about this with me, or anyone."

"I've taken eight months to think about it. This is your lucky day."

"Looking back, maybe it was the kindest thing you could have ever done for him, Pam."

Pam wiped at her face with a sleeve. "Letting him die thinking he was the father of my child? No. I think the kindest thing would have been to tell him. It would have hurt him, deeply, but it would have been kinder than letting him live the last five years of his life in a lie."

"He loved that boy, Pam. Everyone knew that."

"Of course he did. That's not the issue. The issue is I led my husband to his death by telling Virgil to take Ed with him that day. The issue is I let the man of my dreams die without ever telling him the truth. The issue is my son is the illegitimate child of a man I don't know and haven't seen in years...a man, I might add that is still alive. How am I ever going to explain all this to Jonas?"

"Pam, you don't have to. At least not right now. Ed may not have been Jonas's biological father, but he was his dad, the only dad he's ever known."

Pam shook her head and said, "Good speech. But it doesn't matter."

"What? Why not?"

Pam went into the kitchen and returned a moment later with a legal-sized manila envelope. She tossed it on the table in front of Sandy. "Because Ed is gone, Sandy. All indiscretions aside, we were consenting adults that day. I've been living like it never happened, except it did. Guess who wants custody of his son? And if he does get it, he'll also end up with the pension fund money if they ever do release it."

CHAPTER SIX

Virgil and Murton went through the back door, across the deck and out to the yard. The pilot hopped out, opened the passenger door of the Bell Jet-Ranger and tossed Virgil a casual salute as the passengers climbed out.

"Who's the pilot?" Murton asked as they got closer.

"Captain Richard Cool, Director of Aviation, Indiana State Police," Virgil said.

Murton pulled a cell phone out of his pocket and held it close to his side. He looked at Cool and asked him for the phone number of Indianapolis Air Traffic control. Cool hesitated, then glanced at the governor. McConnell gave Cool a slight nod and Murton dialed as Cool recited the number. He pressed send and stepped to the rear of the helicopter.

"Watch the tail rotor," Cool warned him.

Murton gave him a thumbs up over his shoulder.

The governor looked at Virgil. "What's he up to?"

I could ask you the same thing, Virgil thought. "I'm not sure."

Murton finished his call and rejoined the group. "What was that all about?" Virgil said.

Murton winked at him, but spoke to the pilot. "Good name for a guy with your job."

"Yeah?" Cool said.

"Yeah," Murton said. He pointed to the governor. "You work for this cat, and you fly that thing in here and land in someone's backyard on a Sunday afternoon like it's just another day at work. I'd say that's cool." Murton offered his hand. "I'm Murton Wheeler."

Cool shook Murton's hand. "A pleasure. It pretty much is...just another day at the office for me."

"I'm a *cat,*" the governor said to no one.

Cora rolled her eyes, then asked Murton, "Who'd you call?"

Murton looked up and the rest of them followed his gaze. Another helicopter circled overhead. It was high enough that no one else had noticed it. As soon as they all looked up the craft banked away and headed northwest, out of the area. Murton waved. "Air traffic control. I sometimes struggle with privacy issues."

Cora said, "Huh. I thought we lost 'em."

"You good to wait here, Rich?" the governor said. "Gotta talk a little shop with Virgil and Murton."

"I'm cool," Cool said.

"I'll bet that never gets old," Murton said.

"Yes, it does," Cora said.

Cool just grinned. "Mind if I wet a line, Jonesy?"

"Help yourself. Poles are in the shed."

"Catch and release only," the governor said. "I don't want to lose that 'new helicopter' smell."

Cool headed for the shed as the rest of them went up to the house. The governor had a little spring in his step. Never been called a *cat* before.

GOVERNOR MCCONNELL WAS DEVILISHLY HANDSOME in a Pierce Brosnan sort of way. He wore Italian suits, English shoes, and his socks usually carried some sort of design that matched his tie. Today it was fleurs-de-lis. "Those right-wing pricks have got me by the balls," he said. "I swear to Christ, you can't do anything anymore without some idiot sticking his nose in where it doesn't belong. There's no right answer to anything. Not anymore."

They all sat in a circle of chairs in Virgil's living room. "Who's the idiot du jour this time?" Murton said. "Love the socks, by the way."

"There are too many to count," the governor said. He was getting wound up. "It reminds me of the republican presidential primary. About a billion people trying to prove they're crazier than The Donald. It's a race to the bottom."

"The governor is merely expressing his frustration over the house sub-committee's most recent maneuver and their unnecessary involvement in Detective Donatti's death benefit," Cora said.

"I just said that," the governor said. "Although maybe not as clearly. Jonesy, Murton, meet my new chief of staff."

Virgil and Murton looked at Cora. She gave them both

a fake smile. "The governor has tasked me with getting his house in order...literally and figuratively."

"That's no small task either, given what we've uncovered over the last few months," the governor said. "Jonesy, do you remember what I said to you about Pearson the night he died?"

Virgil did. "That guys like him were necessary?"

The governor pointed his finger at Cora. "See? What'd I tell you?" Then he looked at Virgil. "Yes. That's exactly what I said. But here's something I won't often admit: I was wrong...mostly. Guys like him used to be necessary, and it wasn't that long ago, either. But not anymore. Politics as an institution is changing. That cry for transparency we've heard all our lives? It's finally happening. It's a long and slow process—like race relations or marriage equality—but it is happening. Pearson was old school; back room deals and under-the-table envelopes. He knew how to grease the skids and keep things moving. But times change, and so do the institutions of society. Politics is no different, nor should it be. If anything we should be leading the way, except we're usually the last ones to arrive. Have you ever noticed that we don't do anything anymore? Nothing gets done in government, and I'll tell you why. It's because we don't have *time* to do anything. Everyone is running around with their hair on fire. All our time is spent reacting to one crisis after another. Reactions are a necessity, of course, but we need to be more proactive. That's why I've called in the national guard."

"I don't want to speak out of turn here," Murton said. "But calling in the guard seems more reactive than proactive to me."

"You're not speaking out of turn," the governor said. "You're speaking your mind. That's why you're here. And that's what I want. People who'll tell me the truth." He looked at Virgil. "People like you, Jonesy. You've always been straight with me, even when you had reasons not to be. There's nothing more important to me than people I can trust."

Virgil understood. "I appreciate it, Sir. And I believe you. So, with all due respect, why did you call in the guard? Murt's right. That's about as reactionary as you could get."

The governor smiled. "Hell of an article in *The Star*, wasn't it? Except they got one small detail wrong. The ISP hasn't declared a strike. If they had, Cool wouldn't be flying my helicopter, or out there fishing in your pond right now. They were close to calling a strike, and point of fact, they probably still might. In fact...I'd bet on it. But they haven't yet and by bringing in the guard I've taken some of their leverage away."

"What about Pam Donatti?" Virgil said. "The police union is standing with her. As I understand it, that's what the strike is all about."

"Yes. That's what makes politics so frustrating," Cora said. "We're on her side, though you wouldn't know it by speaking with her lawyers. This whole situation is a result of the governor trying to do the right thing for a fallen officer of the state, while an opposing political party is using it as a call to arms. Pam and her son deserve those benefits."

"And they're going to get them," the governor said. "What we need to do is expose the motivations that are driving the sub-committee members. The chair of the committee in particular."

"Kreg Gordon," Cora said. "That's 'Kreg' with a K." She made air quotes when she said it.

"Does he really spell his name that way?" Murton asked.

"He does," Cora said. "That should tell you half of everything you need to know, right there."

Virgil looked Cora. "Congratulations on the new job. I think you're a perfect fit, not only for the position, but for the governor as well."

"Thank you."

"What about the MCU?"

Cora glanced at the governor, who stood and said, "Jonesy, Murton. Hope to see you around."

Murton raised his eyebrows and Virgil said, "Sir?"

"I think I'll step outside," the governor said. "Go for a little stroll. This is a hell of a place you've got, Jonesy. I love the peace and quiet out here. Plus, I'm still *a little* old school."

CORA GOT RIGHT TO IT. "The Major Crimes Unit is expanding. We're splitting the state into thirds, top to bottom. The northern third starts at the Michigan line and extends south to the northern borders of Montgomery, Boone, Hamilton, and a few other counties running east to west, but it's a pretty good line. The center third is from there down to a line based on the northern border of Monroe, Brown, Bartholomew, and Decatur Counties. The southern third gets everything else. There might be a little overlap on the lines. Some of the counties are taller than the others. We'll work out the logistics on a case-by-case assessment. Ron Miles is in charge of the whole shebang and will personally take the northern third until we get more people on board. It's a matter of funding, and I'm working on that as we speak. Rosie is taking the southern third. But anyone can float, as needed."

"That's great information, Cora," Virgil said. "What does it have to do with us?"

"As of today, all members of the MCU are considered special investigators for the state. Like it or not, that means political appointees." She reached into her bag, pulled out Virgil's badge and set it on the table. "There may still be some pond scum on there. Try and get it cleaned up. We need the center of the state covered, effective immediately." She let her eyelids droop when she said it.

Virgil just stared at her.

"There's going to be some paperwork, and you'll be required to undergo infrequent and random drug testing."

Virgil continued to stare.

"You'll be part of the MCU, but—and this is important —officially you'll be listed as the director of public safety and oversight. That's a fancy way of saying you'll be the governor's political fixer. The rest of the unit will run everything up through the chain of command, but you'll report directly to the governor through me."

Virgil said nothing.

"You'll be running your own intelligence. If you need something, you'll have it, within reason, of course."

Virgil remained silent.

"You can pick whomever you'd like to replace Ed." She glanced at Murton. "No questions asked."

More silence.

"You'll receive back pay for the time you were, um, on sabbatical."

Virgil continued to stare.

"In one lump sum. With interest."

More silence still.

"A nice fat check. Lots of zero's." Cora took an envelope from her bag and set it on the table. "Payable immediately."

Virgil opened the envelope and looked at the check. He set it back on the table and frowned at her.

Cora tossed her arms in the air, then let them flop down by her sides. "Okay, okay. I'm sorry. It was a mistake. The biggest professional mistake I've ever made."

"What mistake are you referring to, Cora?"

She pointed a finger at him, a little gravel in her voice. "Don't push me, Jonesy." A hint of a smile, though. After a moment or two she said, "It was a mistake to fire you. I'm sorry. Can we get on with it now, please?"

"I forgive you," Virgil said.

"So are you coming back or not?"

"I'll think about," Virgil said.

VIRGIL THOUGHT ABOUT IT...FOR approximately two half-seconds.

He picked up the badge and the check and put them in his pocket.

Murton looked at Cora's bag. "Got anything in there for me?" He wiggled his eyebrows at her.

Cora pulled an Indiana State Police Detective's badge out and tossed it to Murton. "No cowboy shit. You're lucky you used to be a fed because we do need a replacement for Donatti." She tipped her head toward Virgil then said, "And someone to look after this one. In the meantime, raise your right hand and repeat after me."

Murton got his hand half way up, then stopped. "Wait a minute. Do I get a signing bonus too?"

"No, you do not. And it's not a signing bonus. It's money he should have had all along."

"Still," Murton said, "It seems like I'm getting the short end of the—"

"Do you want the job, or not?"

Murton still had his hand half way up in the air. "Well, yeah, of course I do."

"Then raise your goddamned hand and repeat the fuck after me," Cora said. She was practically shouting.

Murton looked at Virgil and said, "See? Very direct sometimes."

They discussed the administrative minutiae for a few minutes, laying out a rough outline. "We'll want Becky for sure," Murton said.

Virgil agreed. "Yes, we will."

Cora leaned forward in her chair. "No, you will not."

Murton cocked his head at her. "Yeah...pretty sure we will."

"You two still dating?" Cora asked Murton.

"No, he married Sandy. Don't you remember? Delroy

walked her down the aisle and gave her away. I was the best man. I think you drank too much at the reception. You were sort of listing to port there, by the end of the evening."

Cora held her hand out. "Give me back that badge."

Murton smiled at her and put the badge in his pocket, out of reach. "I'm just messing with you. Yes. Becky and I are still dating."

"There's your bonus, then. I'm not sure how she does it. Listen, we want Becky left out of all this. We want her on the outside, so to speak. We're aware of her talents with databases and the net. The thinking is we'd have some deniability there. If you were to keep the business open—let's say strictly a research function—then Becky would have some room to, mmm, maneuver, through your firm." Cora looked at Virgil. "You can pay her with the discretionary fund. Whatever you guys agree to."

"This is already starting to sound a little shady," Virgil said.

Cora dismissed it with a wave. "Nothing shady about having a contracted researcher. Way of the world these days. Listen, you guys are going to have to get up to speed as quick as you can. I don't care what Mac says about leverage and the guard and all that. The union is voting tonight. They're going to walk."

"You sure?" Virgil asked.

"Yes. There's no question. We've got over ninety counties in the state and by this time next week the sheriff of every one of them will be asking for some kind of help until the troopers come back. The Indiana National Guard can't really do anything except provide visibility, and that's a double edged sword. They're going to be a deterrent to crime, but that's about it. They're mostly regular folks. Accountants, Wal-Mart clerks, used car salesmen, whatever. The majority of them do it out of a sense of duty and honor for their country. Or to get away from their screaming kids one weekend a month. The problem is a lot of them are gun nuts. Mac might think the republicans have him by the balls now, but the first time one of the guard opens up on a civilian over some bullshit traffic violation, the governor's going to look back on this like it was a Swedish massage with a happy ending. We don't want this to start looking like a militarized state. That part is mostly on Mac, which means it's mostly on me. But I need you guys to do your jobs. I need your help, Jonesy."

"You can count on me, Cora. You know that. We'll do our best."

"I know you will. Let's hope it's enough. Your old office is waiting for you." To Murton: "Get over to the state's HR department today. You'll find someone there waiting for you. Do the paper. I'll set up the backend paper for Becky myself. We'll want to keep that quiet. I don't want anyone to know we've got outside assets."

"You got it," Murton said.

"Virgil, can you do anything about Pam?" Cora asked. "We really are trying to help her, but she keeps getting in her own way. What's going on there?"

"I'm not sure. She's awfully wound up. I'll speak to Sandy about it."

"Do that. Figure out a way to...unwind her. If the governor can get in front of the committee and she can get paid, the troopers come back and the guard goes away. In the meantime, there's something happening down in Shelby County. You know the sheriff down there?"

"Never met him, but I know of him."

"Yeah. Me too. He used to own a dry-cleaning service. I don't think he could solve a two-piece crossword puzzle."

"Sounds like we're thinking of the same guy. Holder or Hopper or something like that?"

"Yeah. They've got a missing farmer down there, part of some co-op deal with a natural gas company."

"The MCU is doing missing persons now?" Virgil said. "That's a little...dry."

"You've got the center of the state...and Mac wants you on it." Cora looked like she wanted to say more, but she looked at her watch instead. "Okay. Get to it. The case file for the Shelby County thing is on your desk. We're out of here. Mac has a meeting..."

THEY WALKED Cora out to the helicopter. "Everything in order?" the governor asked to no one in particular.

"It is," Cora said.

The governor clapped his hands together. "Wonderful. Murton, welcome aboard. I can't begin to tell you what a pleasure it is to have a former federal agent working for the MCU."

"The pleasure's mine, Sir," Murton said.

"Listen, about the socks...thank you," the governor said. "Do you really like them or were you being facetious?"

"No, I'm serious. Not my style, you understand, but I appreciate the effort. Of course, you have to remember it's coming from a guy wearing a shirt with a bunch of drunk broads all over it."

"Nice try," the governor said. "I've seen that shirt. You got it from The Pop-Up, downtown, didn't you? I'm in there every chance I get...when I can find them. I love the fact that they try to hide their store. No advertising, no Facebook or Twitter or any of that crap. You have to *know*, you know?"

"I do," Murton said. "Everything they have is a one-off custom. A little pricey, but a guy's got to look the part... make an impression. Sometimes you wonder if anyone notices."

They were both looking at Virgil who pretended like he wasn't listening.

The pilot was already on board, flipping switches and going through the checklist. "Virgil," the governor said as he pulled open the passenger door for Cora before climbing in the helicopter, "welcome back." Then to the pilot: "Cool, goddamn it, I said catch and release."

"I did, boss. Honest."

"Honest my ass. It smells like carp in here." He made a twirling motion with his hand before he pulled the door shut. "Let's go."

The main rotor began to turn and Virgil saw Cool motion him over to the pilot's side door. He stepped up, unconsciously ducking the rotor even though it wasn't necessary. Cool stuck his head all the way out the window so the governor wouldn't hear him and said, "I borrowed one of your small coolers. The blue Coleman. I pulled a half-dozen bluegill and a bass that's going to be grilled to perfection later tonight. Anyway, the cooler...I'll get it back to you."

"No problem," Virgil said with an evil grin. He stocked his pond with bluegill, bass, and perch. Clearly the governor didn't know his fish, but still. *Carp?* He was mildly offended.

CHAPTER SEVEN

I t didn't take much effort to convince Pam it would be a good thing if Sandy got Jonas out of the house. "You can get some rest, and I'll take Jonas over to my place. He can go fishing with Virgil and I'll have him back here tonight." Then another thought crossed her mind. "You know what? Can we have Jonas for the night? I know it might sound silly to you, but I sort of feel like I need the practice. I need to know what it'll feel like to have a child in the house. What do you think?"

Pam wasn't so sure. "I think you think I'm a bad mother, that's what I think."

"Pam, I don't. You're a great mother. I just believe you're exhausted and you could use a break. Let me help you. Besides, I really do need the practice. I'm not kidding. I've never even been a babysitter. That probably doesn't make you want to say yes, but it's the truth. If you don't want to do it for yourself then do it for me, as a friend. I need it...the practice."

Pam thought it over and eventually agreed that she was awfully tired. Maybe it would be best if she could get a little time to herself. If she could get a good night's rest things might look better in the morning. She deserved that, didn't she? Could Sandy get the booster seat hooked up without her?

"Of course. Just sit right here and relax. You want me to make you some coffee or something before we go?"

The alcohol was running through her system and Pam mumbled something that could have been either a yes or a no. Sandy decided it was a no. She got the booster seat transferred to her own car and then went back inside to collect Jonas. By the time they were ready to go, Pam was asleep on the sofa.

Jonas tugged at her hand, and they were out the door.

———

Murton watched the helicopter until it was out of sight, then turned and looked at Virgil.

"What?"

"Do we need to keep an eye on him?"

"The Governor? No." Then Virgil thought about it for a few seconds. "We need to keep an eye on us."

"That's what I thought," Murton said. Then, "A little old school, my ass."

They let that lie there for a minute before agreeing that they'd meet at the bar first thing in the morning to close up the private investigation side of things, get Becky organized, and let Delroy know that he'd be short staffed for a while. "He's not going to be too happy with us," Murton said.

"He'll be okay," Virgil said. "He's running the place as it is, anyway." Murton wasn't quite so sure, but they left it at that. After Murton was gone Virgil walked down to the pond and stood next to the cross that he'd carved from a fallen willow tree. The tree had been planted as a memorial to his father, Mason Jones, who'd been killed during one of Virgil's previous cases. When a tornado took the tree down earlier in the year, Virgil used what was left of the stump to carve the cross. He set his badge on the arm of the cross, then called Sandy from his cell.

"Have I got a surprise for you," he said when she answered.

"That makes two of us," Sandy said.

"Oh yeah?"

"Yeah. I'm about twenty minutes away. Get your fishing gear out, will you?"

"Ah, listen, I don't think I'm going to have time today. Some things have—"

"Virgil?"

"Yes?"

"Get your gear out."

Virgil, like most men, recognized the tone of a wife who was going to have her way. He didn't push it. "See you in twenty, then," he said.

Sandy clicked off.

Virgil went and got his fishing gear.

WHEN HE RETURNED from the shed, Virgil felt like something had changed. He could actually feel it in the air. He had that long-time cop-sense that most cops have...the living ones, that is. If you didn't have it, well...

He set his gear down and turned a complete circle. He scanned the woods line on the far side of the pond, but saw nothing out of the ordinary...no one lurking in the trees, no glare from binoculars, or worse, a rifle scope. He stared at the woods for a full minute, then walked the perimeter of the house. Everything *seemed* in order, but something felt off. When he got back down to the pond he set up two folding chairs and a small table. He propped two cane poles against the table and when he glanced at the cross he suddenly knew what had changed.

His badge had been moved from one side of the cross to the other.

───────

OR HAD IT? He stopped and turned away from the cross, closed his eyes and replayed the last five minutes in his head. He'd walked down to the pond, over to the cross, set his badge down on the arm closest to him, which, given the direction he'd come would have been on the left side if facing the cross with the shed in the background. Yes, he was sure of it. But now it was on the right side. He left his eyes closed and stood quietly.

"Don't over think it, son," Mason said.

Virgil turned slowly, his eyes still closed. He was, in a way, afraid to open them.

"If you're going to take a nap, you might want to sit down."

When Virgil opened his eyes he saw his father sitting in

the grass, next to the cross. He was dressed as he always was, in the same clothing he'd been wearing the day he was shot and killed. Except for the shirt. The bloody shirt had been buried under the willow tree. Virgil picked up one of the chairs and turned it so it faced the cross, then sat down and leaned forward, his forearms resting on his thighs. "I've missed you, Dad."

"I've missed you too, Son...in a way."

"What do you mean?"

"Things are different over here. I've told you that. Time is...well, not quite so linear would be the way to put it, I guess."

Virgil couldn't quite wrap his head around that statement, and he knew better than to ask for an explanation. "Where exactly, Dad, is 'here?'"

"I really can't say, Virg. I wish I could."

"Against the rules?"

Mason laughed. The sound made Virgil's heart ache. "No, it's not. There are no rules here. There's no right or wrong, or good or bad. There just...is."

Sometimes, Virgil would admit, the conversations he had with his dead father were frustrating. "That makes no sense to me at all."

"I'm sure it doesn't. It's not that I can't tell you. I just don't know how. It's too...complex for words."

"Are you happy?"

"Happy is a human emotion, Son."

"I know that."

"I'd say I'm well. How's that?"

"I guess it will have to do."

They were both quiet for a beat. Then Virgil said, "Why today?"

"There's a reason for everything, Virg. Every single thing. Don't ever forget that."

"Okay. I won't. But you haven't answered me."

"I am trying. Let me ask you something. Do you think your mother and I made the right decision when we took Murton in after his mom died and his father disappeared?"

"Of course. Murt's the best. You know that. You and mom get all the credit for that."

"Do we? I'd say a fair amount of credit goes to you. Maybe more than you think."

"I don't know, dad. We were just kids."

"But you held each other up, every step of the way, didn't you?"

"To a point."

"I suppose that's true," Mason said. "But the past is more than the past, no matter what you've made of it."

"Excuse me?"

"He never really disappeared from our lives. He was just working undercover."

"He disappeared from mine," Virgil said.

"Yes, he did. But the two of you have put that behind you now, and I'm proud of both of you. Where do you suppose Murton would be right now if we'd turned our backs and let him go in the system?"

"I don't know, Dad. It was a long time ago."

"Was it?"

"Would you stop that, please? You guys did take him in and everything turned out fine. What difference does it make?"

"It makes all the difference in the world, Virg. Everything matters. That's the message I'm trying to convey here."

Virgil was mildly frustrated. "Message received. I get it. Everything matters."

"You sound irritated."

"It's hard sometimes. It's like you're speaking in code or something."

"There's only so much I can say."

"I thought there weren't any rules."

"I said there weren't any rules *here*. That doesn't apply to you. Try to keep that in mind, will you?"

Virgil took a deep breath. "Okay, Dad. I will."

"Your boy is almost here, Virg."

Virgil smiled at his father, the frustration gone. "I know, Dad. Sandy's never been happier. Me either."

"Sometimes a father has to make difficult decisions and when that time comes you've got to rely on what you've learned. The hard choices are the ones that matter most. You're about to discover that. Just remember what I said. There's a reason for everything, and everything matters. Every single thing."

Virgil felt a chill in the air. "Is someone in danger? What are you trying to say? What am I about to learn?"

Mason stood and moved Virgil's badge back to the other side of the cross. "You think you're in control, Virg, but you're not. No one ever really is. That day I took Murton from his father and brought him into our lives...it changed everything. I set a course without even realizing it. I didn't know. How could I? I was operating on pure instinct, doing what I thought was best."

"What do you mean, *thought?* You make it sound like it was a mistake."

Instead of answering, Mason looked past Virgil and said, "Now there's a beautiful soul if I've ever seen one. Keep your powder dry, Virg. Things are going to get interesting."

Virgil turned in his chair and saw Sandy and Jonas walking toward him, hand in hand. When he turned back to the cross, his father was gone.

CHAPTER EIGHT

S andy and Jonas made it back to her house and went inside. "I've got to go potty," she told him. "Wait right here and then we'll go down to the pond and you can do some fishing. How's that sound?"

Jonas said it sounded okay.

After she finished in the bathroom Sandy called out to Jonas. "Do you want a drink of water before we go outside?"

No answer. "Jonas?"

She walked down the hall and into the living room. Empty.

"Jonas? Are you hiding? Come on, you silly goose." She looked out the kitchen window and saw Jonas standing in the middle of the back yard. Further away, Virgil sat in a lawn chair. He was bent forward, his arms resting on his thighs. He was staring at the cross.

Sandy went out the back door and across the lawn.

Jonas took her hand and said, "Who's that man Mr. Virgil's talking to?"

Sandy couldn't see him...not this time, but she knew who it was. "That's Mr. Virgil's daddy."

"But you said in the car that Mr. Virgil's daddy is in heaven just like my daddy."

Yep, Sandy thought. I sure did. "Come on, sweetheart, let's go back inside for a few minutes. Mr. Virgil probably needs some privacy."

But Jonas wasn't having it. He pulled free from Sandy and ran toward the pond. He began shouting: "Mr. Virgil, Mr. Virgil, can I talk to my daddy too?"

VIRGIL WRAPPED Jonas up in a hug and caught Sandy mouthing *sorry* to him, her arms spread out in a *what do we do now* gesture. Jonas squirmed away from Virgil and put his hands on the cross. "Is my daddy in there too?"

"No, buddy. He isn't," Virgil said.

"I want to talk to my daddy. If you can talk to your daddy, can't I talk to mine?"

Virgil gently turned Jonas away from the cross and looked him in the eyes. "Did you see my dad?"

"Yeah. He didn't have a shirt on. He must be cold."

"I think he's okay. You know what? Your daddy is okay too."

"But I want to see him."

"It don't think it works that way, little buddy. Say, how about we catch some fish? How's that sound?"

Jonas looked at Virgil for a long time without speaking.

Sandy walked over and put her arms around both of them and then to Jonas said, "You can talk to your daddy anytime you want. Did you know that? I believe he hears you when you do."

Jonas looked up at her. "I do talk to him. I talk to him all the time, mostly with my prayers at bedtime. Mommy says prayers are how we talk to people in heaven. But he doesn't answer me."

"I think maybe he does answer you, sweetheart. Sometimes it's just hard to hear."

"I never hear him."

Sandy placed her hand on Jonas's chest. "That's because you have to listen with your heart instead of your ears."

"I don't know what that means."

"You will someday, honey. I promise."

Virgil gave Sandy a look that said *careful*, but then thought, who was he to be handing out advice? The three of them talked around it for a while until, like most children, Jonas grew bored with the subject when it became clear that the ghost of Ed Donatti wasn't going to appear.

They fished for a while and when Jonas hooked a large mouth Virgil let him haul it out of the water by himself. They got the hook out and Jonas held the fish above the water until it flopped out of his hands and swam away. After an hour or so Sandy insisted that she take Jonas inside for a bath and a nap. Virgil took his time putting the fishing gear away and when he got inside Sandy had Jonas tucked in bed in one of the spare bedrooms.

Despite the cool temperature, they went back outside

and sat on the deck. Sandy said, "Virgil, I'm sorry. I had no idea."

"It's okay," Virgil said. "You couldn't have known. Hell, I never know. Can't expect you to, can I?"

"I guess not," Sandy said. "So, what's up?"

Virgil looked down at the pond and the cross near the water's edge. "Did you see him?"

"Your dad? No, I didn't."

Virgil didn't want to hear that. "I have a hard time believing I'm able to communicate with my dead father, you know?"

Sandy reached over, put her hands on the sides of Virgil's face and turned it back toward her. "I know you do. And he's not...dead. I can't explain any of it...I don't know what's going on but I sort of think you should stop saying that."

"I just don't get it."

"Probably because you're not supposed to," Sandy said.

"When you guys—you and Jonas—were walking toward the pond he said, 'Here comes a beautiful soul.'"

Sandy smiled and put her hands on her stomach. "Our boy."

Virgil thought otherwise. "I don't know. I think he might have meant you."

Sandy let out a chuckle. "Me? I doubt it."

"I wouldn't doubt it if I were you."

Sandy shook her head. "Are you even listening to yourself?"

"Tell me the rest of it," Sandy said.

"I don't know how to explain it. It was almost kind of dark. He kept saying everything matters. Every single thing. What's that supposed to mean? I know everything matters. When doesn't it? Then he said something about not being in control...that no one is in control of anything, and he was talking about me and Murt and how my parents took him in when we were just kids and the way everything turned out. It's like he wants to tell me something but he just won't say the words."

"That's not what I meant," Sandy said. "Start at the beginning. When I was at Pam's and turned the TV on I saw our backyard from a news chopper. What was that all about?"

Virgil reached into his pocket and pulled his badge out. "It's about this," he said. "Cora and Mac came over. The state troopers are going to strike, the governor is calling in the guard, and they want me back." He spent the next ten minutes bringing her up on everything, including Murton joining the MCU.

"What about the private investigation business you guys have going? What'll happen with that?"

"This is supposed to remain quiet, so keep it to yourself. We're going to keep it open, except it will be used strictly as a research operation. Becky will handle all of it. You know how she is with the computers."

"Is that legal?"

"Cora says so. Independent contract researcher. Says it happens all the time."

"I've never heard of it before. Who'll be paying her?"

"Me and Murt...with state money. Cora said it'll come out of the discretionary fund."

"That seems a little...odd."

Virgil grunted. "Yeah. I used the word 'shady' but I know what you mean. Mac's just covering his ass."

"At whose expense?"

"You're usually the one advocating for him, you know."

"That's not exactly accurate," Sandy said.

"It's not exactly inaccurate, either. Anyway, you should have seen the look on Murt's face. I don't think I've ever seen him so excited."

"What about you? Are you excited?"

Virgil had shifted the conversation away from Becky and the research aspect, and didn't fail to notice that Sandy let him. They talked it over for a while, looking at it from all the different angles, Sandy asking him all the right questions...questions that made him *think*. In the end, though, he decided he was excited about it. Made him feel like his life was back on track. "Yeah, I guess I am. Excited." Virgil pulled the check out of the envelope and handed it to Sandy. "I'll tell you what, if nothing else, I'm excited about this."

Sandy looked at the check. "Oh my god, that's a hell of a signing bonus."

"Don't let Murt hear you call it that. Besides, like Cora said, it's money I should have had all along, plus interest. Money I would have had if they would've just hung in there with me. Guess it doesn't matter now. Tell me about Pam."

Murton came around the corner of the house. "I'll tell you about Pam," he said.

The sound of Murton's voice caught Virgil off guard. He turned in his chair. "What are you doing here? You're supposed to be over at H.R. getting your paperwork done."

"That's exactly what I was going to do. Except I had a visitor just as I was leaving my place."

He handed a bundle of papers to Virgil. "I got served walking out my own front door. Pam is suing me for the wrongful death of her husband."

Virgil read through the complaint, shook his head, and handed the papers to Sandy. "This is nothing, Murt. She's got nothing. I'm not a lawyer, but you know as well as I do that there has to be intent. They have to *prove* intent. She can't prove you were trying to harm Ed. You were doing the exact opposite. You were trying to save him."

Murton bit his lower lip, then said, "Yeah, except I didn't. They're going to say that if I hadn't cut him open, that if I'd just waited for the medics he would have made it."

"Except that's not true. Cutting him open was the only thing that gave him any chance at all. The ER doc said so."

"Let's hope he remembers that at the next deposition," Murton said. "Anyway, I just wanted you guys to know. Pam's on some kind of rampage. And listen Small, I know you guys are sort of friends or something, so you can take this for whatever you think it's worth, but I'd keep a little distance from her if I were you. At least for a while."

Virgil gave Sandy a quick look and Murton caught it. "What?"

Sandy reached over and took Murton's hand. "I love you, Murton Wheeler. I know you know that. And I appreciate your situation, I really do, but it's not that simple. I was at Pam's house this morning. She was already drunk when I got there. Jonas was filthy. He hadn't had a bath in days and I don't think she's feeding him with any regularity. We went through the drive-through on the way over here and he ate so fast I thought he was going to be sick. She's neglecting him and she's neglecting herself. I'm really worried about her. She says she's going to lose the house."

Murton pulled his hand from Sandy's. "Jonas is here?"

"Yeah, he is. He went fishing with Virgil for a while, then I gave him a bath and now he's napping in the guest room. He's going to spend the night with us. Why does that bother you?"

Murton turned and gave Virgil a look that could have meant anything at all.

"Say it," Virgil said.

"I'm going downtown. See you in the morning."

"Murt?"

Murton shook his head and walked away. Virgil wanted to press it, to sit him down and talk it out, but he knew from a lifetime of experience that Murton wouldn't share his feelings unless he was ready.

They watched him go, then Sandy said, "What just happened?"

"I don't know. I'm not in control of it, remember? But everything matters, right?"

CHAPTER NINE

They had coffee together early the next morning as the sun struggled to work it's way through the tree line behind the pond. A local news channel was still in the first block of their morning show. Virgil had it on in the background—an endless, annoying sequence of teasers, commercials, and weather reports that cycled through every third minute without giving any real information. It pissed him off. If you wanted the entire story on anything you had to sit through ninety minutes of utter bullshit and piece the segments together yourself.

It was another cool day...a cold front was sluicing over the top of the country and according to the meteorologist on the television—a tall, thin, unbelievably pretty redhead with fantastic teeth and carefully calculated cleavage—this one would be dipping as far south as the Florida panhandle. Based on her looks alone Virgil was certain she didn't know any more about the weather than he did...a pretty face to read the teleprompter. She'd do a year or two...three at the most before heading to either Hollywood or New York. Anymore than three though, and she was doomed, a weatherperson for life, using way too many words to talk about dew points, cloud cover, and temperature inversions.

She was right about one thing though. It was cold, which, Virgil knew because he'd gone ahead and checked the old-fashioned way...by opening the back door and stepping outside.

Sandy was talking to him about Jonas. "I'll take him back late this morning, or maybe after lunch. I'm not sure it matters. To Pam, I mean." Then, "Would you two like some privacy?"

"What? What does that mean?"

"You're practically drooling is what it means. You're old enough to be her father."

Virgil chuffed. "Yeah, if she was like, seven or eight."

Sandy picked up the remote and killed the TV. "Well, she clearly is not."

"I was just wondering about the temperature," Virgil said.

"Uh huh. Keep wondering, and it'll be below freezing tonight...and that's *inside* the house."

Virgil stood and grabbed the coffee pot and refilled their cups. He put the pot back, grabbed a handful of tit then kissed the top of her head. "You're all bark. You don't have it in you...the frosty thing."

"You don't think?"

"Nope. It's genetic. Would have shown itself by now."

They sparred good-naturedly for another minute or two before Sandy told him about the rest of the conversation she'd had with Pam. Virgil couldn't quite believe it.

"My god. She had an affair? Who was it, and why didn't you say anything last night?"

"I meant to, but we were both already processing a lot of new information."

"That's true. So, who was it?"

"She didn't say, and I don't think it was an affair. It was more like a one-time thing. I think she was about to tell me...in fact, I'm sure of it, but she was in such bad shape we never got to that part. To tell you the truth, even after she told me, my main concern was getting Jonas out of there. I've never seen her like that before, Virgil. She's right on the edge of a breakdown."

"That's a hell of a thing to carry around all this time. I'm having a hard time believing Ed never knew."

"She says he didn't."

"No, no...I believe you...I believe *her*. I'm just saying it surprises me that Ed didn't know...or figure it out."

"Is there any chance he did know and kept it to himself?"

Virgil thought for a beat, then shook his head. "I don't think so. We were pretty close. I think he would've said something. I could check with Rosie."

"Do you think that's a good idea? It's a pretty delicate matter. And private."

"Delicate or not, it doesn't sound like it's not going to be private for very long."

Sandy nodded. "Mmm, you're probably right about that. Let me talk to her when I take Jonas back. See what she has to say." She put her hands on her stomach. "Our plates are full right now as it is. Do we really want to get wrapped up in someone else's drama?"

Sandy might not have the frosty gene, but Virgil had the gene that allowed him to raise a single eyebrow.

"Okay, that's not what I meant...exactly," Sandy said. "I just don't want us to lose our focus, especially now, with Wyatt on the way."

"Speaking of that," Virgil said, "what about work?" Sandy was the director of training at the Indiana Law Enforcement Academy.

"I've already told them I'm going to take some time."

Virgil was encouraged. "Good. As far as I'm concerned, you should take the rest of the year off. We can afford it, you know. Now more than ever."

"I know we can. But I like the work, Virgil. And I know that you, of all people, should understand that."

It was something of an ongoing debate that started when Sandy entered into her third trimester. "I do understand. You know I do. But you'd have to agree that you're getting close enough that you're going to have to be careful."

"Virgil, you know as well as I do that even though I am technically still a cop, ninety-eight percent of it is a desk job. There's no danger."

Virgil put his coffee cup in the sink, kissed his wife, then grabbed his gun and badge. "Yeah, and it's the other two percent that bothers me. There's always danger, baby."

She laughed at him. "That sounds like a line from a bad movie."

Virgil flapped his arms as he moved to the door. "Just... just, be careful."

"I will." Then, "Virgil?"

He had his hand on the door knob. "Yeah?"

"Genetics or not...I *can* bite."

"Yeah?"

"Yeah. What time did you say you'll be home tonight?"

VIRGIL GOT INTO HIS TRUCK—A brand new black Ford Raptor—and fired it up. His previous truck had been destroyed by falling debris from a natural gas explosion and when he went looking for a new vehicle he didn't have anything particular in mind, he was just...looking. But when he saw the Raptor the salesman didn't exactly have to sell it. In fact, he did everything in his power to try to talk Virgil out of it. The truck belonged to the owner of the dealership who was going to keep it for his private collection.

So Virgil met with the dealer, promised him a 'Get Out Of Jail Free' card, and bought it on the spot, the Raptor being the only truck that somehow managed to survive what Ford aficionados everywhere he'd later discovered were calling the Aluminum Apocalypse.

He headed north into the city, toward the office. He needed the Shelby County file before he left. He arrived early enough that no one was in yet and he was quietly pleased. He was happy to be back, but didn't feel like doing the dance that went with it.

He grabbed the file, jumped back into the truck and took 465 around the city to avoid the downtown traffic. He wanted to let the truck run a bit. He'd have to be a little careful though because he didn't have the flashers installed yet. But then he thought, what the hell, the troopers *were* on strike. He'd pieced that much together from the morning news between the teasers and weather reports—so he pressed the accelerator to the floor and let it out.

A white-haired old lady gave him the finger when he went ripping by and he laughed out loud.

He was worried about it though…Sandy and the pregnancy and her job, although technically she was right…it was an office job. But she was still a cop…and with all the guns, still a target. The guns were everywhere now and people were practically using cops as target practice. Okay, that's a little extreme, Virgil thought, but police deaths from gun violence nationwide were at an all-time high.

Twenty minutes later Virgil turned into the bar's parking lot and shut the truck down, its engine ticking from the hard run. He went in the back through the kitchen, where he heard his head chef, Robert, arguing on the phone about an overdue delivery. Robert waved and smiled at him, never letting the tone out of his voice. He found Delroy, their manager, in the bar area turning chairs, getting ready for the lunch crowd.

"Hey Delroy. What's happening?"

"Ha. Maybe you tell me, mon."

"Did I miss something? By the way, have you seen Murton yet? We were going to meet up here this morning."

Delroy turned a chair and set it down a little harder than necessary. When he spoke, it was with his back toward Virgil. "He upstairs with Becky."

"What is it, Delroy?"

"What you tink, you?"

"I guess you heard I got my job back."

"Yeah, mon. Congratulations. Tanks for the call, too. Delroy couldn't be happier for you."

"You don't sound very happy. And I was going to call you, but I thought I'd just tell you in person, today...sort of like I'm doing right now."

Delroy walked behind the bar while Virgil was still talking and returned a moment later with two cups of Jamaican Blue Mountain coffee. He set the cups down on a four top, took a seat and waited. Virgil felt rushed, itchy. He wanted to get going. He brushed the feeling away, sat down, bit the inside corner of his lower lip and arched his eyebrows at Delroy.

"What you do, you?"

"I was offered my old job back, Delroy. I took it. It's as simple as that. Murt's joining me. Why is this bothering you?"

Delroy took his time answering. "Maybe sometimes people know tings day shouldn't know. Or tink day know tings."

"Meaning what, exactly?"

"Your job...Murton's job." Delroy pounded his index finger on the table. "Day here, mon, here. How many times you and me have this conversation? How many times Delroy have to say it before you understand?"

"Delroy, I'm a cop. I've always been a cop. I started the bar with my dad because that's what *he* wanted."

"That's not all he wanted, and you know it." Delroy's finger was off the table now and trembling as he pointed it at Virgil. "He wanted you off the streets. You going to be a father now too. Who'll take after your boy and dat beautiful soul of a woman if something happen, huh?"

Virgil had his cup halfway to his mouth and held it there, the steam rising then dissipating away. "What did you just say? You said beautiful soul? You're speaking of Sandy?"

"Yeah, mon. Who else? You telling Delroy you haven't noticed?"

He let his irritation deflate. "Delroy, thank you. I appreciate your concern. But nothing is going to happen to me."

Delroy clamped his hand around Virgil's forearm, hard...one of only a handful of men Virgil would allow it from. "You and Murton are family. Dat what you are, mon. We don't need to bury another Jones." Then, as if his point wasn't quite clear: "One was enough."

They stared at each other for a long time. Finally Virgil said, "There's nothing to worry about, Delroy. I'll be careful. I *am* careful."

Delroy stood from the table. "Yeah mon. But are you careful enough? There's more than one Jones to tink about, now. Tree...maybe four, huh?" He let go of Virgil's arm.

Virgil tipped his head. "Four? What are you talking about?"

Delroy turned away. "I'll be behind the bar. Message delivered, huh, mon?"

Virgil didn't know what Delroy meant, but he didn't have the time to dig any deeper. He'd have to come back to it later. He yelled up the stairs at Murton, then went outside to wait in the truck.

He'd forgotten something during his absence from the

MCU...someone always seemed upset with him about something.

TEN MINUTES later they were rolling south, toward Shelby County. Virgil drove while Murton worked the phone, getting routed around the county building trying to locate the Shelby County sheriff. Eventually he got kicked through to the county's dispatch center and left instructions for the sheriff to call him back.

"Why'd you walk out on us yesterday?"

Murton flipped through the case file and instead of answering, he asked a question of his own. "How long has this farmer been missing?"

"A few days now. It's right there on the summary page...in the notes at the bottom. Little less than a week, if I remember. Why does it bother you that we had Jonas at the house? Sandy said Pam was drunk before noon. What should she have done? Left him there? He's going back today."

"It's not my business, I'm sure."

"Then why are you acting like it is?" He tried to keep the irritation out of his voice, but when Murton answered him he knew he'd been unsuccessful.

"I barely know the woman," Murton said without unclenching his teeth. "Her husband screwed up and got his ticket punched. Becky had her face smashed in and Pate had a shotgun against my head. I was just trying to help and now I'm on the hook for Ed's death and you and Small are taking care of her kid. *Why am I upset?*"

"That's what I'm asking."

"Then how about this: You're the only family I've got left. Your wife and Pam have become close friends. What happens when it all goes to shit and you've got to choose?"

"I don't think it's going to come to that, Murt. It's not as bad as it looks."

"I'm not sure which of those two sentences are worse. Maybe you didn't hear me before. Pam is suing me for the wrongful death of her husband. She's going broke because the state won't pay and we just took jobs from the one guy who could probably make it all go away with the stroke of a pen, but for some reason that's not happening. Have you asked yourself why? I have. The problem is I don't have an answer. So instead, here we are, looking into a missing farmer down in hump-river, USA."

"It looks to me like he's trying—Mac is—and I don't think it's quite that simple."

"Who said anything about simple? It sure as hell wasn't me. Sometimes I wonder about my own thought processes."

They rode in silence for a few miles. Eventually, Virgil said, "She likes it that you still call her that."

"What?"

"Sandy. She likes it that you call her Small. You've always called her that and even though we're married now you still do."

"No shit. It's a sign of respect. It's my way of telling her I haven't forgotten who she is or where she came from."

And there it was. Virgil finally understood. Murton wasn't upset that Jonas was at the house. He probably wasn't even upset about the lawsuit. He was upset about his own past.

Virgil took a moment and thought carefully before he spoke. When he did, his question hit the mark. "Do you miss him?"

Murton laughed without humor. "My old man? What's to miss? The drinking? The abuse? The fact that he walked out on me? I barely remember what he looked like."

Virgil pulled the truck over and stopped on the shoulder of the road. "I didn't make the connection. I'm sorry. You've been a part of my family for so long I don't think of you in any other way."

"What's to be sorry for? It's not your fault. The truth is, I think about him every day. The last time I saw him was the night your dad beat the shit out of him. If he hadn't intervened on my behalf I don't know what might have happened. I honestly thought my own father was going to kill me. Do you know what the last memory I have of him is? It's his fists flying at me."

Virgil placed his hand on Murton's shoulder. It was as hard and solid as a Hickory stump. "You've never been a spectator in your own life, Murt. It's the quality I most admire about you. I wish I could be more like you than you'll ever know."

"Oh yeah? You know what the worst part is? After everything he did to me and my mom, the way he treated us...abused us, physically and emotionally, I really *do* miss him. How fucked up is that? If I saw him today I don't know if I'd shoot him or hug him. Maybe both, in no particular order."

The pain and disappointment in Murton's voice made Virgil realize he'd taken his own childhood for granted. The things that grounded him and made him whole were all part of a comfortable screenplay that had never quite come into focus for Murton, or at the very least, his way of thinking about the mental film reels that defined his life.

Murton's phone rang. He answered, listened for a moment then ended the call. "The dispatcher said the sheriff is still at the crime scene," he said. "You know what it means when you hear the words 'missing person' and 'crime scene' used in the same sentence?"

Virgil turned the truck back onto the road and accelerated hard, the rear end fishtailing for purchase. "Yeah... when they find the missing person."

Murton nodded. "Yep. Our missing farmer isn't missing anymore. The dispatcher said the sheriff didn't quite have the words to describe the condition of the body."

Virgil couldn't let it go. "Nothing comes between us, Murt. Nothing. Are you hearing me on this, partner?"

But as was often the case with Murton, there was never any uncertainty about when the conversation was over. "Who are you trying to convince, me or you?" He tossed the case file on the dash and stared out the window, his face as fixed and blank as a piece of slate.

THEY RODE in silence for a few more miles then Virgil began to talk about Delroy and Robert and the bar and his own father and the history of it all; the short version of what brought them to the here and now. "I think he'll come around," Virgil said. "Delroy. He's just worried."

"Of course he's worried. Everyone is worried about something except—" Murton's phone rang again, cutting him off. "Wheeler." He listened without saying a word, pinched the phone against his ear with his shoulder, then scribbled an address on his palm. "Yeah. Ten minutes. Tell your guys to get them out of there. Yeah, all of them. We don't want the areas contaminated." A pause. "Yeah, yeah. Just do it." Another pause. "I don't know. I'll have an answer by the time we get there. Yeah. Nine minutes, now." He clicked off and punched the address into the nav system on Virgil's dash. "There's our destination. One of them anyway."

"What's going on?"

"You're not going to believe it."

"Did you say areas? As in plural?"

"Yep."

"An answer to what?"

Murton was dialing another number and had to stop, his annoyance at the interruption evident. "*What?*"

"You told whomever you were speaking with you'd have an answer by the time we got there. An answer to what?"

"How many crime scene people we have. So far they've found at least two separate locations that have different parts of the victim's remains." Murton finished dialing and put the phone to his ear. Then, with a sideways look: "Did you just say 'whomever?'"

He was already coordinating the locations with the crime scene supervisor before Virgil could answer.

CHAPTER TEN

Virgil pulled a wool hat from his pocket and covered his head. It was cold and getting colder as they day went on. The main crime scene looked like something out of a half-completed movie set, one where the director hadn't quite decided what direction the plot should take.

There were three Shelby County squad cars, a fire rescue vehicle, one national guard armored troop transporter, two bulldozers, an excavator, three large dump trucks, a 7-series BMW that looked like it'd just been driven from the showroom floor, and a dusty Chevy station-wagon with wooden side panels that might have been from the late 60's. A hand-painted sign was stenciled on the side of the station-wagon that read *Holden's Dry Cleaners*. A red jackpot flasher like the kind still used by the Michigan State Police was mounted on its roof, which at first glance made it look like an emergency dry-cleaning delivery vehicle.

The guardsmen had positioned themselves in a semi-circle around a large pile of rubble, their rifles at parade rest. Their expressions displayed a mixture of generational humanity that ran the gamut anywhere between lock-and-load, to outright boredom, as if objectivity wasn't a way of life but a state of mind...one they'd been ordered to leave back at the barracks.

A drilling rig sat across the open field less than a hundred feet away, the workmen leaning against the platform's steel support structure and corrugated galvanized siding. They were drinking coffee from tin cups, the type that screwed on top of a working man's thermos and smoking cigarettes even though the side of the structure was posted with warning signs that stated smoking was strictly forbidden.

The cold air felt bent and heavy and smelled of diesel exhaust, sulfur, and molded corn. An industrial generator the size of a semi trailer hammered out a continuous thrum that was felt as much as it was heard. Virgil and Murton had seen it all before; war, bodies, murderous pumps who never should have been born, theft, arson, torture, drug trade, and lowlifes of every stripe. They'd fought together in the desert, almost gotten each other killed, and had, on more than one occasion saved each other's lives. None of that prepared them for what they saw when they stepped out of Virgil's truck. The entirety of the scene reminded Virgil of something he couldn't quite pin down.

The demolition of the co-op and the setup of the drilling platform had been halted by the discovery of the body, or what was left of it, anyway. All together, between the cops, paramedics, guardsmen, drillers, equipment operators, and fire-rescue personnel there were about fifty people standing around listening to one well-dressed man shouting his displeasure over the shutdown...something about unnecessary cost overruns cutting into his profit margins. When he saw Virgil and Murton approach, his wrath turned on them.

"Who the hell are you, now?"

He wore a dark gray business suit that was the exact color of the sky, like he might have checked the morning weather report before he decided on his wardrobe for the day. His glossy black shoes were covered with a thin layer of dust. They were pointed at the toes, a statement that left him slightly behind or just in front of the fashion curve. Virgil didn't know. He didn't care either.

He held his badge out. "Virgil Jones." He tipped his head to the left. My partner, Murton Wheeler. "We're special investigators with the state's Major Crimes Unit and we're the ones you'll be speaking with from here on out. And by speaking, I mean just that. How about you dial it back a little?"

He turned his back on the man before he could answer, his attention now on the uniformed sheriff, his eyes just brushing the name tag on the way up. "Sheriff Benjamin Holden? Virgil Jones. The governor sends his regards and wants you to know we are at your disposal." They shook hands. "I've heard a lot about you."

"Some of it might be true," Holden said. "Call me Ben, would you? The only thing I hate more than this job is the title that goes with it."

"Yeah, call him Ben," the gray suited man said. "As in, been holdin' his dick."

Murton turned his head and said, "Be quiet."

"Quiet my ass. I've got millions of dollars circling the drain because of a farming accident and this flat-footed buffoon—"

Murton got right in his face, his voice no more than a whisper. "I said shut the fuck up. My partner and I are going to be here for a while. How long you're here is entirely up to me. Now you can stand here and act like the gentleman you're dressed up to be, or I can put you in handcuffs and you can wait in the back of one of those squad cars over there. The back seats are molded out of a single piece of hard plastic. That means they're puke-proof. I heard they have to hose them out three or four times during the night shift around here."

The man turned his head away and lifted his chin in profile.

"Yeah, that's what I thought," Murton said. "Nice shoes." He winked at Virgil then looked at Holden. "Show us what you've got?"

"Follow me," Holden said as he walked away from the gathering. He was watching Murton out of the corner of his eye. "What'd you say to him? I didn't think he was ever going to shut up."

Murton shrugged. "I delineated his morning schedule for him."

The sheriff gave him a skeptical look, opened his mouth to say something, then let it go. He looked at Virgil. "Listen, I'm glad you guys are here. I really do mean that. And I don't want to sound disrespectful when I ask, but do you think we could cut the guard loose? When I called the state for help I didn't know they were going to send me GI Joe and the third battalion."

"The troopers are officially on strike."

"Yeah, I heard. But even if they weren't, how many of them would have shown up?"

The sheriff had a point. Usually only two or three uniformed troopers were on patrol in any given county, their duties focused primarily on interstate traffic control. "Who's in charge?"

Holden looked over Virgil's shoulder. "The one talking to the suit. Oh great, he's headed our way now. He thinks he's General Patton, by the way."

Virgil turned and saw the soldier approaching. He wore a standard desert-colored field uniform with silver double bars pinned to his collar and front and center on his helmet. The name tag sewn to his breast read 'Decker.' He stopped no less than two feet from Virgil and stood at ease, his hands behind his back, his elbows jutting out at perfect angles.

"Sir, this is a restricted area under the command and control of the Indiana National Guard. Please state your name and the nature of your business here."

Virgil took off his hat and stuck it in the side pocket of his Carhartt jacket, letting his hair fall across his ears and forehead. He wore it long for a cop and it was streaked with gray at the temples. His eyes were the color of green steel and often looked charged with static electricity. He had an angular face, one that had become taut and lean with the workouts he'd become accustom to since getting free of the drugs. He'd replaced the pull of the chemicals with his own endorphins, lifting weights every other day and running five miles at least three times a week. In his prime, and now the best shape of his life.

"I get the impression that the fellow you were just speaking with has already told you who we are. But maybe not. In any event, you're half right, Captain. This is a restricted area. Tell your men to pack it up and ship out."

Decker took a half step forward. "Sir, you haven't answered my question."

Virgil smiled at him. "Relax, Decker. This isn't a field-op and we're not in the sandbox. And it wasn't a question...it was request. In fact it was two. I'll answer because that's the kind of guy I am. My name is Jones. Detective Virgil Jones. This is my partner, Murton Wheeler. We're special investigators with the state's Major Crimes Unit. That means we're here to investigate a crime. It also means you and your men are no longer needed here unless you believe that a fugitive or fugitives are in the immediate area. Do you believe that to be the case, Captain?"

"You don't look like a cop. You look like a roadie, or something."

Virgil pulled the edge of his jacket back and revealed his badge...and the .45 clipped to his belt. He thought he heard Murton say, 'Oh boy.' "How I look is my business. Answer the question."

"Sir, no sir. My men and myself have been in position since 0600 hours. The area is secure."

"Well done then. Drive carefully, soldier." He turned away.

Decker reached out and grabbed Virgil's elbow and held him in place. The remaining guardsmen began to fan out, forming a half-circle around their commander, their weapons now at port arms. "Sir, until and unless ordered otherwise by my commanding officer, my unit is to remain in place."

Virgil looked at Decker's hand on his elbow, then right in his eyes. "Take your hand off of me right now. I won't ask you again." When Decker didn't reply or remove his hand, Virgil took the hat out of his pocket and put it back on. As he did, his forearm and bicep began to crush the captain's fingers in the crook of his elbow. When Decker finally did try to remove his hand it was too late. Virgil squeezed tighter until he heard a crunching sound and Decker made a noise that might have been a word except for the lack of consonants.

Murton was speaking to someone on the phone.

When the soldiers saw what was happening with their commander they began to move in closer, tightening the circle. Virgil relaxed his arm and Decker yanked his hand away like he'd just pulled it from a pot of boiling water. When he tried to bend his fingers, he winced in pain.

"Put some ice on that when you get back," Murton said to Decker. "Maybe get an x-ray. I thought I heard something crack." Then he held out his phone. "It's for you."

Decker took the phone with his other hand, his men now at his back, their index fingers pressed straight and flat just above the trigger guards of their rifles. He put the phone to his ear, stated his name and rank, then listened, his face reddening by the second. A few moments later he said, "Understood," and tossed the phone to Murton.

He looked Virgil square in the face. "Sir, I apologize. My men and I are at your disposal."

"No, you're not. Like I said, drive carefully."

As they turned to leave Virgil's phone rang.

"Tell me I haven't made a mistake," Cora said. "Please just tell me that one thing."

"Have you ever made one before?" Virgil asked.

"Plenty. I'm hoping this isn't one of them."

"They were in the way."

"They're a presence, one that the governor is counting on."

"Sort of like me and Murt, if I understand our job descriptions."

"I won't argue that. Do you know who Captain John Decker works for when he's not on guard duty?"

"No, and I don't care."

"Yes, you do, you just don't realize it yet. He's a bean counter for the state. He's low level...no doubt about it, but his office falls under the purview of Kreg Gordon, the Chair of the house sub-committee. You know...one of the guys who have the governor by the balls."

This time it was Virgil who winced...but only a little. "I'll leave the politics to you, Cora. Just let us do our thing here, okay? Cora?"

The line was already dead.

Virgil told Murton and the sheriff to give him a minute. He jogged over to the troop carrier. "Hey, Captain Decker, hold up a minute."

Decker had his foot on the running board of the transporter ready to climb in. He turned but didn't speak. Virgil saw him flexing the fingers of his hand. They weren't broken, but they'd be sore for a while.

"Did you do any time over there?"

Decker's eyes went flat and Virgil knew. "So did I.

Murton too. We were part of the first wave of ground troops in Iraq one."

"I did two tours in the 'Stan,'" Decker said. "They wouldn't take me for a third."

"Why not?"

He took his foot off the running board, bent over and pulled his other pant leg up revealing an artificial limb. "RPG took out our chopper. We'd just taken off from the field hospital for another run. I don't think we were more than fifteen feet in the air. The only thing left of the pilots and the door gunners were their tags. Don't ask me how, but I was blown clear. The hell of it is, other than the ringing in my ears I didn't have a scratch on me. Except when the main rotor hit the dirt it came apart and a piece went through my leg just above the knee. The docs said it was the cleanest cut they'd ever seen. It didn't really hurt all that much. I think I must have been in shock or something."

Virgil looked away for a moment. "You know, for a guy with a peg wheel you're pretty quick to make judgments about how other people look."

"I probably could have handled myself a little differently back there."

Virgil thought Decker had to make a conscious effort to leave the word 'asshole' off the end of his sentence. "So how can I get a hold of you if I need to?" he said.

"Call your boss, asshole."

Virgil turned away so Decker couldn't see his smile. "I'll do that. Take Murt's advice and get an X-ray. The state will cover the bill."

CHAPTER ELEVEN

After the guardsmen left, Holden again asked that they follow him. He moved with the awkward gait of a man whose knees had gone bad some time ago. He was skinny and wore an oversize all-black uniform that gave him the appearance of a walking bag of sticks. His gun belt was cinched so tight it caused his pants to ride higher than normal revealing white athletic socks that sagged around his ankles. They walked in a line without saying anything, Virgil at the tail end. Murton and Holden drifted ahead as he looked around the field.

The file report he'd read hadn't done the scene justice. What was once the central hub of a thriving farming community had been reduced to a pile of rubble. He'd never seen the co-op in person, but there'd been photos in the file. The building had been demolished and was now nothing more than a heap of dusty red cinderblocks, shingles, copper tubing, electrical wiring and broken furniture. Half of it was gone, all ready hauled away by the dump trucks. The excavator and dozers had taken care of the structure in short order, probably without ever scratching the paint off their blades and buckets. Three of the ten silos remained standing, the work stopped when the body had been discovered.

The silo's, Virgil thought, with their tubes jutting out at odd angles looked a little like giant upside-down bongs.

He turned a full circle and took it all in...the cops, the business man with the pointy-toed shoes, the workers, the drillers, the guardsmen, the demolition equipment, the drill rigging, the generator and single-wide trailers converted to field offices. It reminded him of how Ramadi and Mosul and Baghdad looked after they'd torn through with their single-minded objective that, in the end, only made things worse.

Armageddon, Virgil thought. That's what it reminded him of.

Maybe Delroy was right. Maybe he should just stay behind the bar. Take a private case once in a while...chase down bail skips, cheating spouses and corporate embezzlers. Why not simply raise his family and let the lowlifes settle their own score?

Then he saw the body and even though it was one of the worst he'd ever seen, he knew he was right where he belonged.

God help me, he thought. *I love this shit.*

———

DECKER...PISSED, and trying not to show it. So pissed, in fact, he was having trouble thinking straight. He sat in the passenger side of the troop transporter, a five-ton flatbed with a hard-topped front and a black canvas tarpaulin hovering over the men in back. The truck didn't look much like a troop transporter. It looked more like something a mid-level Mexican landscaping crew might use. The only thing that even remotely hinted at a military element was the dull green paint job and the men in the rear of the truck.

His driver, a black sergeant named Tom Ford worked the truck, grinding away at the gears as they made their way out of the co-op and on to the highway. Ford kept his head still, but let his eyes slide over to Decker every few seconds. Decker caught it. "What?"

Ford was short, his legs barely long enough to reach the pedals of the truck, but he was square and solid, built like a boulder. In his uniform, he looked like a black and green fireplug. "Shit ain't right."

Decker flexed the fingers of his hand. Tried to redirect him. "Ordered out is ordered out. Eyes on the road, soldier."

Ford wouldn't let it go. "That's not what I meant. That hot-shot cop...putting his hands on you like that? That's not right. Not right at all."

"Just drive, will you?"

"All's I'm saying is every one of those boys in back are talking about how that cop got over on you. Then each one of them is going to say something to someone else and the next thing you know ain't no one gonna respect—"

"Tommy, I said drive."

Ford hit the clutch...he had to slide the left side of his ass forward to move the pedal far enough to shift, and even that was barely enough. He went from third to forth, slid his ass back and the truck lurched forward. They could hear the groans of the men in back. "I am driving, case you didn't notice. But that cop, man..."

Decker held his rifle on his lap, the muzzle pointed at the floorboard. When he turned in his seat, the muzzle just naturally turned with him and ended up pointed at Ford's groin. "Tommy, I swear to god, you better shut the fuck up and drive."

Ford shut the fuck up and drove.

"NAME'S CHARLIE ESSER," Holden said, his back to the body. "We was friends." They were standing close to the body, but not hovering over it. The county medical examiner was still working. "I've done plenty of farming accidents over the years, but nothing like this. Figured maybe the state could help us out. We're just not equipped for this, this..." He shook his head, his voice trailing away.

Murton cleared his throat. "Where, uh..."

"Is the rest of him?" Holder said. "I can't hardly stand to think on it."

The medical examiner snapped off his gloves and dropped them in a sack. He was bald, with hound dog jowls, the skin under his eyes so puffy they looked like they'd been stuffed with grapes. His skin was the color of parchment paper and his eyebrows were almost non-exis-tent...like you had to imagine they were there.

"Don't study on it too much, Ben. He was dead before he went through the auger. At least he was spared that much. But like I suspected, this wasn't an accident. It'll be in my report when I'm done with the post, but he was murdered. I'm sure of it now. He's got a compression fracture of the skull on the back of his head. Probably a baseball bat or something like it. That's what put him down. But he was still breathing. Not sure how long, but his airway's packed with silage. I just popped a lung, right there at the bottom of his right side and you can see the particles plain as day. Looked like he might have been kicked around some too. Got a couple of busted ribs."

"You're saying he was buried alive?" Murton said.

"That's exactly what I'm saying. Tell your crime scene people to call me when I can take him. I'm headed over to Sunnydale. They've got what looks like a femur in one of the hog pens." He shook his head and his jowls wiggled back and forth.

"Any chance at a time of death?" Virgil said.

"Exactly none. The silage kept the body temp up much longer than normal. Factor in the dismemberment, the time from silage removal until discovery...there's just no way. I think the best estimate you're going to get is who saw him last and when. Work it from there."

"Okay," Virgil said. "Listen, I don't want to get off on the wrong foot here, but your office was a little slow in responding."

"And now you want to know why it took me so long to get out here. Is that it?"

"The thought did cross my mind," Virgil said.

The ME looked at Esser's body, sighed, snapped off his gloves and said, "What a gol-darned mess. I'll send the wagon back when you're ready." Then to Virgil: "My wife is...well, she's dying. Got here as soon as I could. What's left of Charlie wasn't going anywhere."

"I'm sorry about that, I really am," Virgil said. "But the duties of your office dictate that—"

"The duties of my office don't mean dick to me right now. You married?"

Virgil nodded.

"Then I hope you never understand. Besides, from the looks of it, seems to me that you were the last one to arrive on the scene." He shook his head walked away.

VIRGIL, feeling a little like an ass, turned to Holden and said, "Tell us what you know for sure." He looked at him with his skinny frame and lightweight uniform. "Aren't you cold?"

Holden was staring at what was left of Charlie Esser. The body looked like someone had run it halfway through a wood chipper, feet first, before changing their mind and hitting the reverse switch. The only part of Esser that remained intact was his upper torso. From his breastbone down, there was nothing.

"I don't feel much anymore," Holden said. "It's the dry-cleaning chemicals. I think they've changed me over the years. I truly believe that."

Virgil had to prompt him to continue. "Sheriff?"

"Sunnydale Farms was storing some feed stock in the silo where the demo crew found Charlie. They'd hauled the last of it out yesterday. Everything is pretty automated these days, but about half of Charlie went through the auger when they emptied the silo. The crime scene people over at Sunnydale are saying that most of the lower half of Charlie has already been eaten by the hogs. There's a few bones left, but not much of anything else.

"The guy with the shoes is named J. Conner Westlake. I don't know what the J stands for. Maybe it's just Jay, but I doubt it. I carry a profound dislike for people who use an initial as a replacement for their given name. Anyway, he's a lawyer. Represents the group that's raping the land down here. It's a buyer's market down river if you're thinking of moving. They can't keep the bottled water in stock at the grocery store. Did you know that the state of Oklahoma used to average one or two small earthquakes a year? That was before they started fracking. Now they average eight a day."

Virgil cared, but he didn't want a geology lesson or the philosophical debate that went with it. "Tell us about Mr. Esser, Sheriff. Start at the beginning."

"He was the hold-out. This was Charlie's land. Technically it still is. Westlake's group bought the mineral rights from all of the farmers who were in on the co-op."

"Who are the other farmers?"

Holden gave them the names and took fifteen minutes to lay it all out for them.

"Why didn't the others just do the deal without Esser?" Virgil asked.

"Couldn't. Word is, Esser wouldn't let them. They each owned their own land, but it was all held in a trust, controlled and maintained by the co-op. It's like a bunch of smaller companies under one holding company. It's really the only way farmers can survive anymore."

"Let me make sure I've got this right," Murton said. "This group of farmers were all going broke because of a dry season and while drilling for water they hit natural gas instead. Then Westlake and company offer to buy them out but Esser, who was the co-op's chairman says no? Why?"

"There's some speculation that he wasn't exactly saying no. He was just biding his time."

"To what end?" Virgil said.

Holden didn't answer for a long time. Eventually he said, "Look, Charlie wasn't perfect. I meant what I said earlier. We was friends and I don't like to speak poorly of the dead."

"But..."

"But there was two sides to the man, which," the sheriff said as he pointed his finger at no one, "is true of just about anyone I've ever known. I seen him get rough with Martha when he thought no one was looking and I don't approve of that type of behavior, but I also seen him untangle a dead doe that got caught up in barbed wire a few winters back. It was frozen solid. He could have skinned that deer, ate venison all winter and made a profit off the hide. Instead he got a pick axe and shovel out of his truck and chopped through the frozen ground and buried the damned thing right on the spot. The air was so cold and dry the tears were frozen to his cheeks by the time he finished. He wouldn't let me help him none, either."

Virgil was losing patience. "Biding his time for what, Sheriff?"

"An end run at the other members," Westlake said. He'd come up from behind them. He also looked like he'd adjusted his attitude. "Listen, I'm sorry about all this." He glanced at Murton. "Really. I know you guys are simply trying to do your job. I'll stay out of the way. But I'm trying to do mine, too. This delay is going to cost a fortune. Every minute those pumps aren't running cost my investors money."

"I'm sorry for your loss," Murton said, his voice dry with sarcasm. "It'll be just a few more minutes and we'll have this carcass out of your way and you can get back to poisoning the planet and saving capitalism."

Westlake raised his voice. "Hey, that's out of line."

Murton spat on the ground, right next to Westlake's pointy shoes. "Take it up with the governor. We're here on his nickel, not yours."

"How about everybody just relax a little," Virgil said. "Mr. Westlake, what did you mean about an end run at the other members?"

"It wasn't true," Westlake said. He peeled his eyes off of Murton and looked at Virgil. "It simply wasn't." He took a deep breath, got his voice under control and started over. "There was a rumor going around that Mr. Esser—because he was the majority land owner and chair of the co-op—was holding out on the deal. The thinking was, if he held out long enough the others wouldn't be able to make it through the winter, much less next spring. They'd all go up at auction, Esser would buy them out at a greatly reduced price and then take the deal. But it just wasn't true."

"How do you know that?" Virgil asked.

"Because I'm the one who put the deal together for the gas companies. My job is to make the deals, then see them through to completion. Completion for me is defined as a fully functioning and producing well. Once that's been accomplished, I move on to the next operation. Mr. Esser and I had many conversations and he never once indicated to me that he was willing to take our offer, now or in the future. He wanted nothing to do with it. As far as an end run goes, he couldn't have pulled it off if he wanted to. The gas companies weren't willing to wait it out. They get enough bad press as it is. The last thing they want is a messy court battle over who screwed who by waiting it out."

"Whom," Murton said.

Westlake ignored him. "When the other members of the co-op approached me about an extension I made it perfectly clear that I was unwilling to grant them one."

Virgil almost laughed at the absurdity of it all. "Yet here we are, ready to drill baby, drill. How did you get Esser to sign?"

Westlake looked away for a moment. "We didn't actually."

"Then how is it that you've set up operations against the wishes of the majority land owner, a land owner who, I might add, has been cut to shreds by the auger coming out of the bottom of that silo?"

"We pride ourselves on being equipped for most any contingencies that may arise. This isn't our first well, you know. We were almost ready to commence with operations until this, uh, unfortunate discovery."

"I'm so happy for you," Virgil said. "Now how about you answer the question."

Westlake lifted his chin. "We did have consent. The majority land owner signed the contract. Perhaps you haven't you heard. Martha Esser...Charlie's wife? She woke up. The doctors say with time a full recovery is not only possible, but probable. She's having some minor difficulty with her speech, fine motor skills and so forth, but she signed the contract the moment we presented her with the deal. I'll tell you something else: she didn't seem all that upset about the news of her husband's death."

"Is that right?" Murton said.

Virgil shot Holden a look, and noticed that the sheriff was somehow managing to nod and shake his head all at the same time. He looked like a bobble-head. "It's true. I guess I should have brought that up already. If Charlie wasn't laying here ripped to shreds, he'd be sitting in the county lock-up charged with attempted murder. Martha said he tried to kill her by throwing her down the stairs. Damn near got away with it too. I'll tell you something, we've had a pretty good run lately, crime wise. It's been nice and quiet. Couple of minor burglaries, an occasional bar fight, and other than Esser here, only one other domestic. This is something I'd expect in the city, not out here. We haven't had a murder in over fifteen years. Sort of stains our record. Did I mention that I hate this job?"

***

"WHERE IS YOUR OFFICE, MR. WESTLAKE?" Virgil said.

Westlake handed Virgil his card. "I'm based out of Irving, Texas, but I've set up a temporary office in Indianapolis. I have a short term lease on a condo downtown as well. We're in the process of closing it all up."

Virgil glanced at the card, shoved it in his pocket, then looked back at Westlake. "The sheriff or one of his deputies will escort you to their station where you'll give a full and complete written statement regarding your involvement in this matter. You will document everything you know about not only your involvement with this operation, but anything else even remotely connected to Charlie Esser and the other members of the co-op and you'll give a complete accounting of your whereabouts over the last seventy-two hours. You'll have the right to have your attorney present if you wish. After that you'll be free to go, but I'll expect you to make yourself available to me or anyone on my team at any time until we've completed our investigation. If you have any travel plans in the near future, I'd make other arrangements if I were you. In other words, don't make me come looking for you. Is their any part of that you don't understand?"

The look on Westlake's face was one that Virgil had seen hundreds of times before. It was the look that said the police and other public service personnel were there solely for the benefit of the wealthy and powerful. If Westlake was trying to hide his feelings, he didn't do a very good job of it, his distain clear. "I'm a lawyer, so I won't be needing representation in this...matter. And listen, I don't mean to be a bother, but I really do have to answer to some very... mmm, influential people. Do you have any idea when we might be able to resume setting up the drill rigs?"

"He doesn't mean to be a bother," Murton said to no one. Then to Westlake, "Get the fuck out of here."

After Westlake left, the sheriff looked at Murton and said, "Little rough on him back there, don't you think?"

"Fuck him. Did you see those shoes? What a clown-stick."

At the end of the service road a small gathering of men stood off to the side talking amongst themselves. "Who are they?" Virgil asked.

"Rest of the co-op members," Holden said.

"You talk to them yet?"

"Yup. I interviewed each of them after Charlie was found. They all had the same story. An early meeting here at the co-op to talk about the gas deal. Charlie told them he wasn't interested, though their descriptions of 'not interested' varied somewhat. Anyway, he said he wasn't going to take the deal, and that was that. According to the rest of the co-op members, Charlie went out to clean the silo and the rest them went into town for breakfast. The waitress at the diner backs up their story. Said they were having an argument...trying to be quiet about it, but everybody in town knows what it's about anyway. The argument started to get heated and they all left before their food was ready. Didn't even finish their first cup of coffee."

"What are they doing out here...right now?" Murton asked.

Holden shrugged his shoulders. "I thought you'd want to talk to them. I told them you were on your way."

Virgil and Murton exchanged glances. It was a procedural error on the sheriff's part. The unspoken look said they wanted to talk to the farmers individually...and at a time they weren't expecting.

The sheriff missed the look—and his own mistake. "See the one doing all the talking? That's Cal Lipkins. He's the one who pushed the deal, is what I hear. Stutzman's the vice-chair of the co-op, but it's Lipkins that railroads everyone into doing what he wants."

"Any of them have it in them to do this kind of thing?" Virgil asked Holden. He glanced down at Esser's mutilated body.

"Let's be clear," the sheriff said, following Virgil's gaze. "This is bad, but the auger done most of what you're looking at. What come before, the knock on the head? That's what you're really asking about."

"It is," Virgil said, his annoyance starting to show. "And let me be clear. We're not talking about a knock on the head. You make it sound like a bar brawl. What we're talking about is murder. So what's the answer? Any of these guys capable of that kind of thing or not?"

Holden sucked on a cheek. "Spend your entire life on a farm and you learn how to kill and not let it bother you. I'd say just about any one of them could have done it, but, these are just regular guys. I don't see it."

Murton grinned without humor. "So what? Nothing's perfect. Let's go jack up some farmers and see who starts to sweat."

The sheriff looked at Virgil. "What's that mean? Nothing's perfect?"

Virgil shook his head. "Nothing. Don't worry about it. You did a fine job of gathering information, Sheriff."

CHAPTER TWELVE

S andy wanted to let Jonas sleep for as long as he needed, but she didn't dare let him wake up in a strange house after what he'd been through. She checked on him every ten minutes until after eleven o'clock, then finally sat down on the bed and brushed the hair from the side of his face. "Hey little man, time to wake up."

Jonas blinked a few times, mumbled something that sounded like "mommy" or "potty" then sat bolt upright, his lower lip quivering. He looked around the room for a moment, his anxiety gradually fading as he recognized his surroundings. "Miss Sandy? Where's my mommy? I have to go potty."

"Your mommy's at home. You stayed here with me and Mr. Virgil last night. Remember?"

"I guess."

Sandy took his hand. "C'mon, I'll take you to the bathroom." Jonas hopped out of bed and they walked out of the bedroom and down the hall to the guest bathroom. "Do you need help or can you go by yourself?"

"I can do it." He said it with a sigh, the way an old man would when asked if he was capable of a task that might lead to his undoing. He walked into the bathroom and with the innocence of a child let the door hang open. He pulled down his pants, turned around, pushed himself up on the toilet, gave Sandy a sleepy smile and said, "I'm hungry."

"Mmm, me too. Which sounds better, pancakes or eggs?"

"Both!" It came out 'boaf.'

Sandy smiled back at him. "Okay, little man. Boaf it is. I'll be in the kitchen. Holler if you need me."

"My daddy used to call me that, before he went to heaven."

"Little man?"

"Yeah."

Sandy looked at him for a moment, then kissed him on the top of his head. "That's because it's true." Then, "Quick, give me your hand."

Jonas put his hand out and when Sandy placed it on her stomach he almost jumped off the toilet. "What's that?"

"That's Wyatt. He's kicking. Can you feel it?"

Jonas nodded, his eyes round and wide. "When is he coming out?"

Not soon enough, Sandy thought. "In a few weeks. Pretty neat, huh?"

Wyatt kicked again and Sandy winced. Jonas snatched his hand away. "Does it hurt?"

"No, not really. It just surprises me sometimes, that's all."

"How does he come out of there?"

Oh boy. "Listen...how about you finish up your business and I'll get started on breakfast, okay?"

Jonas giggled. "Business. Okay, I'll finish my business." Then, "Is Wyatt going to be my brother? My mommy said I couldn't have any brothers or sisters because daddy went to heaven. I want a brother."

"No, not your brother. More like cousins. See you in the kitchen, okay?"

"Okay." Then, again, "Miss Sandy?"

She stopped and thought, *better get used to it.* "What, honey?"

"How long do I get to stay here?"

Get to? She looked at him for a long time, then said, "As long as you want, sweetheart."

IN THE KITCHEN: Sandy breaking eggs into a bowl, her anger at Pam growing by the second. Who puts their own child through a particular type of hell? Answer: Someone who's selfish to the core. She picked up the phone and dialed Pam's cell. It rang five times before kicking over to voicemail. She hung up and redialed two more times with the same result. She was either on the phone or the battery was dead or the phone was turned off. Lately with Pam, who knew?

Jonas still had a year before he started school. He was, Sandy thought, still a baby. Was he aware of the words he was using or the meaning they conveyed? *Get to?* Did he mean to say that? Maybe she was reading too much into it, but wouldn't a child his age say it differently? Wouldn't they say something like *have to stay here* or *when do I go home?* But Jonas had said *get to,* as if being at home with his own mother was too much for him to endure.

She dialed Pam again.

Still no answer...

THE FARMERS STOOD in a semi-circle next to the door of the job-site trailer. They watched the National Guard convoy pull away in a roar of diesel and dust. "Don't know much about the law," Stutzman said to no one, "but Biggie told me they're saying murder." Biggie was John Biggs, and he was Hank Stutzman's second cousin, and a Shelby County deputy.

"Biggie's about as smart as a box of shoe laces," Graves said.

Stutzman's face closed in on itself. "I didn't say he solved the crime. Just telling you what I've heard. My point is this: Charlie was murdered and if you think about motive there are exactly five people who'll directly benefit from his death, and we're all standing right here."

"You're forgetting about Martha," Mizner said. "She's still alive and getting better, according to the doc's. That takes the motive away from us right there."

"The hell it does," Stutzman said. "There going to look at it and say if Charlie was still alive there wouldn't be any deal."

"That's what lawyers are for," Lipkins said. "The way I

see it, the motive is off of us, except maybe for good old Vern, here. Ain't that right, lover boy?"

But Conrad wasn't listening. When the sheriff and the other two men started their way, he muttered, "Here they come." His voice almost broke when he said it.

"Get your shit together, Vern," Lipkins said. "You sound like you're about to cry."

Stutzman spoke before Conrad could respond. "Take it easy, Cal. He's just nervous."

"Fuck easy. He sounds like a school girl. And a guilty one at that. If they sense any weakness in any of us, we're screwed."

Vernon Conrad *was* nervous, but cops or no cops, it was time to make a statement. As Stutzman spoke, Conrad —anything but a school girl—slid behind Lipkins, planted his feet and let go with a solid blow to Cal's kidney. Lipkins arched his back, his mouth opening and closing without sound, as if the magnitude of pain he was experiencing was too great for the human voice to express. When he fell to one knee, Conrad moved around in front of him and threw two more punches at his face, the first one connecting solidly to his eye, the last one at the side of his jaw. Eventually, Stutzman, who was right there and probably could have moved a little quicker if he'd wanted to—which he really didn't—grabbed him and pulled him away.

Someone was shouting, "Hey...hey...hey!"

Conrad shrugged away from Stutzman, landed a final blow to Cal's face, his nose crunching audibly. Then they were all on top of him, and it was over.

THEY WERE about twenty yards away from the farmers when Murton said, "Looks like they're tensing up. Look at that guy...the one moving around behind the others. Oh boy, here we go."

Virgil, Murton, and Holden saw Conrad move behind Lipkins and sucker-punch him in the kidney. The sheriff yelled, "Hey...hey...hey," and started to pick up his pace, ready to break into a run, but Murton grabbed his arm and held him back. "The hell you doing?"

"Saving your knees, if nothing else. Let's see how it plays out," Murton said.

Holden looked at Virgil but all he got was a shrug. "Murt's right." They'd stopped now, and Virgil faced the sheriff. He lowered his voice. "Someone's mad about something. I'd like to know what. At its core, anger is nothing more than fear. That means one of them, or maybe more than one might be afraid of something."

"And your plan is to stand here and let them beat the bejesus out of each other to find out?"

Virgil looked at the group of farmers. "Don't need to. Looks like it's over. But we just witnessed an aggravated assault so now we've got a little leverage if we need it."

"This ain't the city," Holden said. "Not exactly how we do things around here."

Murton turned around and looked back at the demolished silo and Charlie Esser's body. "How's that working out for you?"

LIPKINS HAD a couple of loose teeth, but his bent and

bloodied nose was the worst of it. There was no question...
it was broken. Holden disappeared inside the trailer and
brought out an armful of lawn chairs, the kind you'd see
next to a backyard grill or swimming pool, and a marginally
clean shop rag. He dropped the chairs in the dirt and tried
to hand the rag to Lipkins who was still on one knee, his
eyes not quite focused.

"Let me see that," Murton said.

Holden gave him the rag and Murton got down on one
knee, next to and slightly behind Lipkins. He placed the
rag gently under Cal's nose and said, "We're gonna
straighten you out, Bub."

Holden looked at Virgil, who said simply enough, "He's
had some medical training."

"Maybe we should call and get one of the fire rescue
guys over here, or run him in to the doc's."

"Good idea, " Virgil said. "Why don't you go
get them?"

Holden didn't move.

"Sheriff?"

"Is he gonna do what I think he's gonna do?"

Murton reached around from the back of Cal's neck,
placed his palm on his forehead and pulled his head back
tight against his own chest. "Hold on now, this might sting a
little. On three. Ready?"

Lipkins blew a bloody bubble and said something none
of them could quite make out.

Murton said, "One," then pinched Cal's nostrils
together tight and yanked down as hard as he could. There
was a crunching noise, followed by an audible pop. Lipkins
screamed and passed out.

Graves and Mizner turned away. Conrad stared stone faced at Virgil. The sheriff said, "Jesus Christ, you told him on three."

Murton laid Lipkins on his side in the recovery position. "You never go on three. They tense up. That should do it...for now anyway." He stood, used the rag to wipe the blood from his hands, then turned to the other farmers and said, "We've got some questions for you boys. Who wants to go first?"

One of the fire rescue crew had walked over with a med kit. He looked at Murton, then Lipkins, then back at Murton. "I'll get him taped up. Nice work. Did you go on one, or two?"

Murton tipped his head. "One," he said with a measure of interest.

The medic nodded. "Sometimes I go on two, but not very often. Most of the time it's on one. You get to two and you can already feel them starting to get a little stiff..."

WHEN NO ONE VOLUNTEERED, Virgil and Murton took Conrad—the obvious choice—inside and sat him down while the others waited outside with the sheriff. "What was that all about?" Virgil asked.

"That was about Cal Lipkins running his mouth. Who're you, anyway?" Conrad asked. Virgil introduced himself and Murton, pulled up a chair, sat down and gave Conrad the Miranda spiel. Conrad dismissed the lawyer idea away with a wave and a frown, so Virgil asked about Charlie Esser.

Conrad was rubbing the knuckles of his right hand. "Charlie was a miserable, wife-beating drunkard." He sat forward in the chair, his forearms resting on his thighs. He stared at the floor.

Murton threw three quick questions at Conrad. "That why you killed him? Or was it because of the gas deal? Or both?"

Conrad brought his head up. "No. What? I didn't kill him. Quit trying to twist me up. You city hotshots think you can come down here and roll all over us? We're farmers but we're not idiots. Well, except for Lipkins. He's an idiot."

"You sure about that? The killing, I mean. Because someone sure did a number on Mr. Esser and it looks like you've got some anger issues..." He let the statement float around the room.

Conrad didn't let it float very long. "Don't have no anger issues. Ain't never even punched anyone before in my whole entire life. Probably won't ever again, either. It hurts. Am I gonna go to jail? For punching Cal, I mean?"

"That would be up to Sheriff Holden," Virgil said. "We don't really care about that. That's not why we're here."

"Still would like to know why you hit him, though," Murton said.

"Because he's an asshole."

Murton laughed without humor. "Not good enough. You go around punching people because they're assholes, you'd have a full time job."

Conrad leaned back in the chair, his shoulders slumped. "Yeah, you're right. Hadn't thought of that. But Lipkins is a particular type of asshole. The type that doesn't know when to stop spewing shit at other people, me in particular. We've never really liked each other all that much."

Virgil leaned forward. "He sort of looks like an asshole." Playing a little bit of the good guy.

"He is," Conrad said, nodding as he spoke. "I've known him all my life. We've all known each other our whole lives. Cal is a bully. Always has been."

"How'd he get along with Mr. Esser?"

"Cal didn't get along with anybody except Cal, and I ain't even sure about that."

"Do you think he killed Charlie Esser?"

Conrad thought about it for a moment. "No, I guess I really don't. Bullies are cowards. Surely you guys know that better'n anyone. I didn't see Charlie laying over there...they wouldn't let us any closer'n where we are now, but I heard he's flat torn apart."

"Yes, he is. The auger," Virgil said. "But someone beat his head in, kicked him around a little, then locked him in the silo. The medical examiner says he was still alive after the attack. He died of suffocation."

Murton walked over and stood to the side of Conrad. He leaned in close, right next to his ear. "So you're probably right. This wasn't done by a bully. This was done by someone who was mad enough to smash his head in." He backed up a few steps and leaned against a desk. "Someone with anger issues."

"Weren't me," Conrad said. He folded his arms across his chest. "I ain't never tried to kill no one." Then, as if he had to defend his honor, "But I ain't no school girl, either."

Virgil walked over to the window and looked at the

fracking operation outside. "Tell me about all this. How it all came together."

"Thought you'd know all about it by now."

"We want to hear it from you," Murton said.

He let out a sigh, like he was tired of talking about it. "The co-op is a necessity...at least in this area. We all own our individual farms, but we pool our profits and losses together under the umbrella of the co-op. At the end of the season, if we've had a good year, we split the profits proportionally between all the members."

"How many members are there?"

"Just the six of us. I mean, other farmers in the county use the facility, or they did anyway, before the gas people come along, but they weren't shareholders or stakeholders or whatever. They just used it as a terminal...a way to sell whatever they'd grown that season."

"So they didn't share in the profits or losses of the co-op itself," Virgil said. A statement.

"That's right. There aren't that many of them, anyhow. A dozen or so. Small-timers. Me and Hank and Basil, Angus and Cal, and Charlie...we ran the big farms in the county. Even if the other guys pooled their farms together it wouldn't have been enough for a single share in the co-op. They could have had a share or two...nothing against it, but they were just too small. You know...hundred acres here or there. Just enough to get the farm tax credit. As far as the co-op goes, wouldn't be worth the effort, for them or us."

"So what happens in a bad year? You all have to take the hit together, just like you'd take the profits, is that right?"

Conrad was nodding. "That's right. But we didn't have

too many bad ones. Never had one like this year, that's for damned sure."

Virgil didn't know anything about farming and admitted it. "I guess I don't see the logic. If all you're doing is pooling your resources and sharing in the profits...and once in a while the losses if it's a bad year for everybody, what's the advantage? I mean, why not just run your own farm and let everyone else do the same?"

Conrad looked at Murton, then Virgil. "You think we're all a bunch of country bumpkins, don't you?" He pointed his finger at the space between them. "We're not. Me and Basil and Angus all have Bachelor of Science degrees in agriculture from Purdue. Hank does too, with a Master's in business. I know we look dirty and we smell bad and we talk different than you, but if it weren't for guys like us, guys like you wouldn't eat."

"No one's calling your intelligence into question, Mr. Conrad," Virgil said.

"So now it's mister, is it?"

"Just relax," Murton said. "And answer the question. Why not just run your own farms individually?"

Conrad relaxed a little, his defensiveness dropping a notch. "These are mega-farms we're talking about here. Before this gas deal come along I was farming over a thousand acres. We all were. I've got...or had anyway, over thirty people that worked for me. And that's *just* me. Plus, I'm carrying over a million dollars in debt on equipment that I've either purchased outright or leased...some of it long-term, some of it short. Anyway, on top of all that there's the insurance, payroll, taxes, the seed to plant every spring—and fall if you're doing winter wheat—maintenance on all the equipment, fertilizer, fuel, and on and on and on. Farming is a business just like any other business. Most people think it's one or two guys with a tractor and a plow, but it's not. It's much more sophisticated than that. It has to be in this day and age, otherwise there just wouldn't be any profit. And profits are slim enough as it is. We can barely keep up.

"Look, here's a good example: If it were just me going it alone, I've got enough equipment to keep exactly seven mechanics working full-time. *Seven*. That's full-time with salary and benefits. But Basil's operation is a little smaller than mine...he had four mechanics. Now, say one or two of those guys are sick or has some vacation time or whatever. Now someone is short. So...the co-op. It solves everyone's problems. We've got our own mechanical shop for all the equipment and if you pool your resources, including your people you just don't have to have as many employees. If the co-op was just me and Basil for example, we wouldn't need my seven mechanics and his four. We'd only need eight...nine tops. So you save. Next to fuel and capital expenditures on equipment, payroll is one of the bigger expenses when it comes to mega-farming. People cost money. More money than anything else. Same thing with the administrative end of things. We've got central accounting, great buying power from the seed and fertilizer companies, and the fuel distributors. Also, push come to shove, we can in a small way, set the selling price of our corn or beans or whatever by stockpiling until we get the price we want."

"Sounds a little like OPEC," Murton said.

"It sort of is," Conrad said. "Except we deal with food, not oil."

"Not anymore though," Virgil said.

Conrad nodded at the truthfulness of the statement. "Small farms are a thing of the past. They just can't compete. Our grandfathers all saw the future. They knew what was coming down the line. When everyone else began moving toward the mega-farm model, they went a step further and joined forces and created the co-op. It must have seemed bullet-proof to them all those years ago, but now..." he spread his arms then let them fall to his sides.

"The gas deal," Murton said.

"Yeah, except it's not that great of a deal, really. I'll have enough to live on, but after taxes and all, I'm not going to be much better off than I have been. A little, but not much. Certainly not enough to kill for."

Virgil gave him a skeptical look. "You see, that's the part that doesn't make sense to me. We heard you were each getting two million up front with a back end. You make it sound like you might just squeak by."

"Gotta pay off the debt and offer a severance package to all the co-op employees. Again, people are expensive. And don't forget about the taxes. There's the windfall tax, capital gains tax, land tax that still needs to be paid whether you're farming the land or not, loss of the farm tax subsidy, taxes on the earned interest...it all adds up."

"There's some speculation that Mr. Esser was trying to put a side deal together with Westlake and the gas people," Virgil said. "Try to hold out until next spring and take the deal away from you and everyone else."

Conrad nodded. "Yup. That was the talk. But no one knew for sure. City...that's Westlake, said it weren't true, and I gotta tell you, I don't know to believe him or not.

Esser had a little Jew in him and don't get me wrong, if it would have worked out that way, he'd have taken the deal for sure. Cal is the one who thought that's what was happening, but I just don't know what to believe."

"So if we believe your story, you didn't have motive to kill Charlie Esser," Murton said. "Is that what you're saying?"

Conrad smiled for the first time. "Not exactly. Even if you don't believe my story, I still didn't have motive to kill him. Charlie had disappeared, no one knew where or why —though most everyone thought he'd gone on another bender—but it didn't matter in the end because even though Martha Esser was hurt and in the hospital, she was well enough to sign the contract."

"But someone could have disappeared him before Martha signed," Virgil said, slipping in a little country syntax. "As I understand it, she was sort of touch and go there for a while."

"Yeah, she was," Conrad said. "But killing Charlie because he wouldn't take the deal just doesn't make any sense. He wasn't going to sign when he was alive and he can't sign when he's dead. And you just said it yourself... she was touch and go."

Virgil and Murton looked at each other. Conrad had a point. They took down his personal information before Virgil took one last swing at him. "I'm going to tell you something, Mr. Conrad, and you can do whatever you want with it. I think this whole gas deal spun out of control when Charlie Esser said he wasn't going to go along with it. If one or more of you had something to do with it and you cooperate with us right now, it'll work in your favor. We can help you with the prosecutor. Maybe it was an accident, or an argument that just got out of hand..."

Conrad stood up, and the look on his face made Virgil think they had him. Like he was going to let it all spill out. His lower lip began to quiver, but then he got it under control. When he spoke, it was a simple statement of fact.

"I'm a *farmer*. That's all there is to it."

Virgil looked at Murton and got a shrug. They both stared at him for a few moments, then Murton said, "We'll be in touch, Mr. Conrad. Right now, I'd like you to go ahead and leave the property. Do not speak with the other men until we've talked with them. And think about that lawyer."

Conrad shoved his fists into his pockets, like maybe that was the only safe place for them at the moment. Virgil and Murton stared at him until he walked out the door.

CHAPTER THIRTEEN

They spent the rest of the morning speaking with the other farmers. The conversations were virtually identical...nobody knew nothin' about nothin' and everyone except for Cal Lipkins agreed that Lipkins was an asshole. "Even he was sort of on the fence about it," Murton said when they were finished.

"This whole idea that Esser was putting a side deal together with Westlake...it all comes from Lipkins," Virgil said. "Everyone else was unsure except him. He's the only one that believed it. Why is that?"

"If you've got two guys and two stories, one of them is lying. If you've got six guys—I'm counting Westlake here because he does denies it—you've either got a conspiracy or just one guy is lying."

"Lipkins."

"Yep. I'm having trouble with the conspiracy. Most of them seem like regular guys, not criminal masterminds."

Virgil nodded. "I agree. So, Lipkins. Let's have Becky

run some background on all of them, but start with Lipkins. Who knows? We might get lucky. Maybe there's something lurking there that no one knows about. Let's wrap it up with the sheriff and go feel out the Sunnydale guys."

"That's too bad about the medical examiner. His wife dying and all that," Murton said.

Virgil shrugged it off. "Gotta do the job." But the thought lurking at the back of his brain: Everything matters...

THE SUNNYDALE PEOPLE—THERE were only two of them, the owner, Carl Johnson, and a kid named Mike Grey— both said they'd all ready been felt out by the county cops. "Nothing to tell you that we haven't told them," Johnson said. They sat in Johnson's office, a small, single-windowed shed that had been tacked on to the side of the barn. Carl Johnson was heavy and bald-headed with a white beard. He looked like an overweight Mr. Clean in dirty overalls.

"We'd just like to hear it ourselves," Virgil said. "So, you were dropping off a load of beans or something?"

Johnson laughed at him, but in a friendly way. "Not beans. Feed corn. Couple of truck loads."

"Tell him about the rats," Grey said. He pushed himself off the side wall with his shoulder, his face all lit up.

Johnson tipped his head. "New kid," he said, by way of an explanation. "And the rats don't have anything to do with what we're talking about."

"What about the rats?" Murton said. He was interested.

Grey was a teenager who, Virgil thought, might actually be old enough to drive a semi sometime in the next three or four years. He had short orange, straw-like hair with a few unfortunate orange whiskers scattered around a receding chin. He held out his arms like he was telling a fish story. "Must have been about yay big. I didn't actually see them, but man, you could hear them. Even Carl here, uh, Mr. Johnson, that is...sorry Mr. Johnson. Anyway, Mr. Johnson says they make 'em as big as dogs around here and I believe him." His eyes were wide and serious.

"Hey, Mike," Johnson said, "how about you go check the temporary hog pen for me. I think the water line's plugged up again."

"You bet, Mr. Johnson." He went out the door with a flurry of orange enthusiasm.

Johnson puffed out his cheeks. "He's a good kid. A little—"

"Young?" Virgil said.

Johnson pinched a corner of his lip. "They start out young around here. Know what it means to work for a living. His old man died two winters ago...heart attack. I'm trying to help the family." The statement wasn't quite an insult at Virgil and Murton. "Anyway, I was gonna say slow. But even that's not exactly right. He ain't slow, slow. He just sort of rows his own boat, if you know what I mean. Hard worker, though."

"Any reason you don't want him in here while we talk?" Murton asked.

Johnson nodded. "Yeah. I've got work to do and the longer I talk to you boys the less time I have to do it. We wouldn't get any talking done with him in here. He's like a fly buzzing around your head when you're trying to sleep. You can talk to him all you want. Won't bother me a bit. You'll just get an earful about rats and all the body part out there in my hog pen, is all." He waved at the door. "Have at it."

Murton said he'd take care of it, and followed Grey outside. Virgil turned back to Johnson and said, "So take me through it, from the beginning."

Johnson did—from the time he first called the co-op and asked about the availably of a silo until they dumped their loads and left.

"But when Esser's truck passed you, you didn't actually see him driving, is that right?"

Johnson closed his eyes and tipped his head back in thought. A moment later he opened them and shook his head. "It was just too damned dark. You sit up pretty high in the cab of the semi and we passed pretty close to each other so the angle was bad, so, no. I couldn't see who it was. Safe to say it wasn't Charlie, huh?"

"Looks that way," Virgil said. "And no other vehicles around the co-op?"

"Nope. Just us." Johnson fidgeted around in his seat for a few seconds. Then: "Listen, I gotta ask because no one's come right out and said so, but it ain't too awfully hard to do the math on this here, but me and Grey...we buried Charlie in that silo, didn't we?"

"Were you friends?"

"Nope." Johnson said it in such a matter-of-fact way that Virgil believed him. "I don't keep with wife beaters. Neither does anyone else around here. Charlie was running short on friends the older he got. This was pure business. I needed the silo to rotate my stock. Simple as that. But business or not, friends or not, I don't like to think that what we done killed him."

Virgil tried to gloss over it by keeping the medical examiner's statement to himself. "He'd been severely beaten, Mr. Johnson."

Johnson was looking down in his lap. "I told Mike what he'd heard was rats. Hell, I thought it *was* rats. Charlie'd said number seven would be ready and it was. And we seen his truck leaving, so I didn't think nothing of it. But we buried him, didn't we? And when we emptied the silo, it cut him to pieces."

"He was already gone by then. It's not your fault, Mr. Johnson."

"That don't help much."

Virgil stood and looked and looked out the window. Four crime scene techs were combing through a hog pen, bagging parts of Charlie Esser, their white Tyvek suits stained brown with mud and pig shit. "No, I guess it doesn't."

"Are you going to get him? Whoever did this?"

Virgil didn't hesitate. "Yeah. We'll get him. Just need a place to start...a thread to pull on. That's why we wanted to talk to you. If you could give me one name...if not someone who did it, then someone I can talk to who could tell me who did."

Johnson let his chin fall to his chest and shook his head.

"What?"

"The one person I'd tell you to talk to is the one person who couldn't have done it because she's laid up in a hospital bed."

"Martha Esser?"

"Exactly."

VIRGIL FOUND Murton chatting up one of the crime scene techs. "What'd you get from Grey?"

"He's a smart ass, is what I got. Fifteen years old, says he's been hauling corn around in a semi for two years. I told him to knock it off and he laughed at me, the little shit. He's scared of rats, though. Wouldn't shut up about them."

"You tell him it wasn't rats he heard?"

"No. I told him to check under his bed at night." Then: "The little orange-headed shit."

VIRGIL AND MURTON returned to the drill site, where Sheriff Holden gave them Martha Esser's location. As it turned out, she'd been transferred to Methodist Hospital in Indy. "Probably what saved her," Holden said.

"Okay, we're going to check out the Esser residence before we head back to the city. Get me a copy of the crime scene report when the techs are finished, and a list of all the co-op employees...the mechanics, bookkeepers, everyone."

"Will do," Holden said.

"And Sheriff...?"

"Yeah?"

"Just the list, okay? Let me and Murt talk with them, if you don't mind."

The sheriff rolled his tongue around the inside of his

cheek. "Fine by me. What about Westlake?"

"What about him?"

"He's going to be breathing down my neck to resume operations here. I suspect you know that."

"I'm not unsympathetic to your situation here, Sheriff," Virgil said.

Holden turned and looked in the direction of the Flatrock's dry creek bed. "Meaning what, exactly?"

Virgil was all business. "Meaning we were tasked by the governor to assist you in this matter and that's exactly what we are going to do. But I suspect the matter at hand is a little bigger than the murder of your wife-beating friend over there. Whatever lies behind it is our job, not yours. When the crime scene people are finished you can let Westlake do whatever you think is best. My advice is to stall him as long as possible, but good luck with that. Keep us up to date with any new information on this end. We'll interview Martha Esser and be in touch."

"I'll do just that. Thanks for all the help."

"A return to civilization would be nice right about now," Murton said.

Virgil stood and stared at the drill platforms and equipment that stood idle, ready and waiting to bring natural gas to the surface at the expense of clean water and thousands of acres of land which would no longer be fit to produce food of any kind that would be suitable for human consumption. "It sure would."

Murton gave the sheriff an apologetic look and said, "That's not exactly what I meant."

Sandy kept trying to call Pam, and the result was the same every time. Straight to voice mail. Enough already, she thought. She'd go over to Pam's and find out what was going on. But what about Jonas? She didn't want to take him in case something was wrong, and she couldn't leave him alone either. She ran through a mental list of who to call then picked up the phone. Less than an hour later Delroy and Jonas were playing cards together on the living room floor.

"Thank you, Delroy. I didn't know who else to call."

"Don't you worry about it, you."

Jonas looked at Delroy, then at Sandy. "He talks funny."

Sandy tried to give him a stern look, but failed. "Jonas, that's not polite. Delroy doesn't talk funny. He has an accent, that's all."

Delroy laughed, then said, "Yeah little mon, I got an accent, me. You know what, you?"

"What?"

"So do you." He looked at the cards he was holding. They were playing Go Fish. "Now...got any trees?"

Jonas gave him a funny look. "Trees?"

"Yeah, little mon. Trees." He held up three fingers. "Trees. Day come right before da fours. How many you got, you?"

Jonas giggled at him. "You mean *threes*."

"Ya, mon. What I just say?"

"You said trees, like trees that grow in the yard."

"No, mon, I said trees."

Jonas smacked his forehead with his palm. He thought for a moment then said, "What comes after thirty-two?"

"Tirty-tree."

Jonas rolled over on his back and laughed.

"What so funny, you?"

"It sounded like you said dirty tree."

Sandy knew she'd called the right person to watch Jonas. He was laughing like he didn't have a care in the world. She leaned down, hugged them both and said she'd be back as soon as she could.

Delroy gave her a hard look and pointed his finger at her. "You be careful, you."

Jonas giggled again and said, "Yeah...you be careful, you."

They all laughed but there was no humor in Delroy's eyes when he looked at Sandy. "I mean it."

"You sound like Virgil."

"And you sound like maybe you not listening so good." Delroy stood up, took her by the elbow and led her into the kitchen. "How about I go see Pam and you stay here?"

"Delroy, it's fine. I'm fine. I'll be back before you know it."

"You shouldn't be out running around looking after everyone else. You should be here, looking out for yourself and dat baby of yours."

Jonas shouted from the living room. "Come on, you. Go fish, you!"

"It's okay, Delroy. Go on and play with Jonas. Besides, it sounds like you're converting him."

"Yeah, mon. Day be calling him Jamaican Joe by the time I'm done with him."

She kissed him on the cheek and walked out the door.

CHAPTER FOURTEEN

D ecker and his crew were off shift. When they got back to the barracks he ordered the men to stand down and report back in forty-eight hours for their next stint. Most left the barracks, and the few that remained spent their time on equipment cleanup. He entered the cage where the medical supplies were stored, found what he needed, then hopped in his car and headed out.

Busy day ahead.

LESS THAN AN HOUR LATER, he found the place he was looking for, and when he did, Decker thought: *This is where it could all go to shit.* He killed the engine, slid low in his seat and watched the house. He was about a half-block away on the opposite side of the street. He knew the owner wasn't home, but he wasn't sure if anyone else was inside. Only one way to find out. What was that saying? Fortune favors the bold...? Or some such shit. Whatever, he thought. Time to start kicking ass and taking names.

He walked up the front steps, knocked on the door and waited. If anyone answered, he'd make up some bullshit about being lost, ask for directions and go. Maybe. Because it wasn't exactly ideal, and if anyone did answer, they'd see his face. Then what? He placed his hand on the butt of his gun, knocked again, a little harder this time. Still nothing. He was in a working class suburb and the nearby houses all looked quiet and empty. A typical workday in a midwestern lower middle-class neighborhood.

He stepped off the porch and walked back to his car, started the engine and drove away. So far, so good. He relaxed.

A little.

He circled the block a few times making random turns here and there before backing into the drive. He had a stolen license plate on the car, but still, backing in did two things: It limited his exposure and made for a quicker exit if it turned out he needed one. He pulled on a pair of clear surgical gloves to take care of the fingerprint problem. He'd still have to be careful about the DNA...couldn't leave any traces.

He backed the car up close to the detached garage, closed the door, and went around the rear of the house like he owned the place. The backyard was enclosed by a privacy fence, so unless a neighbor just happened to be peering over the top of the fence he was good.

The back door itself had a double lock just below a set of window panes in the upper half of the door. He used his car key to press on the glass, slowly increasing the pressure until it cracked neatly across the bottom corner. He wiggled the smaller piece out first, then the larger one. Once the two pieces were out, he reached through, unlocked the door and stepped inside. He pulled a roll of clear tape from his pocket—this wasn't his first break-in, after all—and taped the window glass back in place. If you didn't look right at it, you'd never know it had been broken.

Now...time to move. He start in the bedroom closet. Hopefully he'd find it there. He could practically see it in his mind, like he had some sort of ESP or something. It'd be sitting on the top shelf of the closet, in a case, cleaned, loaded, and ready to fire. The caliber didn't matter...any gun could kill if you knew what you were doing, and Decker did. All he needed was the gun.

In the end, his ESP failed him, but he found the gun anyway. It was a .38 revolver, tucked neatly in a holster under the nightstand next to the bed. Decker appreciated the efficiency of the placement. The holster was screwed into the bottom of the table which hid the gun but left it within easy reach in the middle of the night. He appreciated the efficiency because he had the same exact setup himself. Should have looked there first.

ESP, my ass, he thought and let out a little chuckle. Nerves.

He placed the gun in a paper bag, then put the bag in his coat pocket. From another pocket he pulled out a plastic bag that contained a small amount of a brownish grainy substance that smelled, Decker thought, a little like corn flakes cereal that might have been on the shelf a little too long. He took a very small amount of the substance from the bag and dropped it inside a pair of shoes at the back of his closet. The rest was spread around behind the closet door, just a pinch or three. It was a spot, Decker noted, that didn't get vacuumed very often.

Less than a minute later he was out of the house and driving away, his heart hammering inside his chest, the sound inside his head like that of a marching band drum pounding away behind his ears.

———

When Pam Donatti woke she couldn't quite believe how late she'd slept. Then again, after a minute or so, she wasn't all that surprised. Yesterday's bender had been a little over the top. Time to get your shit together, Pamela. Time to get up, grow up and move on. Had she let Ed down? Yes. Had she hidden the truth from him? Yes. But she'd done it out of kindness so as not to hurt him. Wasn't that what you did for someone you loved? It's one thing to deceive someone to hurt them, but what she'd done was the opposite of that. Yes, she'd betrayed her husband, but it was to protect him, not hurt him. It wasn't selfish. It was brave and bold and responsible. Look how happy they'd been since Jonas came into their lives. Why spoil that? Or worse, why spend the rest of her life second guessing something from the past, something she had no control over in the here and now?

All she could do was move forward and take care of herself and her son. Lawsuits weren't the answer. Good decisions were. The money situation would work itself out or it wouldn't. She had good friends who were good people, and they would help her. It saddened her to think of how poorly she'd been handling things. *No, don't kid yourself, Pam.* She hadn't been handling anything, except a bottle of Vodka. That changes today, she told herself.

She sat on the edged of the sofa, rubbed the sleep from her eyes and went to check on Jonas. She was halfway to his room before remembering that Sandy had taken him for the night. When she checked her phone she saw that the battery was dead.

She plugged the phone into the charger, then headed to the bathroom to shower. She'd get cleaned up while the phone charged, then call Sandy to make arrangements to get Jonas. She took her time with it—the cleaning up—and let the hot water soak into her skin. Hopefully it'd pull some of the toxins away.

After thirty minutes or so she stepped out, wrapped a towel around her head, slipped into a robe, and went to sit and cool off before doing her makeup. When the doorbell rang she smiled to herself and thought: *Sandy and Jonas...*

THE DRIVE to Pam's gave him time to think about his past, something Decker tried not to do very often. Last time he'd done something like this—not counting the sand niggers in towel-head central—it had been his old man, and his old man had been a walk in the park compared to what lie ahead.

Decker had been raised on a horse ranch in northern Indiana on ten acres by a loving mother whose spirit and soul was so stifled by her abusive husband that she died of cancer when he was about the same age as his own son was now, her own body turning against her when her heart could take no more.

The abuse Decker's father handed out was predominantly emotional in nature because he was a small man in every sense of the word and to use his fists would have taken a particular type of courage he did not often possess. When Decker thought of those days, the memory that frequented his mind most was the image of his father's teeth, crooked and razor sharp, browned with nicotine stains. Even when he smiled, which rarely happened, there was a feral nature to it, hidden behind a mask of alcohol induced anger that would reveal itself in an instant. It would happen so quickly Decker sometimes thought he was witnessing a portal to hell, a vortex of rage that could open with the flick of a switch where the eyes would change and take on a peculiar cast, a dullness like the sun sliding behind a layer of clouds. He knew if he looked into those eyes for any length of time his own soul was at risk.

Perhaps that's why the teeth remained as the one thing he always thought about when he remembered his father. The brownish, yellowed, razor sharp teeth.

Always the teeth.

To drive past the ranch as an outsider on a summer day must have been idyllic. The tree-lined drive with its white crushed limestone, the perfectly manicured lawn and fenced-in pastures that led to the majesty of the main house gave the illusion of peace and tranquility. On either side of the drive they'd see the magnificent creatures galloping playfully within the confines of those fenced-in corrals and eventually their eyes would catch the barn set back near the edge of the woods, it's indoor riding arena as big as a soccer field. Decker would sometimes walk out to the road and look at it himself and pretend he was someone else, just another admirer, one who was free from the terror and beauty of it all. But he knew the secrets within and it was hard to see the beauty as anything other than the facade that it was, a veneer of goodwill and harmony that fronted the shame and horrors of everyday life led by a moral bulimic who thought dominance and ascendency were Proverbs that somehow got left out of the bible by mistake.

It was, Decker thought, like living in the garden of the mafia.

One day, when Decker was only fifteen years old, a colt had spent the day playing in the pasture and had muddied itself from pastern to crest and everywhere in between. Decker loved the animal and its playful nature. When it was time to collect the colt from the pasture he'd often have to spend the better part of an hour getting hold of the young horse whose personality was that of a playful puppy.

The colt would stand still, his head bowed, his ears forward, his large brown eyes as warm and seductive as a high school cheerleader sitting alone next to the bonfire after a Friday night football game. He'd approach the colt with the halter in plain sight and as soon as he was within reach the colt would let out a snicker, paw at the ground with a front hoof as a distraction, then take the bill of Decker's hat in its teeth and gallop away, his head bobbing in delight.

Decker finally learned the only way to halter the animal was on its own terms. He did it by sitting on the ground, his back turned, and let the animal come to him. It worked every time. After a minute or so the young colt would trot over and stand behind him and nuzzle his hair. Decker would then hold the halter out at his side and the colt would lower his head and practically tether himself.

He led the horse inside the barn and cross-tied him to the support beams on either side of the wash bay, leaving enough slack in the rope so the horse could turn his head and see what was happening. Decker took care with the hose, turning the pressure just high enough to loosen the mud. He started at the front hooves and worked his way up slowly. At the back, the colt had a ticklish spot near his gaskin and when Decker sprayed the animal on that spot the colt would smile and stomp his back hoof and let out a snicker that reminded Decker of a child giggling with delight.

These were the times that Decker enjoyed the most, alone and at one with the animals, times where he could almost convince himself that the garden was just that, a thing of beauty and there was no evil nearby, no secrets hidden within the majestic house of horrors, no vortex that could swallow him whole and leave nothing behind save a memory of something that never existed in the first place. But as he was once again about to learn, the endless complexities of humanity hold few boundaries and not only children see monsters.

He'd finished bathing the colt and was sluicing the excess water from the horse's coat with a sweat scraper, a flexible blade with leather hand grips at both ends. The scraper had a smooth edge on one side and short metal teeth on the other. By flexing the blade and bringing the handles together as one the tool formed a loop that could be dragged across the horse's coat to wick the water away.

Decker was working the scraper when he heard the back door of the house slam shut.

It must have been another bad day at the office because his father was already drunk, shedding his suit as he approached the barn. He removed his coat and let it fall to the ground, then yanked at the front of his vest until the buttons gave way, sailing across the lawn like acorns blown from a tree during a storm. He pulled his tie loose, ripped open his shirt and let them fall in the grass as well. By the time he made it to the barn and the wash bay, he was down to his slacks and undershirt. His wing-tipped shoes were covered with dirt and dust. Decker thought if he ignored his father he might go away, but he was mistaken.

"What the fuck are you doing?"

"I'm cleaning up the colt. I let him play out in the pasture while I mucked out the stalls. He rolled around in the mud and made a mess of himself. I think he enjoyed it, though," Decker said.

"Enjoyed it? You think he enjoyed it?"

"Yeah, you should have seen him. He looked like a giant puppy rolling around in the yard."

"Let me see that scraper."

"It's okay. I've got it, Dad. In fact, I'm almost finished."

"Almost finished? You're a pathetic piece of shit, you know that? You call that clean? I've seen pigs in slop that are cleaner than this."

The colt was named Broker and Decker's father now had his hand wrapped firmly around the halter, his knuckles right next to Broker's right eye. He pulled and twisted the halter, his knuckles grinding into the side of the colt's face between his eye and jowl. Broker's eyes were going wide and his ears worked back, almost flat against the top of his head.

"I said give me that goddamned scraper, boy. I'm sick and tired of the half-assed job you do around here. As usual, I'm going to have to handle the hard work."

Decker could have taken his father. Even at only fifteen years old, he was already bigger and stronger than his father. The problem was, he didn't see himself that way. He saw himself as a little boy, one who'd been beat down mentally and emotionally his entire life. He handed the scraper to his father and stepped back out of the way.

"Fucking almost finished. What a joke. Look at this mud...it's still caked on here."

"I hadn't gotten to that part yet."

Decker's father stopped and turned, his teeth bared, his jaw clenched so tight it seemed it might be wired shut. "If you hadn't gotten to that part yet, then what are you doing with this?" He held the scraper out to his side and when he did one end of the handle slipped from his grasp allowing the blade to become unslung and it hit Broker across the top of his nose, the metal teeth leaving a gash that began to bleed.

"Dad, watch out! Broker's bleeding."

"He's bleeding because of your half-ass work. And because he won't hold still. Bring me those ropes. I'm gonna tie him off."

"Dad, let me finish. I'll take care of it."

"Like you take care of everything else around here? Forget it. Now get me those goddamned ropes."

Decker got the ropes while his father picked up the hose and began spraying the colt's face with water, the blood pouring down across his nose before dripping on the ground and flowing into the drain set in the concrete. By now, Broker was fully panicked, his ears laid flat, his hooves slipping and skittering on the wet concrete. Decker's father took the ropes and tied one at barrel height directly across Broker's hind quarters so he could not back up and tied the other between the bottom of his halter and the D-ring on the floor. He then cinched the cross ties tight, effectively immobilizing the colt.

Decker began to panic and back away. He backed up until he bumped into the side of the wash bay in fear and shame as his father began whipping the colt with the scraper, his teeth bared, spit flying from his lips as he shouted over and over, "Who's the boss? Who's the fucking boss? I'll show you who's boss."

Broker, unable to move or escape the beating began to grunt, then he did something Decker had never seen a horse do, something he didn't even know was possible.

Broker began to cry.

He let out a painful combination of neighing and screaming as Decker's father continued to whip the colt until it was bleeding not only from its face, but from its forehead, muzzle, crest, and shoulders. Broker's lower lip was extended and stiff, drool spilling from his locked-open jaw, his square teeth that only moments ago had been smiling with delight were now bared in contrast, his eyes full and unblinking and open so wide you could see the sclera. When he could take no more, Broker finally collapsed on his front knees, his head twisted to one side against the restraining cross-ties.

When it was over Decker's father dropped the scraper

and stood bent forward with his hands on his knees, his undershirt covered with Broker's blood, sweat dripping from his hair. He was breathing hard and fast, taking in huge gulps of air. He finally stood upright, shook a cigarette out and lit up, exhaling smoke into the colt's face. When he spoke his voice was distant, like he might have been remembering something from long ago.

"Sometimes you've got to show them who's boss. It's good for them and they don't even know it." He had a smile on his face, his cigarette pinched tight between his yellow teeth. "Get this cleaned up. I'm sick and tired of doing your work for you, you half-assed piece of shit." He walked out of the barn and after a few steps stopped and turned back and pointed his finger at Decker. "That's how you whip a horse into shape, by the way."

What happened next changed Decker for good. When he tried to approach Broker, the colt panicked and wouldn't let him near, as if it had been Decker himself who had whipped the horse. After three or four tries, Decker finally closed all the barn doors and simply cut the ropes and let the animal wander loose in the main arena.

Broker never let Decker get close to him again, and in Decker's mind the reason was obvious. The horse knew Decker could have stopped the beating, but had been too afraid of his father to do so.

His father, on the other hand, would get drunk and tell that story over and over again to anyone who'd listen until the day he died, four years later. It was the first time Decker killed anyone. He was surprised how easy it was. He simply let him drink until he passed out, took the tumbler of vodka from his hand and replaced it with his father's pistol, carefully wrapping his index finger around the trigger, placed the gun against the side of his head and blew the top of his skull across the room.

Once that was done, he stripped down to his shorts, put his clothes in a garbage sack, took a quick shower, called his girlfriend and took her to the movies. The garbage sack went into a drugstore dumpster on the way over to pick up his girlfriend, and after the movie was finished they went back to Decker's house. His girlfriend loved horses.

As they walked in the house Decker opened the door and let her lead the way. When she saw the carnage she began to scream and cry. She was still crying when the cops showed up, explaining between sobs how she'd found her boyfriend's father. Decker was crying now as well, but his tears came from a sense of relief and liberation. When the cops began asking questions Decker answered them all and even showed them the ticket stubs from the movie.

The cops never even looked at him. A month later he joined the army and was gone...in every sense of the word.

Decker was nuts.

Pam went to the front door, pulled it open...the smile still on her face, one hand holding the door knob, the other holding the towel in place on her head.

Decker pushed her backward, hard. She bounced on her butt and smacked her head on the floor. Even with the towel protecting her skull, it still dazed her. Decker followed her right in, kicking the door shut with his prosthetic leg. He rolled her, quick, then hit her at the base of her skull with the butt of the gun. The blow knocked her out cold.

In the back of his mind, he thought, *pretty nice entry.*

He took a quick peek though the front window to make sure no one was watching the house—no one was—then turned back to Pam. He pulled her through the house, back to the bathroom and closed the door behind him. The noise could be a problem, but he couldn't really do anything about that. He pulled the hammer back on the gun, then hesitated for just a moment—thinking about the one time they'd had sex, how good it had been. He even remembered thinking that maybe she was the one who could...repair him, return him to some sense of normalcy.

Then he remembered the look on her face when he happened to run into her at the grocery store months later, how she tried to shrink away from him, the swell of her belly and the fullness of her breasts evidence of their single encounter. He tried to explain that he was nothing like his father, that he was a good man who didn't drink and would care for her and their son. He remembered how all he wanted to do was be open and honest with her. It was the most vulnerable he'd ever been with a woman, right there in the grocery store next to the produce, and she looked at him like he was some kind of freak. She told him to get away from her, that she never wanted to see him again. She hissed it at him, then abandoned her cart and ran to her car, one hand holding her stomach, the other covering her bouncing breasts.

Decker had been so stunned he didn't respond. He looked only at her teeth when she spoke and when she hurried away he simply stood there and watched her go. He stood in the same spot for so long that a grocery clerk finally approached and asked him if he was all right. Decker told the clerk he was going to be a father, then walked away...

He wrapped her hand around the gun, put the barrel against the side of her head and pulled the trigger. He leaned down next to Pam's ear and whispered, "Who's the boss? Who's the fucking boss now?" At least he thought he'd whispered. He may have shouted. The blast from the gun within the confines of the small bathroom had been deafening.

A flood of panic rippled through him. This wasn't like his old man...out in the country in the middle of nowhere. There were houses right next to each other. Had any of the neighbors heard the shot? There were no windows in the bathroom, so that helped, but if someone had heard...

He let go of the gun and stepped back. He wasn't quite satisfied with the position of Pam's body, but he knew that moving her was too much of a risk. He'd have to let that part go. He pulled two strands of her hair from a brush on the edge of the sink. Then he took two vials of morphine and carefully rolled her thumb and forefinger across the containers. The vials and hair went into a separate bag.

Had to hurry now.

He moved to the front of the house, sprinkling a smattering of a powdery substance in his wake. A quick check outside a few windows helped with the panic. No one was running toward the house, no curious neighbors were sticking their heads through their front doors with a 'What was that?' expression. In fact there was no one at all. He checked the back windows from the kitchen and saw the same thing. He could see a neighbor three houses down mowing a backyard. If anyone had heard the shot, maybe they'd think it was the mower backfiring.

He was safe. His breathing and his pulse began to return to normal. He took the other vial of morphine and hid it in a top drawer of the master bedroom dresser. After that he watched the front of the house for another agonizing minute before opening the door and walking down the block at a leisurely pace...just a regular guy out for a stroll. He turned the corner, forcing himself not to run to his car.

One down, one to go. Decker, crazy as a loon, had one thought running through his brain: Who's the boss now? Who's the boss now?

Like loons everywhere, he wasn't even aware of the thought. His phone buzzed at him and brought him out of the trance.

"Where are we at?"

"Right on schedule. One down, one to go."

"You're going to have to disappear for a while when this is done. You realize that, don't you?"

Decker did, and he didn't care. As long as he got the money. "I do. In fact, I can't wait." He tossed the phone on the seat and drove toward the hospital. He didn't really care about what he had to do next. He just didn't know why. And the why—the not so loony part of his brain told him— might be important.

Still, work to be done. He knew the consequences of a half-assed job.

CHAPTER FIFTEEN

He parked near the hospital's receiving docks and pushed through a set of swinging double doors. He wore tan canvas pants, a buttoned denim shirt, and a plain black baseball cap. He also wore his combat boots. That was strictly for comfort. It was, he thought, the one fucking thing the government did right—they knew how to make a comfortable boot. He kept his head down in case of security cameras, made a hard left as soon as he was inside and found himself right in the middle of the janitorial supply room.

The room itself was institutional gray and seemed to be the source of origin for the hospital smell that everyone always commented on or complained about. There was a time clock just to his right with a slotted card holder mounted next to it. The opposite wall was lined with lockers painted the same dull gray as the walls. A large bay contained four-wheeled pushcarts stocked with spray bottles, disposable rags, buckets, a mop, toilet paper, and other cleaning supplies. No one was in the room. He moved quickly to the lockers, opening each one until he found what he needed: A hospital uniform shirt with a name tag. This particular shirt belonged to someone named Sam, and Sam, God bless him, had left his hospital I.D. clipped to the shirt pocket.

Decker snatched the shirt off the hook and put in on. It was slightly large, but not overly so—apparently Sam had little regard for the dangers of processed food—but he tucked it in tight around his waist and made do with what he had. There were boxes of light-blue hospital shoe covers, the kind doctors and nurses wore in surgery, and still more boxes filled with paper head covers done in the same pale blue with a thin band of white elastic around the edges. He wished there were some of the paper face masks. That would have been ideal. Or would it? Did janitors wear those? He didn't think so. No sense in trying to blend in to the point where you stuck out like a donkey at the Kentucky Derby.

He rolled the bill of his hat and shoved it in his back pocket, put one of the covers on his head and pulled it low, right down to his eyebrows, then slipped his shoes inside the paper covers. He grabbed one of the four-wheeled custodial carts and pushed it out to the hallway. With a little luck, he'd be in and out in less than fifteen minutes. Without a little luck, he'd resort to plan B, which was locked and loaded with the safety on, strapped to his one good ankle.

He pushed the cart along, turned a corner, kept his head down, whistled softly the way janitors do and headed for the elevators.

No one even looked at him.

THE FIFTEEN MINUTES came and went. He was still on plan A, but he was starting to sweat. Finding Martha Esser was harder than he thought it might be. He emptied a trashcan next to the elevator and studied the directory that hung on the wall.

He made his way to the ICU, thinking that if she'd just woke from a coma caused by severe head trauma, that's where she'd be. So far he'd discovered two things: the fucking hospital was huge, and they didn't put the patient names next to the individual rooms like they used to. After circling the floor twice and peeking in on several patients, his luck finally ran out.

"Excuse me. May I help you?"

Decker jumped at the voice behind him and spun on his good leg. A young nurse in yellow scrubs and white tennis shoes stood right behind him. She had jet black hair pulled back and tied in a bun. A single mole, no bigger than the head of a pin was centered right below her left nostril. Decker thought it looked like she had a little booger trying to get away. She was maybe twenty-five, and other than the unfortunate booger-like mole, very pretty. He forced himself not to stare at the mole, the same way others often tried—and failed—when they saw his artificial limb. The nurse looked at the I.D. badge clipped to his shirt. Fortunately, he'd had the sense to turn it so the back side faced out and the picture was hidden. But the uniform shirt had done its job because people see what they expect to see.

The nurse looked away from the I.D. and to the name tag sewn on the familiar shirt, one that had the hospital logo on the opposite breast.

"Sam, is it?"

"Uh, yeah," Decker mumbled. "Sorry, I'm still a little new. And a little lost."

She smiled at him. "I thought so. I haven't seen you around here before. And, you don't look like you're cleaning. You look like you're looking for someone."

"Actually, I am...Amber." He'd glanced at her name tag and smiled. "Hey, my mom's name was Amber," he said. Decker was crazy, but he wasn't stupid. He knew how to turn on the bullshit a little when he needed to. His mother's name was Ruth. Amber sounded like a stripper name.

Amber reached out and touched his arm lightly...just a brush. "Was?"

"She passed just last year. Right here in this ward."

"Oh, I'm so sorry."

Decker leaned on his cart, let his head hang, and turned the bullshit up a half notch. "Still miss her. Guess I always will. I see these rooms and, well..." He spread his arms out a bit and let the gesture speak for itself. The gesture had to because his mother, the one good thing in his life had been gone for almost thirty years now.

Another touch. "It gets better. It does. You just have to take it one day at a time."

"I guess. Lot of days, though. Listen, you were right. I am sort of looking for someone. One of my mom's old friends. I thought she'd be up here, in the ICU."

"A patient, you mean?"

"Yeah. Her name's Martha Esser."

Amber looked around before she answered. "We're not supposed to give out patient information..."

"Well, we do both work for the same hospital, you know," Decker said with a chuckle. "Not exactly crime of the century if you know what I mean."

"Yeah, I know what you mean, but it's the HIPPA laws. I'll tell you something, Sam, they're getting worse every year. Pretty soon the patient is going to have to sign a piece of paper that says they can look at themselves in the mirror." She laughed at her own nurse humor.

Decker smiled at her. "Yeah, I get it. That's okay. Sorry to have bothered you. I better get back to my floor. She probably wouldn't even remember me, anyway."

"Oh, I'll bet she would. You know what? What's the harm? I mean, from what I hear, she doesn't have any family left after what happened to her husband. You heard about that, right?" Amber was a talker. She thought for a moment, then said, "She's been moved to the rehab wing. Do you know where that is?"

"I'm afraid not. But I'll find it. Listen, you've been a huge help. Thanks a lot, and it was nice to meet you, Amber." He pushed at the cart and started to walk away.

"Hey, Sam?"

He stopped and turned back. "What's that?"

"I'm getting ready to go on break. Come on, I'll take you right there."

Decker didn't want that. Didn't want that at all. "Oh, no. That's all right. You've been very helpful. Take your break. You deserve it. I know how hard you all work up here."

"No, really. I insist. Plus, I haven't seen Martha for a

few days and I'd like to see how she's progressing. Besides, everyone knows it's impolite to deny the insist."

Decker looked at her for a moment. "You sure you want to do that?"

Amber caught a look in his eyes, just a flash. Something in her gut tried to tell her something, but she pushed it away without ever realizing she'd done so. "Sure. Why not?"

Plan B, then. "Okay. Lead the way, Amber."

Decker followed her down the hall, watching her ass jiggle inside the yellow scrubs. Amber was already dead. She just didn't know it.

Probably would have made a good stripper though, with that ass.

CHAPTER SIXTEEN

Murton took the call from Becky and told her she was on speaker with Virgil. They were about halfway back to the city. They'd been to the Esser residence and saw that there was exactly nothing to see. The crime scene techs told them that the truck had been wiped clean and there was nothing in the house that constituted a crime other than the rooster wallpaper in the kitchen. "That's a misdemeanor-level crime right there," the tech had said.

"Hey Jonesy."

"How's it going, Becks?"

"Going well...considering."

"Considering what?"

Murton slapped his own forehead and interrupted before Becky had a chance to answer. She was just as upset about Pam Donatti's lawsuit as Murton was. Virgil, on the other hand, seemed to have already forgotten it. "What have you found so far, baby?"

There was a pause before she answered, and when she did her voice was flat. "Westlake is exactly who he says he is. In fact, so are all of the farmers. Other than a few traffic violations there's no real background on any of them, unless you consider the fact that Charlie Esser married into his fortune. He clearly didn't marry out of love and respect. Cora has given me access to the state databases as well as the NCIC. Martha Esser filed two separate complaints against her husband, one just over a year ago and the other six months before that. But both were eventually dropped. If there's two complaints filed, you know there must have been on-going abuse that didn't get reported at all. Other than that, everyone's taxes are in order and no one is involved in any radical organizations or anything like that. The co-op books are clean as well. Not counting the Esser's, reading about the entire group of them is a safe substitute for sleeping pills."

"How'd you get the taxes?"

"Hey, Jonesy?"

"Yeah?"

"Don't ask questions you don't want answered."

"Mmm, okay." Becky, Virgil thought, had hacked the federal database, probably through a backdoor from the NCIC. "Is there anything else?"

"Yeah, Jonesy, there is. Just where in the hell do you get off siding with Pam Donatti and this ridiculous lawsuit she's—"

"The governor's calling, baby-doll," Murton said. "Thanks for the intel. I'll see you tonight." He clicked off, glanced at Virgil and noticed the cartilage flex as he ground his jaw tight. "Women, huh?"

"Murt, Sandy and I are not siding with Pam on this lawsuit. I thought I made that clear."

"Relax, Jones-man. I know you're not. I was just a little hot for a minute. The whole thing caught me off guard... and you know how much I like that. I told Becky about it and frankly, she's upset. Got a right to be too, if you ask me. She'll cool off. I'll take care of it. I just haven't had the chance to talk to her since this morning."

"You know what I remembered this morning?"

"What's that?"

"When I was with the MCU...before they sacked me, it felt like someone was always upset with me about something. Wait, that's not exactly right. It's more like someone was always upset with me about something and I either didn't notice or didn't care. I'm not exactly sure which. But after I spoke with Delroy earlier, I did notice. I'm not talking about the lowlifes and scumbags. I'm talking about people I care about...you and Becky, Sandy, Cora. Like that."

"Ah, Cora's always upset. I think it's part of her personality. And you were in charge. Not to sound too unsympathetic, but that's the breaks, Jonesy. It goes with the territory. Meet the new boss...same as the old boss."

"I think you might be missing my point."

Murton looked at him without expression. "Then how about you dumb it down for me a little."

"There's something I didn't tell you yet. I saw my dad yesterday. By the tree. We spoke to each other."

Murton turned away and stared at the countryside sliding by. After a few moments he turned back and looked at Virgil. When he spoke, his voice was at once full of pain and anger. "I'm going to ask you something and I'm only going to ask you once and you better tell me the fucking truth."

Virgil knew what was coming. "So ask."

"I swear to Christ, Jonesy, if you try to bullshit me on this I'll know it. I will also personally kick your ass so bad you *will* need those fucking pills again."

Virgil nodded. "That wasn't a question, but I believe you about the ass-kicking. If you think you could, that is." Virgil knew he could. Murton was the toughest fighter he'd ever met. "I'm not on the pills. I'm as clean as the day I was born."

Murton stared at him, hard, for a full minute. Because Virgil was driving he had to watch the road, but he turned and looked at him a few times without blinking, his face open and honest.

"Okay," Murton finally said. "I believe you. The offer of the ass-kicking still stands though."

"Noted." Then: "It makes me feel like there might be something wrong with me."

"Why? Because you can talk to him?"

"No, because..." Virgil was going to give him a smart-assed response but cut himself off. "Yes, because I can see my dead father. And not only that, I can talk with him. Jesus, I feel like I need a shrink, or something."

"Ah, that's bullshit, and you know it. You're fine. Besides, Small has seen him, and so has Robert. There's nothing wrong with them. Especially with Small." He wiggled his eyebrows. "Nothing wrong with her at all."

"You know, I'm really starting to worry about you and her."

"You should."

"Maybe Becky can give me some guidance on the issue."

Murton called his bluff. "Hey, that's a great idea. Becky's a wild one. I'll bet she'd go for it...me and her and Small. It's more common than you think these days. Besides, after Sandy spits out that kid and he's got my steel gray eyes, my square jaw and over-all dashing good looks you're going to know what's what. She'll probably get your house after the divorce which means I'll be living there. Man, I've always loved that place. Can't believe it's going to be mine. You can still fish in the pond if you want. I'll let you have Wednesdays and one weekend a month. Hell, I'll even rent you my place at a reduced rate until you get back on your feet."

Virgil picked up his phone.

"What are you doing?" Murton asked.

"Calling Becky back. You just said it was a great idea, remember?"

Murton held up his hands in surrender. "All right, all right. I'm just fucking with you. Hey, give me that phone."

"Yeah, Becks, it's Virgil. Listen—"

"Hey, c'mon man, quit fooling around..."

AFTER THE COP humor had run its course: "So every once in a while you get to talk to your old man. So what? I'd give my left nut to be able to see him—Mason, I mean—let alone talk to him. Count your blessings, brother."

"I'll tell you exactly three things," Virgil said. "One, it makes me feel a little like a freak or something."

"Everyone's a freak in one way or another."

"Would you please just let me say it? B, he's always speaking in some sort of code. He never just comes right out and says what he means. This time the theme was a combination of 'everything matters, and I'm not in control.' He just kept driving that point home. And three, deep down in my heart—and I've never really told this to anyone —a tiny part of me wants it to stop. It's like every time he shows up by that tree my grieving process has to start over. It's not natural."

Murton shook his head. "Don't be an idiot."

"What's that supposed to mean?"

"It means here's three things right back at you," Murton said. He ticked them off his fingers. "A, you just said one, B, and three. Try to stay with the same system, like I'm doing right now. B, I just said it, but clearly you didn't hear me... Count. Your. Blessings." He poked his finger into Virgil's shoulder, hard, with every word. "And C, stop saying you want it to stop, because if you don't, it just might and then you'll really be fucked up about it."

"Ah, I don't really want it to stop. It's just...hard. He's there, but he's not there, know what I mean?"

"No, I don't," Murton said. "I guess some of us just aren't as fortunate as others." He turned away and stared out the side window of the truck.

———

THE REHAB WING of the hospital, Decker thought, was

almost as depressing as the V.A. facility where he'd done his own rehab after the war. The floor was tiled in a dull cream color, the walls were painted cream, the ceiling was cream, and so was the furniture. Even the physical therapists wore cream-colored scrubs. Decker discovered that if he squinted just so, he could make their scrubs fade into the background to the point where it seemed that the attendants all looked like a bunch of floating heads.

"What's with all the cream?" he asked.

Amber chuckled at him. "Some big study from a few years ago. It's supposed to have a calming effect or something." She lowered her voice then said, "Personally, I think it's bull. I mean, if you're on this floor, you've got some serious problems to try to overcome. Most of the patients are recovering from closed head injuries...or something just as bad. I doubt they care much about the décor."

Decker didn't answer, but thought she was probably right.

The floor was quiet. They only passed two patients, both in wheelchairs pushed by creamy attendants whose facial expressions were much the same as the people in the chairs, as if being on the floor was its own kind of hell. Whether you were pushing the chair or sitting in it made little difference.

Decker pushed the janitorial cart with one hand and slipped his other hand in his pocket, feeling the syringes that held the lethal doses of morphine. When they turned from the main corridor and into the short wing he knew they were close so he popped the cap from one of the syringes with his thumb and forefinger, careful not to poke himself.

"Here we are," Amber said. She'd stopped in front of a door to a private room. Decker glanced at the placard on the wall, made a mental note the room number, smiled and said, "After you." He swept his arm in front of the door in a gentlemanly way. Amber blushed slightly, gave the door a polite knock and placed her hand on the knob.

Then something happened and it saved her life.

Her hospital pager began to buzz.

———

"OH SHIT...WHOOPS, I MEANT SHOOT." She blushed again. "I've got to run. Something's happening on my floor."

Decker was momentarily caught off guard. His instinct was to grab her and pull her into the room. He even found himself reaching out for her arm, but he stopped himself. If she screamed, or it went bad in any other way he'd be screwed. Plus, she was already moving, out of reach.

"Nice to meet you, Sam," she said over her shoulder. "I'm sure I'll see you again. Take care."

"You too," Decker said, in spite of himself. Two seconds later she was around the corner and gone. And now he had a decision to make. He could go in and take care of Martha Esser, or he could come back and do her later. The one thing he knew he couldn't do was continue to stand outside her door doing nothing at all.

He moved the cart to the opposite side of the hallway and pushed it two doors down. The smallest of distractions in case anyone turned the corner. He grabbed a spray bottle and a rag from the cart, then stepped back to Martha's room, opened the door and slipped inside.

The blinds were closed and the lights were off so he had to stop just inside the doorway to let his eyes adjust. A faint green glow from a heartbeat monitor cast a pale light over the bed. Martha Esser was on her back, with one arm hanging clumsily over the side. Decker stood there for a moment, his eyes adjusting, and watched her breathe. The monitor bleeped out the rhythm of her heartbeat and as it did, Decker noticed that his own heart was beating almost twice as fast as hers. He could see that her head was heavily bandaged on one side and she had some sort of apparatus attached to her shoulders and skull.

A bracing system of some kind with rods that ran vertically from her shoulders that attached to a set of double rings that encircled her head. A halo. He didn't know how he knew what the device was called...he just knew. Probably from a TV medical drama. He liked to watch those.

An oxygen tube ran under her throat and behind her ears before making its way to her nostrils. An IV drip bag hung from a pole on the opposite side of the bed, the line snaking awkwardly across her body before reaching the back of her wrist where it was held in place by a clear bandage. There was an injection port poking out of the tape. That's where he'd inject the lethal dose of morphine.

From the looks of her, Decker thought, he'd be doing her a favor. He was no doctor, but if the shows on TV were at least somewhat authentic—and he thought they were— then Martha Esser didn't look like she was quite ready to be out of intensive care. She looked like she was ready for the morgue.

He had the syringe in his hand now, and began to move towards the bed. It was filled with enough morphine to kill a horse...not that'd he'd ever do anything like that. Horses were kind, intelligent beautiful animals. His mind was racing, wandering, and he knew it. Adrenaline.

He took another step and stood right next to Martha Esser's bed. He stuck the needle of the syringe into the injection port, placed his thumb on the plunger, and thought...

Amber.

He'd have killed her. Had been ready to do so simply out of necessity. The fact that he hadn't created a problem. He stood there with his thumb on the plunger and thought it through. Could she identify him? She didn't know his name. His head was covered with one of those ridiculous blue paper caps pulled low over his forehead. He'd avoided eye contact with her as much as possible. Was that suspicious? It probably was.

And what about his leg? People with a prosthetic leg move with a certain gait. She was a nurse. She'd probably known all along and was simply too polite to say anything. He imagined the conversation she'd have with the cops:

"Oh, yes, Officer. He's the one, I recognize his voice. And he seemed lost, like he didn't know which end of the hospital was which. I remember after they hired me we got the full tour and during our training we had to learn where every department was located, you know, in case anyone asked, or in the event of an emergency or whatnot. And it's not only the nurses. It didn't matter if you were a doctor or a cafeteria worker, you had to do the tour. And I'll tell you something else, I knew all along about the prosthetic. I see those every day of my life. I'd be ninety percent sure anyway, but that leg of his? You can always tell. Yep, that's him all right. Unless he's got an identical twin brother with a prosthetic leg, he's the one who murdered Martha Esser. Take him away. Testify in court? Of course. I'd consider it my civic duty."

Shit.

He'd have to deal with the nurse later. Maybe. This wasn't her floor. She might not even hear about it. And if she did, what were the chances the cops would end up talking to her? Slim? None? Likely? He simply didn't know.

What he did know was this: If he didn't do this and do it now, some very dangerous people were going to be extremely upset with him. He was just about to push the plunger down when Martha's eyes popped open. She reached across the bed and clamped her hand around his wrist. He tried to pull away but Martha, a strong country woman, held him tight and wouldn't let go. Decker began to panic. He tried to pry her fingers away without success.

"Bitch." He hissed it at her. He grabbed the frame of the halo and twisted it violently to one side. Martha tried to let out a scream so he punched her hard in the gut and that took the air out of her. The plunger was still in the port and he pushed it all the way down, then watched as her breathing began to slow almost immediately.

Less than a minute later she exhaled one final time— her lips making a little motorboat noise—and that was it. He placed his hand on her heart...it was quivering, more like a muscle spasm than a beat, but after a few seconds that stopped too. The heartbeat monitor was showing a flat line and making a continuous screeching noise. Decker pushed a few buttons but couldn't find the right one to turn it off. He followed the power cord to the wall thinking he'd simply pull the plug but the machine was hard-wired into the wall. He took a knife from his pocket and sliced the cord in two that caused a brief shower of sparks, but the machine finally stopped screeching at him. With that done, he pulled the syringe from the injection port, capped it, and put it back in his pocket. Martha Esser was gone.

Strong as a fucking ox, though.

He pulled on a pair of latex gloves, took the bag that held the extra vial of morphine and Pam Donatti's hair from his pocket. His hands were shaking badly, but he managed to get one strand of hair on the center of the bed, and let the other fall on the floor next to the IV stand.

His own heart was pounding away, the adrenaline running strong and he had some trouble deciding the best placement for the morphine vial. He wanted it to either look like she'd dropped it and lost it, or that she'd simply forgotten it. Ultimately he decided that the forgetting option was the way to go, so he set the vial on the table next to the bed. It occurred to him though, if someone other than the cops touched the vial, Pam's prints could be covered up and ruined. He couldn't have that, so he placed the vial on the floor behind the table, as if it had been dropped and lost. The crime scene techs should find it before anyone else did. He hoped so, anyway. Said, *fuck it* to himself because a clock was ticking in his head and he knew it was time to boogie. If he stood there any longer trying to decide on the perfect placement he may as well just cuff himself to the bed and wait for the cops to show up.

Decker moved across the room, put his ear close to the door and listened. The hallway was quiet. He was going to crack the door and take a peek, but he'd learned in the army that if you were going to be somewhere you shouldn't, the best way to pull it off is to act like you were supposed to be there.

In the end it didn't matter. When he pulled the door open the hallway was still empty. He retrieved his cart, put the spray bottle and rag back in the side bin and moved back down the hall, toward the elevators. There were a few other things he needed to do, and soon. He was running through the list in his head, all the while thinking that he almost got his ass kicked by a woman in a hospital bed, but when he turned the corner at the end of the hallway he forgot all about the list and the strong-as-an-ox bitch.

The two state cops, Jones and Wheeler were at the far end of the hall, coming right at him.

When they arrived at the hospital the parking garage was full and Virgil ended up circling the campus twice looking for a place to park. After the third circuit he gave up and parked his truck in one of the valet spots right by the front entrance. He tossed an oversized "State Police Official Business" placard on top of the dash and locked the doors.

"That right there is an invitation to be towed," Murton said.

"Hasn't ever happened."

"Doesn't mean it never will."

"I've had it for years," Virgil said. "Issued when I made

detective. Besides, it has the official seal of the state on it, right there at the top."

Murton leaned over the fender and looked closely at the sign through the windshield. "I'm telling you, it looks like you made it yourself at Kinko's or something...about twenty years ago. The font alone is grounds for a misdemeanor. I'm tempted to write the ticket myself."

"Are you coming or not?"

"I don't know. If you're really going to park here, one of us should stay behind and guard the truck."

"Fuck that," Virgil said. " I'm the fuzz. I can park wherever I want. That sign on the dash says so."

"That sign on the dash says 'Tow me,'" Murton said as he moved toward the hospital entrance. "But whatever, dude. It's your truck. You should at least let the valet guy know."

"Yeah, yeah." Fucking partners.

Virgil stopped at the valet station inside the double doors, identified himself to the kid behind the stand, and told him where he'd parked. In retrospect, he'd used a little too much attitude.

"I'm sorry, sir, but those are reserved spots. You can't park there. Hospital security has sanctioned me to have any unauthorized vehicles towed from those spots."

Sanctioned? "That's an official state police vehicle. You have it towed and I'll have you arrested."

The kid turned around and looked out the window at the spot where Virgil had parked. "That's a Ford Raptor. Hell of a nice truck. Do all official state police vehicles have vanity plates, sir?" Virgil's plate said 'Jonesy.'

"Did you not hear me? I'm authorized to take you to jail," Virgil said.

The kid rolled his eyes and held out his arms, his wrists turned upward, the palms of his hands hanging limply upside down. After a beat: "No? I didn't think so. I've got the towing company on speed dial, by the way."

Virgil gave in. "Okay, how much does authorization go for these days?"

"Twenty bucks."

"Twenty bucks? That's crazy. How about ten?"

"You have exactly three choices, sir. Move the truck, get towed, or pay the twenty-five dollar courtesy fee."

Virgil shook his head. Courtesy fee. "Twenty-five? Two seconds ago you said twenty."

"Yes sir, I did. But that was before you decided to negotiate."

Virgil wasn't backing down. "All right kid, look, I want to talk with your supervisor. Right now."

The kid gave him a slow blink. "Yes, sir. That's fine. He's in his office, right down the hall. I'll have him here in less than thirty seconds. But before we get to all of that, may I ask you a question?"

Virgil had him now. "You just did."

"Indeed I did, sir. May I ask you another question following this one?"

Virgil sighed. "What?"

"Do you have a supervisor?"

"Yeah, I do. So what?"

"Well, I'd like to have a word with yours as well." He took a pen from the pocket of his vest, clicked it a few times and waited. "The number, please. Sir?"

People were beginning to stare and Virgil was turning red. "Oh, fuck it." He took out his wallet and tried to hand the kid a twenty and a five. The kid just clicked his pen a few more times, then looked at Murton. "He's not very good at this sort of thing, is he?"

Murton covered his mouth with his hand, like he was scratching his cheek. He just shook his head.

"What are you doing?" Virgil said. "Do you want the money or not?"

"Yes sir, I do. The pay isn't too great around here, as I'm sure you might imagine. But I'm still waiting for the number of your supervisor. That's what we agreed to, is it not? You give me the number of your supervisor and I'll have my supervisor come down here and everything will be all squared away."

"How much if we leave the supervisors out of the equation?"

"That would be forty dollars, sir."

"Fort—" Virgil caught himself before he did any more damage. He looked in his wallet, then over at Murton, who was bent over with his hands on his thighs. "I need five bucks."

IN THE ELEVATOR: "That's extortion. I should lock his skinny ass up."

Murton, still laughing. "Extortion? Man, that was a thing of beauty. That kid took you to the mat. You should have seen your face when he asked for Cora's number."

"I did okay. He had me at a disadvantage, is all."

"Okay? When is Small due again?"

Virgil gave him a skeptical look. "Little less than a month. Why?"

Murton clapped him on the back. "No reason. You're going to make a hell of a good father, I'm certain of it, but when it's time to teach young Wyatt how to negotiate, maybe you better leave that part to Uncle Murt."

Virgil finally laughed. "Yeah, you're probably right. Don't even ask me what I paid for the truck."

Murton turned slowly until his entire body was facing Virgil.

"What?"

"You paid sticker, didn't you?" Murton said.

Virgil didn't answer.

"Oh man...nobody pays sticker. Nobody."

"Yeah, yeah. Whatever. It's a Raptor. They don't make them anymore and it was the last one on the lot. It was a holdover or something. I'm not sure what that means, but the guy who owns the dealership was keeping it for himself."

"That's what they told you, huh?"

"What do you mean, that's what they told me? It's the truth."

"How do you know that?"

"Well, I don't...exactly. But so what if it wasn't? I got the truck, didn't I?"

"You owe me ten bucks."

"Ten? I borrowed five."

"Gotta pay the vig, brother. You can pay me or I'll give the kid your number and let him collect."

They stepped off the elevator and turned down the

main hall. It was empty, except for a janitor pushing a cart toward them.

WHEN DECKER SAW the cops he immediately looked straight down to hide his face. Then he got down on one knee with his back turned and began rearranging the items on the cart. The cops were laughing about something...he didn't know what. He didn't care either. Probably some bullshit cop humor. All he needed was for them to pass by without saying anything so he could make it off the floor and out of the hospital without being recognized...or getting caught.

It felt like it took them forever to pass by. He never looked up, but sensed them slow down as they walked by, like maybe they were looking him over, but then he heard one of them say, "They said down here, but...ah, here we go...on the right. Right there at the end."

CHAPTER SEVENTEEN

S andy parked in Pam's driveway, went to the front door and rang the bell. When no one answered she went to the rear of the house, thinking Pam might be in back, but when she rounded the final corner she saw that the backyard was empty. She knocked hard on the backdoor but got no response.

After a moment she took out her phone and made the call.

"Are you sure about this?" Cora said.

"As sure as I can be. When I saw her yesterday she was a mess." Sandy spent a few minutes bringing Cora up to speed with the rest of the story, then said, "You know how it is, Cora. If I call the locals for a wellness check I'll be here for an hour waiting on them to show. If the governor's chief of staff calls, they'll be here in two minutes. Probably less."

Cora was quiet for a moment, then said, "If the governor's chief calls and it turns out that Pam is at the mall or getting groceries or whatever, the governor is not going to be very happy with you know who."

"And does You Know Who really care, or is You Know Who just busting my chops for the fun of it?"

"The word 'fun' doesn't exist in my life these days. What about her car?"

"What about it?"

Cora sighed heavily into the phone. "You've been hanging out with your husband too much. A little alone time might be good for you. Is her car *there*?"

"The garage is attached. There aren't any windows."

"How about a side door?"

"Hang on..." Sandy went around to the opposite side of the garage and found the side door. When she turned the knob she was surprised to find the door unlocked. She pushed it open and saw Pam's car. "I'm in the garage, Cora. Her car is here."

"Go back to your car and wait there," Cora said. The tone of her voice had changed. "I'll have a city patrol car there in five minutes or less."

Sandy placed her hand on the hood of the car. It was cool to the touch...it hadn't been run recently. When she tried the interior door to the house the knob turned easily. She cracked the door. She could hear Cora in the background, over the phone.

"Sandy, I said go wait out front. I've already got the city units rolling."

"The door is unlocked. I'm going in."

"No, you're not, Sandy. Do you hear me? You're eight

months pregnant for Christ sake. Go back to your car and wait for the city units. Sandy? Sandy?"

As soon as the cops entered the room, Decker abandoned the cart and hurried down the hall. He pressed the elevator button and got lucky when the bell chimed right away. The doors opened and he rode all the way to the ground floor before ducking into the men's room for just a moment. He shed the hospital gear...the gloves, the shirt, the bonnet, the paper shoe covers, then stuffed everything into a trash can and covered it all with a healthy supply of paper towels. He pulled his ball cap back on and walked away, just a guy leaving the hospital. He never saw the cops.

Never realized the mistake he made, either.

Something was tugging at the back of Virgil's brain when he and Murton entered Martha Esser's hospital room. Something about the janitor they'd just passed in the hallway, but he couldn't quite get a hold of the thought. There was a familiarity there, though he didn't know why. He didn't know any hospital janitors...did he?

Inside, with the lights off and the curtains closed, the room was bathed in black. Murton made his way to the window and pulled the curtains halfway open.

"What are you doing?" Virgil whispered. "She might be sleeping."

"We're here to talk to her aren't we? Besides, everyone

knows they never let you sleep when you're in the hospital."

He had a point, Virgil thought. The last time Virgil was in the hospital was the most sleep deprived he'd ever been. They tell you to get some rest, then come in every hour and wake you up to check your vital signs. It was exhausting.

He turned back toward the door, pulled it open and looked back down the hallway. The janitor's cart was still there, but the janitor was gone. He let the door swing shut and turned his attention back inside the room. "Did you get a look at that janitor?"

"No, why?"

"I don't know. Something about him. Like I knew him or something."

"You want to go say hi or you want to talk with the victim?"

Virgil didn't bother to answer. With the curtains open and a little light in the room he noticed that Martha Esser was a hard looking woman. She might have been pretty at one time, but the years had not been kind to her. Her skin was gray and covered with deep wrinkles, her hair was thin and held no real color. Virgil thought it looked like curled fishing line...maybe two-pound test.

They were standing at the foot of the bed when Virgil said, "Huh."

"What?"

"Why is that machine turned off?"

"That's the one that monitors heart rate and pulse," Murton said. He looked at the cord under the machine and said, "Uh oh. Look at that."

"What?"

"That machine's not turned off. Somebody sliced the cord."

Virgil moved closer to Martha Esser and saw that her lips were starting to blue, as were her eyelids, the tops of her ears and her fingertips. He yanked the blanket back and placed his hand on her chest. She was warm, but there was no heartbeat.

"Murt, start CPR," Virgil yelled as he ran toward the door.

Murton moved to the bed, lowered the rail and immediately started chest compressions. "Where are you going?"

"To get some help...and to find that janitor we saw in the hallway."

"What? The janitor?"

Virgil didn't answer. Just ran out the door and down the hall.

"Sandy, they're a half-block away," Cora said. "Do not go into that house alone."

"Too late. I'm already in." Sandy had made her way from the garage and stood in the laundry room that gave way to the kitchen. She stopped for a few seconds to listen and didn't hear anything out of the ordinary. Just regular house sounds...the fridge kicking on, a slow but steady dripping sound from a leaky kitchen faucet, the furnace fan running in the basement. The house had an open floor plan, laid out in an L-shape. She was in the long section of the L that gave her a view from the garage entrance through the kitchen and into the living room, but that was all. The front of the house and the hallway that led to the bedrooms was around the corner. She could hear Cora saying something in the phone but couldn't make it out. When she brought the phone back up to her ear, she caught the tail end of it. "...at the front door."

"What? Say that again," Sandy said as she moved into the kitchen.

"I said two squad cars are there now. In ten seconds they're going to be knocking at the front door."

"I think maybe we're over-reacting here," Sandy said. "It's quiet. She's probably still sleeping it off in her bedroom." She was through the kitchen, moving into the living room, almost at the junction of the L now, ready to turn the corner. She heard the doorbell ring and someone pound on the front door. "I'll unlock the front door and let the locals in and—"

That was as far as she got. The door of the hall bathroom was open and when Sandy glanced that way she saw Pam on the floor, the white bathroom walls covered in blood.

Cora heard Sandy scream Pam's name over and over, then she heard the phone hit the floor and the connection went dead.

VIRGIL RAN to the central nursing station near the elevators and was so amped up he didn't realize he was yelling at the nurses.

"Sir, you'll have to calm down or we'll be forced to call security and have you removed."

It finally dawned on Virgil that he hadn't identified himself to the nurses and he must look like a madman. He took a deep breath and forced himself to slow down. He pulled out his badge and said, "I'm Detective Virgil Jones with the state's Major Crimes Unit. You've got a dead woman, Martha Esser, down the hall. My partner is giving her CPR right now." Then he slowed down, "Ah man... she's gone. Did you see a janitor come by here?"

The nurses were already moving. One of them grabbed a crash cart and ran down the hall. The other picked up the phone and gave a code over the intercom that Virgil didn't recognize. She started to follow the other nurse, but Virgil grabbed her arm and stopped her. "Listen to me for a minute."

She tried to yank her arm away. "Let go. You're hurting me."

Virgil let go and held his arms up. "I'm sorry, I'm sorry. Just give me a second, please. Did you see the janitor? It wouldn't have been more than two or three minutes ago, tops."

"No, I didn't. I wasn't at the desk. Neither of us were. We just finished turning a patient." She was rubbing her arm where Virgil had grabbed her. When she continued, her voice had changed, now thick with contempt. "The main janitorial station is on the ground floor, near the south entrance by the shipping and receiving area. Try there. I've got to go."

"I'm sorry about grabbing..." Virgil let her go. She wasn't listening to him anyway. He spun around in a circle looking for the elevators, caught them just around the corner, pushed the button and waited, his heart rate beginning to slow. He'd seen enough dead people in his life to know that Martha Esser was gone. They might hook her up to the machines, but she'd never be back.

He pushed the elevator button again, then again and thought, janitors don't wear army issue combat boots, do they? Virgil had seen the tops of the boots poking out of the blue paper shoe covers while the janitor had been kneeling next to his cart. He ran it through his head all the way down to the ground floor. He was headed to the south entrance where the janitorial department was when his phone rang. He pressed the answer button, brought the phone up to his ear and said, "Jones."

"Virgil, it's me. Where are you?"

Cora. "I'm at Methodist. Martha Esser is dead. I think somebody killed her in her hospital bed."

"Is Wheeler with you?"

"Yeah. What is it, Cora?"

"All right...leave him there for now to handle Esser. I'll get some extra help headed his way. You need to get over to Pam Donatti's place."

Virgil could hear the tension in her voice. "Cora, what's going on?"

"Listen, Jonesy, I don't know exactly how to say this..."

"Just say it." When Cora didn't respond, Virgil started to put it together. "How bad is it?"

"First glance says suicide."

"Ah, Jesus." Virgil collapsed back against the wall and slid down to the floor, his free hand pressed against his forehead. After a moment he said, "Tell me what happened."

"We don't know anything yet...other than it looks like a single GSW to the head. Homicide is on the way as we speak. The uniforms said the gun was still in her hand."

"I knew...I mean Sandy and I both knew that she'd been struggling, but...suicide? I didn't think it—"

Cora cut him off. "Listen, Jonesy...Sandy is there. She's the one who found the body."

"*What?*" That got him up and moving. The elevator doors had opened and were just starting to close again. He squeezed through the doors and punched the button for the ground floor. Cora filled him in with the details as he headed for his truck.

"She went over there...I don't know why, but when she couldn't get an answer at the door she called me and told me she wanted a city patrol to go over for a wellness check. I had two units rolling while we were on the phone, but she went in anyway without waiting."

"And you let her?" Virgil was hot, and his voice didn't hide the fact.

"What was I supposed to do? Her mind was made up before she ever called me. She went in through the garage, saw that Pam's car was there—"

"All right, all right...I get it. Is she okay?"

"Pretty shook up, but yeah, I think so. I couldn't get ahold of her for a few minutes. She dropped her phone. I think it's busted. But I've talked with the medics. They're with her and said she's okay."

"Where in the hell is Jonas?"

"Jonas? Uh, I don't know about Jonas. Becky told me that you guys had him last night...I thought he was with Sandy."

"You mean he's *there*?"

"No...I mean I don't know where he is. He's not there... at the scene."

Virgil was running toward his truck as they were speaking. "Okay, I'm on my way. Can you get me an escort? I don't have any electronics on the truck yet."

"Yeah...let's see, you'll be going, what, southwest out of there?"

"Yes. And I'm not waiting. Have them pick me up on 465, at exit...uh, shit I can't remember the number."

"Don't worry about it. I know where you mean. Just go. There'll be two units waiting for you at the ramp. They'll box you and you can go."

Virgil yanked open the truck door, fired the engine and took off. "I'm rolling now," he said as he turned the corner out of the hospital valet lot, his tires squealing in protest.

"I can hear that," Cora said. "Take it easy until you get to the highway."

"Fuck that," Virgil said. "Make sure they keep up." He ended the call and pressed the accelerator to the floor.

MURTON CONTINUED DOING CPR until the nurses came in with the crash cart. A doctor showed up a few minutes later and pronounced Martha Esser dead. He noted the time of death, made a few marks on her bedside chart and left the room. Murton followed him out to the hallway.

"Hold on, Doc. I'm going to need that room sealed. Let's get the nurses out of there."

The doctor cocked his head. "I think you can relax,

Detective. I'm guessing she probably had a clot that let go. We see strokes in patients with the kind of head trauma she'd suffered. Even with the preventative meds, sometimes it's simply not enough. It'll all be in the autopsy report."

"That may or may not be true," Murton said. "The information we had indicated she was well enough to sign some pretty important legal documents. Plus, she was moved from intensive care to the rehab wing. Doesn't that mean she was going to make it?"

The doctor scratched the back of his neck, then tipped his head, an indication for Murton to follow him away from the room. "Not necessarily. She was transferred out of intensive care because she was breathing on her own and had regained consciousness. We needed the beds in the ICU, so the rehab floor took her because if she did make it, this is where she'd have ended up anyway. Happens all the time."

Murton thought the doctor's statement had a touch of bullshit mixed in there somewhere, but he took it in stride, mostly because he didn't think it mattered. "Look, you're the doctor, okay, but I think someone came in and...suffocated her or something. I'm not sure. So we're going to treat it as a crime scene, at least for now and that means I need that room cleared. I don't want the area contaminated anymore than it already is."

The doctor let out a heavy sigh, like the whole thing was inconvenient and unnecessary, but when Murton told him about the power cord that'd been cut the doctor walked back into the room, looked at the cord and nodded. "Okay, listen up, please. Stop what you're doing and step out into the hallway."

The nurses were unhooking the IVs and monitor leads from Martha's body. They looked at the doctor, then at Murton, then back at the doctor. "Don't touch anything else please," Murton said. "Just step away from the bed and move out to the hallway."

One of them looked at the doctor and said, "What's going on?"

"This is officer..." The doctor looked at Murton and said, "I didn't get your name."

"I'm Detective Murton Wheeler with the Indiana State Police Major Crimes Unit. We're investigating the death of Mrs. Esser's husband, Charles Esser. We have reason to believe that Mrs. Esser's death was not a result of her injuries. We think she's been murdered, possibly by one of your hospital employees, or someone posing as an employee."

Both of the nurses put their hands to their chests, like they'd been trained to do so if they were ever informed of that type of news. "That's ridiculous," one of them said. "You think one of us killed her?"

"I didn't say that. I said it was possible someone posing as a hospital employee. Now, please, do not touch anything in this room. In fact, put your hands in your pockets and step out in the hallway and wait for me there. Doctor, you too."

The three hospital employees left the room and once they were outside, Murton opened the curtains all the way and turned the overhead lights on with his elbow. He stood at the foot of the bed and looked at the entire room without moving. Other than the monitor cord being cut, he saw nothing out of ordinary, nothing out of place. He took his phone out of his pocket and tried to call Virgil. When he didn't get an answer he went out to the hall and spoke to the doctor.

"Can you get someone from hospital security up here to guard the room until I can get our crime scene people here?"

"That shouldn't be a problem," the doctor said. "I'll get someone started this way right now." He made a call and a few seconds later said, "They're on their way." Then, "You really think she was murdered?"

"Looks like it, unless she got out of bed, cut the cord on her own monitor, then got back in bed and coincidentally had a stroke."

The nurses looked at each other, then at Murton. "Are we in any danger here?" one of them asked.

"I don't think so, especially if you didn't see anyone. You didn't see anyone going in or out of the room, did you?"

"No, but the other gentleman...I guess he's your partner? He was going on like a crazy man...something about a janitor. But I didn't see a janitor. He grabbed my arm really hard. Look at this bruise."

Murton tried to give her a sympathetic look, something he knew he wasn't very good at. He looked at the other nurse. "How about you?"

She closed her eyes for a moment, thinking. "No, I don't think I did, but I don't know that I'd remember if I did or not. You get so used to seeing certain things and after a while you don't even know you're seeing them. Like that janitorial cart right there." She pointed with her chin. "I see those carts all day long. I don't even notice them anymore. I probably wouldn't even remember seeing that one, except your partner mentioned a janitor. Does that make sense?"

It did, Murton thought. "Okay, listen, you guys can get back to work, but stay close until the crime scene people arrive. They're going to want to get your fingerprints." The nurses started to make a fuss, but Murton waved them down. "It's just so we can eliminate you. You're not suspects. Also, there's going to be some other detectives showing up, and a few uniformed cops as well. They'll want to question you. If you remember anything that might matter, anything at all, tell the other police officers when they arrive."

"I'll tell them about how your partner grabbed me. You guys go around thinking you can just put your hands on anyone you want and no one will say anything, but you're wrong. I'm going to file a complaint." Her adrenaline was running now, the gravity of the situation settling in.

"Are you hurt?"

"Well, no, not really, but—"

"If you are, see the doctor. There's one standing right next to you. If you want to file a complaint, you're free to do so. I'm sure my partner meant you no harm." When he glanced down the hall, Murton saw two hospital security officers headed his way. He walked over and gave them instructions that no one was to enter or touch anything in Martha Esser's room. Then, almost as an afterthought, he said, "And don't let anybody touch that cart, either." One of the security officers grabbed his belt and hitched up his pants, then moved over to the room and stood with his back to the door. The other stood next to the cart and stared at the wall.

With that done, Murton tried calling Virgil again, and still got no answer. Finally, he called Cora. "I'm at Methodist. Jonesy and I were going to try to speak with Martha Esser. She's dead, and I can't say for sure, but there's a good possibility that someone killed her in her own hospital bed. There aren't any visible signs, but I'd bet Jonesy's signing bonus that she was murdered. Why? I don't know. At least not yet."

"I already know about that. Jonesy filled me in. Stay at the hospital until homicide gets there and get them up to speed. When you're through with that I want you to come directly to my office."

"Where's Jonesy?"

"I'll fill you in when you get here. Do not call Jonesy. That's a direct order, Detective."

"Don't call Jonesy? What the hell's going on, Cora?"

"Tell me what you're going to do, Murton."

Murton squeezed his phone so hard he thought it might crack in his hand. When he answered it was through a clenched jaw. "I'm going to follow orders."

"And what are those orders?"

"I'm going to wait here until homicide shows up, hand off to them, then go straight to your office."

"What else?"

"I'm not going to call Jonesy."

"Exactly. Metro Homicide is already on their way. I'll expect you in an hour or less," Cora said, then hung up.

Murton walked over to the nurse. "Listen, on behalf of my partner, I'm sorry, okay? We've got some crazy person running around killing people. File your complaint if you want, but don't expect much." He held his thumb and forefinger an inch apart. "You were this close to a madman who probably would have killed you without thinking twice and you didn't even know it." He pointed at the room behind her. "Would you rather be dead in there or standing out here with a little bruise?"

CHAPTER EIGHTEEN

Ninety minutes later, Murton barreled into Cora's office without knocking. She stood with her back to the door, smoking a cigarette and looking out the window behind her desk.

"It's illegal to smoke inside a state building. Do you mind telling me why I'm not allowed to speak with my partner during an ongoing investigation we're both working?"

"You're late. Sit down, Murt."

"Tell it to Metro Homicide. Their modus operandi revolves around the theory that the body isn't going anywhere. They showed up with a box of doughnuts and jelly stains on their ties. Where's Jonesy?"

Cora turned from the window and sat down at her desk. She pointed at a chair and waited until Murton sat down before she spoke. "He's at the Donatti residence."

"Why? What's happening there?"

Cora didn't dance around it. "Pam Donatti is dead. That's what's happening there."

Murton could feel the slack in his face. He stood up, ran his hands through his hair, and said, "Jesus Christ. She's dead? Why didn't you just tell me that on the phone? I could have been there by now." He turned to leave. "All right, I'm on my way."

"No, you're not. You're staying right where you are. When we're finished here, I want you at your desk writing up your report on Martha Esser and how it may tie in with the murder of her husband in Shelby County. Are we clear on that, Detective?"

"Why are you shutting me out on this, Cora? What's happening?"

"It's called allocation of resources. The Shelby County case...the Esser murders...those are yours for now."

"What do you mean for now?"

"It's a fluid situation, Murt."

"Cora, in case you've forgotten—and I know you haven't—I used to be a federal agent. The bureaucratic bullshit that went with it was epic. It makes things at the state level look like reruns of The Romper Room. So you'll forgive me if I get right to the point and say, fluid my ass. You ordered me away from one of the murders you just said I'm investigating. What's the real reason?"

"Okay, have it your way. It's for your own protection. Use your head for a minute, will you?"

"What's that supposed to mean?"

"It means exactly this: Pam Donatti, the woman who was suing you for the wrongful death of her husband was just found with a single gun shot wound to the head. I've been back and forth with the homicide detective at her house. He thinks it was set up to look like a suicide."

"And it's not? According to Small she's been so depressed lately that she's been neglecting her kid and drinking her breakfast. I hate to say it, but suicide doesn't surprise me."

"Let's hope you're right, because if you're wrong, you're probably going to end up as the number one suspect."

"Cora, that's insane. I didn't have anything to do with her death. Surely you know that."

"Of course I know that," Cora said. "But just because I know something doesn't mean that certain accusations won't be made, or that certain procedures can be ignored. We'll protect you to the best of our abilities, but we've got to keep everything above board. The lawsuit against you is a matter of public record. That means that you stay away from the Donatti investigation. You don't ask questions about the Donatti investigation. You don't even talk about the Donatti investigation until we figure out what's going on. Are we clear on that?"

Murton slumped back in his chair. "I told Jonesy this was going to happen. I told him we were right in the middle of this thing from the get-go. He didn't see it, but I did. All I was trying to do was save Ed's life. The doctors said he'd have died anyway. I did the best I could with what I had. I'm no more responsible for Ed Donatti's death than you are, Cora. The fact that Pam was going to try to sue me should have no bearing on any of this."

"You're right. It shouldn't. But you know as well as I do that it will. That's why you are going to continue to work the Esser case." She pointed her finger at him. "But I'm warning you, right here and right now, you stay the fuck away from the Donatti investigation. It's for your own protection. Internal Affairs is going to want an interview and they'll be conducting their own independent investigation...on you. The governor and I expect you to cooperate fully in their inquiry. If you do, you'll have our complete support."

Murton leaned forward in his chair, a snarl on his usually smiling face. "And if I don't?"

"You will," Cora snarled back. Then, a little softer. "You don't have a choice, Murton. The governor and I hired you because of the strike. Pam Donatti's death effectively ends that strike. By this time tomorrow—maybe even earlier—the troopers will be back to work because there's no reason for them not to be. And the fact that you're probably going to wind up as the main suspect in a murder investigation is not going to sit very well with the governor. Don't you get it? It's going to look like the strike and everything behind it was ended by assassination."

"I really don't care about the politics of it all, Cora. Besides, who's going to believe that kind of bullshit conspiracy? A few political nut jobs, that's who."

"At least we see eye-to-eye on something. Except you're forgetting one thing. The media is going to have a field day with this."

Cora was right, and Murton knew it. "So what am I supposed to do?"

"Normally I'd tell you to talk to the union rep, except as a political appointee you can't do that. Get a lawyer, Murt. You're probably going to need one. In the meantime, figure out who killed Charlie and Martha Esser, and why."

CHAPTER NINETEEN

Decker, sitting in his trailer, was pleased with himself. In less than twelve hours the troopers had returned to work, the guard was officially released from duty, and the conspiracy nuts were having a field day...all at the governor's expense. Martha Esser hadn't been mentioned. Not yet, anyway.

It really was the best of both worlds, he thought. If the cops bought the suicide angle with Donatti then no one would even think, let alone bother to look at him when he showed up to collect his son. On the other hand, if they didn't buy the suicide, then their number one suspect would be Murton Wheeler, the hotshot former fed that was being sued by the victim. And since Wheeler worked for the state and was practically one of the governor's button men—the media was already saying as much—there'd be enough confusion and political bullshit floating through the air they wouldn't even get a whiff of Decker himself.

Then again...

Another thought occurred, one that increased his heart rate, if only a little. The only other evidence besides the lawsuit that qualified Wheeler as a suspect was the gun and the bits of silage he'd spread around. It was good evidence, but was it enough? Couldn't Wheeler just say he'd given her the gun for her own protection? He could, but would anyone buy that story? He didn't think so, but he didn't know, either. It seemed unlikely that a guy being sued by someone would give a gun to that same person. Plus, Donatti was the wife of a cop. A dead cop, but still... wouldn't it be likely that she had a gun of her own? Maybe she had a houseful of guns. Decker didn't know. He didn't even know if it mattered.

What he did know was there were going to be a few hard questions for Wheeler, questions about how she had his gun and why. What would he say? He'd either have to lie about giving her the gun or admit he didn't know she had it. Neither of those options were perfect for Wheeler, but he'd find a way around it. Cops protect their own. All you had to do was watch a little evening news to figure that out. And if they didn't charge Wheeler, they'd keep looking. They'd keep looking because eventually Wheeler would convince them that he didn't do it. And when that happened it would only be a matter of time before they started looking at other possibilities.

The bottom line was this: If Wheeler didn't go down for Pam Donatti's death, he'd never get the boy. What he'd get was life without the possibility of parole, or worse...he'd get the needle.

One thing was certain...he couldn't show up and claim Jonas as his son until and unless one of two things happened: Wheeler had been charged in the death of Pam Donatti, or it was ruled that Donatti killed Martha Esser and then herself after the fact. He'd planted enough evidence that it could go either way. He didn't care which.

Another question: Why was it that the media was ignoring Martha Esser and putting so much coverage into Pam Donatti? From a media marketing standpoint he could see the Donatti reports for what they were...pure money. What was that saying the media didn't want anyone to know? If it bleeds, it leads? Something like that. It was odd though, he thought, that the Esser bitch hadn't been mentioned yet.

He turned on the TV and cracked a beer. Time to stop worrying about what he couldn't control and start thinking about how to get the kid...and his money.

The fucking kid, Decker thought, was a rich little prick and didn't even know it. But with Pam Donatti out of the way, and as the boy's biological father, the pension money was his. The waiting though...that was a bitch. Couldn't do anything about it.

Christ on a bike, he thought. Nothing's easy.

WHEN THEY FINALLY MADE IT home that night, Jonas jumped up from the floor, ran over to Virgil and Sandy and gave them both a big hug. Virgil scooped him up and said, "How you doing, little man?"

"I'm...I'm—" He looked over at Delroy.

"Irie, little mon."

Jonas threw his arms up. "Yeah, I'm irie!" he shouted.

Virgil set him down, looked at Delroy, and nodded toward the kitchen. Delroy followed him over.

"I can tell by the look on your face dat someting not right, mon. What going on?"

Dr. Bell, Virgil's physician, knocked quietly on the back door and stepped inside. "Virgil, Delroy."

Delroy shot Virgil a look. "Where's Murton?"

That, Virgil thought, is why I love you, Delroy. Delroy knew that Robert was at the bar and the only other person Virgil loved who wasn't present at the moment was Murton. Virgil threw his arm around his Jamaican friend's shoulder and pulled him close. "Thank you, Delroy. Murton's fine. He's um, still working, I think."

"If you *tink* he still working then how you know he fine, you?"

As usual, Delroy had a point. "Well, I haven't spoken with him since this afternoon—things got a little crazy—but I'm going to talk to him in a little while. Listen Delroy, we've got some bad news. Jonas just lost his mother. She was killed earlier today. The official story right now is suicide, but it looks like she was murdered." He hesitated, then added, "It also looks like someone is trying to frame Murt for her murder. We don't know why."

Delroy stared hard at Virgil for a moment, then said, "But you tink Murton okay, you?" He shook his head. "Maybe I go say goodbye now. Go to the bar and get back to work, huh?"

"That's probably a good idea, Delroy," Virgil said. "Thanks for watching Jonas for us."

Delroy gave Virgil a look, patted Bell on the shoulder,

walked into the other room, bumped fists with Jonas, kissed Sandy and then walked out the front door.

Thirty seconds later Virgil's cellphone dinged at him. A text from Delroy. It read: Talked to Robert, me. Murton at the bar. Says he home soon.

Virgil and Sandy spent the better part of the evening carefully explaining to Jonas what had happened to his mother. They left the heavy details out and delivered the news as simply and gently as they knew how. Bell sat quietly in the corner of the room, watching Jonas, looking for any signs that he might need immediate professional help. By the time they got him in bed and asleep, Virgil was flat out relieved. Jonas seemed to be okay. Maybe even better than okay. Virgil thought he looked and acted remarkably well.

"He's not though," Bell said to them both. "He's in shock. His world has just been turned completely upside down...again. That's twice in less than a year. He hasn't even begun to process what you've just told him. In fact, I wouldn't be surprised if he woke up tomorrow morning and asks when he's going home or where his mom is. Did either of you notice that he didn't cry?"

"I thought maybe that was good," Virgil said. "Like maybe he was being strong or something."

Sandy shook her head. "What do we do, Bell?"

"Well, for a while, you're going to have to be with him all the time. And I do mean all the time. Sandy, I think you should sleep in the same bed with him tonight. For the next few weeks he's going to need to see one or both of you almost every single moment he's awake. He seems to have bonded with Delroy, so time with him would be good too.

His grieving process will be the same as a healthy adult...all the stages and all that, but as a child he's going to need someone he trusts to help him navigate his way through it all. Right now he's in denial. That's why he hasn't cried. But he will. The information made it in, but he doesn't really believe it yet. He hasn't processed it. In his mind it's not real and his mother is still alive, which is the same way of saying it hasn't really happened. Does he have any other family?"

"No," Sandy said. It came out fast and she jumped a little when she said it.

"Well—" Virgil said, but that was as far as he got.

"He doesn't have any other living relatives that we know of," Sandy said, this time with a little steel in her voice.

Bell raised his eyebrows. "I see." After a moment of tense silence, he stood and slipped into his jacket. "You have my number if you need me. I'll put together a list of child psychologists and email them to you tonight. A few sessions would be a tremendous help in getting him started along the right path. That sound okay?"

"That sounds fine, Bell," Virgil said as they walked toward the front door. "We can't thank you enough for coming out. We didn't know who else to call."

"Don't worry about it, Virgil. I'm always available for you." They stepped outside and Bell stopped for a moment. "Anything else I should know?"

Plenty, Virgil thought. "We don't quite have a handle on it just yet. Its...sort of complicated."

"Everything that matters usually is, Jonesy. Look, I want you to think about something. Unless you or someone you know...someone with some *juice* intervenes, CPS is going to come knocking, and soon. They don't like complicated, Virgil. They have their forms and their procedures, and they like to make sure every box is checked. They want the facts and they want them in order. It's been my experience that they'll go to extraordinary lengths to make sure they find what they're looking for."

"What do you mean?"

"I mean they want *family*. Things aren't as simple as they used to be. You know, back in the day when you and Murton were kids. Murton and your father in particular, if you take my meaning."

"I'm willing to entertain suggestions."

"Then replay what I just said. Goodnight, Virgil. And good luck. Take care of that boy."

THEY ARGUED ABOUT IT, Virgil and Sandy. It was the kind of argument neither of them would win. Sandy, still a cop and not wanting to be...reduced.

"How can you say that?" Virgil said. "Being a mother isn't being reduced to anything. I believe it's going to be your greatest accomplishment."

"Do not try and steer this conversation, Virgil. That's not what I'm talking about and you know it. The only reason you're upset with me is because I walked into Pam's house without any backup. It doesn't have anything to do with anything else."

"Yes, it does, Sandy. You're pregnant. Pregnant with

our son. And pregnant or not, you had no business going into that house alone."

"Like you would have waited."

"Of course I would have," Virgil lied.

Sandy knew he was lying and let it go. "I thought she was in trouble."

"All the more reason to wait."

"I'll say it again: Like you would have."

"That's not the same thing, and you know it."

Sandy shook her head. "Why not? Because you're a man?"

Virgil was trying to stay calm. Felt it starting to slip away. "No goddamn it, because I'm not pregnant." He paused. "Look, this isn't getting us anywhere."

Sandy sat back, her arms crossed and resting on her belly. "You've got that right."

"I think we're both just upset about...everything."

"What exactly, Virgil, is everything?"

Virgil puffed out his cheeks and glanced down the hallway where Jonas was sleeping in one of the spare bedrooms. "You know. Everything."

"No, I don't know. Explain it to me."

Virgil was pacing. He flapped his arms. "Just...everything. Everything was going fine until Pam went off the rails and now she's dead. What are we going to do? We can't let Jonas go into the system. Bell said that Child Protective Services is going to be coming out and asking questions. Hard questions. What are we supposed to tell them? That Jonas still has a father out there, except we don't know who it is? A father, I might add, that Pam wanted nothing to do with and went to extraordinary measures to make sure he stayed out of their lives. Even if we had any control over it...and it doesn't look like we do, how are we going to stop CPS from doing their job? They'll find Jonas' father, and do you know how they'll do it? They'll come out here—with a court order, if necessary—and get a DNA swab from Jonas. Then they'll run that through the system and if Jonas's father has ever been in the system for anything, or in the military or with the government in almost any capacity whatsoever they'll know who he is within a matter of weeks. Maybe even within a matter of days. These are bureaucrats were talking about. They won't care about a struggling marriage and a momentary lapse of judgment, because that's all it is. She never told anyone except you. I know you believe her, and that means I do too. If they find this guy, Jonas will be his."

Sandy walked over to Virgil and put her arms around him. "It's okay. You can say it."

"Say what?"

"Whatever is on your mind."

Virgil's phone rang. Murton. He'd have to call him right back. He silenced the phone then was quiet for a long time before he spoke. When he did, his voice was ragged and filled with regret. "She had a right to be angry with me all these months. It *is* my fault that Ed died, and because of that it's now my fault that Pam is too. All of it. The whole entire thing is my fault, and now Jonas is alone. That's what my dad was trying to tell me the other day."

"That's just not true, Virgil, and you know it. Now listen to me. Things happen. Things that you can't control. These things are not your fault. They just happen. It's what we do after they happen that matters."

"Meaning what?"

Sandy gripped him by the shoulders. "If you won't say it I will. That's not all your dad was trying to tell you. He was telling you like father, like son. Jonas is ours now. Every single event since the afternoon of that party eight months ago has led us to this very moment. We are all he has."

"Are you sure about this? You've got to be sure."

"I am sure. As sure as I've ever been about anything in my life." Then she gave Virgil a kiss. "And I do mean anything." She turned and walked toward the bedrooms.

"Where are you going?"

"To lie down with Jonas."

"It's still a little early."

"You heard what Bell said. We shouldn't leave him alone."

"And what do we do if his biological father turns up?"

"We'll figure something out," Sandy said. "We'll take care of it."

"How?"

Sandy stopped. She had her back to him, and when she answered, Virgil found himself relieved that he couldn't see the look on her face. "Any way we have to, Virgil. Any way at all."

VIRGIL WALKED down to the pond and sat in one of the chairs by his father's cross, thinking about what Sandy had just said. Or more to the point, what she had meant. She was going to have her way, that much was clear. Virgil was fine with it. More than fine, in fact. He wasn't exactly sure how they'd pull it off, only that they would. But there was a problem and Virgil had no one to talk to about how he felt.

He had always considered himself his father's son through and through, not only because he was exactly that, but because of the way their lives had blended together and mirrored each other's. They were an amalgamation of sorts. It was like a line graph, Virgil thought. If you charted Mason's life and projected it on a screen, then overlaid his own, their paths were virtually identical. Mason had been in the military...so had Virgil. Mason had been a cop...so was Virgil. After Mason retired, they ran the bar together before he died, thus cementing that part of Virgil's life. They both had wives who were strong, independent women, and Virgil, as an only child was about to have a child of his own.

He'd never told anyone—not even Sandy—of his secret fear. The fear that his life so mirrored his father's that he might one day lose Sandy to some tragedy. Maybe not cancer, like his own mother had suffered, but...something. Something completely out of his control. He'd lie in bed at night and stare at the ceiling thinking of all the similarities between himself and his father, all the while knowing that like his father, he'd ever only have one child, a boy of course, and then somewhere down the line at some unde-termined time, Sandy would be gone, taken from him. He'd almost convinced himself that he was full of shit, that fathers and sons everywhere led similar lives, boys growing up and following in their dad's footsteps...it happened all the time. He was ready to let it go...until Jonas came along.

The truth of the matter was this: Virgil wasn't an only

child. His parents had taken Murton in when he was a young boy and raised him as their own. Now, with Jonas in the picture, it frightened Virgil to no end. Somewhere deep down inside, he had the feeling that if they brought Jonas into their lives and raised him as their own—just as his parents had with Murton—something terrible would come of it. Something he didn't think he could handle. He'd lose Sandy to some type of accident or disease just like his father had lost his wife. Even if he was right, how could he say no to Sandy, much less Jonas? Was he so fearful that he'd let one of his best friend's child go into the system, a friend who'd died helping him protect some of the people who were most dear to him? What did that say about him as a man, or a friend?

And even if he let Jonas go, what about Sandy and what she wanted? He knew in his heart that he could never persuade her to let go of Jonas. She'd just said as much. Even if he did manage to convince her, would it cause a rift between them, one that could ultimately lead to their undoing or Sandy's death? Accelerate it somehow? He didn't know.

"You have to listen to your spirit...your soul," Mason said.

Virgil had been sitting forward in the chair, his forearms resting on his thighs, staring at the grass. When he looked up, his father was there. He had a forefinger pressed against the very top of the cross and he walked a complete circle around the monument before stopping.

"What are you doing?"

"Just admiring your handy-work," Mason said.

"I'm stuck," Virgil said.

"No, you're not. You're just a little confused."

"There doesn't seem to be a way forward."

Mason laughed. "There is always a way forward, Virg. The question is, are you willing to move down that path?"

"When I was on the pills you told me that I was losing Sandy."

"That's because you were. You just didn't know it. I seem to recall that you didn't believe me, either."

"I wasn't thinking clearly. But I am now. I don't know what to do. If I put my foot down and say no to Sandy about Jonas—"

Mason laughed again. "Let me stop you right there. How many times did you see me put my foot down with your mother?"

"Plenty of times."

"Right. Now think for a minute and tell me how many times that worked out for me."

This time Virgil laughed. "Not very many, I guess."

"Not very many at all. I'll tell you something, Virg, your mother and I had a rule that served us well over the years."

"What was it?"

"It was simple. 'No' always wins."

Virgil tipped his head. "Care to explain that?"

"On big decisions, each of us had veto power. It's a good rule for married life. Think about it. If you're both in agreement there's no problem, right?"

"Yeah, I guess."

"But if you're not, then the person who says no has the last say in the matter. I remember once when you were little...this was before Murton came into our lives, I wanted to buy a new car. There wasn't anything wrong with the car we had. I just wanted a new one. But your mother knew it wasn't a good idea at the time...money was tight and all that, but I really wanted that car. We talked about it, argued a little, but in the end she said no and we didn't get the car. It's also how we came up with the rule."

"That's great stuff, Dad. So it's as easy as just going up there and saying no to her about Jonas, huh?"

"Not exactly. You only use the no rule when you really need it...for the big issues."

Virgil felt his jaw go slack. "And this doesn't qualify as big?"

Mason shook his head. "Nope. This one is a no-brainer."

"I guess I don't quite see it that way."

"That's because you're not doing what I told you. You've got to listen to your spirit and your soul, Virg. When you do, everything that doesn't matter falls away and your path becomes clear...and simple. Try to manipulate things to achieve a certain outcome, or protect a way of thinking and it'll all fall apart."

"I guess I don't know how to do that. To listen to my spirit, my soul." When he said it, it reminded him of what Sandy had said to Jonas...that he had to listen with his heart.

"Of course you do. You're doing it right now. I couldn't control cancer, Virgil, and I couldn't control what happened with Murt's parents, especially his dad. All I could do was the right thing. That's all you can do now, and I know you know what the right thing is. Are there similarities to our situation? You bet. Just don't overthink it."

"Let me ask you something, Dad."

"Sure."

"Last time we spoke, when Sandy and Jonas were in the yard, you said, 'Here comes a beautiful soul.' Which one of them were you talking about?"

"Why does it matter?"

Virgil pointed his finger at him. "See. That's what I mean. Why does everything have to be a puzzle with—"

Virgil's phone buzzed at him. He pulled it out of his pocket and looked at the screen. Murton again. He'd forgotten to call him back. When he looked back up at the cross, his father was gone and he was instantly pissed. He pressed the answer tab and said, "What?"

"How soon can you get over to my place?"

The sound of Murton's voice helped the anger fade. "What's wrong?" Virgil said. "Is Becky okay?"

"Yeah, she fine. She's still at the shop. I just got home. Delroy seems pissed off at you about something, by the way. Can you get over here or not?" Murton was tense. Virgil could hear it and it was something he didn't hear very often.

"I'll be there inside a half hour. You okay?"

"Yeah, yeah, I'm fine...but I've got a problem."

CHAPTER TWENTY

Virgil turned into Murton's drive—the house where they'd both grown up—and found Murton sitting on the front porch, a beer in one hand, and his Smith .45 in the other, hanging down between his knees.

"You shoot somebody again?"

Murton stood up, tucked the gun away, and downed the last of the beer. "Not yet, but I'm a little rattled. I just had to clear my own house."

"What?"

Murton came down off the steps. "Come on, let's go around back. There's something I want you to see."

They made their way around the side of the house and into the backyard. Murton walked up next to the backdoor and stood off to the side. "Notice anything?"

Using Murton's position as a tight perimeter, Virgil looked around without speaking until he got to the door and saw the taped glass. "How long has that been broken?"

"Good question. The honest answer is I don't know for

sure. But what I do know is this: I sit at that kitchen table every morning and drink my coffee and stare out that back door, just like Mason used to. That cracked pane sticks out like a sore thumb. I noticed it right away when I got home tonight. Walked to the fridge, grabbed a beer, turned and glanced that way...just glanced, and I saw it. If it had been broken this morning, I don't see how I could have missed it. My best guess is sometime earlier today while Becky and I were out."

"Maybe Becky—"

Murton cut him off. "That was my first thought. But after what happened before, you know with Pate and Sigara, I wasn't taking any chances. I decided to clear the house right away."

Virgil had just been through this with Sandy. "Jesus Christ, Murt. What were you thinking? Why didn't you call me?"

"I did. Twice. But for whatever reason you didn't answer the first time."

"Ah, I'm sorry. Sandy and I were in the middle of something."

"How's Jonas holding up?"

"Bell says he's in for a rough ride. He's probably right." They walked inside and Virgil looked back at the door. "I assume when you cleared the house no one was here."

"Yeah, and I talked to Becky. She was out all day and doesn't know anything about this, which means I've got a problem and a busted window pane ain't it."

"Tell me."

"They got my dog."

Virgil knew about the watchdog. Murton joked that it

only barked once...per intruder. "The .38 under your nightstand?"

"That's the one."

"Anything else?"

"Nope. I carry everything else. The long guns are in the safe in the basement and they're all still there. I've got a couple grand in the top dresser drawer, Becky's got some minor jewelry, and it's all there too. This wasn't your typical robbery. They just took the dog."

Virgil walked over to the kitchen sink and stood with his hands on the counter, his back turned. "You're right. This wasn't a robbery, Murt. This is a setup."

"No shit."

They stood in silence for a moment before Virgil turned around. "Is it registered?"

Murton nodded. "Yep. I picked it up at a gun show. Licensed seller. I knew I wasn't going to carry it though... just wanted it for easy reach in the bedroom. I wasn't looking for a throw-down."

"That's a problem. You know where that gun is right now, don't you?"

"I'm not a psychic, but I'm guessing it's sitting in an evidence bag downtown. You know, the one with big red letters that says Donatti-comma-Pam on the side. How long before they trace it back to the seller, you think?"

"They probably already have. How long it takes to track him down and get a look at his records to see who he sold it to is another matter. Could be a couple days if he's the fuck-you-show-me-a-warrant type...or a couple of hours if he's cooperative."

"Ah, he'll cooperate. He's a good guy."

"You know him?"

"Not exactly, but I've dealt with him before." Murton said. "And you can tell about people, you know? Just one of those guys. One of the good ones."

Virgil took out his phone. "What are you doing?" Murton asked.

"Calling the crime scene tech. I'll get them to read me the serial number from the weapon."

"Why bother? I'm being set up, man. You know it as well as—"

"Yeah, Lou, it's Jonesy. Yeah, yeah, I know, sorry. Do you have your case notes with you?"

Lou did, and told Virgil to hang on. A minute later he was back. "The caliber and serial number of the gun," Virgil said. "Yeah. No, that should do it...for now anyway."

Virgil listened, trapped the phone between his ear and his shoulder and wrote something on his palm. "Thanks, Lou. I owe ya. Dinner on me next time you're in."

"What'd he say?"

"It was a .38 done up with jacketed HP's."

"Uh huh."

"Would you know the number if I read it to you?"

"What do you think?"

Virgil knew he would. He read off the number and saw Murton's shoulders slump.

"Shit."

"You've got to report it as stolen."

"I know that. I also know it won't make a damn bit of difference. I'm about to be hung out to dry for the murder of Pam Donatti."

"No, you're not. And one thing at a time, okay?"

Murton waved him off. "Yeah, yeah."

"Let's take a look around," Virgil said.

"Why?"

"They took your dog."

"We've already established that," Murton said. A little harsh.

"If you're being set up, and they wanted to do it properly, they wouldn't only take something."

Murton finished the thought. "They might have left something."

"Exactly."

"Man, Becky is going to kill me."

Virgil clapped him on the back. "We knew that eventuality was a foregone conclusion out of the gate though, didn't we?"

Murton finally broke a smile. "I guess. Not a bad way to go, if you think about it."

It took them the better part of two hours, and in the end, Murton, deciding it might be something subtle, was the one who found it. He shined the flashlight behind the closet door. Virgil couldn't tell what he was looking at. "What, they planted dust? Christ, when was the last time you ran the vacuum?"

"It's not dust...and I vacuum once a week like everyone else," Murton said.

"Only once a week, huh?"

"The traffic areas, anyway. Would you give it a rest, please? I guarantee, behind the doors at your house are exactly the same."

"Well, they're not, but whatever. What are we looking at here?"

Murton pulled at Virgil's jacket sleeve. "Over here...the same thing that you'll find in my closet, inside my shoes." They went to the closet and looked in Murton's shoes. Virgil got right down on his hands and knees and looked closely.

"What is it?"

"It's silage. From the Shelby County thing. Except I wasn't wearing those shoes. Just the ones I've got on now."

"You know where else they're going to find that same silage, don't you?"

Murton's eyelids drooped. "Yeah, the thought already occurred to me. It going to be all over Pam's house, isn't it?"

Virgil took out his phone again. "Only one way to find out. Lou's going to love me."

"Quit giving away dinners at the bar, will you? Our profit margins are thin enough as it is."

"Says the guy with a couple grand in his dresser drawer and, what did you call it...some minor jewelry? You want to give away a few meals or have your permanent address listed as the Super Max pen down in Terre Haute? That's where they hold all the terrorist these days, you know. I heard they hand out free prayer rugs and your own personal copy of the Quran. If you convert, maybe you'll get one of your own. You and all the post 9/11 boys will have a great time together."

"You're a laugh a minute. Anyone ever tell you that?"

Lou, the crime scene tech answered before Virgil could respond.

"Yeah, Yeah, Lou, I'm sorry, but this is important. I'm going to need you to read me the entire list." A pause. "That's what I said, Lou, the entire list. No, I can't tell you what I'm looking for. That's why I need you to read the entire list. What's that noise in the background? Okay, okay. None of my business. I've got it. Are you going to read me the list or not?"

Virgil winced at the sound the phone made, then glanced at Murton. "He's getting the list back out."

"I gathered that."

When Lou came back on the line, Virgil listened. Fortunately—and to Lou's relief—he didn't have to listen very long. "Okay, thanks, Lou. That should do it for now. Yeah, yeah, drinks *and* dinner." Another pause. "For two? Jesus Lou, you're killing me here. Besides, I didn't think you were the type. What's his name, anyway? Uh huh, right, right. Sure Lou, whatever you say. Hey nothing to be ashamed of these days. Okay, well, fuck you very much then."

After he'd ended the call, Virgil saw the look on Murton's face. "What? Just a little cop humor."

Murton shook his head. "You didn't know, did you?"

"Know what?"

"About Lou."

"What about him?"

"He *is* gay."

Virgil didn't believe him. "Lou? No way."

"Yep. And you just insulted the hell out him."

Virgil put his hands to his face and rubbed his cheeks. "Ah, that's bullshit. He's been in the bar dozens of times, all with the same woman."

"Ever take a close look at her?"

"Yeah...she's a handsome woman."

Murton raised his eyebrows. "Interesting choice of words."

Virgil finally got it. "You mean she's a—"

Murton cut him off. "Careful. Use the wrong word and I'll be forced to write a report."

"Jesus Christ, I was just kidding around with him."

"Can't do that kind of thing anymore. Didn't you read the employee manual that H.R. handed out?"

Virgil didn't answer.

"Well, you should. You can get fired for that type of thing. Who knows, maybe we'll be cell-mates. I heard you get your own prayer rug if you—"

"Yeah, yeah." Then: "She really is sort of attractive. I mean, it's always sort of dark in the bar and I've never looked closely, but, jeez...with the hair and the make-up and the heels and everything."

"Caught your eye, did she?"

Virgil held up his hands in shock and horror. "No, no, no. I'm just saying it's getting harder and harder to tell sometimes..."

Murton was nodding slowly, his eyes opened wider than normal. "Thus the employee manual."

"Maybe I should call him back. He sounded pretty offended."

"I'll bet. And I wouldn't. Relax Jones-man. I'll smooth it over for you. And leave the cop humor to the professionals, will you? So, what'd he say?"

Virgil puffed out his cheeks. "He said they found trace evidence of silage at Pam's house. There was practically a trail of it from the front door all the way back to the bathroom."

Murton's mood changed. "That's it, then. My gun, and traces of silage from the Shelby County scene? I'm surprised SWAT hasn't rolled up here already."

"Nobody works that fast, especially state government."

"They'll get to it soon enough though. You know they will."

And they might have, except Virgil and Murton caught a little break.

MURTON'S PHONE RANG. He answered, listened for a full minute, told the caller he owed him and he'd let him know, then ended the call.

"Who was that?" Virgil said.

Murton smiled. "My new best friend. Metro Homicide has already started running the dog. They've traced it back as far as the guy I bought from. That was him. He was calling to give me a heads up."

"That doesn't leave much time."

"It gives us as much time as we need. A week should do it though, I think."

"I don't get it."

"He's on vacation...down in Marco Island. He's got a place down there. When it starts to get cold up here, he takes off for the season."

"They'll just search his place up here and take the records, Virgil said."

"Won't do them any good. He's licensed to sell in

Florida too. All his records are on his laptop, and he's got that with him. He said Homicide wouldn't tell him which record they needed because it's an ongoing investigation. They want to see all his records, which they have a right to do under the law, and he's even willing to cooperate."

"So how does that help?"

"This isn't his first records request. The paperwork has to come through the ATF. He says it'll be at least a week because the feds don't have a central database of gun sales."

"I find that hard to believe."

"It's true," Murton said. "Federal law prohibits the ATF from maintaining an electronic database."

"Jesus Christ, that's the most ridiculous thing I've ever heard of. The branch of the federal government that's responsible for firearms isn't allowed to have computers? Who thought that up?"

Murton wagged a finger at him. "I didn't say they don't have computers. I'm sure they do. They just aren't allowed to maintain a computerized database of gun owners at the federal level. And to answer your question, it was probably the NRA. I'm considering membership right about now."

"So you've got a week."

"Yup, at least" Murton said. He clapped Virgil on the back. "Don't sweat it, Jonesy. We've been in tighter spots than this before. It'll all work out."

Virgil turned and looked at him. "Uh, listen, I don't mean to sound unsympathetic to your situation, and you know I'd do anything for you, but what, exactly, do you mean when you say 'we?'"

"DID CORA MENTION to you that I'm not to go near the Donatti investigation?"

"I haven't spoken with her since Sandy found Pam," Virgil said.

"You know her better than I do. Does that sound like her?"

"What do you mean?"

"I mean if she really didn't want me involved in an ongoing investigation that will either convict me or clear me and tells me that to my face, does it seem logical that she doesn't say anything to you?"

"You're suggesting that she's trying to have it both ways?"

"That's what I'm asking you."

Virgil thought it over. Cora had always known how to play the political aspect of any given situation. "I guess I could see it, but what I can't see is why."

"Me either," Murton said. "Maybe it doesn't matter. She's probably just watching out for Mac-Daddy. That is her primary job."

Virgil rubbed his temple. "Please tell me you've never called him that."

Murton ignored him. "Either way, I got a call while I was waiting for you to get here. You know that janitor you were yammering about?"

Virgil gave him a look. "Yammering isn't exactly the word I'd use."

"I know. That's the sort of thing that sets us apart. That and your wardrobe. Did you find him?"

"No."

"Well, guess what, hotshot? I did. Crime Scene lifted a

set of prints from the cart he was pushing around. No other prints in the hospital room, the door handle, the monitors, nothing. But he either wasn't thinking or simply made a mistake, because he left prints on that cart. Maybe things didn't exactly go as planned and he got the gloves on a little late. I don't know. But I got the call while I was waiting for you to get here. They ran the prints and got an immediate hit."

Virgil's face lit up. "You are one-hundred percent shitting me."

"I one-hundred percent shit you not, Jones-man. Remember Captain Attitude from the Shelby County crime scene?"

"Decker? You're saying Decker killed Martha Esser?"

"I'm saying I left instructions to have the janitorial cart included as part of the scene at the hospital before Cora called me away. I'm saying Decker's prints were on that cart. I'm saying you noticed something about that janitor—though it pains me to say it, you really don't miss much—and I'm also saying that it doesn't take a very big leap of imagination to conclude that if Decker killed Martha Esser, he's probably responsible for Charlie Esser as well. Given the current situation I'm in, it also doesn't take much of a leap to include Pam. Either way, it's time to look up Decker and get some answers."

Virgil shook his head. "We can't do that, Murt."

CHAPTER TWENTY-ONE

"What? Of course we can," Murton said. "That's what we do. We find the bad guys, lock them up, and let the prosecution do their thing."

Virgil pointed at him. "That right there is why the Feds have the lowest prosecution rate of any law enforcement agency in the country. Think it through, Murt. We've got one piece of evidence against a guy we know nothing about. Could we go pound on his door, cuff him up and take him downtown? Sure. But you know what his lawyer is going to say? Burden of proof is on the state. He's going to say Decker was at the hospital. No crime there. He's going to say he grabbed the handle on the cart...to move it out of the way or for some other reason—there are about fifty different scenarios where his prints get on that handle that mean absolutely nothing—no crime there, either. Then the whole thing gets tossed out."

"But it was a crime to kill Martha Esser and we were

right there, minutes...maybe even seconds after it happened."

"I know. You're right about that. But as soon as we take Decker into custody the game changes. If we can't or don't charge him, he walks. And unless we get a confession out of him, that's exactly what will happen. If we try to charge him without a confession his lawyer will rip our evidence to shreds and that will only serve to magnify the evidence he planted against you. We need more, because if Decker is our guy, he not only killed Charlie and Martha Esser, but he's set you up to take the fall for Pam."

Murton knew Virgil was right. "It's a risk, you know. What if he goes after someone else?"

"I don't think there's anyone else to go after. Charlie Esser was killed because he wouldn't take the deal. All the other farmers wanted it, so they're probably safe."

Murton was shaking his head. "Can't make that assumption, Jonesy. Martha wanted the deal and she's dead too. Why is that?"

Virgil didn't have a direct answer to that question. "You're saying the other farmers are in danger?"

"I don't know. What I am saying is this: We've got two people on opposite sides of the same deal and they're both dead. The fact that they were married to each other may or may not be a factor."

They talked it around, looked at it from every angle they could think of and ended up right back where they started. "Here's what I don't understand," Virgil said. "Why Pam? And why go to the trouble to set you up for her murder?"

"That's what I'd like to know," Murton said.

Virgil smacked his forehead.

"What?"

"I just remembered something," Virgil said. "When we were out at the fracking site, right as Decker was leaving, Cora called me. Remember that?"

"Yeah. So what?"

"She asked me if I knew who Decker worked for. I blew it off at the time…said something like, 'I'll leave the politics to you, Cora,' but it's not what I said that matters. It's what she said right before that."

Murton made a twirling motion with his hand.

"She said Decker worked for Kreg Gordon."

"The sub-committee guy?" Murton asked.

"Yup."

Murton stared at nothing. "This is getting worse by the second. At least we know why he's setting me up for Pam's murder."

"What re you talking about?"

"C'mon, Jones-man. How do you think this is going to play out? Decker works for Gordon, a guy who is demon-strably going after the governor in one of the most public ways possible. As if that isn't enough, Decker is a wounded war veteran, and a member of the Indiana National Guard. You know what I've got? I've got a dead woman who was suing me over the death of her husband, and the people I work for are holding evidence that shows I killed her and did it either for my own gain to make the lawsuit go away, or on behalf of the governor to end the strike and every-thing behind it."

"That's a pretty short-sided outlook."

"How's that?"

"You forgot to mention the one thing you've got that they'll never have."

"Which is what?"

Virgil clapped him on the back "You've got me."

THE NEXT MORNING Virgil brought in three veteran ISP Troopers, put them in plain clothes and told them what he had in mind. "I want you to sit on Decker around the clock. We don't want to get too close and spook him, we just need to keep an eye on him. So. Keep it loose. If he even get's a sniff of one of you guys, we're toast."

"Three of us is a little thin," one of the troopers said. The other two nodded in agreement.

They were right, and Virgil knew it. "I know. But right now I want it wide and casual. We know where he lives and where he works. Basically I want one of you to take him to work, and the other two to cover his off time and put him to bed. One of you can cover as a janitor in the building where he works, one of you can float through his off time, and we've set up a short term watch point in an empty double-wide in the trailer park where he lives. You can divide it up any way you like."

One of the other troopers cleared his throat. Virgil looked his way, expressionless.

"How sure are you that this is your guy?"

"We're not to one-hundred percent yet."

"What percentage are you at?"

Virgil let the corners of his mouth turn down, thinking

it over. "Ninety...maybe ninety-five. He looks extremely good for one of three murders."

All three troopers were leafing through the notes Virgil had provided them. The youngest of the three...and the most eager, said, "Martha Esser?"

Virgil nodded at him. "That's right. There's almost no question regarding her. I was right there and missed it, and I'm pissed about it. But this whole thing has a deeper level that we're not seeing...at least not yet. So we want to know where he goes, who he talks to, and all that. I've already got the paperwork started for his phones, so leave that to me. Get pictures if you can, but be careful. That's the main thing. This guy is a nut. I had a run in with him down in Shelby County and he left me with the impression that it doesn't take much to set him off. He's former military and is active with the guard, so he's trained and he knows his weapons."

They all nodded. The young guy again: "What if we see him—"

Virgil cut him off. Knew where he was headed. "Unless you see him with a weapon pointed at someone or have reason to believe he is about to take action that could lead to the injury or death of another, you are to remain at a distance and disengaged. Are we clear on this?"

They were. "One more thing," Virgil said. "No disrespect, okay, but try not to look so...coppish. Every one of you guys look like you might as well have ISP tattooed on your foreheads."

The older trooper laughed. "Regulations, Jonesy. You used to be uniformed. You know the drill."

"Yeah, yeah, just...I don't know, try to look a little more—"

"Like you?"

Virgil nodded. "Exactly."

"I've done this before," the older trooper said. "Guarantee you, I could pass you on the street and you wouldn't recognize me."

"Let's hope you're right," Virgil said. "Work out your rotation, let me know what's what, then report to the motor pool. You can have your pick of vehicles. Watch your asses."

They stood to leave and the younger trooper held back a step or two. Virgil raised his eyebrows at him.

"Heard you might be looking to expand."

"That's the word," Virgil said.

"Keep me in mind?"

Virgil grinned at him. "There's a special sort of mentality that goes with the MCU. Show me what you've got, kid. If you've got it, I'll see it, then we'll talk."

"Fair enough," the kid said. He closed the door on the way out and Virgil made a note to himself to go through the kid's jacket.

THE TROOPERS SAT ON DECKER. They spent a week taking him back and forth, from home to work and from work to home. For the first few days, Virgil got multiple reports throughout the day. By the end of the week it was down to one report in the morning and one in the evening. Decker, according to the troopers, was as predictable as the cycle of the sun. "He gets up, goes to work, comes home. Not much else. Grocery store, drug store, that sort of thing."

Virgil told them to stay with it. He took his truck down to the motor pool. The shop had his lights and siren ready to install.

SANDY SPENT all her time with Jonas—didn't leave him alone for a second. She showered when he napped or when Virgil was home...which lately, wasn't often. Bell's predictions proved true. Jonas struggled a great deal, even with constant care and attention. Bell had stopped in twice during the week, spent some time observing, and maintained that Sandy was doing an excellent job.

"I just now got him down for a nap. And it doesn't feel like I'm doing an excellent job," she said. "It feels like I'm second-guessing myself about everything. Do I do this, or that? I'm never sure what the right thing is."

"Parenting doesn't come with an instruction manual, Sandy."

"It should. And I'll tell you something else: It seems like he's mad...at me. I'm the one who's doing everything for him—Virgil's helping of course, but he's busy with everything that's going on right now—and he gets angry with me. He tries to hide it, in his own little way, but I can see it. It's there."

"That's one of the stages. It's natural and it will pass. Sooner than you think, too. Look, you really are doing a great job. It's just hard for you to see. Like him, you're right in the eye of the storm. Pam was your friend and it's your loss as well. Don't forget that."

"How could I?" Sandy said. She stuck out her bottom lip and blew a strand of hair away from her face.

They were sitting across from each other and Bell, in a doctorly way, leaned forward and touched Sandy's knee with his index finger. "What about you? How are you holding up?"

"It's...harder than I thought it might be."

Bell lifted his finger and pointed at her abdomen. "That's not exactly what I meant. You're getting close now. So let me ask you again: How are you holding up?"

Sandy placed her hands on her belly. "My answer isn't much different. I *am* getting close. I'm scared, I'm nervous, and I'm exhausted. I think everything I'm feeling right now would be exactly the same, but with Jonas thrown into the mix, it seems much harder. I feel like I've lost my focus. For eight months I've been thinking only of Wyatt and his birth and our future. But now, caring for Jonas..."

Bell held up his hands. "Sandy, you're not neglecting your unborn son or your future or anything else for that matter...except maybe yourself. You're just tired."

"Tired doesn't quite say it."

"Why not get some help?"

"I've got this, Bell. Really. I'm putting a family together. It's just happening all at once and it's sort of exhausting."

"Have you heard from CPS?"

"Not a peep," Sandy said.

Bell pressed his lips together, a frown forming on his face. "That's a little odd."

"I was thinking the same thing. On one hand, I'd like to

get it over with...the interviews or questions, or whatever. But on the other hand, I'm thinking why rock the boat? There must be some reason they haven't shown up. Should I call them?"

Bell shook his head. "I don't know. You're not doing anything wrong or illegal. You're taking care of a friend's child...a child in need. He's much better off here, with you and Virgil than he would be in any sort of foster care. I think you need to factor in the ultimate question and let that be your guide."

"The ultimate question?"

"Are you and Virgil..."

"Going to adopt him? Yes. I mean, we want to, but there may be some complications that need to be sorted out. That's why I'm not sure what to do. I feel like if this goes on much longer and I don't call, it might look like we're trying to hide something."

"And these complications are connected to the case Virgil is working?" Sandy let her eyes slide away and Bell caught it. "I understand if you can't talk about it."

"It's not that I can't, Bell. I just don't want you to get the wrong idea. It looks like Pam was connected somehow to the Esser case that Virgil and Murton are handling. But the truth of the matter is this: no one knows exactly how."

"Is there any chance that it's coincidental?"

"I'm not sure. Based on what I know, I'd have to say that it probably isn't. That's what makes our decision to reach out to CPS so difficult. If the cases aren't connected, I don't think it will matter. But if they are, then there might be some trouble."

"You've got friends in all the right places, Sandy. Why not take advantage of that?"

"Because we can't simply pick up the phone and call the governor every time we want or need something."

"Why not? That's one of the perks of being friends with someone like that."

"But it's also our jobs, Bell. I'm the director of training at the Indiana Law Enforcement Center. Virgil just got his job back at the MCU. He reports directly to the governor's chief of staff. If it ever got out that we asked the governor to intervene on our behalf to adopt Jonas, we'd not only lose him, our jobs could be on the line as well."

"You're over-thinking it, Sandy. You're also part of a small and elite group...the kind of group where people who need something turn to the people who can make it happen. Do you think the governor would ever hesitate to contact you if he needed something only you could provide?"

"He never has before."

"Then there's your answer. You want Jonas? Make a few calls. Make it happen."

Sandy said she would. Then Bell said something that surprised her. She put her hands on her hips the way her mother used to do after hearing something she didn't want to hear. "You want to what?"

Bell held up his hands. "I know, I know. It's just something I've always wanted to do."

"Helicopters?" Sandy said. She moved her hands from her hips and crossed her arms.

"Why not? I can afford it. I love flying—I've got a friend who's a fixed wing pilot, but helicopters have always fascinated me. And riding along is fun, but I want the control...I want the stick." He held up a finger to emphasize his point, "But I also want to do it right. I was hoping Virgil could maybe call Mac's helicopter pilot and get me an introduction. I'm sure he could steer me in the right direction."

"Oh, Bell. If you hurt yourself..."

"Sandy, I'm doing this whether you help me or not. I just want to talk to the right people before I start taking lessons. So will you help me? Say something to Virgil?"

Sandy was against it, but how could she say no to Bell after everything he'd done for them? He'd saved Virgil's life. Given that, she couldn't turn him down no matter how she felt. She told him—with some reluctance—that she'd talk to Virgil, and even though she didn't like the idea, she did like the look on his face when he walked out the door.

CHAPTER TWENTY-TWO

B ecause of the outstanding evidence against him in Pam Donatti's murder, Murton got pulled from all active investigative duties and was placed on administrative leave. With nothing better to do, he was back working the bar with Delroy and Robert. Short on help, Virgil brought Tom Rosencrantz in to assist with the case load. He bounced it off Cora before doing so, mainly because Rosencrantz had been Ed Donatti's partner, but also because Virgil found himself increasingly unable to trust his own judgment, no matter the speech Sandy had given him only days ago.

Over the course of the next week, Rosencrantz worked the Esser murders down in Shelby County, painstakingly interviewing all the co-op employees, re-interviewing the farmers, and following up on everyone's alibis.

The toxicology on Martha Esser came back and showed an overdose of morphine as the cause of death and the crime scene report showed something that, in Virgil's opinion, simply had to be wrong.

"I don't care what the report shows, Rosie," Virgil said. They were in Virgil's office at the state building, Virgil tipped back in his chair with his fingers interlaced behind his head, one heel up on the corner desk, and Rosencrantz in a side chair, a look of defeat on his face.

"I don't like it any better than you do, Jonesy, but the facts are right there in the report."

Virgil leaned forward, picked up the report and looked at it for a moment. He waved it in the air before tossing it on his desk. "Fuck the facts. The facts are wrong."

"You're not going Republican on me, are you?"

Virgil gave him a dirty look instead of an answer. The facts went like this: The toxicology showed that Martha Esser had enough morphine in her system to kill three people. The medical examiner's report wasn't the part that bothered Virgil. The part that bothered him was what the crime scene people found in Esser's hospital room.

"It's all very fitting, isn't it?" Virgil said. "If you read that file cover to cover you could come to only one conclusion: Pam Donatti walked into the hospital and murdered Martha Esser by injecting her with enough morphine to take down an elephant. The DNA, the hair samples, the fingerprint on the vial of morphine, not to mention the other vial of morphine at her house...it's all very tidy, isn't it?"

"It is awfully convenient that the person who allegedly killed Martha Esser is also dead and unable to defend herself."

"If Decker killed Charlie Esser because he wouldn't

sign the fracking deal down in Shelby County, that means he's part of it somehow, possibly through his boss, Gordon. Except when Martha Esser signed, the deal went through and Decker kills her too and then the whole thing is set up to look like Pam Donatti was a part of it. Murton too. It's not making sense. There's too much noise."

"Here's the part that doesn't make sense to me," Rosencrantz said. "Why would you kill both of the Esser's if they were on opposite sides of the same deal? According to everyone we've talked to down there—and that's almost one hundred people—everyone is saying the exact same thing: Charlie Esser was against the deal. Period. But most of those same people—I'd have to check my personal notes to give you the exact number—say they didn't know where Martha stood on the deal or what her actual position was."

"Meaning?"

"Meaning she signed the deal right from her hospital bed without so much as batting an eyelash. We know she knew about the deal...hell everyone in the county knew about it. So she must have been for it, right?"

"Yeah, but was she for it because she simply wanted the money, or because her husband was dead and she couldn't run the farm without him?"

That triggered something in Virgil's brain. "You know what, Rosie? We've been looking at this whole thing backwards...maybe." He was excited, but trying not to get in front of himself.

"What do you mean?"

"I mean this whole time we've been looking at all of this with the murder of Charlie Esser at the center of the entire case."

Rosencrantz let his eyelids droop. "Yeah, that's sort of what we do around here. You should know. You run the joint, remember?"

Virgil ignored the sarcasm. "But we didn't start at the beginning of the case. Sheriff Holden told me as much last week when Murt and I went down there after they discovered Esser's body. He said something to the effect that if Charlie Esser wasn't dead he'd be sitting in county lockup on attempted murder charges for tossing his wife down the stairs and trying to kill her."

Rosencrantz thought about that for a minute. "So you're saying even though Martha Esser is dead, her murder happened out of order?"

Virgil pointed a finger at him. "That's right, and I think it's the order that is important."

"So it goes back to motive." A statement.

"Yep. I think we need to refocus. The entire time we've been trying to figure this whole mess out we've been looking at Charlie Esser's murder as the starting point, but the truth of it is, we should be focusing on Martha Esser's murder. She *wanted* the deal to go through, just like every other farmer on the co-op board."

"You may be right," Rosencrantz said. "But all that does is bring us back full circle because the guy that tried to kill her—her own husband—is dead."

Virgil was already shaking his head, his impatience growing by the second. "No, no, no. That's wrong, man."

"How can it be wrong? That's exactly what happened."

"That's not what I'm talking about. Yes, Esser tried to kill his wife, but you're trying to fit the puzzle together the wrong way. We can't twist the order of the facts to make them fit the way we want."

"What do you mean?"

"We're talking about motive, remember? And there's no motive in your full circle scenario. I can see someone killing Charlie Esser because he wouldn't sign, either because they knew or at least hoped that Martha Esser would if Charlie was out of the picture, or maybe even out of pure hatred and revenge for ruining the deal. That's motive...plain and simple. But then why kill Martha Esser after the fact? That's the part that doesn't make sense."

"Yes, it does. That's what I'm saying. If someone didn't want the deal to go through—" Rosencrantz caught himself and stopped.

Virgil saw his wheels turning. "That's right. It makes no sense whatsoever to kill Martha Esser. She had already signed. The deal was done. Killing her after the fact doesn't stop the deal. It's a non event...deal wise. The Esser's didn't have any heirs."

"What about the other farmers?"

"What about them?"

"If both Charlie and Martha Esser are dead, and they are, what happens to their portion of the deal. Does it go back into the co-op? Do the other farmers benefit?"

"Not according to Westlake. He showed us all the paper, and Becky researched the hell out of it. With both Charlie and Martha Esser dead and without heirs, their estate, including their portion of the gas deal goes to the state. There's something missing...some element that we're not seeing. Something that ties Pam Donatti's murder to the Esser murders. And we need to find it."

"Have you considered the fact that they may just be coincidental?"

Virgil leaned across his desk. "Of course I have," he snapped. The look on Rosencrantz's face left Virgil ashamed of himself. "I'm sorry."

Rosencrantz raised his eyebrows. "You want to tell me the rest of the story?"

Virgil looked at the clock on the wall. "We have to find out how Pam Donatti's murder ties in with the Esser killings because if we don't I'm afraid that I'm going to lose the best friend I've ever had."

"Why? What are you talking about?"

Virgil looked at the clock again. "Pam Donatti had filed a lawsuit against Murton, Rosie. She alleges that Murton was directly responsible for Ed's death."

"I know. I read the paper. I also know it's bullshit. Everyone knows he was trying to save him."

"It is bullshit, and it probably would have all gone away eventually, or at worst settled by the insurance carriers. But then Pam turned up dead. Internal Affairs is having a field day with this. Gordon is leaning on them hard and they're ready to hang Murton from a meat hook. The only thing stopping them is the evidence that Pam killed Martha Esser."

Rosencrantz thought it over. "So you're stuck. If you follow the physical evidence it smears the wife of a former member of this unit, and if you don't, Murt is hung out to dry."

"That about says it."

"There is no fucking way that Murton murdered Pam Donatti."

Virgil rubbed his face with both hands. Tired. "I know that, Tom, but try telling it to IA. The gun records came through from the ATF. If something doesn't break, they're going to bring him in and once that process starts, he'll have a hell of a time getting out from under it."

BECKY WALKED into Virgil's office. Her face was waxy, her eyes tired and red. She sat down next to Rosencrantz, put her face in her hands and choked back a sob. When she raised her head the look on her face was like someone who didn't exactly know where they were. "Cora told me to get over here. I don't know what's happening, but I really don't have time for it right now. If you want to know the truth, the only reason I'm here is I had to get out of the house. I couldn't take it anymore. They're tearing the place to pieces. These are *our* people, Virgil. They're treating my home like their own personal stomping ground."

"It's okay, Becks. Everything is going to be all right."

Becky stared at him with an intensity he'd not seen from her before. "It better be." Then after a few seconds she softened and said, "I think I've got something, but I don't know if it matters."

"What?"

"Before he got pulled, Murt asked the hospital for a list of all the people who'd been in to visit Martha Esser. Unfortunately they don't keep a list or a sign-in sheet or anything, so I had to do it the hard way."

Becky's main job was to compile every scrap of evidence and enter it into a useable database. Every single person listed in a case—suspect or not—got entered into the list with as much information as possible. If there were blank spots in the information, Becky had talents and resources that no other agency in the state had access to. But the information was just that...little bits of data that didn't always have much meaning unless you knew how to look at it. That's what made Becky good at her job. She not only knew where to look, she knew how to look at what she saw.

"What did you find?" Virgil asked.

"Pretty much what I expected," she said. "And one thing I didn't." She pulled a sheaf of papers from her bag and sorted through them, taking her time. Virgil looked at Rosencrantz who simply shrugged. Becky caught it out of the corner of her eye. "Just give a girl a minute, will you?"

Virgil tried to help. "Maybe if you told us what—"

She stopped shuffling her papers and looked at him with a wooden expression. "Virgil?"

He knew what was coming. "Yes, Becky?"

"Shut up."

Rosencrantz looked over at him. "Cool. I didn't know we could talk to the boss that way."

Virgil and Becky both said the same thing at the same time: "You can't."

After another full minute of organizational madness, she had it in order. "Okay, Rosie. You interviewed everyone down in Shelby County, right?"

Rosencrantz nodded. "Yup. Spent the whole week down there."

"And everyone has a rock-solid alibi for Charlie Esser." A statement.

"Well, I don't know that I'd say rock-solid. Most of them. The rest are fairly tight. The coroner couldn't get an exact time of death because of a number of mitigating factors, but we narrowed the window down to a twelve hour period based on when he was seen last and when he was expected to be seen."

Virgil tried to interrupt. "Becky, we're sort of thinking that Charlie wasn't the beginning of whatever's going on here. Martha is. Charlie tried to kill her, which sort of makes her the center of the case, not Charlie."

Becky shook her head. "That's...wrong. Sort of. I think."

"Meaning what?"

"That's what I'm trying to get to...in a reasonable and logical fashion. Except you keep interrupting me."

Virgil held up his hands in an 'I give up' gesture.

Becky paged through her notes. "The last group of people who saw Charlie Esser alive...that would be the other members of the co-op, correct?"

Rosencrantz nodded.

She turned to Virgil. "And of that group, you and Murton both stated that you witnessed Vernon Conrad assault Cal Lipkins. You also listed Conrad's excuse for the assault as, and I quote, 'Conrad stated that Lipkins was a bully and always had been.' You both also said that Conrad further stated that no one got along with Lipkins and he was the one who was trying to push the fracking deal through. Lipkins was the one who set up the tests, made contact with Westlake's group, and was trying to get everyone to go along with the deal. Is that an accurate portrayal of the facts?"

Virgil leaned forward in his chair. "Yes. Go on."

She turned to Rosencrantz again. "You corroborated all this in your reports as well."

"I did," Rosencrantz said.

"And Martha Esser wanted the deal, even though her husband didn't."

"That's right," Virgil said.

"Martha Esser also stated to various hospital employees and Sheriff Holden that her husband, Charlie, tried to kill her by throwing her down the stairs. I called the sheriff earlier and confirmed this with him. I also asked him a question that probably got overlooked."

Virgil was already shaking his head. "Becky, we asked all the right questions. I know we did. I was there."

"Relax Jonesy. I'm sure you did. But you were there investigating Charlie Esser's murder. I asked the sheriff if Lipkins pressed charges against Conrad for punching him. I was just gathering and entering information into the database. He said no charges were ever filed."

"So what?"

She shuffled her notes again and read directly from the page. "The sheriff is a talker. He gave me all the boring details of life in the country. But it wasn't *all* boring. He said Vernon Conrad and Martha Esser had had an on-again, off-again romance going back to before Martha and Charlie were married." She handed Virgil a piece of paper with a set of fingerprints on it. "Guess whose prints were all over Martha Esser's hospital room?"

Virgil looked at the paper and thought, son of a bitch.

"How DO we even have Conrad's prints to begin with?" Virgil asked.

"Carry permit from the state. They were right there in the database."

"So you're saying Vernon Conrad killed Charlie Esser, not because he wouldn't go through with the deal, but because he tried to kill Martha?"

"Not exactly. The coroner said Charlie Esser was still alive when the silo was filled. Technically, he died of suffocation after he was attacked and locked inside the silo. I'm simply telling you that the sheriff said Vernon Conrad and Martha Esser had been in love with each other for years. Decades, even. Then Charlie starts knocking her around and eventually tries to kill her. If you were Vernon Conrad, what would you do?"

Virgil stood up and looked at Rosencrantz. "Want to take a drive down to Shelby County with me?"

"You got it, Boss."

Virgil turned to Becky. "Nice work, Becks. Really."

"I love me some detective work," Becky said. "I told the sheriff to expect you. He says he'll be waiting in his office. What are you going to do about Murt?"

Virgil chose his words carefully. "I'm handling it, Becky. I promise."

She stared at him for a full minute, then walked out the door. Virgil pulled out his phone and called the bar. He looked at Rosencrantz and said, "I'll be right there."

Rosencrantz closed one eye and squinted at him. As soon as he stepped outside, Virgil got Delroy on the line. "He still there?"

"Ya mon. Where else he gonna go, him? Hang on."

A few seconds later Murton was on the line.

"How are you holding up?" Virgil said.

"As well as can be expected, I guess."

"We caught a break in Shelby County. We're headed there now."

"Not to sound too selfish, but does it do anything for me?"

"I don't know...at least not yet. But don't worry. Everything is under control," Virgil said. It was a bald-faced lie and they both knew it.

CHAPTER TWENTY-THREE

An hour later they turned into the Shelby County Law Enforcement Center parking lot and entered the building. The sheriff was standing behind a glass wall partition speaking with one of his deputies. When he saw Virgil and Rosencrantz he walked over to meet them, grabbing his jacket from a coat tree. His gait reminded Virgil of a turtle with bad knees. Did turtles have knees? He wasn't sure.

"I don't know about all this, Detectives. Known Vern a long time."

"I appreciate your position, Sheriff, but how long you've known someone can't be the determining factor on whether or not they've committed a crime."

The sheriff gave Virgil a look like he'd just spit in the punch bowl. "I know that. I'm only suggesting that you use a little discretion is all. I know I will. In fact I already have. I called Vern and told him we were on our way out to talk to him."

Rosencrantz looked down at his shoes.

"I wish you hadn't done that, Sheriff," Virgil said. "We've just lost the element of surprise."

"Ain't any surprise to be had. Vern's about as violent as a church mouse on Easter Sunday. You riding with me or you gonna follow? Never mind. I think you should you follow."

WHEN THEY TURNED into Conrad's driveway, Virgil pulled his truck right up behind the sheriff's station wagon. The three men stood in the cold for a moment, Virgil and Rosencrantz looking over the property. "Doesn't look like much," Virgil said to no one.

The sheriff, still somewhat offended by the accusations against Conrad said, "Folks live a simple life out here. How about you show a little respect? What were you expecting, a four-storied mansion?"

Virgil, already tired of the huckleberry routine turned and glared at him. "I had no expectations, sheriff. It was just a statement. These guys run mega farms...thousands of acres, but all I see is a small ranch house, a barn, and a few out-buildings."

The house *was* small, and old. But it appeared well-kept, the design simple and functional. Virgil could practically see the inside in his mind. A kitchen and bathroom in the front, a one-room common area, two bedrooms and a hall bath in the rear. The annuals and perennials that fronted the landscaping and rounded the corners of the house had withered with the season. A wooden rocking chair with the finish worn away and a small side table sat next to the front door. The roof looked new, except there was one solitary shingle just below the chimney chase that was askew. It was, Virgil thought, the kind of place you wouldn't give a second look if driving past.

"What else do you see?" the sheriff asked.

Virgil looked around. "Nothing."

"Exactly," the sheriff replied. "The house ain't much because the money is in the land."

"Look, sheriff, it was just a simple observation. You seem to take offense at everything I say. I mean you no disrespect. Nor Mr. Conrad, for that matter. We're simply here to ask him a few follow-up questions and try to either clear him as a suspect in the murder of Charlie Esser or—"

"Arrest him," Holden said. He shook his head the way an adult would when trying to explain something complex to a child. "C'mon, if I know Vern, he's in the barn getting his equipment put up for the winter." They turned that way and as they did the jackpot flasher on top of Holden's station wagon blew apart, followed almost immediately by the sound of a rifle shot. Virgil and Rosencrantz ducked behind the vehicles and pulled their weapons. Sheriff Holden looked at the ruined flasher, then the barn, then back at the flasher. "Damn it, Vern."

"Sheriff!" Virgil yelled. "Get down. Get back here before you get killed." Another shot, this one taking out the front tire of the station wagon. Virgil looked at Rosencrantz. "If that motherfucker shoots my new truck I'm going to—"

The next shot went through both side windows of the truck and continued on and cracked the upper part of the rocking chair before burying itself in the side of the house. Rosencrantz brushed the broken glass out of his hair and off his shoulders. "You were saying?"

"I've got to get the sheriff. Throw everything you've got at the barn. Aim high. I don't want you to hit him by accident. Ready?"

Rosencrantz nodded. "Go." He leaned over the bed of the truck and opened up on the barn. Virgil ran around the front of the truck, grabbed the sheriff by the arm and yanked him back behind the truck. They landed in a tangle, the sheriff grabbing at his left knee. Rosencrantz kept firing until the slide on his gun locked open.

"Ah, shit, I think you popped me loose partner."

Partner?

"What the hell were you doing just standing there, Sheriff?" Rosencrantz said. "Are you trying to get yourself killed? Your Easter Sunday church mouse is shooting at us. That sort of changes things."

Holden was breathing hard, his teeth clenched, both hands wrapped around his knee. "I could stand there all day and not get killed. Vern's the best shot I ever seen. If he wanted me dead, I'd be dead."

"Still think he's innocent?"

"I think he's scared and confused." Then: "I am too."

"I can see that," Rosencrantz said. "Every time I'm scared or confused I do the same thing. I get my rifle out and start shooting at the cops. Makes perfect sense."

Virgil looked down at Holden. "Where's your weapon, Sheriff?"

"Where it usually is. Top right hand corner desk drawer in my office."

Enough of the down-home bullshit, Virgil thought. He reached up and opened the door of his truck, unlatched the shotgun behind the seat and handed it to Holden. "There's five shots in there."

"I'm not shooting Vern. You boys have got him mixed up with someone else."

"We're past that, Sheriff. And I don't want you to shoot him. Rosie and I are going to get him out of the barn but we've got to get there first. I want five shots from you, three seconds apart. That means you shoot, count to three, then shoot again. Think you can handle that?"

"What am I shooting at?"

"Anything but us. We just need the noise to pin him down for a few seconds."

"Don't kill him."

"It's time to do your job. I'm looking for a yes or no answer, Ben."

Holden sucked in his cheeks, then nodded at Virgil, the shotgun pointing straight up in the air. "Just say when."

"Rosie, take the left corner. I've got the right. You ready?"

Rosencrantz had reloaded and positioned himself at the back bumper of the truck. "Say the word, Boss."

Virgil looked at Holden. "Get ready, Sheriff. I'm going to move up as far as I can, then try to get him to fire again. As soon as he does, you do what I said. And for Christ sake, stay out of sight. When we get to the barn, I want you to try to talk him out of there."

"What? Talk him out? I ain't exactly a skilled hostage negotiator."

"We're not dealing with hostages, Sheriff."

"How do you know that?"

Good point. "I don't. Will you do it, or not?"

"Yeah, yeah, I can talk to him."

"Good enough. Just try to get a dialog going. We'll handle the rest." He duck-walked all the way to the front of the station wagon, turned and nodded at Rosencrantz, then shouted at the barn. "Conrad...It's Virgil Jones, I spoke with you last week about Charlie Esser. Stop shooting at us, will you? You're only making things worse. We just want to—"

Another shot came from the doorway of the barn and even though he didn't know where the bullet went, Virgil got a glimpse of the rifle flash and saw Conrad duck back behind the left side of the door. Holden sat with his back against the side of Virgil's truck. As soon as he heard the shot he fired the shotgun in the opposite direction, over the roof of Conrad's house. Virgil and Rosencrantz ran for the barn, the shotgun blasting away every three seconds.

THEY MADE it to the corners of the barn, but their line of sight was a problem. Conrad had been shooting from inside the doorway, not exposing himself to return fire. Virgil looked at the walls of the barn and noticed the dry rot and the gaps in the boards. He caught Rosie's eyes and motioned him forward. Virgil was waiting for the sheriff to start talking, but it was Conrad who spoke first. Virgil and Rosie were each about halfway in from the corners, working toward the door, their backs flattened against the exterior wall, their handguns pointed down at the ground. When they heard Conrad, they both froze in position.

"Hey Ben, that you out there with the scatter gun?"

Holden worked himself off the ground and stared through the broken windows of Virgil's truck. "Yup. Don't know why you're shooting at us, Vern, but it'd probably be best if you set your rifle down and came on out. Nobody wants to get hurt here. I know I sure as hell don't."

"Ain't gonna come out, Ben. You shouldn't have called and you shouldn't have come out here. You and those state boys best leave my property and we'll pretend this never happened."

"That's not going to happen, Vern. Man's got a job to do and this one's mine. I've got to tell you, I ain't enjoying it too damned much right about now."

"You ain't never have enjoyed it, Ben. Ain't that what you go around telling everyone all the damned time. You should have stuck to garment cleaning and the like."

"That might be true, but I didn't and here we are, Vern. We can't change the past but we can control what happens next. Now come on out before these state boys decide to take matters into their own hands. They're not exactly what you'd call the patient type."

Virgil and Rosencrantz were inching their way toward the door as the two men shouted at each other. They were now only about ten feet from either side of the door. Virgil held his hand up, palm out, and stopped their approach. He caught Rosie's eye and held it, then motioned for him to get low so they wouldn't be directly in line with each other. Virgil moved in tighter on the door.

"I ain't coming out because I know why you're here. You think I killed Charlie, but I didn't."

"Then we don't have a problem. Put your gun down and come on out. You know me, Vern. We'll get everything straightened out. Nothing's happened here that can't be fixed. I was going to replace that jackpot anyway. It never did turn proper, and as for the tire, that thing is so bald I'm surprised it didn't blow apart on the drive out here. What do you say?"

"I say you should have done something about the way Charlie was treating Martha. She'd still be alive if you'd have listened to me. That's what I say."

"Did all I could do under the law, Vern. You know that. Having a shootout here isn't going to change anything except your situation."

"I didn't kill him, but they're going to say it was murder just the same. He was beating on Martha so bad she couldn't hardly take it no more. Then when he thrown her down the steps that was it for me. He was working in the silo and I went in there and knocked him around a little. At least that's what I meant to do, but I think I must have snapped or something because I got a little carried away. I didn't know that silo was gonna get filled. It hadn't been used all season. How was I supposed to know?"

Rosencrantz looked at Virgil and held up his finger in a 'wait a minute' gesture. He belly crawled forward another foot or so to a gap between two boards of the outside wall. He looked into the gap and saw Conrad just behind a vertical beam, his rifle pointed straight out the door. He pulled his head away, nodded at Virgil, then looked back through the hole.

Virgil understood. Rosencrantz had him spotted. He moved forward until he was right at the edge of the door.

"I understand that, Vern. That's what I've been trying to tell you. People under stress react differently than they might otherwise. Sort of like right now. If you say it was an accident, I believe you. We can fix this whole mess if you'll just put the gun down and come on out before anyone gets hurt."

But Conrad had already made his choice. He cycled the bolt action on his rifle and reversed it in his hands, his thumb now inside the trigger guard. Rosencrantz saw what was about to happen. He yelled "Go!" to Virgil and jumped up.

Virgil spun inside the door just in time to see Vernon Conrad shoot himself under the chin. His head jerked back and his arms flew out away from his sides as he fell to the ground. He landed on his back like he was about to make a snow angle in the dirt, the top half of his head gone, the back wall of the barn painted in red.

HOLDEN MADE THE RADIO CALL, then sat in his wagon, his left leg extended out straight, his knee swollen tight inside his uniform pants. Virgil walked over and stuck his head down inside the door. "You okay, Sheriff?"

When Holden didn't answer, Virgil tried a little diplomacy. It was genuine. "You did a great job, Ben. You said you weren't a negotiator but that was pretty amazing what you just did. We got a confession by way of a dying declaration."

The sheriff turned his head slowly and looked up at Virgil. "You call that a nice job? The man just blew his brisket across the hayloft. He lost his farm and the only woman he ever loved. He beat his business partner half to pulp, an action that led directly to his own death. On a more personal note, that's the second friend I've lost in just over a week. No offense, Detective, but I'd call it anything but a nice job."

"They did it to each other, Ben."

The sheriff looked away and didn't say anything else.

CHAPTER TWENTY-FOUR

The next morning they all crowded into the conference room just down the hall from Virgil's office. Coffee and doughnuts and juice and fresh fruit were on the table. The group consisted of every single person who knew Martha Esser was dead...every cop, all the hospital employees who'd had any interaction involving her care...the nurses, doctors, rehab staff, the medical examiner, all the crime scene techs, Sheriff Holden from Shelby County, and the assistant district attorney.

There were so many people in the room that all the seats were taken and a couple of the crime scene techs went out in search of folding chairs. Virgil wasn't there yet and they were all waiting on him.

The techs came back a few minutes later with a couple of armfuls of folding chairs and everyone settled in and waited. The doctors kept looking at their watches. "Well, we're all here as promised. Anybody have any idea why?" one of them said.

"Maybe he's going to give us a medal or some shit," one of the crime scene techs said. That got a small chuckle from everyone.

Sheriff Holden popped a giant strawberry in his mouth and packed it into the side of his cheek. "I doubt it," he said. "Every time I'm around the guy, someone ends up dead."

That ended the chuckling. A nervous sort of quiet settled over the room, like they were all together in a crowded elevator. They sat and waited.

VIRGIL, with the help of Murton and Rosencrantz had spent most of the previous evening working the phones in order to get everyone there. Didn't tell them why, other than to say it was part of the on-going investigation. A few of them didn't like it, but they all eventually agreed to come in. He emphasized the timing of it all. It was critical that they be on time. He secretly enjoyed the fact that the doctors were waiting on him. Rosencrantz popped his head in the doorway and said, "They're all here. Waiting on you, big guy."

"What about Becky?"

"Haven't seen her yet. Any minute, I'd guess."

"I'm right behind you," she said to Rosencrantz. "I need a minute with Jonesy, if you don't mind."

"No problem," he said as he turned to leave. Then he saw the look on Becky's face and stopped. "Hey, Becky...are you okay?"

Becky visibly swallowed, nodded and put her hand on Rosencrantz's shoulder. "I'm fine. I'll tell you what I really am is tired. Up all night researching for this one." She tipped her chin at Virgil.

"He is a slave driver," Rosencrantz said. Then to Virgil: "Anyway, the conference room..."

"Be right there."

———

HE LOOKED at everything Becky handed him. "You're sure about this? Decker is Jonas's father?"

"Yep."

Virgil couldn't quite believe it. "You're saying that Pam Donatti and John Decker had an affair and Jonas is their child?"

"Yes, Jonesy...that's exactly what I'm saying. You can keep asking the question, but the answer isn't going to change. He filed the paperwork with the state. Pam had a copy of it at home. I pulled it from the evidence room. No one had seen it yet because they're still inventorying every-thing they took from the house. Short of a DNA test, that's as good as it gets. With Pam dead, he not only gets custody, he gets the pension money."

Virgil held up the custody paperwork. "You're sure about this?"

"One hundred percent," Becky said.

"How did you find it?"

"I almost didn't. It was wiped off the system, but whoever did it either didn't get to the backups or didn't have the clearance and couldn't get in. I only had to go back a couple of days and it was right there." Becky caught the look on his face. "What are you thinking?"

"I'm thinking he never could have pulled it off by himself. This isn't just Decker. He's had help all along, and I think I know who it is. I've known it from the start, I just didn't realize it."

"Who?"

"It's Decker's boss, Kreg Gordon. Mac wanted us on this from the get-go and Cora never did tell us why. She just let us believe the obvious. But Gordon has been after Mac in every way possible. And Mac drops in on me and Murt and sends us to Shelby County to track down a missing farmer?"

"Are you saying Mac knows more than he's telling us?"

"I think Mac always knows more than he tells. He's a master politician. I don't think he knew anything about Decker, but he knew Gordon was involved somehow because he was the one pushing for the fracking deal, something that Mac was adamantly opposed to."

"So he's killing two birds with one stone," Becky said. "He gets Gordon off his back and stops the fracking ops in Shelby County."

"He's no dummy, our governor. He comes off as this affable sort of goof—charming and even a little...thick sometimes. But he's not. He's ten steps ahead of everyone in the room."

"And he's using you and Murt to do his dirty work."

Virgil sucked in his cheeks. "That's the job, Becky. I wouldn't call it dirty work either. He pointed us at a crime and told us to solve it. It looks like we're almost there."

"At what cost? What if Murt gets hung out to dry?"

"That won't happen, Becky. I guarantee it."

"Says the guy who got fired by the same man we're talking about right now."

"Different set of circumstances back then, Becks."

"And a different guy to take the fall now," Becky said.

Virgil shook his head. "Look Becky, I know the man. We have a history. He'll back Murt. I know he will."

"I hope you're right."

Virgil changed directions. "Let me ask you this: What if someone realizes their mistake and tries to go in and rewrite or overwrite or whatever you call it?"

"The back-ups? Give a girl some credit, will you? It won't do them any good. I put a little code in there. If they try, it will just make another copy. Plus I downloaded a digital copy for safekeeping."

"Is that...can you...?" Virgil stopped himself. "I probably don't want to hear anymore, do I?"

"Mmm, probably not. Virgil?"

"Yes, Becky?"

"You needed absolute proof to get to Decker, and to get Murton out from under these charges. I just handed it to you. Those are official state documents. They're straight out of the state's court system, sitting behind one of the lamest firewalls I've ever encountered. Murt's in the clear, and you've got your killer. How about you go pick him up and we can all get on with our lives?"

Virgil picked up the phone and called the trooper who currently had Decker. "He still there?"

"Yep." It was the young trooper. The kid. "He must have taken a sick day or something because he didn't leave for work this morning."

Virgil felt a thump in his chest. "You're sure?"

"Positive. I was in place and watched him come home last night. His car's still there and I've been sitting by the window all night. You getting ready to move?"

"Yeah...won't be long now. There's a press conference about to start and we're going to take him right after that. In fact, be ready to run. If he's watching, I expect him to panic and make a run for it."

There was a moment of silence and Virgil caught it. "What?"

"Well, I was just thinking that you might have filled a guy in, is all."

"That's what I'm doing now. Can you see the entrance to the park from your position?"

"Hold on." Ten seconds later the trooper was back. "Old school...but nice. I appreciate the subtleness. Nobody does that anymore. Now it's all armored vehicles and flash-bangs and—"

"Glad you approve, Trooper." Virgil had a SWAT team positioned at the entrance. They were disguised as a water and sewer crew. "Listen, I'm on the clock here. Set your radio to SWAT's frequency and be ready."

He ended the call and went back to Becky. "Are you sure you don't mind covering Jonas for us? Murt said you'd be fine with it, but I want to make sure you are too. There's just about zero chance that anything could happen...and I really do mean that. Less than one percent. But this guy wants his kid and he wants the pension money, and he's a total nut job. But we've got him pinned in his trailer and he doesn't even know it."

Becky ran her hands through her hair. "Yeah, I'm fine with it. If the state wants me to babysit, I'll babysit."

"Okay. I want you to take him to the office at the bar. Delroy is there and Jonas needs lots of friends around him. Normally I'd say your place is fine, but we know Decker has been there, so that's out of the question. Plus, you'll be surrounded by cops downstairs. Couldn't be safer. Sandy's waiting for you at our place. We'll pick him up after her doctor appointment."

"No problem." Then, "Jonesy, is Murton going to come out of this all right?"

"He's one of the most important people in my life. I'd die for him, Becky."

"I know you would. That's what scares me."

"What are you talking about?"

"Only that I can relate to what Pam must have been going through over the last eight months. How do you think Murt feels about you, Jonesy? Do any of you guys ever wonder how it lands on the women in your lives? The brotherhood and all that."

Becky had a look on her face that suggested she was focused on something else. Virgil watched her for a moment, then said, "Becky, are we okay?"

She took her time answering. "I don't know, Jonesy. Are we?"

"Becks, we've known each other a long time. I've always trusted you because I know your loyalties to the people in your life...and mine. You have to know that I've got Murt's back on this. I would never let anything happen to him."

"I know that's your intention, Jonesy, but the fact of the matter is this: I still think about being dragged naked from the shower and having my teeth knocked out by Hector Sigara. I think about waking up and seeing a shotgun pressed to the side of Murt's head. I think about all of it every single day. Who had our backs then, Jonesy?"

"I did, Becky, and you know it. I was there."

"A little late to the party though, weren't you?"

"That's not fair and it doesn't honor the man who died saving your life. We got there as soon as we could. We came on a hunch, for Christ's sake."

"Look, no disrespect to Ed. He's a hero to me. And so are you. But my point is this: Murt's life could be on the line here. How many hunches do you have left?"

Virgil didn't know what to say. "Becks, I promise you, this is going to work out. Hang around for the press conference before you get Jonas. You've got time. Maybe you'll see what I mean." Then before she could add any more: "Listen, we still need to find the connection between Pam and Martha Esser. Keep digging, will you?"

Becky wanted to question him but she let it go. "I will. Besides, Cora still has me working on something. I was going to work on it at home, but I'll just do it from the office."

Virgil arched his brow. "Working on what?"

"Stop with the eyebrow thing, will you? You've got a little Mr. Spock sort of habit going there and it's creepy. I keep expecting you to show up with pointy ears and bangs."

"Yeah, yeah." Fucking researchers.

"Anyway, I'm following up to make sure the Esser's didn't have any heirs. You know, covering their butts when Mac and Cheese go on TV and say Martha Esser isn't dead even though she is."

Mac and Cheese? Virgil put his face in his hands. If Cora found out people were calling them that...

CHAPTER TWENTY-FIVE

Virgil ran down to the conference room and told everyone what they were doing. Everyone agreed to go along with it, mainly, Virgil thought, because they really didn't have to do anything except keep their mouths shut. He naturally got some pushback from the doctors. "I don't know if that's legal," one of them said.

"I'm a cop," Virgil said. "There's nothing illegal about it."

"That sounds a little like, 'I'm from the government and I'm here to help.'"

"Look, we just don't want anyone talking to anyone who doesn't know. Especially the press." Virgil glanced at the assistant district attorney and tipped his head back. The ADA caught it.

"I have a form here for everyone to sign. You'll notice that I've already signed each of them myself," he said. He began handing the papers out. "There's no legal mumbo-jumbo. It states very clearly and simply that what we're asking of you is perfectly legal, that no one is forcing you to do anything, and that your cooperation or lack thereof will in no way result in the state taking any legal action against you or—"

Virgil interrupted. "Listen, I'm sort of in a hurry here."

The ADA waved him off. "It's all good, Jonesy. I've got this. Go ahead and take off."

DECKER SAT in front of the TV watching the coverage. He couldn't believe how well his plan had worked out. It'd taken a little longer than he expected it would—but it looked like an arrest warrant would finally be issued for Murton Wheeler. According to the talking heads, he was going to be charged with the murder of Pam Donatti, and even better—this was something Decker hadn't even considered—the state was re-examining the evidence surrounding the death of Ed Donatti. The heads were already saying for reasons not yet known, there was speculation that it had been Murton Wheeler's plan all along to eliminate both Ed and Pam Donatti.

A press conference was scheduled to start soon where the governor and other state officials would give a briefing.

He sat back in his chair and clicked through the channels, thinking the whole thing through. The paperwork he'd filed with the clerk of the court seeking custody of the boy had been a risk, one he felt he had to take. His thinking had been that once he'd gotten rid of Pam—messy, but necessary—he, as the boy's biological father would have everything he needed, not the least of which was the money that would have gone to the Donatti's. But then the people he worked for told him Martha Esser had to go, so that's what he did. It surprised him, but these weren't the type of people you said no to. These were the type of people that tapped you on the shoulder and quietly whispered a name in your ear. They didn't give you a reason or an explanation, just a name. If you asked for a reason or even looked at them the wrong way, someone else would get a tap on the shoulder and your name would be whispered, and that would be that.

So. He hadn't told them about the paperwork, and with good reason. They would not be happy. They had their own agenda, and Decker knew that if he got in the way of that he was expendable, which not only pissed him off, it scared him. They knew he was responsible for Pam's death and his desire for the pension money. Gordon, his boss acted like it was nothing to him. A minor detail. Yes, yes, take care of business, as long as Martha Esser died, they didn't care. He wanted to know more about the Esser bitch and the fact that he didn't know was driving him crazy. What were they hiding?

So he'd gone along with their plan for two reasons. He didn't have a viable plan of his own, and he wanted his boy and the money. When he forced himself to think about it, he had to admit that he didn't really give two shits about the boy. In fact, the more he thought about it, the more despondent he became. What, now he had to drag a kid around with him everywhere he went for the next fifteen years? Fuck that.

Was there a way he could get rid of the kid and still get the money? He'd have to think about that. Definitely have to get the kid first. The kid was the key. Once paternity was established and the money came in the kid could...what? Disappear? Have a tragic accident? Whatever. He'd figure something out. He had to. It's not like he could just send him off to boarding school. That wouldn't work. No way he was going to let the little shit turn eighteen and walk up to him one day and say, "Where's my money, dickhead?"

He was still thinking it through when he looked out the window, lost in his own deluded thoughts, and noticed something odd. Someone was in the trailer across the way, two spots down. That trailer was vacant and had been for some time.

A sudden flood of panic ripped through him. Were they on to him? Were they *watching* him? He moved over to the side of the window and cracked the blinds...just a fraction. There was movement. He could see it. He glanced at the roof and saw a thin trail of steam rising from the furnace's exhaust stack and when he did the panic grew stronger. He ran to the other side of the trailer and looked toward the park entrance. There was a water and sewer truck parked across the exit lane of the park's main drive. He counted six men. None of them were doing anything, which, even Decker had to admit didn't necessarily mean anything, especially with a water and sewer crew. But it was the way they weren't doing anything that bothered him. They all stood next to the rear of the truck and looked like they were looking in every direction except his trailer.

Fuck me, he thought. Cops. Probably a SWAT team. He took out his field glasses from his gear bag, inched up to the window as close as he dared and took a quick look. When he did, his heart sank. Definitely cops. He could see the outline of the armor they wore under their clothing. In addition, they all wore black combat boots and tactical gloves.

But why were they just sitting there?

On the television he heard rather than saw the governor and his contingent as they walked up to the podium. He grabbed his tactical vest, already loaded with a handgun, extra ammo, and his K-bar. He moved to the back of the trailer and checked outside. The angle was bad and he couldn't see the front entrance or the other trailer...the one that was supposedly vacant. But that meant they couldn't see him either.

Virgil was in his truck, headed toward Decker's residence. He'd had an emergency service replace both side windows the previous evening—it had cost him a small fortune, but it was worth it given the cold. Virgil thought if felt like it might start snowing any day now. With a little luck they'd yank Decker from his trailer without incident and let him sit in lockup for a few hours after he was processed. Virgil needed the time because he was meeting Sandy at the doc's for one of her weekly checks... they were that close now. Wyatt was almost here, and the thought both thrilled and terrified him. His phone chirped at him. He grabbed it off the dash and said, "Jonesy."

"I got every last one of them," the ADA said. "Had to give away a few handshake deals to the doctors on future speeding tickets, though."

Despite everything that was going on, Virgil had to laugh. "I'm surprised everyone didn't ask for something."

"They were smart about it. They knew if they asked in front of everyone else then everybody would want something and that my answer would have been no. I mean, you can't start giving away the farm on this type of thing. So they sort of hung back until everyone else left before they asked. I'll tell you something else too...these guys were at opposite ends of the table and they both knew what the other was thinking. I watched it happen. They did it with a *look*. Fucking doctors."

CHAPTER TWENTY-SIX

K reg Gordon, the house sub-committee chairman, and J. Connor Westlake were together at Gordon's house. They sat in the library and Gordon was nervous. Westlake could see it. There was a thin line of perspiration on his upper lip reflecting from the light of the television and it looked like a translucent pencil mustache.

"I don't believe I've ever seen you quite so anxious before, Kreg," Westlake said.

"Lot on the line." Gordon sat forward in his chair and rubbed both eyes with the heels of his hands. He pulled a bottle of scotch and two glasses from a desk drawer. "Drink?"

"Thank you, no. It's a little early for me."

"Suit yourself. The press conference is about to start and the governor may as well show up holding a shovel. His political career is about to die."

"Then why do you look so nervous, Kreg. Maybe it's because you know everything is not in order."

Gordon froze, his glass of scotch caught halfway between the desk and his mouth. It looked like he was about to propose a toast. "What are you talking about?"

"Your man, Decker? You've lost control of him."

"The hell I have. Decker does what he's told."

"Then maybe the problem is with you. Either way, he's decided to take matters into his own hands."

"Meaning what, exactly?"

Westlake reached into his pocket and pulled out an envelope. "I have contacts at every level of the court system. My people go in ahead of me and set everything up. It's easier than you might imagine. It probably wouldn't be if government employees were paid a little better. Your state is no different from any other. It's one way we stay in front of our competition."

Gordon was annoyed with Westlake's dramatics. "Yes, yes, you're good at what you do. I already knew that. If you weren't, you wouldn't be sitting here right now. What's the problem with Decker?"

"This," Westlake said. He tossed the envelope on Gordon's desk. "Apparently Decker is tired of waiting, or he senses a weakness in you. He's taken matters into his own hands. That's a copy of the paperwork he filed with the court. He's seeking custody of the boy, something you told me he wasn't going to do until we had everything else in order. I've managed to clean all the originals from the system. It wasn't easy, even for me."

Gordon set his drink down and snatched up the envelope. "What? That's insane. I specifically told him not to do that until—"

Westlake didn't let him finish. "Well, he specifically didn't listen, Kreg."

"I'll take care of it."

"No, I'm afraid you won't, Kreg. That particular ship has already sailed, as they say."

Thirty seconds ago, Gordon felt like a man at the top, in charge and in control of his own destiny. As chair of the sub-committee looking into Bradley Pearson's botched prison privatization scheme, Gordon knew an opportunity when he saw it. With Charlie and Martha Esser out of the way, the money from their portion of the fracking operations would go directly to the state—through his committee. It wouldn't be enough to get them out of the red—Gordon didn't care about that. That would be someone else's problem down the line.

What he cared about was wiping the smug look off the governor's face and positioning himself for a run in the next gubernatorial race, a race that would be backed in full by Westlake and his consortium...but only if Gordon helped the deal in Shelby County go through. Gordon, who knew of Decker's desire to get his kid—and the pension money that went with it—had used Decker to take care of Martha Esser, eliminating obstacles and creating confusion along the way.

"That son-of-a-bitch is going to ruin everything," Gordon said.

"What did you tell him?"

"Only what he needed to know...that the kid comes with the pension money."

Westlake was staring at a framed photograph on the

wall. In the photo a much younger Kreg Gordon was dressed in a three piece suit and was shaking hands with Ronald Reagan. Gordon was beaming at Reagan. Reagan, on the other hand, wore a cowboy hat and jeans with a flannel shirt, his faced turned away as if he might be having a conversation with someone just out of view of the camera's lens. His grasp of Gordon's hand appeared to be no more consequential than that of a waiter handing him a napkin or a piece of junk mail addressed to 'Occupant.' Westlake took the photo from the wall and held it in his hands.

"What are you doing? Put that back."

"Decker was useful, Kreg. But he was useful to you, not me. Letting you use him instead of bringing in our own people was a mistake. I accept responsibility for that."

"What are you saying?"

Westlake picked up the remote and turned the volume up on the television. "I'm suggesting that you sit down and shut up. I want to hear this."

Gordon, who had never had anyone speak to him in that manner was outraged. "Now you wait just a goddamned minute," he said, pointing his finger at West-lake. "Just who in the hell do you think you're talking to? You're in my home—"

Westlake held up his hand to silence Gordon. "You know what the difference is between guys like you and guys like me, Kreg? Guys like me know how to insulate themselves." Then, as if to clarify his point: "We use guys like you to do it."

On the television, the governor and a small group of people were gathering around a podium. There was a blue curtained backdrop with the flags of the United States and the state of Indiana behind them. Westlake turned the framed photo of Gordon and Reagan over and pealed a small electronic device from the back, then smashed the framed photo against the corner of Gordon's desk, breaking the frame in half, pieces of glass flying everywhere. He walked to the rear corner of Gordon's desk, reached underneath and pulled a similar item out and inspected it before placing both listening devices in his pocket. He pulled two more from their hiding places, one from a bookshelf and the other from the underside of a small table that sat between two leather chairs.

The look on Gordon's face was beyond disbelief. "You've bugged my home?"

"Don't look so surprised, Kreg. Even though it's fairly obvious, I'll answer your question. Yes. We bugged your home. And your office. Decker's too. Boy, he sure lives in a dump, doesn't he?"

"He got a divorce. She took everything he had," Gordon said, surprised that he felt it necessary to defend Decker's living situation.

"Maybe he should have hired a better lawyer. Someone who knows how to think more strategically, someone more like, well...me."

Gordon picked up his phone. "I will not stand for this. I am going—"

Westlake yanked the phone from his hand and placed it back in the cradle. "You're going to what, Kreg? All the bugs have been removed. There's no proof they were ever there. My people have taken care of everything. And I do mean everything. We've got you and Decker on tape. It makes for great listening...all the planning, the strategy, the...killings. All ordered by you. Boy you really strung him along, didn't you? Hanging the kid's pension payout in front of him. It's the one thing you did well. Too bad you didn't keep a closer eye on him."

"What, I'm supposed to have him followed around twenty-four hours a day?"

"Why not? We did. Are you aware that he's been under police surveillance for the past few days?"

"*What?*"

Westlake lifted a finger to his lips and made a shushing noise and pointed at the television. "I really do want to hear this. You do too, whether you know it or not. Your future sort of depends on it."

CORA LARUE STOOD in front of the microphone, the governor just to her right. "For those of you who might not be aware, my name is Cora LaRue and I'm the governor's chief of staff. The governor is here today to make a statement regarding some operational issues surrounding the Major Crimes Unit and to clarify some details that seem to have somehow been twisted into something other than—"

One of the reporters wanted to get the jump. "When you say twisted, are you referring to the arrest warrant that has been issued for one of the members of the MCU, the governor's—"

Cora wasn't having it. She spoke right over the reporter, the gravel in her voice leaving no room for misinterpretation. "Here's how this works. I'm making a brief introductory statement to tell you why we're here. The governor will give you the details. There'll be no questions at the end, and there'll be no interruptions. Is everyone clear on that?"

The governor stepped forward, placed his hand on Cora's shoulder and gently moved in front of her. He waited until he had everyone's attention. "As most of you know, I campaigned on lowering crime in our state, specifically major crimes. The MCU was my idea and my way of sending a message that corruption of any kind, especially from within the ranks of our own state's government would not be tolerated. Has it been successful? Yes. But that's not to say it hasn't come without cost, both personally and professionally. Eight months ago I not only discovered that Bradley Pearson, my former chief of staff—a man who'd been both a colleague and a friend—was a part of the problem I was trying to fight. When Bradley was killed I discovered that he had betrayed me, betrayed our friendship, and betrayed this office. While the MCU was working with me to fight corruption within our state's government, Bradley was working against me. Doing so led to a series of events that culminated not only in his death, but the death of one of the MCU's finest officers, Ed Donatti.

"Officer Donatti was killed in the line of duty. Period. His family is owed by the state his pension and death benefits, benefits that have been withheld by members of our state's government as a bargaining chip as leverage against me for no other reason than political gain. It is gamesmanship at its worst. While the republican house of our state has been doing everything in their power to withhold the funds due to Ed Donatti's family, tragically, Ed's wife, Pam Donatti was murdered in her own home, leaving a young boy without any family whatsoever. I know that most of you here today already know everything I've just told you. I also know that you're probably aware that an arrest warrant has been issued for Detective Murton Wheeler, a former special agent with the FBI and current member of the MCU." The governor paused for effect, the clicking of camera shutters the only sounds in the room. "Let me be perfectly clear. Detective Wheeler has been framed for the murder of Pam Donatti. The MCU and Metro Homicide have evidence that support this theory, evidence that completely exonerates Detective Wheeler. As such, the warrant for his arrest has been vacated and Detective Wheeler has been taken off administrative leave and will be returning to duty within a matter of a day or two."

The governor glanced at Cora, then he smiled and said, "Perhaps a quick question or two. I think we have the time." The smug, I-told-you-so look back on his face.

Every reporter in the room began shouting questions at him. The governor held up his hands to quiet the reporters. "You'll have to forgive me, I almost forgot. As the murder of Charles Esser is tied directly to the fracking operations down in Shelby County—something I've been against since its inception, by the way—I've ordered the state's attorney general to include that operation as part of the ongoing investigation. As such, the state has filed a motion to halt all drilling procedures down along the Flatrock."

The reporters didn't care about Charlie Esser. That was already yesterday's news. A lover's quarrel gone bad. "What about Martha Esser's murder?" one of the reporters shouted out.

The governor let a mask of confusion cross his face.

This was the part he and Cora had rehearsed before the start of the briefing. "I'm sorry...Martha Esser? I think you're confused—"

Cora leaned over and whispered in the governor's ear, then stepped back. The governor continued. "My apologies. I thought we'd already released this information. Apparently we have not, so I guess you'll hear it here first. Martha Esser wasn't murdered. While an attempt was made on her life, thanks to the heroic efforts of some highly skilled medical personnel she is alive and well, recovering from her injuries. Her attacker tried to kill her in the hospital with a lethal injection of some sort. Fortunately the doctors were able to revive her. Mrs. Esser is cooperating fully and has identified her attacker. The MCU and other agencies are positioning themselves as we speak to apprehend the suspect."

The reporters shouted more questions, but the governor held up his hands, thanked them for their time and walked away.

OUT IN THE HALLWAY: "You're sure the Esser's didn't have any heirs?" the governor asked.

"No kids, and no other blood relatives, Mac," Cora said. "Becky's taking a deeper look, but there's nothing there. Nothing to worry about."

"Good. I'm going to be in enough trouble when the fucking press finds out I just lied about Martha Esser being alive."

"We'll spin it...somehow. And keep your voice down,

for Christ sake. If they hear you call them 'the fucking press' your career will be over."

Becky came around the corner and gave the governor a hug. "Thank you."

The governor hugged her back, his right hand about a half inch too low on her back. "It's my pleasure, Becky. We take care of our own." Then he smiled his thousand watt political smile and said, "My God, I love it when beautiful young women hug me."

Cora looked down the hallway. "Jesus, Mac, let's go, huh?"

CHAPTER TWENTY-SEVEN

Westlake clicked off the television, took out his phone and pressed a button.

"What are you doing?" Gordon said.

"Calling for my ride."

Gordon heard the car doors and looked out the window. "You need two cars? Who are those men? Why are they here?"

Westlake sat down on Gordon's couch like he didn't have a care in the world. It was an act that indicated anything Gordon said or did had little to no consequential value whatsoever. "Have you ever heard the expression 'You win some, you lose some, and some are rained out?'"

Gordon picked up the phone. "I don't understand what's happening here." He picked up the phone but couldn't get a dial tone. His cell phone wasn't on his person.

"Categorically, it covers just about everything, doesn't it? This one looks like a rain-out to me. The governor just said so. The Flatrock's history, but I've won before and I'll win again. You, Kreg, on the other hand, probably won't."

Gordon thought it was time to get the upper hand. He pointed his finger at Westlake. "I want you and these men you've brought here out of my house and off my property."

"Consider it done, Kreg," Westlake said. "Once we've taken care of a few things we'll all be gone. Out of your hair forever, you might say."

The meaning wasn't lost on Gordon. "You won't get away with this."

"Get away with what, Kreg? The fact is, I haven't done one single thing wrong." He paused, then said, "Well, that's not entirely accurate, is it? I've done a number of things wrong. But I haven't done anything illegal. Nothing that can be proven, anyway. I should know. I'm a lawyer." He stood, slipped into his jacket and walked toward the door. "I'm going to leave now, Kreg. I think some very bad things are about to happen here...things that if I were to witness or have direct knowledge of might put me in a rather compromising position. We can't have that now, can we? Historically speaking, the people I work for have never been very forgiving, as I suspect you're about to discover. Maybe. Like I said, I have no direct knowledge of anything." Two well-dressed, hard looking men stepped into the room. They didn't speak or even look at Westlake.

"I have a family," Gordon shouted at him.

Westlake tipped his head just so as if he was going to say something else, but he didn't. Gordon was sitting behind his desk, the heels of his hands pressed tight against his forehead. When Westlake didn't respond, Gordon began to beg. "We can work something out. I'll do whatever you want."

"Take it up with these gentlemen. I don't think they're willing to negotiate, but who knows? I hope you'll forgive me for the lack of introductions. The fact is, I don't even know their names. In any event, your business is with them now. I don't mean to be rude, but I really do have to be on my way."

Westlake turned and walked out of the library. When Westlake stepped out of the room and into the hallway, one of the men pulled out a silenced handgun and shot him in the back of the neck, the cycling action of the weapon louder than the shot itself.

Gordon yelped like a dog, then choked out a noise that was either a laugh or a sob. He did it with relief, his hand over his heart, trying not to hyperventilate. When he could finally speak he was surprised that his voice was an octave higher than normal. The words he spoke spilled from his mouth without control. "Dear God, I thought you were going to shoot me. Did you hear that idiot with his win some lose some bullshit? That's why you needed two cars, right? You're going to put his body in one and, what, take it somewhere and burn it or something? Isn't that how these things get handled?"

"Sometimes, yes," one of the men said. His english was good, his accent vaguely Russian. The gun in his hand hung loosely by the side of his leg. "That is one way it is done. But there are others as well. Do not worry about that right now. You have other problems, my friend." He raised the gun and pointed it at Gordon's head.

Gordon tried to run. He never even made it out of his chair.

DECKER WAS ONLY VAGUELY aware of what the governor was saying on television, but he'd processed enough information to know that he was in serious trouble. He opened the back window, kicked the screen out of its moorings and tumbled awkwardly on the ground. He stayed low and crept along a path that kept his line of sight away from both the other trailer and the front entrance. If he could make it to the back of the trailer park he had a chance. Maybe. There was a wooden privacy fence he could bust through—the fence was absolute shit—and beyond that a shallow ravine with overgrown vegetation that would provide some cover. It wasn't much, but it would have to do. He wouldn't get far on foot...not with his prosthetic leg, that much he knew for certain. He'd have to find a car, and quick.

He stumbled through the ravine, pushing the weeds and brush away from his face as he went, the branches and brittle vines slicing his face and hands with tiny incisions that stung like paper cuts. The going was tough and despite the cold, sweat was already pouring across his face, chest, and down his back. When he reached the end of the ravine he was about a quarter-mile away from the trailer park. He wiped the sweat from his face and his hand came away bloody from all the little cuts. He was surprised by the level of pain. The sweat flowing into the cuts hurt like a bitch. *Pussy*, he thought.

He pushed the discomfort to the back of his brain and tried to think. He needed to concentrate.

The trailer from where they'd been watching him was completely out of his line of sight because of the fence, but the water and sewer truck wasn't. He turned and brought the binoculars up and focused on the park entrance. The men posing as city workers were still there, but something had changed. Another man who Decker had not seen earlier was standing there and it looked like he might be giving direction to the other men.

Decker couldn't tell who it was...his back was turned, but he knew a command presence when he saw one. He was about to lower the binoculars and keep moving when he saw another vehicle pull up and stop by the sewer truck, the entrance to the park now completely blocked off. When the group of men turned to look at the truck, so did the man who'd had his back turned. Murton Wheeler. The same Murton Wheeler who was supposed to be in jail.

And the one who'd just arrived? The one who got out of his truck smiling like he didn't have a care in the world? The one who was keeping him from his boy and his money? It was that fucking cop who didn't know when to quit, Virgil Jones.

He revised his thought process. He wasn't in serious trouble...he was absolutely fucked.

Now what? Decker was so miserable he almost gave up. And he was tired. He was so tired that he thought if he were to lie down he could fall asleep right there in the weeds. It reminded him of all the times his father used to come home drunk and start screaming and shouting at him. It didn't really scared him all that much. It simply made him tired. He never did understand that. Maybe it was his body's way of tuning it all out...by shutting down. Maybe it was more than his body...maybe it was his soul.

Whatever. Enough with the thinking, all ready. Maybe he should simply stand up, wave his arms and start walking their way. When he got close enough he'd pull out his weapon and they'd shoot him down and the whole thing would be over. Suicide by cop. Fuck you very much and goodbye. But the more he thought about it the madder he became. His plans for the boy and the money and every-thing else vanished in an instant, replaced with something primitive, primal. He knew his life was over and it looked like he wouldn't get what he wanted or what he deserved. But Decker never did anything half-assed. He learned that particular lesson the hard way, a long time ago. Thanks, a pant-load Dad, you miserable piece of shit.

If he was going out, he was going to do it on his terms, not theirs. He wasn't going to give up or give in. He was going to fight and make them pay. And he knew exactly how to do it. You don't go after the ones who have hurt you. There was very little satisfaction in that, and it was short-lived. So what do you do? How do you repay the ones who would destroy your life and keep you from your own son? How do you give them a lifetime of pain and suffering and regret? For Decker, the answer was simple.

You go after the ones they love.

―――――――――

When Becky showed up to collect Jonas for the after-noon Sandy led her into the kitchen, out of earshot.

"How's the little guy holding up?" Becky asked.

Sandy didn't answer her right away. She took her time thinking about the past week and everything Jonas had been through. "I think he's doing pretty well, all things considered. The one thing he needs right now more than anything, I think, is some outside stimulation...even if it's only for a day. I'm so grateful that you're willing to do this for us, Becky."

"It's my pleasure. Really. I'm going to take him to the office, so Delroy will be there. That's enough stimulation for anyone."

Sandy laughed, holding her stomach. "I know. He was here with him the other day, last week...the day Pam was killed. They were having a great time together, until that happened, of course. Since Virgil and Murt are out picking up this Decker lunatic and Delroy couldn't get away, I didn't have anyone else I trusted to keep him. Virgil's going to meet me later, either at the doctor's office if he's done in time, or at the bar. Either way, we'll pick him up there when we're finished."

"That sounds fine. Take as long as you need. Besides, if things keep going the way they are with me and Murton, who knows? I might need the practice." Then, Becky saw something that frightened her. "Hey, hey, what is it? You look like you're about to faint. You're as white as a sheet." Sandy had one hand on her stomach and one hand pressed flat against her chest at the base of her throat. "Sandy, are you okay? Is it the baby?"

Sandy swallowed hard and tried to wave it away, but Becky wasn't having it. "Talk to me, Sandy."

"It's nothing. You caught me off guard is all."

"Caught you off guard with what? What are you talking about?"

"What you just said...that whole 'I might need the practice' thing. I think I said almost those exact words to Pam the day I went over to see her. I asked her if I could have Jonas for the night. It was the last time Jonas or I ever saw her alive."

"Ah, jeez, I'm sorry. I didn't know. Maybe you should sit down for a minute or something."

Sandy looked at the clock. "I'm okay. Really. Plus, If I don't get moving I'm going to be late for the doctor. I made that mistake once before." She puffed out her cheeks, then said, "I won't do that again." She walked over to where Jonas was waiting, turned the television off, then helped him into his coat and hat. "You'll be a good boy for Aunt Becky?"

"I want to go with you," Jonas said.

"I know you do, sweetie. But it's just for a few hours, then me and Mr. Virgil will pick you up and we'll all go out to dinner tonight. How's that sound?"

Jonas shrugged. "Okay, I guess."

"Hmm. You don't sound too excited. How about ice cream, too?"

That got her a small smile. "Ice cream *and* cookies?"

"Tell you what...we'll have boaf," Sandy said, already aware of the fact that she was mastering the bribery part of parenting. She kissed him and gave him a hug that lasted so long he got squirmy. When Becky and Jonas walked out the door, Sandy stood on the porch and watched them until they turned out on the road and were out of sight. All she could think of was the message Mason had given Virgil over a week ago.

Everything matters...

Then her phone rang and her schedule changed. The call was so matter of fact she didn't give it any more attention than it deserved. But still, it changed everything.

CHAPTER TWENTY-EIGHT

Virgil and Murton moved around to the public side of the water and sewer truck, out of sight of the park entrance. They leaned against the side of the vehicle with the rest of the entry team, all of them now relying on the trooper in the stake-out trailer for observation reports.

The SWAT commander was going over the entry plan with everyone when Virgil's phone buzzed at him. Sandy. He stepped away to answer. He didn't need the hard details of the entry—SWAT would handle that by themselves. Virgil and Murton were there only for the official arrest and to provide transportation...or to assist in a chase if necessary, though that was unlikely given everything they already knew about Decker.

"Hey baby. I'm not interrupting, am I?"

"Not at all. You know I wouldn't answer if you were."

"Is that right?"

"Well, yeah," Virgil said. "You know how hard it is to

shoot and run at the same time. Throw a phone call into that mix and I'd be dusted."

Sandy chuffed. "Virgil, I've seen you shoot standing still. If you try to shoot *and* run that would probably be defined as a public health hazard. Someone should report you."

He smiled through the phone. Virgil was an excellent shot and Sandy knew it. A master marksman herself, she'd improved his technique over the last two years by spending time with him at the range. They both enjoyed it tremendously, blasting away at the paper targets. "I see the pregnancy hasn't affected your sense of humor. If you were any funnier I'd probably wet myself. Seriously though, we're about to grab Decker. The briefing is happening right now. Is everything okay?"

"Everything is fine, baby. Just wanted to let you know that I got a call from the doc's office. She had to run to the hospital and cover for another O.B. I guess she's handling some sort of emergency—which I don't even want to think about—so my appointment is going to be delayed."

Virgil was relieved. He'd felt sort of rushed and now he could take his time. "Did they say how long?"

"She's already on her way back, but now she's about an hour behind schedule. Just wanted to let you know."

The SWAT commander caught Virgil's eye, his palms turned upward in a 'what gives' gesture. Virgil ignored him. This was his show and SWAT could wait. Decker wasn't going anywhere. "Tell you what, Baby, I think the timing will work out. We'll just arrest him slow." Virgil strung the vowel out on the word 'slow.'

"Virgil?"

"Yes?"

"Don't do that."

He smiled into the phone. "I'll meet you there. Sound good?"

"That'd be great. Becky has Jonas at the office. I told her we'd pick him up after the appointment."

"All right, then. I'll see you when I see you."

"Hey, Virg?"

"Yeah, baby?"

"Be careful."

"Always. Besides, nothing's going to happen to me. I'm surrounded by cops."

Had Virgil known the way things were going to turn out, he would have told Sandy he loved her. No, that's not quite right...had he known how things were going to turn out, he would have dropped everything and gone straight home.

———————

AFTER DECKER GOT clear of the trailer park he ran as well as he could with his bad leg. It pissed him off, the leg. They had Olympic runners with prosthetics competing in sprints and marathon races, yet he found himself hobbling along like a lame horse in desperate need of an emergency farrier and some equine hoof care. That's what's wrong with the entire half-assed country, he thought. A champion athlete gets the best of the best and goes on to fame and fortune. Lose part of your leg in combat with the rag-heads fighting for your country's freedom and you get an ill-fitted piece of shit from the

V.A., one that in all likelihood Captain Ahab would have tossed back into the sea.

He passed by a small nondescript warehouse of some sort and found that it backed up to a quiet residential area. He cut through a back yard and wound up on a street that ended with a cul-de-sac at the ass end. The houses were modest, built sometime in the late seventies or early eighties, he thought. The trees were mature, the streets needed repaved, and the sidewalks were buckled here and there, but overall it seemed nice enough. He didn't see any bicycles or basketball hoops in the driveways, which meant an older demographic, and that was good for what he needed.

It was almost exactly the type of neighborhood where he'd lived before his bitch wife gave him the boot over a year ago, forcing him into poverty, despair, and the dump where, he suddenly realized, he'd never be able to go back to. It might have been a dump, but it was *his* dump. The thought of it depressed him to no end. It also deepened his resolve for revenge against the cops, one cop in particular.

He moved toward the end of the street and made his way back between two of the houses at the end of the cul-de-sac and noticed an elderly woman in one of the back-yards. She wore an ugly purple parka that went down to her knees and rubber boots that met up with the bottom of her jacket. She had a small bag of birdseed and was filling a feeder as he came up behind her.

Decker was a mess and knew it, so he did the only logical thing he could think of. He played the hand he had. "Excuse me, Ma'am?"

The woman turned, saw his face and hands, the cuts and dried blood from his mad dash through the ditch and dropped the bag of seed. It landed with a dull thud and the seed spilled everywhere. She made no sound, put her hands to her face...not out of fear, but surprise. "Oh dear," she said. Decker didn't know if her statement was about him or the bag of seed that had spilled across the ground, or both.

He thought the woman must have been at least eighty. Perfect, he thought. Then he remembered the struggle he'd had with the Esser bitch and remind himself to be careful. He put a little whine in his voice. "I'm sorry if I've startled you. There's been...I mean, I've been in an accident. May I use your phone? Mine was broken in the crash."

"Oh dear," she said again. She looked at her house, then back at Decker.

"I understand your concern. You can't be too careful these days. I can wait out here if you like. Maybe I could sit down? Would that be all right?"

The woman turned and looked at her house again. "I don't have a cell phone, the buttons are too small. My phone is mounted on the wall. Your face...did you go through the windshield?"

Decker touched his face with a dramatic wince. "No, but I smashed it pretty hard. It cracked the glass. I guess that's how I got all these cuts. I'm not feeling too well. Could I maybe get a drink from your hose over there?" He limped a few steps in that direction.

"Is your leg injured as well?"

Decker shook his head and pulled the bottom of his pant leg up. He put a sad look on his face and simply said, "The war."

That did the trick. He knew he was good to go when he heard the magic words: "Thank you for your service."

What a crock of shit, he thought. Every time some idiot thanked him for his service he wanted to remove his prosthetic leg and beat them to death. "Just doing my job, ma'am. Protecting our country."

"Come on in. The phone is right here in the kitchen," she said as she led him inside. "Maybe we should call an ambulance. You don't look well at all."

"I think you might be right. In fact, I feel like I'm about to pass out. Maybe your husband could drive me to the hospital? I hate to ask."

"Oh, no dear. He's been gone for almost eight years now. I'm all alone."

Then something about him changed and she must have seen it in his eyes because she started to tremble, first in her hands, then both her arms. Before long her entire body was shaking like she was about to have a seizure. Decker just stood there and watched it happen. Watched her realize that she'd reached her end.

"Please. I have grandchildren. My daughter lives right next door. The keys are on the hook. The car is in the garage. I don't have any money in the house." She was moving toward the phone that was mounted on the wall. It had giant buttons. One was labeled 'emergency.' "Please don't—"

Decker ripped the phone from the wall then grabbed the old woman by the back of her neck and smashed her face on the edge of the kitchen counter. She dropped to the floor with the same dull thud as the bag of seed.

God, people are stupid, he thought. She mentioned money. He'd need some. She had a stash hidden somewhere or she wouldn't have tried to convince him she didn't. It took him about three minutes to find it. Old coffee can, middle shelf of the pantry, next to a bag of flour and a jar of peanut butter. A small bundle of fifties and twenties. He rifled through it and put the amount close to three-hundred bucks. Good enough for gas and grub. Maybe a night in a cheap motel if things got that far. He wasn't sure they would. The thought of food made him realize he'd not eaten since yesterday. He was suddenly starving. He stepped over her body, opened the fridge, made himself a ham salad sandwich—delicious—and ate it over the sink like he did at home.

He looked at the old woman and realized he felt nothing at all for her. Everyone goes sooner or later.

He washed his face in the bathroom sink and checked himself in the mirror. The cuts were minor and the bleeding had stopped. He looked a little rough, but that was okay. The rougher you looked, the less shit anyone gave you. Time to boogie. He didn't know if the bit about the daughter next door was true or not and he wasn't going to wait around to find out. The cops would have a perimeter up soon—if they didn't already—and he needed to be outside that circle when it was established. He grabbed the keys, went to the garage and found a mid-nineties Lincoln Continental, a huge four door boat of an automobile. He backed the car out of the garage, hit the button to close the overhead door and sailed down the street, the boat floating through the curves like a ship at sea.

What was it he'd thought all those months ago at the cop's funeral? Oh yeah...Hell of a storm coming.

Not exactly the way he would have predicted it, but here it was. Here he was...running hard.

Headed for his boy...

———

THE SWAT COMMANDER, an ex-marine sergeant and fifteen year veteran named Jon Mok gave Virgil the tiniest bit of shit. "We try not to take personal calls in the middle of our briefings."

He and Mok had known each other for years and got along well. "Blow me, Jughead." Virgil said.

Mok laughed. "It's Jarhead. God you Army wipes are all the same. I'll let the 'blow me' comment slide though. I remember what it was like when my wife was pregnant."

That got a laugh from everyone then Mok got serious. "Okay, strip out of those costumes. It's time to rock and roll."

The team began to remove their water and sewer coveralls as Mok continued with his instructions. "Jonesy, we're all armored up and we do this for a living. You and Murt don't. So you'll let us make the entry, take him down and cuff him. After that he's yours. Until then, hang back, okay? Nine times of out ten these things go down like clockwork. But that means one time out of ten they go to shitsville on a sled. So stay back and stay out of sight. If I see you before I call for you, I'll shoot you myself."

Virgil started to protest, but Murton interrupted. "Don't worry, Gunny, we'll stay put."

"See that you do," Mok said, his expression stiff and serious. Then, with a little light in his eyes: "Say, what's Robert have on the menu tonight?"

"I don't know," Virgil said dryly. "I'd call and find out, but no personal calls while you guys are working."

Mok frowned at him, gave a hand signal to his men and they fanned out and began their approach to the trailer.

Sixty seconds later it was over.

And just getting started...

CHAPTER TWENTY-NINE

Virgil was hot and didn't care who saw it or how it looked. They were standing outside Decker's trailer, which was empty. Andrew Ross, the young ISP Trooper who'd been watching him was dumbfounded. "I'm telling you, he was just there. I saw him moving around inside."

"Well, he's not there now, is he, Ross? It was your fucking job to keep him in sight and inform us of his movements. But you didn't do that, did you?"

"Sir, I don't know what happened. I never took my eyes off that trailer. His car is still there. He didn't go out the front or side doors. If he's on foot he couldn't have gotten far."

"I told you last week to show me what you've got. If this is it, you'd better make sure you don't lose your fucking ticket book. You'll be on patrol for a while. Quite a while."

Most of the SWAT team members were looking away, their discomfort growing by the second. Mok came out of the trailer and walked up to Virgil. "Looks like your man Decker climbed out the back window. Take it easy on the kid, will you? The line of sight was bad. Two of my guys followed Decker's path to the back of the park. He punched through a wooden privacy fence and took off through the weeds. You can see the trail he left."

Virgil nodded to Mok. "All right. Get everyone out until we can get the crime scene techs over here to start bagging evidence." He then turned and looked at Ross. "Now Decker's either holed up with hostages or he's stolen a car and is on the run, or both."

"Sir, I—"

Virgil had calmed...a little. "Ross, don't speak, okay? Just listen. Get on the radio and a get a perimeter set up. I want this area flooded with patrol cars. Right now."

"Yes, sir." Ross turned away and began speaking rapidly over the radio.

Murton walked over. Virgil looked at him and said, "What?"

"Little harsh on the kid, weren't you?"

"Yeah, yeah. You know who's fault it is? It's mine. We should have taken him sooner like you wanted to. Instead we sat on him and didn't get any substantial evidence in the process. Then we rolled up here like we didn't have a care in the world and all the while we knew Decker was good for at least one killing...Martha Esser, and probably good for Pam's as well. I should have had that trailer covered better. Should have had more men out here."

"Maybe," Murton said. "But then he might have spotted them. More men means more visibility. If that would've happened we'd be in the same boat we're in now. Relax, Jonesy. We'll get him."

Virgil turned and began to walk away. "Hey, where you going?" Murton said.

"Can't do anything here. Sandy has an appointment with her O.B. doc. I'm going to take her. You good to work the trailer?"

Murton nodded. "Yeah. I'm gonna go walk the path that he took first. See if I see anything."

"Well hell, go ahead. One more set of eyes won't matter much though."

"Probably right. I'll come back and tear into this shit hole when I'm done. Good luck at the doc's. Tell Small I said hey."

"Call me if you get anything."

Murton waved him off. "Yeah, yeah, go be a dad. I've got this."

———

BEFORE HE LEFT, Virgil walked over to the other trailer. "I've got the perimeter set up six blocks out. SWAT is going to help. We'll have patrol cars going door to door," Ross said. He was in the middle of packing up his gear. "I'm going to help with the search as soon as I'm squared away here."

"Sounds like you've got it covered, then. Listen, I shouldn't have jumped on you like that and I'm sorry. I'd like you to forget everything I said back there. It wasn't your fault. It was mine. We should have had more men out here. You did the best you could with what you had."

Ross looked relieved. "These trailers, the way they sit angled in here...it never occurred to me that he might slip out a back window. I thought we were good, but he must have made me somehow."

"Forget it. I got my Amygdala hijacked there for a minute is all." Virgil was looking at Ross's equipment. He had a sniper rifle mounted on a tripod that rested on a table, the barrel pointed at the window. "You any good with that thing?"

Ross shrugged. "I'm the guy they usually call when they need somebody on a rooftop. Doesn't happen too often, but when it does..."

Virgil was interested. The sniper rifle was a pure killing machine. "How many?"

"I don't keep a running total in my head." Ross let his eyelids slide down to half-mast, then said, "I've got a little log going in the back of my ticket book though, if you're that interested."

Virgil grinned at him. "Really, I'm sorry. I was out of line. Come see me when this is over. We'll talk about your future if you want to."

"I'll think about it," Ross said. He was smiling when he said it though.

DECKER MADE it through the perimeter, but the old lady's fridge and the spur-of-the-moment ham salad sandwich had almost cost him. He turned left out of the cul-de-sac, went south for two blocks, made a quick right and saw the first patrol car coming in hard, its light bar flashing, its siren off. He kept his speed down and his eyes straight ahead. He made a few more turns, gradually working his way to the Southwest, and saw three more cop cars before they started to thin out.

Five minutes later he was far enough away from the residential area he felt safe. He got on one of the main streets that would take him out to 465, hit the ramp and was lost in the six lane madness of metal circling the city. He was headed south, the Continental gliding along effortlessly. The airport drifted by on his right, and a few minutes later the highway made a bend to the left and he was headed east on the giant loop at the southern end of the city. He'd take highway 37 south for a few miles, out into the country. There was a little side road off 37 to the left, further to the East, and then he'd be there.

He thought the Jones bitch probably had his boy at her house. If not, he'd try that stupid bar they owned next. He wouldn't have to worry about her husband, the cop. He was busy looking for him...in all the wrong places.

SANDY HAD some downtime before she had to leave for her appointment. She set the alarm on her phone as a reminder then thought through the different things she could do with the gap in her schedule. She was exhausted, but the house needed cleaning—Jonas had demonstrated the effects a young child could have on the cleanliness of a household. There was also grocery shopping, laundry, bills to be paid, insurance forms for their upcoming hospital visit for Wyatt's delivery, paperwork for her extended leave from work, funeral arrangements for Pam once her body was released by the coroner, and on and on and on. She sat on the couch in the living room and ran the list through her head. It was, she thought, a little like counting sheep.

She leaned her head back and closed her eyes. Two minutes later she was asleep.

CHAPTER THIRTY

C ool was buttoning up the engine cover on the Jet-Ranger when Bell walked up and introduced himself. He wiped his palms on a shop rag then shook hands with Bell. "I spoke with Virgil a few days ago. He told me you might stop by."

"Virgil's good people. From what he said it sounds like you are too. I really appreciate the time."

"No problem," Cool said. "How can I help you?"

"What I'm looking for is guidance. I want to learn how to fly helicopters. Take flight lessons, do the ground school, the whole bit. The problem is, I don't know what I don't know. There are a bunch of different places I could start, but I want the best, not something like Chuck's Discount Chopper lessons."

Cool laughed. "Yeah, Virgil told me you had the bug. I know what you mean, about the schools. I learned in the service, but I know a couple of places I wouldn't hesitate to recommend. These guys do it right. And by right, I mean exactly that. If you don't cut the mustard, they'll drop you from the program and do it with a smile on their face. It's not about the money for them, it's about safety. Plus, they don't want or need the liability."

"That's exactly the kind of thing I'm looking for."

"And speaking of money, I've got to tell you, it's pretty expensive. There are minimum requirements for flight time, both dual instruction—that's when you have the instructor with you in the aircraft—and solo flights by your-self once you're ready. So there's that, but as far as expense goes, a lot of it is based on your ability...how quick you catch on. Some guys take to it like a duck to water. Others... not so much. They need extra time. You should budget at least twenty grand. If you turn out to be a duck, you'll spend a little less. If you can't quack, you'll spend more."

"Twenty grand is doable. I'm a doctor, so I can afford it."

Cool's face turned a little red. "Maybe I should have used a different analogy...the quack thing. I didn't know you were a doctor."

Bell smiled at him "No problem. I've been called worse."

"You didn't blink when I said twenty-K. Maybe I should have been a doctor."

"Do you love what you do?"

Cool didn't hesitate. "Absolutely."

"Then you made the right choice. Money isn't everything."

"That's true enough," Cool agreed.

"The main thing is, I'm single, so I don't need anyone's permission."

Cool pointed a finger at him. "That's a big step right there." Then he chuckled a bit and said, "I heard you sort of had to talk Sandy into it though."

"Wow. You got the whole story, huh?"

"Sure did. She's just worried about you."

"I know. And I love her for it. But I'm going to do it, no matter."

"You know, there's an old saying: Doctors and lawyers make the worst pilots."

"Why is that?"

"Mostly because it's true," Cool said, suddenly serious. "As a group, or groups I guess you'd say, they're control freaks, right down to their core."

"And pilots aren't?" Bell said, a little skepticism creeping into his voice.

"Oh we absolutely are. There's no question about it. But that's our job. We're not flying around thinking about a patient or a lawsuit or whatever, we're thinking about flying. Doctors and lawyers have lots of money, so they take their lessons, get their license, buy a plane or helicopter and half the time end up flying the damned thing right into the ground. Pure pilot error. Why? Because they're thinking about a patient or a client or something when they should be focusing on piloting their craft. They've done studies on it...the FAA."

"That does make sense. I'm all but retired from my practice, so I think I'll be okay. Something to think about, anyway. And I will."

Cool had the impression he would...think about it. "Well, you've got the name for it anyway...Bell. As in Bell Jet Ranger."

Bell grinned at him. "It sounds ridiculous, but that's one of the things that got me started on all of this. It's like a little seed got planted. The more I thought about it the more I couldn't quit thinking about it. I guess the seed sprouted and well, here I am."

Cool shook his head. "Not silly at all. I knew a pilot once...his name—and I'm not making this up—was Larry Landing."

Bell nodded. "Same here. I met a guy years ago, back in med school. His last name was Doctor. He's got a practice up north now. I mean, with a name like that, what else are you going to do for a living? Sell used cars? You'd never live it down. Every day some schmuck would come up to you and say something like, 'You know, with a name like that, you should have been a doctor.' Who wants to hear that their entire life?"

Cool scratched at the back of his head. "You know, now that I think about it, I went to a dentist once whose last name was Molar...

So they talked about it, flying, and funny names and careers and life. Cool gave him the names of a couple of instructors he trusted, then told him, "Just remember, pick your school based on the instructor, not the school itself. It's better to have a good instructor at a lesser known school, than a bad instructor at an otherwise great school. Find someone you like and stick with them."

Bell took the names, thanked Cool for his time and told him he'd let him get back to work.

"No problem. It's been pleasure talking with you." Then, almost as an afterthought, Cool said, "Do you have anyplace you need to be for the next hour or so?"

Bell shook his head and waved the piece of paper Cool had given him. "Not really. I was going to go home and research these names. Why?"

He smacked the side of the Jet-Ranger with his palm. "Because I just changed the oil and I've got to take it up for a test flight. I need three take-offs and landings, and about an hour of total flight time. You're welcome to ride along if you like."

"Are you kidding me? Let me get my bag and I'll be ready to go!"

"Your bag? What for?"

"Old habit. I never go anywhere without it. A doctor without his bag is like a pilot without his wings." Bell went back to his car and got his bag while Cool pulled the helicopter out of the hangar. He waited for Bell, then did a full preflight inspection. He talked him through everything he was doing and explained why he did it. A few minutes later they were strapped in and Bell watched with fascination as Cool began running the checklists and flipping switches. The main rotor began to spin up slowly, and as it did, Bell turned around in his seat and looked at the back of the cabin.

"What is it?" Cool asked.

Bell turned back. "Is it just me, or does it smell like fish in here?" When he saw the look on Cool's face he laughed and said, "Virgil told me to say that." They both laughed.

"Well, I don't know what kind of pilot you'll make, but you've got the sense of humor for it."

Bell couldn't remember the last time he was this excited. He felt like a teenager who about to get laid for the first time. "That's another reason I want to do this. I'm tired of being so stuffy all the damned time. If you're a doc, it's sort of expected from you. It's like no one will take you seriously unless you've got a stick up your ass. But this...this is a whole other world." He rubbed his hands together then slapped Cool on the thigh and said, "Come on, let's launch this motherfucker."

WHEN MOLLY JACOBS looked out her kitchen window she saw something that simply didn't make sense. It was her mother's Lincoln Continental driving away from the house. There were two things wrong with what she saw: One, her mother's eyesight had deteriorated to the point where she could no longer drive—she'd lost her license over a year ago, and two, it was the way the car was being driven. It wasn't exactly reckless, but it was...aggressive. Even when her mother had still been able to drive, she drove, well...like a little old lady.

Did her mother lend the car to someone? It was possible, but not likely. Even if she had, it was the kind of thing they would have talked about. They talked about everything. Something didn't feel right.

Molly grabbed her jacket and hurried next door.

ONE OF THE SWAT team members, a guy named Leach, was showing Murton the trail through the weeds on the opposite side of the fence. Murton looked around trying to get into Decker's head. With all the time he'd spent working undercover for the FBI, it was something he was fairly good at.

"What are you doing?"

"Trying to be Decker. I discover I'm being surveilled and I've just climbed out of my own back window—probably in full panic mode—then busted through the fence and crawled through a ditch full of weeds to get away. Where do I go from here?"

The SWAT guy named Leach looked around. "Need wheels." He pointed to his right and said, "Closest residential area is right over there, just past that tree line."

"Lets go check it out. Ever catch any shit about your last name?"

Leach gave him a look. "Not too much. Once or twice a year, maybe, when being introduced to someone or something like that. If they're an asshole they might say something or get a look on their face...you can always tell. Then they find out I'm SWAT and suddenly it all goes away and they want to be best friends."

Murton was nodding. "I hear you."

They moved through the tree line—a single row of densely packed Arborvitaes that separated the trailer park from the back lot of a warehouse. When they got to the far side of the warehouse they passed through a residential backyard and ended up in the middle of the street. To the left was an intersection with a four-way stop. A patrol car was sitting at the intersection and the officer who'd been driving it was standing on the front porch of a house close to the intersection, speaking with a man dressed in a bathrobe and slippers, a cup of coffee in his hand. The man pointed with his cup and the cop turned and looked at

Murton and Leach. He keyed the microphone attached to the upper part of his vest and said, "Starting the door-to-door." Murton heard it come through on the SWAT frequency.

They waved to the cop, looked around for a moment and were about to turn and go back to the trailer when a woman came running out of a house at the end of the cul-de-sac. She was screaming something—Murton didn't know what—and pulling at the hair on both sides of her head. She stopped, doubled over like she'd just been punched in the gut, then began screaming again. She stood upright then spun in a full circle, still screaming, like she was having some kind of fit. Then she stopped and collapsed backward on the ground, smacking the back of her head on the pavement.

"What the hell?" Leach said.

Murton ran toward her, his gun drawn. "Cover the back of that house," he yelled to Leach. "And get that other cop down here."

The last part of his instruction wasn't necessary. The cop was already running their way.

———————

DECKER TURNED off of highway 37 to the East, down an unmarked gravel road that snaked its way along a dry creek bed and skirted the edge of a large wooded area. Once he was past the woods he saw the house. It was a modern looking log cabin style home that sat about a quarter-mile back from the road. The road curved just enough that he could see a large shed and a pond in the back yard. He'd

seen it all before of course, when he'd done his reconnoiter-
ing, but that had been in the middle of the night. Now, in
full daylight, he could see all the details of the property. He
wasn't very familiar with acreage and how it was calculated, but he guessed the cop was sitting on at least twenty
acres...maybe more. Where'd he get the money for this type
of setup? Why did everyone seem to have it so easy
except him?

That was about to change. He'd go in and grab the
boy...his boy, and get the hell out of Dodge. They'd have to
leave the country, probably go to Mexico, he thought. Then
what? How was he going to get the pension money? He'd
have to lean on Gordon to make that happen. He had
enough dirt on him that he'd have to pay. Either that or end
up in jail. He knew all about the back-room dealings and
under-the-table money that had changed hands between
him and Westlake and the Russian oil men.

But what if Gordon wouldn't pay? Then what? Could
he sell the kid to the Mexicans? It wouldn't be as much as
the pension fund money, but it'd be something. Enough to
hold him over until he figured out his next step. Whatever.
One step at a time. Right now he needed to get the boy and
get gone.

He turned into the cop's driveway and rolled up on
the house.

CHAPTER THIRTY-ONE

The impact of Molly Jacobs' head against the pavement when she fainted would have been much worse were it not for the hood of her jacket. The coat was a thick, heavy parka and the hood itself had a pocket for storage of mittens, scarves, gloves and the like. Molly had packed the hood full last spring—a convenient storage place —and had yet to unpack it for the upcoming winter. When she fell, it was like having a giant pillow on the back of her head. So the impact didn't render her unconscious, but it dazed her. It was still, she'd later admit, one hell of a knock.

Murton got down next to her and quickly checked her over. Other than the bump on her head, she appeared to be uninjured. She tried to get up, but he persuaded her to remain on the ground. She was crying, her gaze going back and forth between Murton, his gun, and her mother's house.

"Why do you have a gun? Who are you," she asked.

"My name is Murton Wheeler. I'm a police officer. You're safe."

"My mother...I need to get up. Can I at least sit up?"

Murton scooted back and made room, then gently pulled her into a sitting position. Her legs were splayed like a doll left on the living room floor. "What about your mother?"

"She's...she's...someone attacked her or something." She started crying again. "Her face is smashed in. There's blood everywhere." She grabbed Murton's arm and the strength of her grip surprised him. "You've got to call an ambulance. She might still be alive."

The city cop who'd been doing the door-to-door jogged down to the end of the driveway just in time to hear Molly's last statement. When Murton glanced at him, he shook his head.

"An ambulance is already on the way," Murton said. "What's your name?"

"My name is Molly Jacobs. My mother is Mary Budman. That's her house," she said, pointing behind herself.

"Tell me what happened," Murton said, although he already had a pretty good idea. "What happened to your mother?"

"I don't know what happened. I saw her car speeding out of the driveway. She doesn't drive anymore and my father has been gone for years—heart attack—and when I went over to check on her I found her lying on the kitchen floor all bloody. Her face...it looks like someone hit her with a sledgehammer. If I didn't know who she was I don't think

I would have recognized her." She gripped Murton's arm tighter. "Where's the ambulance? Why is it taking so long?"

She was in shock and Murton knew it. He turned his back so she couldn't see and looked at the city cop. He raised his eyebrows and slowly mouthed the words 'you sure?' to him. The cop nodded, lowered his eyes and mouthed either yes, yeah or yep, Murton wasn't sure which. But there was no question, Mary Budman, mother of Molly Jacobs was dead.

He placed both hands on Molly's cheeks and gently turned her face toward him. "Ms. Jacobs, I need to speak with this officer for a moment. I'll only be a few seconds. Please stay right here. Can you do that for me?"

Molly nodded, then wiped the snot and spit from her chin. Murton stood, wiped his palms on his pants and tipped his head at the city cop. They stepped a few feet away.

"Victim's in the kitchen," the city cop said. "Blood everywhere. Looks like one massive blow to the face. There's quite a bit of blood on the edge of the countertop, like maybe he had her by the neck and face-planted her. I checked for a pulse, but it wasn't necessary. She's gone. I backed straight out. The SWAT guy is still guarding the rear of the house. It feels empty."

"Okay, good work. Wait right here for a minute." Murton turned and went back to Molly. "Ms. Jacobs, you said you saw your mother's car speeding away?"

"Yes. That's what got my attention. I just happened to be looking out the window and I saw it shooting out of the drive. My mother doesn't drive anymore...her eyes are bad. Someone stole it, didn't they? If she were going to lend it to someone, she'd have told me. We talk about everything."

"What kind of car is it?"

"What? I don't care about the car. Where's the ambulance?"

"Ms. Jacobs, we need to know the make and model of the car. The color too. How long ago did you see the car leave?"

Molly again pulled her hair at the sides of her head, her eyes closed so tight her teeth were showing. "It's a dark green Lincoln Continental. I don't know the year. It's old. Late nineties, I think. It was about ten minutes ago. *Is the ambulance coming or not?*"

Murton looked at the cop. The cop nodded at him, then began walking away, relaying the information about the car over the radio.

Molly Jacobs stood suddenly and tried to run toward the house. The city cop heard, then saw her coming. He did a little juke and cut her off. Murton was there two seconds later.

"I need to get inside. I need to get to my mom."

Murton tipped his head, his mouth a thin line. "Ms. Jacobs, I'm sorry, but your mother didn't survive. She's gone. Come on, lets go over here, out of the street. We can't let you go back inside right now."

Two more City patrol cars turned the corner and pulled right up next to Mary Budman's driveway.

"That's right, right over here," Murton said as he steered her toward one of the cruisers. One of the city cops opened the front passenger door and they helped Molly inside. When the door was closed, Murton looked at the cop. "Her mother is the victim. Keep her here." He then ran to the back yard and told Leach they needed the house cleared.

Five minutes later they were back out. Except for the victim the house was empty. The city cop told him that a BOLO had been put out on the Continental. Murton did a little quick math in his head. With at least a fifteen minute head start a perimeter was out of the question. All they could do for the moment was hope that the car was spotted. He got everyone squared away and up to speed, then headed back to Decker's trailer.

SANDY WAS HOVERING in the stage of sleep that left her not fully out, but not fully there, either. A dreamy nowhere land where bills and laundry and insurance forms and to-do lists were forgotten, replaced by images of a family that was taking shape all around her. She had the man of her dreams, a man who, with her help, was going to raise two fine boys into strong young men. Wyatt and Jonas were going to be just like Virgil and Murton. It was fate, no different from the fate that had brought her and Virgil together.

Had there been adversity along the way? Tragedy? Yes, but things happen...*life* happens. They'd face their own challenges in the years ahead, but they'd do it together and they'd do it with hearts that were full of hope and joy and laughter and love. Sandy, floating along in her dreamy netherworld, had never been happier. When her cell phone rang it brought her part of the way back. When the house phone rang a few seconds later she was almost up.

In her half-sleep state she heard the car pull into the drive and stop by the front of the house. She rubbed her eyes with the heels of her hands and thought...*Virgil*. She may have even said it out loud. Then the front door exploded inward and shards of glass and wood fragments flew through the air. Sandy was suddenly no longer just thinking her husband's name, she was screaming it. Except Virgil wasn't there.

Decker was.

MOK STEPPED out of Decker's trailer just as Murton returned. "You're going to want to see this."

They went inside the trailer and made their way to the rear. There were two bedrooms at the end of the hall. One was obviously Decker's bedroom. Murton was surprised by the neatness of the room. The bed was made, the pillows squared, and the personal items on the dresser were arranged with precision. Other than the open window and torn screen, the room was in perfect condition. "Huh."

"Huh, what?" Mok said.

"I don't know. Everything we have on this guy suggests he's a nut. I was expecting the place to be trashed...you know, clothes on the floor, no sheets on the bed, that sort of thing."

"He's military. It gets wired into your brain. He doesn't know how to do it any other way. But don't worry, you're not too far off. This isn't the room I wanted you to see. Follow me."

They stepped out of the bedroom and backtracked down the hallway a few feet. Mok opened the door to the other bedroom and stood back to let Murton enter first. "Here's your nut," Mok said.

Murton looked around with dismay. The room instantly unnerved him. There was no furniture at all...just four walls and a dirty laminate floor. Except every inch of all four walls were covered with photographs of various sizes. There were so many that they overlapped each other. Some were color, others black and white. Most looked like they'd been taken from a distance with a powerful lens. Others looked like they were shot up close, the subjects slightly blurred and always in profile, as if they had no idea their image had been captured as they walked by the photographer. But it wasn't the photography itself that unnerved Murton. It was the subjects in the photos. Most of them were shots of Jonas Donatti. A few of them featured Pam and Jonas together. In each of those photos, Decker had either scratched Pam's face out, or colored over it with a black marker. "Jesus," he whispered.

"That's the Donatti kid, isn't it?" Mok said.

"Yeah. And his mother, Pam."

"Step a little further into the room."

Murton looked at Mok. "Why?"

"Because Decker is on the run and there's something else you need to see and see right now."

Murton moved into the center of the room. Mok followed him in, closed the door, then shined his tactical light on the back of the door. When Murton saw the photos on the back of the door he yanked it open and ran from the trailer, dialing his phone as he went. He made it outside and began running toward his vehicle at the end of the street. When Sandy didn't answer her cell, he tried her home number. When that failed he dialed another number.

When Virgil answered he sounded happy, like he didn't have a care in the world.

CHAPTER THIRTY-TWO

Decker felt like he was moving at light speed, like there was a pressure wave pushing him forward, clearing obstacles from his path, leaving nothing except destruction and devastation in his wake. He felt like nothing could stop him now. He ran up the steps, pulled out his pistol and fired three quick shots at the deadbolt, then kicked the door in.

Glass and wood flew everywhere and even though the gunshots left his ears ringing, he heard, then saw the Jones bitch on the sofa. He saw her turn and face him, heard her scream something he couldn't quite make out. The sofa was about six steps into the room from the front door. He'd already covered half of that, the pressure wave carrying him forward when the bitch stopped screaming. She stood from the sofa and darted to the end. She was going to try and run for it, which, Decker thought, was foolish because he had the gun and she looked like a whale, her stomach bigger than that fat fuck of an old man that used to beat him down at every opportunity.

But then something happened he didn't expect. Decker discovered he wasn't going up against a whale.

He was taking on a tiger.

Virgil's phone buzzed at him and Murton's name popped up on the nav display. He hit the green button on the steering wheel to answer the call, enjoying all the conveniences of modern technology. "Hey Murt. You guys track him down yet?" He was speaking of Decker.

Dear God, I hope not, Murton thought. "Virgil, where are you?"

The sound of Murton's siren came through over the cell phone and Virgil was instantly worried. But it wasn't the sound of the siren. Murton had called him by his proper name, something he only did when he needed Virgil's full attention or when something was seriously wrong. "I'm on my way to the doc's office. I'm meeting Sandy there. What's the matter?"

"Where's Sandy?"

"Should be on her way. Murt, what's going on? I can hear it in your voice."

"I just tried to call her. Cell and landline. She's not answering."

"She might be driving. She doesn't like to—"

"Virgil, shut up. Listen...Decker is still on the loose. We found hundreds, hell maybe thousands of photographs in his trailer. Most of them were of Jonas, or of Jonas and Pam together. All the ones with the two of them together had Pam's face scratched or blacked out. But there were a lot...*a lot*, Virgil, of Sandy and Jonas together. This guy's done his recon. I think he's making a run for Jonas. If he thinks Jonas is with Sandy..."

Virgil felt his heart sink. His breathing became rapid and shallow. He hit the switch for his lights and siren, then made a U-turn in the middle of an intersection, his tires squealing in protest. A car swerved to avoid him and sideswiped a telephone pole before running down in the ditch. "Murt—"

"I'm on my way, brother. How far out are you?"

"I'm fifteen minutes at best. You?"

"I'm a little closer than that. I'll probably beat you there."

"Don't bet on it. If that motherfucker—"

"Bury it, Jones-man. You push it down and bury it. Get those thoughts out of your head, you hear me? Concentrate on your driving. We'll get to her. She's going to be fine. Jonesy?"

———

SANDY WAS YOUNG, in shape, in the prime of her life, and as a police officer had years of advanced hand-to-hand tactical combat training. She knew how to fight and she knew how to disarm an adversary with moves that often left them wondering if they'd ever had a weapon in their hand to begin with.

She was also exhausted, eight months pregnant and carrying over thirty extra pounds. The extra weight threw off her balance and her center of gravity left her unable to maneuver in any sort of meaningful way that might give her an advantage over her attacker. In short, she only had two things working in her favor: A mother's instinct to protect her child and the element of surprise.

She waited until Decker was about six feet away. She moved to the end of the couch like she was going to try to make a run for it, then stopped, grabbed a table lamp by its base, yanked the cord free from the outlet and flung it at Decker's head. He raised his hand to block the lamp and Sandy followed with the only other thing on the table, a hardcover book she'd been reading, a wonderful novel titled *Feast Day Of Fools*, by James Lee Burke. Decker raised the gun and fired, hitting the book and ripping it to shreds.

Sandy moved right at him. Decker was so surprised by her movements and her aggression that he found himself backing up to get some distance between them. When Sandy saw the fear in his eyes she pushed forward, her adrenaline kicking into what Burke would have called E-Major overdrive.

She grabbed the barrel of the gun, ignoring the heat that seared her palms and pushed the gun up, above her head. Decker squeezed the trigger again and the blast from the gun forced her to let go. A chunk of drywall fell from the ceiling and covered them both with dust and bits of pink insulation. She swung a hard right that caught him on the shoulder and sent him sidestepping away. She followed his movements but got tangled up in the lamp cord and fell to one knee. She was halfway up when the gun went off again and her eyes went wide before she collapsed on the floor.

THE TOWER GAVE them clearance for takeoff. Cool's instructions to Bell were simple and straightforward. "Keep your hands in your lap and don't touch anything."

Bell assured him he would. "Where are we headed?"

"Anywhere you'd like," Cool said. "Within reason, of course."

Bell smiled. "You know what would be really neat? Let's go to Virgil and Sandy's and land in their backyard. Is that allowed?"

"Of course it's allowed," Cool said. "I'm the cops. Besides, I flew the governor in there last week."

"How long to get there?"

Cool laughed. "In this baby? From here? About six minutes."

The sky was a bright blue, clear and free of clouds. The rotors chewed through the thick cold air with a forceful- ness that Bell could feel in the seat of his pants and the soles of his feet. The tower handed them off to departure control and vectored them to the Southeast. Right into the storm...

MURTON CALLED Becky and told her what was happen- ing. She assured him that Jonas was safe. They were in the office above the bar.

"I need two things," Murton said. "First, tell Delroy to get everyone who isn't a cop out of the bar. There's a chance that Decker might show up there. It's small, but I don't want to risk it. He's after Jonas and I don't think he's going to stop until he gets him."

Becky wheeled her chair over to the window that looked out across the bar from the upstairs office. "It looks pretty busy down there."

"I don't care. Tell Delroy he can hand out vouchers for free drinks, just get them out. How many cops are there?"

Becky looked around. "No uniforms, but I see four...no wait, five guys that I know. One county, four city."

"Good. Go take their drinks away and tell them to stay put. Drinks on the house for a month if they cooperate. Send them away with the civilians if they don't."

"What's the second thing?"

"Get into the phone company. See if you can get a ping on Decker's phone."

"That's going to take a warrant and that takes time, Murt."

"Get Cora on the warrant. Tell her what's happening. She'll get it done. But why not get started in the meantime?"

"Anything else?"

"Yeah. What's Jonas doing?"

"Napping on the sofa."

"You know what sits on top of the bookcase, right?"

Becky did. It was a Mossberg twelve-gage pistol grip shotgun. "Yeah, I do."

"Keep your eye on that window. If Decker shows up, remember what I taught you."

"We're good," Becky said. And she was. Her voice was calm. She sounded like they were talking about the weather or their dinner options. "Go get this asshole, will you?"

———

SANDY WAS CONFUSED. She couldn't piece together what had just happened. She was on the floor, her feet tangled in the lamp cord. Her side burned like someone was holding a blowtorch against her skin and she felt a wave of nausea that made her gag, biliousness fluid filling the back of her throat. She coughed and spat the fluid out and when she did her side flared with a type of pain she'd never experienced. When she touched her left side, her hand came away bloody. When she tried to stand she only made it as far as her hands and knees before the pain and dizziness overcame her and she collapsed back on the floor. She felt a wetness between her thighs.

She'd been shot. It came back in an instant, like a slap in the face. Then she heard the sounds in the house...the ranting and raving. She was going to try to get up again when she saw him come around the corner.

He stood over her, his face a twisted mask of hate and rage. "Where's my boy?"

Sandy swallowed. She felt Wyatt move inside her but the movement was wrong. It was...off. She didn't know how she knew, only that she did. She felt it again and began to cry.

Decker pointed the gun at her head. "Where's Jonas? Where's my boy?"

"Not here." Sandy said. "The county took him away."

"Don't lie to me, bitch." When Sandy didn't speak, Decker squatted down next to her and put the barrel of the gun under her chin, forcing her to look at him. "I'm only going to ask you one more time. Where's my boy?"

"Please. He's not here. I'm pregnant. I'm hurt badly. I need help."

"Have it your way then. I think you know where my boy is. That means you've decided to hold out on me. Now you've got another choice to make. Which child do you want more? Mine, or yours?" Decker kicked her in the stomach, hard, three times. One for every word. "Where's...my...boy?"

Sandy curled into a ball and felt the unnatural movement from Wyatt again, this time much weaker than before. More like a tremor than any kind of actual movement. The last thought she had before she passed out was, boaf. I want boaf.

DECKER SLIPPED on the last kick, his prosthetic leg giving way. He landed in the puddle of blood that surrounded Sandy and when he did his leg came loose. He was rigging it back in place when he felt the windows start to rattle. When he looked out the window he saw a blue and white state police helicopter circling the pond in back, its nose turning into the wind as it crept forward, ready to land in the backyard. He kicked Sandy one more time, And his leg came loose again and he fell back down, cursing.

The two men from the helicopter were headed his way. Decker got his leg reattached, fired three quick shots out at the men through the back window, then ran out the front, pulling the door shut behind him.

CHAPTER THIRTY-THREE

C ool brought the helicopter in with a dramatic flare, a little hot-dogging for Bell's benefit, then touched down softly in the grass by the pond.

"Man oh man," Bell said as he unhooked his harness. "Wait till Sandy sees this. She'll be so excited she'll probably pop her water bag on the spot."

"Let's hope not," Cool replied. "The governor wasn't too happy with me about the fish smell. I don't want to even think about what he'd say if we have water-popping fluid or whatever you call it all over the carpet back there."

"Relax, I'm just messing with you. She's still got another few weeks yet. Come on, let's go say hello."

THEY WERE WALKING across the grass when one of the back windows of the house shattered, followed by three loud pops. Cool recognized the shots for what they were right away and pushed Bell to the ground. "Stay down," he yelled. "Get back. Take cover behind the chopper."

Bell wasn't hurt, but he was confused. Who was shooting at them, and more importantly, why? Cool stood in a crouch, pulled a gun from an ankle holster and ran around the corner toward the front of the house. He saw Decker hobbling toward his vehicle. He brought his gun up and yelled, "Freeze. State Police. Drop your weapon and get on the ground."

But Decker had already made it to the relative safety of his vehicle. He spun, fired once, and yanked the car door open. Cool, who knew how to live up to his name didn't duck or even flinch at the shot fired his way. He took careful aim and returned fire just as Decker was lowering himself into the car. He saw a spray of blood and knew he'd hit his target. Nevertheless, the car pulled away with a squeal of rubber, cutting through the grass before finding the driveway.

Cool ran back around to the rear of the house. Bell was nowhere to be seen. He jumped into the chopper and fired it up. He'd be on top of the car within seconds. He'd just lifted off when he saw Bell come running out of the back of the house, frantically waving his arms. Cool put pressure on the right rudder pedal and moved the stick to the left. He crabbed the chopper in sideways right up next to the house and set it back down.

Bell yanked the door open and yelled, "Get inside. I need you."

Cool shook his head, the rotor still beating away. "Can't. He's going to get away."

"It's Sandy. She's hurt badly, Cool. Follow me." He

turned and ran back into the house. Cool shut everything down and climbed from the chopper. When he got inside, he felt his heart begin to break.

DECKER TOOK off down the long driveway, barely keeping the car under control as he turned out on the gravel road. He had his hand on the top front of his left shoulder and blood was seeping through his fingers. He'd been shot, he realized. He pulled his hand away and looked at the blood. It covered his entire hand. He reached up and pulled the rearview mirror into position for a better view. The bullet had ripped out a chunk of meat and based on how it felt, it might have clipped a bone. He was going much faster than he should, the car bouncing on it's springs, the gravel pinging away at the underside of the vehicle. He turned north on 37 back toward the city. He needed to get out of sight...get somewhere to patch himself up. The boy...his son...that was a lost cause now. He'd left too big a footprint.

There was only one place he could go to get the supplies he needed. He hoped they were still there. He was almost sure they were. The army, the National Guard in particular never did anything with efficiency.

He was five miles north on 37, his shoulder barking at him and barking louder by the mile when a black Ford Raptor went screaming by, its siren blaring, blue and red lights flashing inside the grill. He watched it in his rearview mirror until it was out of sight.

Murton beat Virgil by three minutes. He turned into the drive, fishtailed through the grass and skidded to a stop right by the front porch. Cool yanked open what was left of the front door, and for the first time in his life, didn't live up to his name.

"Murt..." That was all he could say. Tears were running down his cheeks.

Murton looked past him and saw Bell working on Sandy. He was covered in Sandy's blood. She was flat on her back and Bell was giving her CPR and tending to her bullet wound all at the same time. Every time he compressed her chest blood spurted out of the bullet wound. She was bleeding from her genitalia as well. Pools of blood were everywhere. Murton felt his knees start to go. He grabbed the side of the door jamb to steady himself and took out his phone. Virgil answered on the first ring.

"What?"

"How far out are you?"

"Ninety seconds. I'm almost there."

"You better hurry, Virgil."

Virgil gripped the wheel so tight he thought it might break in half. The last time he'd heard those words his father had died in his arms.

"Where's Sandy? Is it Sandy?" He was screaming at the interior of the truck. Somewhere in the back of his brain he wondered where, exactly, was the microphone that let him speak without taking his hands off the wheel.

"Yeah, it's Sandy. Come home, brother. Come home right now."

"You're supposed to call her Small," Virgil shouted. He was banging his fist on the steering wheel. "Why aren't you calling her Small, Murt? Why aren't you calling her Small?"

MURTON DIDN'T ANSWER. He'd gotten past the shock of what he saw, jammed the phone in his pocket and ran over to Bell. "Tell me what to do."

Bell wiped the sweat from his face and left a bloody smear that made him look like an Indian warrior. "In my bag...there's packages of quick-clot. Pack as much as you can into the wound. She's bleeding out."

Murton dumped the bag out and grabbed the packages of hemostatic agents. He ripped them open and began packing the wound. Bell continued with the CPR. Murton looked over at him. "Bell, trade places with me. Let me do the CPR. You look like you're about to have a heart attack."

Bell nodded without speaking and finished packing the wound while Murton continued compressions. He stopped every tenth time, pinched Sandy's nostrils closed and breathed into her mouth. "Keep her head tipped back or you'll just fill her stomach with air."

"I know, I know."

Bell packed the last of the clotting agent into the wound then covered the bullet hole with multiple layers of gauze. Murton was breathing into Sandy's mouth when she coughed once, weakly, then moaned. Bell put his stethoscope over her chest and moved it around to three different places. "Okay...we've got a rhythm, but it's weak. Her pulse is thready. She's lost a lot of blood. She's right on the edge." He moved the stethoscope to her abdomen, frowned, then moved it four more times. On the last movement he bent forward as if the act of doing so might help him hear better.

Cool was standing over them. He turned and looked out the front door. "Here comes Virgil."

Bell looked him. "Cool, go get that chopper fired up and ready to go. Do the back seats come out?"

"Yeah, I can have them out in thirty seconds. You want them all out?"

Bell didn't look up. He still had the scope on Sandy's abdomen. "Yes. Go now. Get the seats out and get it ready. We'll be running hard."

Cool ran out the back and went to work on the chopper. Bell looked at Murt. "I'm going to need your help with Virgil."

Virgil was flying up the driveway and almost there. "What do you mean?" Murton said. "Help with what?"

Sandy coughed again, a touch stronger than last time. She reached out and took Murton's hand.

"I think the bullet ruptured her uterus. She's bleeding internally and she's losing her amniotic fluid. That means the baby isn't going to make it unless we get him out of there right now."

"You're talking about a field C-section?"

Cool had the helicopter started and the wine of the jet engine and the beating rotor blades were growing louder by the second. Bell had to shout at him in order to be heard. "It's the only way to save one of them."

Virgil flew into the room just in time to hear Bell. "What do you mean save one of them?"

VIRGIL GOT down on the floor, down in the blood. He put his hands on his wife's face. "Sandy. I'm here baby. Everything is going to be okay. Come on, sweetheart. Hang in there with me." He looked at Murton. "What happened? What the fuck happened?"

Sandy's eye's fluttered, then opened part way. She tried to speak but coughed up blood instead. Virgil leaned close and she got the word out on her second try. "Decker."

Virgil turned and screamed at Bell. "Do something, goddamnit." Spit flew from his mouth when he spoke, the tears rolling freely down his cheeks.

Murton had both hands on Virgil's shoulders. He pulled him back. "Listen to me now, brother. Your baby is dying as we speak. We've got to get him out or you're going to lose him."

"But...Sandy. Bell, what about Sandy?" They were all yelling at each other, partly to be heard, mostly in panic.

Bell shook his head. "She's losing too much blood, Virgil. If we don't do something right now we're going to lose them both. If we put Sandy on that chopper she might make it, but you'll lose your son. If we deliver Wyatt right now via C-section he'll probably be okay, but Sandy won't survive the surgery. I don't have the blood for a transfusion."

Virgil grabbed Bell's shirt with both hands and pulled him close, ready to scream at him. Sandy reached up and put her hand on Virgil's arm. When she spoke, it was with such effort that every word came out like its own sentence.

"Virgil. Save. Wyatt."

Virgil was shaking his head, like a child who didn't

want to hear what the adults were saying. "No, no, no. This isn't happening."

Then, with surprising strength, like a lightbulb ready to burn out, Sandy pulled Virgil close one final time. "Love. You. Forever. Virgil Jones." Then her grip went soft and her arm fell away and her eyes focused on nothing at all.

Virgil leaned down and put his forehead against Sandy's, his tears running across her face. He kissed her lips, her eyes, her nose. He ran his fingers along the sides of her face, put her hair in his mouth and wept openly in front of Murton and Bell. Outside, the helicopter's rotor blades were beating furiously and the back door flew open, unable to withstand the blast. Leaves and grass and small bits of debris sailed through the kitchen and swirled around the house.

Virgil crawled away from Sandy on all fours and heaved as if he might vomit. When nothing came up, he turned back and sat flat on his ass, his eyes empty, like someone had just switched him off.

Murton, who'd been to war, who'd watched men suffer and die, who thought he'd seen the very worst of what any man should ever have to see, was suddenly certain he'd just witnessed his best friend lose his mind.

Three minutes later, thanks to Bell's quick work, a tiny baby boy named Wyatt Andrew Jones was born. His right eye was as green as the ocean waters of Montego Bay, his left, a deep crystal blue that was as bright and clear as the sky right outside the door.

CHAPTER THIRTY-FOUR

The funeral didn't take place for another week. Virgil spent the entire seven days in complete isolation at the hospital with the only family he had. Jonas was present as well and even though they were stuck there, the nurses all chipped in and helped to keep Jonas occupied, entertaining him when Virgil needed the rest. Wyatt was going to be okay, but they had him under constant watch in the Neonatal intensive care unit due to the nature of his birth. He'd suffered no visible trauma from the beating and all other intensive tests came back normal. The biggest concern was the stress of the birth because of the attack, and the fact that he was almost a month early.

The nurses all agreed his eyes were unlike anything they'd ever seen. He was going to be special and—more than one nurse had commented—quite the ladies man when he grew up. Virgil held him constantly, only allowing the nurses to take him when he needed to sleep or tend to Jonas.

Cora ran the overtime budget through the shredder and made sure they had round the clock protection with two ISP troopers stationed at every entrance and four on the NICU floor itself. No one got close. No one tried.

Murton sat in the office above the bar and watched Becky, waiting for her to give him the information he needed.

"I've got it," she finally said.

"Moving or stationary?"

"Stationary...for now anyway. There's some historical data, but I'd have to run a different sub-routine through their system. Leaves a bigger footprint."

"Let it go then. You can tell me if he moves?"

"Of course, but there's an easier way." She handled Murton a nondescript computer tablet. "I've downloaded the tracking information on that. You'll have real-time updates on his movements...if he moves, that is. I'm surprised he hasn't."

"I'm surprised he isn't dead. Cool said he shot him. He was sure of it." He took the tablet and turned to leave. Becky grabbed his wrist and held him in place. "There's other ways to do this."

"Not this time, there isn't."

"Are you sure, Murt?"

Murton looked at her for a long time before he spoke. "I'm as sure as you are."

"Meaning what?"

"Meaning you knew it was going to come to this. That's

why you never asked Cora to get the warrant. We're a lot a like, Becks. It's why I love you."

"I love you too." Becky let go of his hand and handed him a burner phone. "Destroy this and scatter the pieces if you have to use it."

He gave her a look that said he knew how to handle a burner. She pretended like she didn't notice.

"I will."

"If you go now, you're going to miss the funeral."

"Can't be helped. We've been waiting for a week to get a ping on Decker's phone. It's now or never. My guess is he's finally called for help. I'm going to go help him."

"You could arrest him, Murt."

"You're right. I could. But what about Jonas? I know what Virgil would want. Sandy and Pam too. They'd want me to take care of business so that's what I'm going to do. It's what I've always done, and what I'll always do. You know who I learned that from? Mason. It's time to return the favor and pay the debt I owe to my real family and take care of my brother." He kissed her hard on the lips then walked out the door.

"Be careful," she said, but he was already gone.

THE SERVICE WAS HELD at a small chapel on the outskirts of the northwestern suburbs. While the chapel itself was packed full with cops, their spouses, and a number of politicians, Virgil thought that there would have been more people present. It *seemed* like there were a lot of people because every seat was filled—there were even people lined up along the back and side walls—but the chapel was smaller than most, so it was an illusion. Virgil didn't care. The measure of your life was in how you lived it, not who showed up when you were gone.

The casket was closed, draped with a simple, almost shear white cloth. The pallbearers were all ISP Troopers, hand picked by Cora. Virgil had enough on his plate and Cora knew it, so she'd planned almost all of the service by herself.

Virgil sat in the front row, Jonas and Becky on one side of him, Cora and the governor on the other. The preacher spoke of a life well lived, of sacrifice, dedication and commitment to others. He referenced passages from the bible that he thought fitting, and steered well clear of the violent manner of death that had occurred. He finished with a prayer, then asked if anyone in attendance wanted to say a few words about the deceased. Virgil felt the eyes of the entire chapel turn toward him. He'd known this moment would come and he'd been dreading it. But something wonderful and amazing happened in that moment. When everyone turned and looked his way, their looks weren't heavy and weighted as he thought they might be. Instead they seemed to lift him up and give him strength. He stood, ready to approach the pulpit when Jonas reached out and took his hand.

They walked up together.

"My father once told me something that was so basic, so fundamental and elementary in nature, that I let its true meaning slip past without ever knowing it. In fact, I don't think I realized it until today." He paused for a moment and looked down at Jonas, who was staring at his shoes. There were tears running down his little cheeks. Virgil squatted down next to him and whispered into his ear. "Look at all these people, Jonas. These are our people. Every single one of them. They're not here for themselves... they're here for us. Our lives have been changed, but we're going to move forward, the way she would have wanted. That's how you honor the ones you've lost."

Jonas wiped his face and looked out at the crowd of people, then he turned and looked up at Virgil and squeezed his hand tight.

Virgil stood up and continued. "What my father told me was simple. He said, 'everything matters.' I think what he meant was this: While everything matters, every choice, every decision we make, every direction we turn leads us down a path that we rarely have any control over, even though we think we do. When Sandy and I had that party at our house almost a year ago, I made a choice. The choice was to take Ed Donatti with me to go and look for Murton. It was a simple choice and even though it cost Ed his life, and cost Jonas his father, I believe it was the correct one. And that one little choice all those months ago has led us to this very moment, a moment where we're all here, together, because this is where we are supposed to be right now, whether we like it or not." He shifted his gaze and looked directly at Becky. "For those who couldn't be here today...I believe they are where they're supposed to be as well."

"Today we are saying goodbye to a fine woman, a woman who gave everything of herself in service to not only her husband, but a son she'll never get the chance to see grow up, a woman who endured pain and suffering at the end of her life so that others could have the very best of theirs. I can't think of a better tribute for a wife and mother." He stared at the crowd for a moment, then took Jonas and walked over to the casket. He laid his palm on top of the cloth, then traced the edges lightly with fingertips. He choked back a sob, whispered, "Forgive me," then sat back down. Becky leaned her head on his shoulder. Jonas climbed in his lap and Virgil could feel the moisture of his tears soaking through his shirt and against his skin.

MURTON TURNED into the abandoned airport and pulled his car behind a gatehouse, out of sight from the other buildings. He had a long wait ahead. He wouldn't make his move until in was dark outside.

THE FUNERAL PROCESSION left the chapel and snaked its way to the cemetery. A small tent was set up over the gravesite and it was cold enough that tiny ribbons of steam were rising from the freshly dug mound of soil. The preacher waited until everyone had parked their cars and walked over to the grave.

Once everyone was in place, he said a few more encouraging words about life, the fragility and finite time they all shared on earth, and wrapped everything up by saying, *"In sure and certain hope of eternal life, we commend to Almighty God our sister; and we commit her body to the ground; earth to earth; ashes to ashes, dust to dust. May the Lord bless her and keep her and give her peace. Amen."*

Everyone stood silently as the casket was lowered into the earth where finally, Pam Donatti's body was laid to rest, next to her husband, Ed.

CHAPTER THIRTY-FIVE

When Virgil and Jonas got back to the hospital, they were waking Sandy for the first time. They'd kept her in a medically induced coma to aid in her healing. She was in considerable pain, because the doctors didn't want her over-medicated due to the amount of blood she'd lost. She was still weak, but getting better every day. The doctors assured everyone there were no neurological concerns and they were pumping her full of antibiotics to ward off any infections that might try to creep in. Jonas moved to the bed and took her hand, then crawled up and laid down next to her. Virgil moved to stop him, but Sandy shook her head and told him it was okay.

Virgil leaned in and kissed her, then told her he'd be right back. When he returned, he carried a tiny bundle in his arms. "Say hello to your miracle baby." He placed Wyatt in Sandy's arms. Wyatt opened his eyes and looked at his mother.

Sandy saw his eyes and found she had trouble with her

words. When she finally got them out, they were as simple as ever. "When do we get to go home?"

IT HAD HAPPENED LIKE THIS: While Virgil was saying his final goodbyes to his dying wife, Bell took out a scalpel, cut Sandy open and brought Wyatt into the world. He clamped and cut the cord, wrapped him in a blanket then handed him to Murton who got him stimulated and breathing. When Bell saw that Murton had Wyatt going, he turned his attention right back to Sandy. Because everyone there was either a cop or a doctor, they all knew their own blood types. Murton had to physically move Virgil out of the way. He grabbed him by the shoulder with his free hand and shook him hard.

"What's Small's blood type?"

Virgil looked at all the blood on the floor and didn't respond.

Murton slapped him, hard and screamed at him. "What's her blood type?"

Virgil finally told him and when he did, Bell's shoulder's slumped. She was O-negative. Bell was working furiously to get Sandy's incision closed up, but when he spoke his voice was calm, his thought process clear and completely focused. "O-negative is one of the most rare. People who are O-neg can only take blood from others who are O-neg donors. I'm type B. That means I'm out. Murton, what about you?"

Murton was putting two IV lines into Sandy, one in

each arm. He held the lines, one in each hand and shook his head. "Same."

"Virgil?"

"I'm type A."

Of course you are, Murton thought.

Bell had Sandy as closed up as he was going to get her with the equipment he had on hand. "Come on, let's get her on the chopper. I honestly don't think she's going to make it, but we've got to try. She's not dead yet, but she's knocking on the door. Virgil, get your shit together and grab your son. Let's go."

They went out the back, Murton and Bell carrying Sandy's limp body. They got her into the chopper, and Bell kept saying "Easy, easy," and Murton kept responding, "I am being easy. I am."

Virgil followed them in and handed Wyatt to Murton so he could get right down next to Sandy. Bell climbed into the front seat next to Cool who was just about to pull up on the collective and get them airborne. He leaned over and shouted. "Cool...what's your blood type?"

———————

SIXTY SECONDS later they were flying away, the air traffic controllers clearing the flight path direct to the hospital. Cool had a line in each arm and he was flexing his muscles as hard as he could to get the blood flowing into Sandy. In the end, it saved her.

The story eventually got out. The governor's helicopter pilot had made an emergency medical run to the hospital while having his own blood transfused during the actual flight. When the word started to spread everyone began referring to him as that Cool Motherfucker. The rumor, it turned out, was started by the governor.

———

SANDY SPENT over eight hours in surgery to repair the damage from the gunshot wound. She also had to have a full hysterectomy from the damage to her uterus. She'd never have another child. When the doctors who'd performed the surgeries told her, she nodded and said, "I know. I've always known."

Then they put her back under with the meds, to let her heal. Out in the hall, one of the docs said. "Did you hear that? About always knowing. I think it was the drugs talking."

The other one stared at him blankly. He wasn't so sure, though he didn't know why.

CHAPTER THIRTY-SIX

Nightfall came and Murton made his way across the abandoned airfield and moved toward the large Quonset hut. He opened the outer door and stepped into the darkness, pausing to let his eyes adjust. A portable half-wall was at the far end of the hangar, a dim light barely illuminating the far side of the interior space off in the distance. He took the gun from the holster on his hip and moved forward, slowly, silently.

Decker was unconscious. He never heard him coming.

MURTON PICKED up the weapons and moved them well out of reach, then pulled a chair over by the cot. Decker was on his back, shirtless, a large bloodstained gauze pad taped over his shoulder. It was yellow and brown and smelled of rot. The infection was spreading rapidly, the skin puffy and stretched tight. He sat for a few minutes waiting for Decker to come around, and when he got tired of waiting, he pressed the barrel of his gun into the wound. Decker screamed and tried to sit up. Fluid gushed out of the wound and filled the air with his stink. Murton punched him in the face with his free hand and that flattened him back out on the cot.

"Time to wake up sleepyhead."

Decker was sweating heavily, the fever raging through his body. "I need a doctor."

Murton nodded. "Yeah, you sure do. Funny thing about gun shot wounds, even the minor ones will kill you if you don't tend to them right away. You've got to get the bullet out and all the little bits of fabric that followed it in. If you don't...well..." He pressed the barrel against the wound again. "Exhibit A."

Decker screamed again. "Please, you've got to help me."

Murton wiped the barrel of the gun on the edge of the cot then sat back in the chair and crossed his legs, the gun pointed casually at Decker. "See, that's where you're wrong. I don't have to do anything. You know, you sort of remind me of my old man." When Decker didn't respond, Murton kept talking. "He was a miserable prick just like you. He thought he could bully his way through life, rolling over anything and anyone he wanted, whenever he liked. Treated me like I was a possession. His possession. If I got out of line..."

"He beat you."

Murton nodded. "With some regularity."

"What'd you do about it?"

"Nothing. I was a kid. But I had another man in my life, a real man who came to our house one night and set my father straight. He was a cop. I guess that's why I became one. He beat the hell out of my old man and that seemed to take care of the problem. I never saw dear old dad again."

"So a cop took his boy from him. I know how he must have felt."

"I doubt it. He didn't do anything to try to get me back. The upshot is, I'm glad. If he had, I might have ended up just like him. Just like you."

"Thanks for the trip down memory lane. Are you going to help me or not?"

"No. Maybe I'll just sit here and watch you die."

"You can't do that. You're a cop."

Murton tipped his head in thought. "You're right. I'm a cop. It's my job to protect and serve. I'm about to do both at the same time." He pulled the hammer back on the .45 and pointed it at Decker's chest. He began to tighten the pressure on the trigger when he felt the air move behind him. It took him by surprise.

"Never used to be able to sneak up on you like that, Murt. How's it hanging?"

He recognized the voice and didn't bother to turn around. "I'd love to catch up, Paul, but I'm a little busy right now."

Agent Paul Gibson had been Murton's handler when he worked undercover with the FBI. Over the twenty-plus years they had worked together they never were quite friends, but they'd been good colleagues. "Before you excuse yourself, though, tell me this: Why are the feds here?"

"Just fed," Gibson said. "Singular. I'm the only federal

agent here. And I'm not with the FBI anymore, either. Got a little bump."

"Where to?"

"Homeland."

Now Murton did turn around. "You're shitting me?"

Gibson smiled at him and held out his identification. Murton looked at it and nodded. "Congratulations. I'm happy for you. Why are you here?"

Gibson tipped his head at Decker who was trying to sit up. "Your man there is making a break for it."

Murton rolled his eyes, de-cocked his gun and swung it backwards without looking and cracked Decker across the nose. Decker moaned and fell backwards on the cot.

Murton raised his eyebrows at Gibson.

"I've been wanting to have a little chat with your boy, Decker, here."

"You better talk fast then."

"I'm going to need you to step outside, Murt."

"Not gonna happen, Paul."

"It's not Decker I'm interested in. It's his boss."

"Gordon?"

"That's the one."

"Why?"

Gibson seemed to be examining his options. He tilted his head, an indication for Murton to step away from Decker.

Murton turned back, looked at Decker and said, "If you try to get off this cot, I'll shoot you. Look in my eyes and tell me I won't."

Decker visibly swallowed, but otherwise didn't move.

They walked a few yards away, both of them keeping

an eye on Decker. Gibson lowered his voice. "Kreg Gordon was murdered. We found him and another victim at Gordon's home. Guy named Westlake. You know who he is?"

"Yeah. The lawyer that was setting up the fracking deal in Shelby County."

"I don't care about all the Mickey Mouse fracking bullshit. But Westlake and Gordon were connected to the Russians and *they* were the money behind the fracking deal, among other things."

"What's the rest of the story?"

"Classified."

Murton put it together in about two seconds. "You're not here for Decker. You're here for me." It was a statement, not a question.

"You always were a little too clever for your own good." Gibson nodded in Decker's direction. "I heard all about what this asshole did. She going to make it?"

"Small? Yeah. Looks like she'll pull through. The baby too."

Gibson smiled. "That's great. Happy ending all the way around." He looked at Decker again. "Well, almost all the way. Do me a favor will you? Step outside. There's someone waiting. They'd like a word with you."

"You said you were alone."

"No, I said I was the only federal agent here."

"What about him?" Murton said. He meant Decker.

"As far as I'm concerned, he doesn't exist," Gibson said. Then he turned and walked away.

"The fuck was that all about?" Decker said.

"I don't know yet. But it doesn't concern you. So, where were we?"

"You were trying to be clever, saying you were going to sit here and wait for me to die."

"Yeah, I sort of changed my mind about that." Murton brought the gun up and pointed it at Decker's heart. "You got mixed up with the wrong group, Bub. Nobody threatens or does harm to my family and gets away with it. Look at it this way...at least you won't suffer any longer."

"Fuck you," Decker said.

Murton shot him in the chest three times in rapid succession. "Yeah, fuck me."

When he stepped outside Murton saw Gibson leaning against a black limo. He walked over and stood next to him.

"I really did want to talk to him," Gibson said.

"Too late. And you're forgetting I know you a little too well, Paul." A panel van backed up to the hangar and two men dressed in white Tyvek suits got out and went inside. "What are they doing?"

"Cleaners," Gibson said.

"Uh huh. Wanted to talk to Decker, my ass. You were trying to take the heat off me. I appreciate it, but it's not necessary. I've got it covered."

"So let us handle the cleanup. Why bother doing it yourself when you've got the federal government ready and willing to assist in your time of need? Anyway, hop in. We need to talk about something...and you, in particular, need to listen."

Murton pressed his tongue into the side of his cheek. After a moment they got in the back of the car and when Murton saw who was seated inside, he was at a loss for words.

"Good evening, Murt," the governor said. "You and me and agent Gibson here are going to take a little ride. That okay with you?"

Murton looked over his shoulder at the hangar. The two men in Tyvek suits were carrying Decker's body through the door. They laid him on top of a sheet of plastic, wrapped his body up like a roll of carpet, then put it in the back of the truck and drove away. He looked back at the governor. "You're the boss."

The governor chuckled at him. "Sometimes I wonder, Murt. I really do." Then he slapped his thigh and said, "Let's get out of here before the cops show up, huh? Don't worry, you'll be home before bedtime."

CHAPTER THIRTY-SEVEN

C ora worked with the adoption people and got all the necessary paperwork pushed through. Once the red tape had been cut—something with which Cora was extremely adept—the process was quick and smooth. She even had the judge show up at the hospital to preside over the hearing. After all the required documentation was approved and the papers were signed by Virgil and Sandy, the judge sat down next to Jonas and looked him in the eye.

"Do you understand what's happening here young man?"

Jonas looked at the judge and didn't answer. The judge waited a few moments then tried again. "Everything we're doing here...do you know what it means?"

Jonas remained silent.

Virgil cleared his throat. "Your Honor, may I have a word with you in the hallway for a moment?"

They stepped out into the hall. The judge wasn't

pleased. "You know, When Cora LaRue called, she told me to come over here. She didn't ask me, she told me. Anyway, I knew I couldn't say no. I owe her a few favors. No, no, don't ask. I'm not going to tell you. But she said get over here, so here I am. That means I've reduced my favor count to her by one no matter how this thing turns out." He held his thumb and forefinger an inch apart. "I'm this close to being free. I thought you guys would have prepped him a little better. What's the holdup with the kid?"

Clearly he doesn't know how to deal with selfish assholes yet. "He's just a child." Then, trying to put a smile in his voice: "I don't think he has a full and complete understanding of the complexities of the law. How about we give him a break? To tell you the truth, Judge, I think he's afraid of you. He doesn't know who you are or why you're here."

The judge snorted and looked like he was about to say something nasty, then to Virgil's surprise, he softened. "You know what? He probably is. Do this job long enough and you can get a little rough around the edges. You think criminal court is bad? Try family court. Some of the shit I've seen..."

"I've got an idea if you're willing to entertain it," Virgil said.

"Let's hear it."

"Lose the robe. I think it might be intimidating him. No disrespect, but with that thing on you look like the grim reaper in the room. Without it, you look like you might be somebody's grandpa."

The judge chuckled at him. "I am somebody's grandpa. And you know what? I think you're right." He unzipped the robe, tossed it on the chair, removed his tie and unbuttoned the top button of his shirt. "How's this?"

The judge was making an effort and Virgil appreciated it. He smiled at him and said, "Let's go find out."

They walked back into the room and the judge asked Jonas to come and sit next to him. Jonas walked over and sat in the chair, his hands folded in his lap. He stared at the floor.

"I've got a grandson about your age," the judge said. "He likes to go fishing with me. Do you like to fish?"

Jonas nodded. "I fished in Mr. Virgil's pond. I caught a big mouth but we let him go."

The judge laughed and rubbed the top of Jonas's head. "I think you mean large mouth. That's pretty impressive. Those can be hard to catch sometimes."

They talked about fishing for a few minutes and then the judge reached over and picked up a stack of paperwork from the table. "Mr. Virgil and Miss Sandy have already signed these papers. That means they want to be your parents. Is that what you want?"

Jonas looked first at Virgil, then at Sandy, then back at his shoes. He nodded.

The judge put his hand on Jonas's thigh. "You have to say it out loud. I have to hear you say yes or no."

Jonas looked at Sandy and said, "Does that mean Wyatt will be my brother?"

"It sure does, honey. You'll be Wyatt's big brother."

"I miss my mommy and daddy. I wish they didn't have to go to heaven."

"We all do, little man," Virgil said. "My dad's in heaven

too, remember? I'll bet he's showing them all around. So what do you think? Can you tell the judge what you want?" Virgil put his hand on Jonas's chest. "Just answer with your heart."

The judge knew his opening when he saw it. "What do you say, Jonas? Do you want Mr. Virgil and Miss Sandy to be your new parents?"

Jonas looked at the judge. "Yes, please."

The judge handed the stack of papers to Jonas. "Okay, that's great. Now, I have to sign each one of these papers, and there are a lot of them. How about you hand them to me one at a time..."

Cora took pictures of everyone, tears rolling down her cheeks.

———

FROM SANDY'S PERSPECTIVE, it felt like she might never get to take her family home from the hospital. The docs wanted to make sure she was healing properly, which meant they couldn't let her go until she could prove her body was functioning normally.

"How do I prove that?" she asked. "I'm hooked up to every machine ever invented." She waved her hand around the room. "I don't know what else I can do that you're not already getting from all this."

"You've got to have a bowel movement," the doctor said. If he thought that was going to embarrass her, he was mistaken.

"Wait here," she said. She stood from the bed, pulled

the stand of monitors along with her, then walked into the bathroom and took care of business. The doctor went into the bathroom, flushed the toilet, came back out and shrugged. "That's the rule. Once you've gone, you can go. I'll get the paperwork started and you'll be on your way. You're one hell of a fighter, kiddo. Doctors don't get to say this often enough, but I'm proud of you."

Sandy smiled at him. "Thank you."

Virgil and Jonas walked into the room. They'd been down in the cafeteria having breakfast. Jonas made a funny face, plugged his nose with his finger and thumb and said, "What's that smell?"

"That is the sweet smell of freedom, my boy," the doctor said.

Jonas looked at Sandy. He still had his nose plugged. "It smells like business to me."

Two hours later, they were home.

VIRGIL FOUND himself running around the house doing everything wrong. The crib had to be moved to the master bedroom, he'd somehow managed to buy the wrong sized diapers, there was nothing in the house for Jonas to eat, the electric swing had to be assembled, and when he tried to wrap Wyatt in a swaddle, he ended up looking like a giant doobie on the verge of suffocation.

Fortunately, they'd hired a part-time nanny to help with the kids during Sandy's recovery. It took Virgil about ten whole minutes before he offered her a full-time, live-in position. She readily agreed.

Jonas turned out to be a wonderful helper, except Virgil didn't know what he needed help with until something needed tending to...and as it turned out, everything needed tending to.

They went about setting up baby monitors in all the rooms. His thinking had been, why keep lugging one transmitter to different rooms when you could just put one everywhere Wyatt was going to be and carry the receiver around. It was a fine idea until they were all tuned to the proper frequency and turned on. A loud screeching noise from the feedback filled every room of the house and they had to run around and turn them all off again. That woke Wyatt the giant doobie, who they'd just managed to get to sleep for the first time since they'd been home. Wyatt's crying woke Sandy, who was less than pleased, and on and on it went like that, well into the afternoon.

Eventually Virgil and the nanny, a middle-aged woman named Huma Moon, fell into a rhythm and got everything squared away. Huma explained to Virgil that in addition to being a nanny, she was also something called a postpartum doula. Virgil listened and nodded at her like an idiot. He thought postpartum had something to do with depression and had absolutely no idea what a doula was or what they did. He pretended to know and Huma—who knew he was pretending—let him. Doula? It sounded like some sort of hippy bullshit. He'd Google it later. Her last name was *Moon*, after all. She was good though...he had to give her that.

"Listen, Huma, I need to step outside and get some air. Could you keep an eye on..." He waved his hands around, indicating the entire house. "This?"

"It gets easier, Mr. Jones. I know it's all new and confusing and scary, but you'll get the hang of it."

"I'm sure I will," Virgil said. "And call me Jonesy. But right now—"

She waved him away with a motherly smile. "Go, go."

"I'll be right outside, in the back. I've got some yard work and then I'll probably have to go down to the bar later, and there's that list you gave me for the store—"

"Jonesy...go."

He went.

HE ENDED up down by the pond, next to the cross. "One big happy family...home at last," Mason said.

Virgil spun around. "Is there some sort of rule that says you have to sneak up on me every time?"

"No, but I do enjoy keeping you on your toes."

Virgil zipped his coat and sat down on the cold hard ground. "It looks like everything's working out. Just like you said it would."

"I don't recall saying that. What I said was, everything matters."

"And now Jonas is ours, just like it was with you and mom and me and Murt."

Mason looked at his son and didn't reply.

"What?"

"I think you might have missed my point."

"How's that? You said I'd have some hard choices to make and I've made them. Not only that, I beat the odds. I really thought I was going to have to choose between my wife and my unborn son, but everything worked out just fine."

"Everything that you're aware of."

"What do you mean? What am I not aware of?"

"Plenty. You thought this whole thing was about you and Sandy and Jonas and Wyatt, didn't you?"

"Of course. What else could it possibly be about?"

"I asked you a couple of weeks ago if you thought I made the right decision when we took Murton in all those years ago."

"I remember. So what? It *was* the right decision, Dad. I don't know what I'd do without Murton in my life. He's been a gift to me at every turn. Does this have anything to do with Jonas?"

"No, Son, it doesn't. It's about Murt. It's always *been* about Murt. That's what I've been trying to tell you. I'd go spend some time with him if I were you. He's going to need somebody by his side whether he knows it or not. He's going to need you in particular."

"Are you talking about what he did to Decker? That man almost destroyed my entire family. Murt took him out. He's my hero. And believe me, if he hadn't, I would have."

"I believe you. But to answer your question, no, that's not what I'm talking about."

The baby monitor was still clipped to Virgil's belt. It squawked at him and Huma's voice came through the speaker. "Jonesy, when you're finished speaking with that gentleman could I see you in the house for a moment? There's some things we need from the store."

Virgil turned and looked back at the house. Huma smiled and waved to him from the kitchen window then stepped away. When Virgil turned back, his father said, "I'd keep her around. She's one of the good ones...and she's a doula to boot."

CHAPTER THIRTY-EIGHT

Virgil went down to the bar and spent some time with Delroy and Robert. He showed them pictures of Wyatt and Jonas and thanked them both for the extra work they'd put in since he and Murton had been hired by the state.

"Don't you worry about it, you. Dat's a fine looking family if I've ever seen one."

Virgil hugged them both and thought about how lucky he was...that the people in his life were some of the finest human beings on the planet. "When we get settled and Sandy is feeling better we'll have everyone over for an adoption party. With Wyatt and Jonas coming into our lives so close together we're calling it our family anniversary."

"Count me in," Robert said. "Just let me do the cooking, huh, mon?"

"Deal," Virgil said. "Have you guys seen Murt and Becky?"

"You just missed them," Delroy said. "Dat Becky, she was on fire about someting, mon."

"What do you mean? Was something wrong?"

"No, mon. In fact, I don't tink I've ever seen her so excited."

Virgil thought about it for a minute. "Huh. Did they say where they were going?"

They both laughed at him, then Robert said, "They were looking for you, mon. They're on their way to your house right now."

VIRGIL STOPPED at the store on his way home to get everything Huma had put on the list, plus a few items he needed for himself. He had to stop at two different places before he found the right diapers, then got caught up looking at a contraption called a Diaper Genie. Huma had it on the list, but Virgil didn't think it was necessary. He was about to put it back when a cute young female store employee who was passing by pointed at it and said, "Have one yet?"

Virgil put it back on the shelf. "No. Not going to get one either. Looks to me like it's nothing more than a fancy trash can for dirty diapers."

She laughed at him and walked away. A few minutes later as Virgil was standing in the checkout lane he realized his cashier was the same young woman who'd just advised him about the Judy Jetson dirty diaper disposal unit. He'd already forgotten what it was called.

She scanned all his items and instead of telling him the

total amount due, said, "I'd re-think the Genie, I were you," she said. "It's the last one we have."

He wanted to ask her if she was on commission. Instead, he said, "What's the big deal? Why not just toss them in the trash?"

"Because your whole house will smell like baby poop, that's why. With the Genie...problem solved. Trust me. I've got three kids."

Virgil thanked her for no other reason than to shut her up. He paid, stuffed everything into the truck and headed home. People needed to mind their own business once in a while, he thought. Nannies, Diaper Genies, doulas, baby monitors, electric swings...the whole world was going soft. Although he thought the nanny was good idea, mostly because it had been his.

⸻

When he walked in the back door the smell hit him like a Mack truck. "Dear God, what the hell is that?"

"That's Wyatt's business," Jonas shouted. He was jumping up and down on the sofa.

"Don't do that," Virgil said. "You'll ruin the furniture."

Sandy shot him a look. It was one that Virgil knew well. "I mean, be careful buddy. Not too high."

Huma took the bags from him, "This is what your house is going to smell like for the next two or three years if you didn't get everything I had on that list, which, it appears you did not."

"I thought it was a waste of money." Virgil walked over to the trash can. "How about I just take the trash out? That should help." He removed the lid from the kitchen trash and the smell slapped him again. The can was empty except for one diaper.

"I already did," Huma said. "By the way, you're low on trash bags."

Virgil looked across the kitchen counter and saw Murton and Becky sitting in the living room across from Sandy. Becky was holding Wyatt and making funny faces at him. Murton was listening to the exchange between Virgil and Huma, shaking his head and smiling at the same time. He stood up and made his way into the kitchen.

"Didn't get the Genie, huh?"

Virgil puffed out his cheeks and shrugged his shoulders. "I thought—"

Murton cut him off. "I know, I heard. You thought it was a waste of money. What do you think now? Come on, let's make a run back to the store. We'll get the genie...my treat. Besides, we've got something to talk about."

"Hey, where are you two going," Becky said. "Murt, we've got to tell them!"

Virgil and Sandy looked at each other. "Tell us what?" Virgil said.

Sandy had a look of satisfaction on her face, like she already knew what they were going to say.

"It'll keep," Murton said to everyone. Then to Becky: "Not a peep until we get back."

"Murt—"

"I mean it Becks. Not one single word."

Sandy waved them out the door. "Go ahead and go. Besides, I'm pretty sure I already know anyway."

But she didn't. She had no idea.

VIRGIL AND MURTON went back to the store, grabbed the genie, and to Virgil's dismay the only open checkout line was the same one he'd gone through less than an hour ago. The cashier, trying to be polite, was sucking on her cheeks to hold back her laughter. Her eyes were watering with the effort. Murton, nobody's idiot, put the whole plot together in a matter of seconds. He looked at Jonesy, then the young lady behind the cash register. "You tried to tell him, didn't you?"

She nodded, her hand over her mouth. Finally she couldn't take it anymore and the laughter burst out. Virgil just stared straight ahead at a spot about six inches in front of his face.

"How was it?" she asked Murton.

"Like a bomb went off."

She nodded. "I tried to tell him..."

Murton waved her down. "Oh, I believe you. The other day, at the hospital, he tried to park in the valet lot—"

"Can we go now, please?" Virgil said.

Murton turned, tipped his head sideways and looked at Virgil, who in turn, refused to look back.

"I'll wait in the truck," Virgil said. "Don't forget who drove you here." He walked outside.

"Is he okay?" the cashier asked.

"No, but he's about to be. He just doesn't know it yet."

The cashier had no idea what that meant, so she let it go. "You want the extended warranty? It's an extra fifteen bucks."

Murton didn't hesitate. "Absolutely."

BACK IN THE TRUCK: "Have you ever noticed that I often end up as the butt of your jokes?"

Murton looked over at him. "Have you ever noticed that you set yourself up perfectly for those very same jokes?"

Virgil finally laughed. "I guess so. My god, that smell. He's a baby, for christ's sake. He should be clean as a whistle. Instead it smells like he's been drinking beer and eating boiled eggs and bean soup. It's absolutely toxic."

Murton picked up the box the genie came in and shook it. "Well, problem solved. I got the extended warranty, by the way. You're welcome."

"Thanks."

They rode in silence for a few miles. Virgil knew Murton would come out with it only when he was ready. They were almost all the way back to Virgil's place before he said anything.

"There's something I need to tell...about Decker and Gordon."

"What's there to tell? You took Decker off the board. The guy almost cost me my wife and son. I don't know how I can ever thank you enough."

"Don't ever thank me for killing someone, Jonesy. I did it because it had to be done."

"Ah, come on, Murt, you know what I mean."

"Yeah, I do. I also think it might have been a mistake."

Virgil took his eyes off the road for a second and looked at Murton.

"Watch the road, will you?"

Virgil pulled off to the side of the road and put the truck in park. "Why do you think it was a mistake?"

"You don't know the whole story."

"So tell me."

Murton stared out the side window for a few minutes. Virgil let him. When he spoke, his voice sounded hollow and distant, like they were talking on an overseas call. "Gibson was there."

"Paul Gibson? With the FBI?"

"Yup. I was just about to drop the hammer on Decker when Gibson walked in. He's not with the FBI anymore, either. He's with Homeland now."

Virgil raised his eyebrows. "Huh. Well, good for him."

"Yeah, good for him. Maybe not so good for me."

Virgil thought about it for a minute, then realized the implications of Gibson's presence. "He was either tracking Decker or you."

"That's right. And he never was very clear about that. Either way, he said he wanted to have a conversation with me."

"Listen, this just occurred to me, but you never told me what you did with Decker's body."

"That's because I didn't do anything with it."

"*What?*"

Murton spent the next few minutes telling Virgil how everything happened, including the cleaners and the fact that the governor was there. Virgil felt his jaw hanging open. He had to force himself to keep his mouth closed.

"You're telling me that Mac was sitting outside in a limo waiting to talk to you while you were inside..."

Murton nodded. "Yeah...killing Decker. Gibson's boys

took the body and Mac said let's go for a drive, so that's what we did."

"Where'd you go?"

"Nowhere. We just drove around and talked, then they dropped me at my car and I went home."

Virgil was getting impatient. "What did they want, Murt?"

"Decker was nobody. He simply did whatever Gordon told him to do. Gordon was the one pushing to have Mac hung from a meat hook. Now Gordon's dead. Westlake too."

"I know all that."

"Just let me get to it in my own way, will you? The fracking in Shelby County was backed by the Russians. It wasn't BP or Exxon Mobile or anything like that. It was the fucking Russians, Jonesy."

"All of this from Gibson?"

"Yes. And he's as honest as they come. He might skirt the edges every once in a while to get things done, but he's a patriot through and through."

Virgil thought about it. "I guess I'm not seeing the bigger picture, because the guy that wanted Mac run out of office—the same guy who was in bed with the Russians—is dead, and the fracking operations have been halted."

"You're not seeing the bigger picture because you don't have all the facts yet. According to Gibson, the Russians have bigger plans. Gibson's got intel that puts them behind the theft of nuclear material that was supposed to be shipped to hospitals all over the state."

"Why are we just now hearing about this, and not to

put too fine a point on it, but isn't this a little outside the scope of what we do?"

"We're just now hearing about it because that's the way the federal government works. They keep their mouth shut until they need something. As for the 'what we do' part of your question, normally I'd agree, but in this case I don't. That's why Mac wanted to talk to me." Murton reached into his coat pocket, pulled out an envelope and handed it to Virgil.

"What's this?"

"Homeland found it at Gordon's house. The federal government needs something. Open it up."

Virgil opened the envelope and shook out the contents. There were only two items. One was a small piece of paper, similar to a post-it note. On it was an address for someplace in Louisville, Kentucky. The address meant nothing to Virgil, and he said so.

"Me either," Murton said. "But take a look at the photo."

The photograph was the other item in the envelope. It was a black and white, slightly blurry, and taken from a distance. The picture was that of a man standing next to a locomotive in a train yard.

"That photo was taken less than a month ago. You know who it is?"

Virgil had an idea, but found himself unable to say it out loud.

"Yeah. I felt the same way. That's my old man, Ralph Wheeler. So here's the question: Why did Kreg Gordon, a guy who was mixed up with the Russians and missing nuclear material have information on my father? You know what else is interesting? There's a rail line that runs directly from Louisville to Indy."

"What the fuck, Murt?"

Murton nodded. "My thoughts exactly." Then, as if the conversation had never happened, Murton smiled and clapped Virgil on the back. "Come on. One thing at a time. We need to get back to your place. Becky's got something to tell you and Small." He looked at the box that held the genie. "I wonder if this thing will hold adult diapers?" Then he laughed like he didn't have a care in the world. "You're probably going to need them. Let's go."

CHAPTER THIRTY-NINE

They walked in the back door and even though Virgil didn't think it was possible, the smell was worse than before. Huma grabbed the box from Murton and began assembling the contraption that would hopefully restore some olfactory stability to the interior of the Jones residence. Virgil pulled Murton aside. "Listen, really quick, do you have any idea what a doula is...or does?"

Murton glanced back over his shoulder. "Yeah, of course. Huma's a doula. Becky told me. I thought you knew."

Virgil shook his head. He felt like a dope. "Never mind."

They went into the living room and sat down, Murton next to Becky, and Virgil next to Sandy. Wyatt was sleeping peacefully in the bassinet next to the sofa and Jonas was in the other room crashing toy trucks together and making explosive noises.

"So what's this big news?" Virgil said. "You guys getting married or something?"

Becky frowned at him. "No, we're not. But your comment would have been a great way to take the fun out of telling you."

Sandy punched him in the shoulder. "She's right."

Virgil held up his hands. "Okay. Sorry, sorry. Let's hear it."

Becky reached into her purse and pulled out a stack of papers. Murton was so excited he was rocking back and forth on the sofa. He didn't even realize it.

Becky looked at Virgil. "Do you remember the conversation we had just before the governor held his press conference?"

Virgil thought about it. "Yeah, basically. I thought there must have been a connection between Charlie and Martha Esser and Pam Donatti. It was right after you told me that Decker—" Virgil stopped himself to make sure Jonas was out of earshot. He was. "Right after you told me that Decker was Jonas's father."

Becky nodded. "That's right. But I never found the connection because I wasn't looking at it the right way."

"What do you mean?"

"I was looking for a criminal component. Something that would tie the three murders together. But Vernon Conrad killed Charlie Esser, and after Murt took care of Decker I sort of let the whole thing go because I thought it didn't matter anymore."

"It really didn't," Virgil agreed. "There won't be a trial, and the guilty party is dead."

"Right. But do you remember what else I said during that conversation before the press conference?"

Virgil thought some more. "Well, I remember you were worried about Murt. But that's all been taken care of too."

She shook her head. "Not that. I said Cora had me looking at something. She wanted to cover Mac's butt with that little stunt he pulled at the press conference...about Martha Esser still being alive. They wanted me to be absolutely certain that there were no Esser heirs because Mac and the state could get sued for saying something that they knew to be absolutely false."

"Right," Virgil said. "And they don't. Have any heirs, that is."

Becky smiled at him. Murton winked at Sandy.

"Except they did. I dug a little deeper than I normally would have and found something. Charlie Esser married into his land and fortune. The land from all those generations ago came from Martha's side of the family."

"So what?"

"I'll give you so what, mister," Becky said. "Martha Esser had a half-sister. She died about ten years ago. Her name was Annabelle Mumloe."

Sandy's eyes got wide and she brought her hands up and covered her mouth. "Oh my God." She started vibrating. Virgil could feel it.

Virgil looked at her, then back to Becky and Murton. "I don't get it. Who's Annabelle Mumloe?"

"I just told you, Jonesy. She was Martha's half sister."

"But I don't understand—"

Sandy looked at Becky, who nodded at her...an indication to tell the rest of it. When she tried to speak she could barely get the words out. "Virgil, Mumloe was Pam Donatti's maiden name. Annabelle Mumloe was her mother."

Virgil stood up then sat right back down. "You mean that Jonas is..."

Murton nodded. "That's right, Jones-man. And you guys just adopted him. That means you are now the proud owners of over two thousand acres of farmland down in Shelby County." He reached into Becky's purse, pulled out a piece of straw and stuck it in his mouth. "Virgil Jones. Even sounds like a farmer's name, doesn't it?" He stood up and walked bow-legged around the room.

"He's been waiting all day to do that," Becky said. "We had to stop at Hobby Lobby to buy a single piece of straw."

Sandy looked at her husband. "Oh-My-God. Virgil...we're rich!"

It took a minute for it to all sink in for Virgil. Becky showed him all the documentation and before he knew it they were all dancing around and laughing like they'd just won the lottery, which, essentially they had. Huma was listening from the kitchen.

She walked over, looked at Virgil and said, "It suddenly occurred to me that we hadn't actually agreed on my salary...or benefits."

All the noise woke Wyatt and he began to cry. Huma picked him up and snuggled him. Then she patted Virgil on the shoulder and said, "Don't worry...we'll work something out, I'm sure. Whew, someone needs their diaper changed."

Murton popped the tops on two bottles of champagne he'd brought along, one a non-alcoholic version for Sandy because she was breast feeding, and they toasted their future which looked brighter than ever. The rest of the evening was a roller coaster. One minute they would all be speaking calmly and rationally about what it all meant, then, what it all meant would sink in all over again and they'd get up and hug each other and dance around like a bunch of kids. They were making so much noise that Huma—who was trying to get Wyatt to bed—told them they had to quiet down or take it outside. Quieting down didn't seem possible, so they took it outside.

Virgil went out to the backyard and built a bonfire to keep the chill out of the air and once he had everything set up—the chairs, tables, blankets and a cooler full of Red Stripe beer—Sandy, Becky, Murton and Jonas joined him. They partied into the night, well past Jonas's bedtime, talking and laughing and crying, their futures at once sure and full of hope.

Sandy and Becky and Jonas were all wrapped up in their own conversation on the other side of the bonfire. Virgil went and got a few more logs for the fire then sat down next to Murton and told him about the conversation he'd had with his father...about his secret fear, that his life matched his father's in so many ways that he might one day lose Sandy to some tragedy...something completely out of his control, and how it almost *had* happened. "It scared me, Murt. It still scares me."

Murton shook his head. "What are you going to do, spend the rest of your life being afraid all the time? No one's life should be rooted in fear, Jones-man." He pointed a finger at him. "You gotta let that go."

Virgil had his head tipped back. He was gazing at the stars as Murton spoke. Then something he'd never witnessed happened right above him. He saw a double shooting star. Two of them together, tracing a path side by side through the night sky. "Man, look at that, everybody." He pointed up at the sky and followed the path of the stars across the horizon.

As he did, he noticed two things. The first was Jonas. He'd walked away from the bonfire and was standing next to Mason's cross down by the pond.

The other was a little goofy, he thought, even for this group.

Murton and Becky and Sandy were playing that ridiculous mannequin challenge or whatever it was called. They were all sitting there like they were frozen in time. Becky was leaning forward, a half smile on her face like she'd just said something funny and Sandy had her head tipped back in silent laughter. Murton was looking right at Virgil, his index finger pointed at him, his mouth a thin line.

He shook his head and chuckled, trying to figure out when they'd planned it. Probably when he was setting up the bonfire. He wondered how long were they willing to keep up the charade. Only one way to find out. He pulled his phone out, turned the video recorder on, put it in his breast pocket to capture the stunt then sat back in his chair and decided he'd wait them out. Except he didn't have to wait long because he suddenly realized what he thought was a prank was something else entirely.

Not only were the three of them frozen in time, but so

too were the flames of the bonfire. The light no longer flickered and danced, nor did any sparks or embers shoot skyward from the center of the fire. The noise was gone as well, the crackling and hissing of the burning wood now silent, the air instantly chilled. The fire was visible, it just wasn't giving off any heat. It was like a photograph of a bonfire.

Virgil jumped up from his chair. "Hey...guys? Guys?"

"They can't hear you, Son," Mason said. He stepped through the flames as if they weren't there and walked over next to Virgil. When he passed through the fire, the flames seemed to bend and bow around him then warp back in place, like ripples in a pond after a stone had been tossed in the water.

"Dad...are they okay? What's happening to me?" Virgil was visibly shaking.

Mason put his hand on Virgil's shoulder. " Relax, Son. Nothing is happening to you. Something is happening for you. Look at Jonas."

Virgil turned and looked at the cross. "I don't understand."

"You've been pulled out of time for a moment. I doubt it will ever happen again. You won't want to miss this." Mason stepped closer to the cross and Virgil followed him. They stopped about ten yards away. "That's close enough."

Virgil realized that, like him, Jonas wasn't frozen. He turned and waved at Virgil then focused his attention back on the cross. A radiant light began to emanate from the cross until it glowed with such intensity that Virgil became concerned for Jonas's safety. He stepped forward but Mason touched his arm to hold him in place.

"What's happening, Dad?"

"Just watch. In a sense, your other son is being born right this very moment. He's being welcomed into your family."

"What are you talking about?"

"He's letting go of his grief, Virg."

Virgil watched as the cross continued to glow, its colors changing and multiplying into a spectrum so broad Virgil saw colors he didn't even know existed. Maybe they didn't, he thought. And then without warning, the glow moved away from the cross and enveloped Jonas. He collapsed on the ground and disappeared into the light. Virgil rushed over to him, except when he got there, the light had faded and Jonas was gone.

VIRGIL SPUN around to say something to his father...he wasn't sure what, when he noticed that Jonas was back with Sandy and Becky and they were all laughing and giggling and having what looked like the time of their lives. Murton was poking at the fire with a large stick. He threw another log in the flames and waved to Virgil like nothing had happened at all.

Virgil waved back and looked at the cross. His father smiled at him. "What just happened?"

"You're back, Son. The colors are amazing, aren't they?"

Virgil certainly couldn't argue that. He'd never seen anything like it. "Can you tell me?"

Mason seemed to consider the question. Finally he

said, "Jonas got what he needed. He got to say goodbye. I think I'll do the same now too. Stay tuned, Virg. Dad loves you."

"Dad loves you too." It was their saying.

He watched his father fade then felt the movement behind him. Sandy and Jonas were staring at him.

"Virgil? Jonas says he has something he wants to ask us."

"What is it?" he said to Sandy.

"I don't know. He said he wanted to ask us together."

They both got down low, right at eye level with Jonas. "What is it, honey?" Sandy said.

There was a light in his eyes that was bright and undeniable. "I listened with my heart like you said. They told me it was okay to ask."

"Told you what was okay?"

Jonas looked at the cross for a full minute. Then he turned back to Virgil and Sandy. "Is it okay if I call you mommy and daddy?"

———

LATER THAT NIGHT, after Murton and Becky had gone, after Wyatt was fed and both boys were asleep, Virgil tried to explain to Sandy what happened by the bonfire, only to discover he didn't have the words. Who would? But then he remembered something. He jumped out of bed and got his phone, praying that what he'd experienced had been captured for Sandy to witness. It had. They spent the entire evening watching the video over and over again. They didn't speak. What could be said?

At six in the morning there was a tiny knock on the door. Jonas came in, walked over to the bassinet and looked at Wyatt for a moment. He smiled, then jumped up on the bed and snuggled in between Virgil and Sandy. He wasn't the least bit shy with it. "Hi Mom. Hi Dad. I'm hungry. What's for breakfast?"

Virgil rubbed the top of his son's head and said, "Hey little man. What sounds good? Pancakes or eggs?"

Jonas and Sandy laughed then looked at Virgil, and at the same time said, "Boaf!"

ACKNOWLEDGMENTS

Thank you for reading this story. It's an honor to write for each and every one of you. I really do mean that.

Writing is an absolute joy. I can't think of anything else I'd rather be doing for a living. It's also a tough gig some-times. Why? Because I've discovered that writing—much like the most important and fundamental parts of my life—is largely out of my control. If I try to force it, I find myself floundering around making myself (and pretty much everyone around me) miserable.

But I've also discovered if I surrender and let go...lose control, in other words, something magical happens every single time, both in my work and in my personal life. My wife, Debra has been my teacher, my guide, my champion, my muse, my guru, and most of all, the very best friend I've ever had. She believes in me in ways that are at once beau-tiful and shamanistic in nature. Without her, none of the books I've written would have seen the light of day, much less ended up where they are right now...in your hands. If you enjoy my stories, much of the credit belongs to her.

So. All of that to say this: Debra...thank you.

ABOUT THE AUTHOR

Thomas Scott is the author of the Virgil Jones series of novels. He lives in northern Indiana with his lovely wife, Debra, his children, and his trusty sidekick and writing buddy, Lucy, the cat.

Thomas loves to read and is a self-proclaimed regular guy. He holds an Airline Transport Pilot Rating, is a former airline pilot, Chief Pilot, and Director of Flight Operations for a private corporation. You may contact Thomas anytime via his website (thomasscottbooks.com) where he personally answers every single email he receives.

If you enjoy the Virgil Jones series of books, please help other readers just like you discover Thomas Scott by posting to your Facebook page and leaving an honest review on Amazon.com

For information on future books in the Virgil Jones series, please visit:

thomasscottbooks.com
thomaslscott@icloud.com

The Complete Virgil Jones Mystery, Thriller & Suspense Series of Books

State Of Anger - Book 1 of the Virgil Jones Series

State Of Betrayal - Book 2 of the Virgil Jones Series

State Of Control - Book 3 of the Virgil Jones Series

State Of Deception - Book 4 of the Virgil Jones Series (coming in 2017)

47910804R00244

Made in the USA
Middletown, DE
05 September 2017